The Case of Tiffany's Epiphany

A Richard Sherlock Whodunit

by
Jim Stevens

2013 by Jim Stevens

First Printing

ISBN: 978-0-98492477-6

For Teresa

Thanks for all your help.

Please keep it coming.

CHAPTER 1

"Shoot! Shoot! Now! You got a clean shot. Shoot!"

BANG. She shoots.

DAMN. She misses.

"Again! Shoot." I'm jumping around like a maniac. "Don't wait! Pull the trigger. Shoot!"

Behind me, I hear voices shouting: "Hit it." "Nail it." "Come on, put it down." "Now!"

My lungs ache, I'm screaming so loud. "Shoot!"

And another misfire.

We're dying out there.

The tide turns. *They* take control. They're setting us up for the kill. They're ready to fire. I scream a different tune, "Get down. Hurry. Run. Stop 'em."

I'm wailing so loud my throat is as dry as sandpaper. "Get your hands up."

Nobody listens.

They shoot. They hit. We're getting murdered.

This is the worst basketball game we've played so far, and up to now, we've played some real stinkers.

Time is running out. If they score one more point and we don't score, the first half ends, and we lose by the Slaughter Rule, which would make it six games in a row where we're down by 20 points at the end of the half, and the ref calls the game to alleviate further embarrassment and humiliation. Although the team is so used to getting slaughtered, embarrassment and humiliation are the least of our problems.

"Come on, girls. We got to stop 'em!"

We have the ball, down nineteen, less than twenty seconds on the clock. If we hold the ball for ten seconds we can get to the second half for the first time this season. "Go into a stall," I scream out, knowing full well the team has no clue on how to go into a stall. "Fifteen seconds, just burn fifteen seconds!"

There's only one phrase in the entire world that can break my concentration from the game before my very eyes and unfortunately I hear it loud and clear.

"Oh, Mister Sherlock."

From the opposite side of the gym, Tiffany walks right onto the court in the midst of the action, "I need you."

"Tiffany, get off the court. You're not supposed to be out there. You're in the middle of the game!"

The players run around Tiffany like she's the slow driver in the middle lane on the expressway.

The whistle blows.

Cease fire. Everything stops.

Dead silence, until, "Technical foul."

"What?"

"Unauthorized player on the court," the referee shouts.

"You can't call that," I argue, running onto the court. "I didn't tell her to be out there."

"I'm the ref; I can do whatever I want."

"No, you can't," I argue my case.

"You want another technical?"

"You can't do that either."

The ref points a finger at my nose. "Back on the bench, buddy."

I back up, but I refuse to sit. That'll show him.

"Oh, Mr. Sherlock." Tiffany stumbles across the court on her four-inch heels and heads my way. "It's really important." She's decked out in a micro-miniskirt, black knitted hose, an ivory-colored blouse with a plunging neckline, and an array of gold, equal to a Pizarro find, around her neck. Hardly a Saturday morning gymnasium outfit.

Care, my youngest daughter, calls out to her teammates. "Hey, everybody, that's Tiffany. She's like totally cool." The five ten and eleven year old girls leave the court and surround my self-styled protégé, as our opposition line up for the free throw.

Kelly, my obsessed with fashion, middle schooler, who was sitting at the end of the bench, actually quits texting on her cell phone, jumps up and runs to Tiffany, "I love those shoes."

Behind me, I hear disgruntled parents admonish me in extremely harsh tones. "What the heck is going on, Sherlock?"

"Who is that person?"

"Can't you control the team?"

"They really need help with their transition game." That last unsolicited piece of advice came from Mrs. Whiner, whose kid, Wilma, has the distinction of being the worst player on the team, which is no small accomplishment. Actually, I like Wilma; she fits in with my motley, ragtag crew. Her mother, on the other hand, wouldn't fit into a round hole even if she were a round peg.

"Transition game? The kids are eleven," I say to the woman.

"I put Wilma on the team to learn basketball, not excuses," Mrs. Whiner informs me.

"*Any* lesson learned is a good lesson," I respond taking the high road.

While I'm dealing with Wilma's mother, my whole team stands in front of our bench, instead of out on the court where they belong. They surround Tiffany as if she were Katy Perry, and chat her up like a bundle of baboons.

I turn around and redirect my attention to the team. "Girls, we're in the middle of a game here."

Nobody listens.

"Time out," I call out, using the appropriate T signal with my hands.

"You can't call time out," the ref informs me. "You don't have the ball."

"Girls, get back out on the court."

"Do we have to?" Annie our point guard asks. "You know we're going to lose."

"Don't say that," I tell Annie. "We can't bail out now." This is probably a bad choice of words since the name of the team is the Bailouts, due to the fact that the only sponsor I could find, one of the last businesses on earth that owes me a favor, is Morrie's Bail Bonds.

"We're so far gone in this game we'll never catch up." Kaylyn, our forward, says in absolute desperation.

"We never got going to begin with," Annie adds.

"We got a chance to pull this one out." I say this in my best *Never say die* inflection.

"It's twenty-three to four," she reminds me.

"This is our big chance for a comeback in the second half," I point out.

"Even if we could, Mr. Sherlock, at the present rate of scoring, we would need forty-eight more points to win. That translates into one basket every twenty-four seconds," Shemika informs me. She's not only our best player; she's also the Bailout's math whiz.

"When the going gets tough, girls, the tough get going," I give it my best Knute Rockne impersonation.

"So, let's just get going home," Annie says. "This is dumb."

I feel Tiffany's hand reach over and hold my arm for support. I get my first good look at her. She's as pale as a bleached blonde bimbo's beehive. "Tiffany..."

"Oh. Mr. Sherl-l-l-l....."

I catch her before she hits the floor. Care screams.

I carry a limp Tiffany to the bench, set her down gently, "Somebody get me some water," I say.

Six water bottles come out of nowhere and are thrust at me.

"Kelly sit behind Tiffany and hold her head while I take her pulse," I tell my eldest.

I count beats, and thank God, there're plenty. "Care," I tell my youngest. "Soak one of those small towels with water and wring it out."

My entire team, the ref, the opposing team, and an assortment of parents are huddled around me and Tiffany, in morbid curiosity.

I place the wet towel on her forehead. "Drink some water," I say as I tilt a bottle to Tiffany's lips. She sips. A little color comes back into her cheeks. She tries to sit up, but I won't let her. "Just relax."

"Should I call an ambulance?" the ref asks.

"No," Tiffany protests.

"You sure?" I ask.

"Absolutely not. I'm not dressed to go to the hospital," she says.

After that comment, I know she's going to be okay.

"Tiffany, take some more of this." I keep trying to get some water into her.

The ref blows the whistle. "Play ball."

Our opponents return to the free throw line.

"Girls get back on the court," I tell my team. "Everything is going to be fine here."

Not one kid moves. Nobody listens to me, and I'm the coach.

The next sound I hear is the *swish* of the ball going through the net. 24 – 4. The Slaughter Rule kicks into effect. The Bailouts are locked out of the second half. This makes six games in a row. A new record.

The next two teams are coming on the floor for their game. "Girls, go shake the hands of the other team, find your parents, and I'll see you all Tuesday for practice." I say this half-heartedly as I help Tiffany to her feet.

Tiffany tries to walk, but her legs are like cooked spaghetti. I carry her around the bleachers and into the boys' locker room, which I know will be empty. Luckily there happens to be one of those canvas chairs there, the kind you can fold up and take along to sit anywhere. Unfortunately, it's right in front of the urinals. I sit her down without moving it and wonder who would ever want to sit in such a weird spot.

Care and Kelly are behind me. They're scared.

"I haven't felt like this since I overdosed on that mango juice diet I went on," Tiffany manages to say.

"Just relax, get some strength back," I tell her.

"Hey, you, lady, there you?" a voice comes from outside the door. This is no Midwest accent. It's not even a Southside Chicago accent. "How you, lady, how you?" It's coming closer.

A swarthy man enters. His body odor reaches us before he does. However, its unpleasant aroma has an unexpected side benefit since it acts like a vial of smelling salts on Tiffany, who is now going in and out of consciousness.

"Meter read sixty-three, and ten dollar charge for suburbia," he bellows loudly.

"Who are you?" Care asks.

"My name, Anwar. I come to America to study chemistry at university."

This guy might want to start with the chemical compound to make soap.

"I cab drive."

Kelly has no problem pulling my wallet out of my back pocket, opening the fold, and removing the last two fifties, leaving me twenty dollars of mad money for the weekend. She hands it to the cabbie. "Keep the change," she says like she's Bill Gates.

Anwar doesn't bother to say thanks. I hope he takes a course in manners in between his chemistry classes.

Tiffany stirs. I hold the wet cloth across her forehead. In a few moments she comes to again, grips my arm, and pulls herself upright. She grabs the water bottle, puts it to her mouth, and chug-a-lugs the entire eight ounces like a frat boy at a kegger. "Whew," Tiffany says. "I needed that."

"Tiffany, what happened?" I ask.

She turns to me slightly, takes a breath, and says, "Mr. Sherlock, I got roofied."

My name is Richard Sherlock. I spent nineteen years on the Chicago Police Force, sixteen as a detective. I got kicked off the force due to a very uncharacteristic temper tantrum. I took a swing at my superior's face and made a solid connection. I lost my job and my pension, and couldn't find another job. I ended up as an on-call investigator for the Richmond Insurance Company, where I'm forced to investigate settlement frauds, suspected frauds, or any settlements that can be proven fraudulent.

I hate my job.

I'm also a divorced dad of two girls, almost eleven and almost thirteen. I have a bad back, no savings, and an ex-wife who hates me. I live in a crummy, one-bedroom apartment. I'm a lousy dresser, I can't find a steady girlfriend, and I drive a 1992 Toyota Tercel. Could life get any more pathetic? Yes. I am also the coach of what is probably the worst basketball team since James Naismith hung up his first peach basket.

A major portion of my job with the insurance agency is mentoring (aka babysitting) the twenty-something, spoiled heiress of the Richmond fortune, Tiffany Richmond. On the surface Tiffany is a vapid, spoiled-rotten, rich, self-centered, egotistical girl who will never experience an "I can't afford it" moment in her life. Down deep, Tiffany is a vapid, spoiled-rotten, rich, self-centered, egotistical girl with a good heart. I've found in life if you have one of those, all other frailties diminish. Plus, my kids think the world of her. I suspect they like her more than they like me. I really can't blame them.

"Tiffany, are you okay?" Care asks.

"You can't have anything wrong with you," Kelly says just as worried as her sister. "Who's going to take me shopping if you're sick?"

My oldest is a bit more self-centered than her sister. She gets this from her mother, no doubt.

"Girls, leave her alone," I tell them. "Let her get her breath back."

"I'm in this club, sipping on a Cosmo," Tiffany says as best she can.

"Which one?" the detective in me immediately asks.

"Kumquat," she answers.

"There's a club called, Kumquat?" I again ask.

"No," Tiffany says. "A kumquat *cosmo*."

I stand corrected.

"All of a sudden, my head starts spinning faster than a strobe light in a disco." Tiffany takes another water bottle from Care and sips. "I try to get up and, let me tell you," she says. "It's tough enough to balance on four-inch Christian Louboutin's when you're sober, but doing it with your head spinning like a break dancer on speed, that's impossible."

"Tiffany, we should really get you to a hospital."

"No, Mr. Sherlock, the first thing we have to do is find out if anyone snapped my picture when I was down. If an Instagram of me sprawled out against a bar rail goes out, and shows up on somebody's Facebook Page, I'll never live it down."

"What's an Instagram?"

"Dad," Kelly says, "you are so lame."

I admit I'm a bit behind the times when it comes to technology. I still use a flip phone.

"Don't argue with me," I say in no uncertain terms. "You're going to get checked out and checked out right now."

Tiffany half-collapses back into the chair.

"You two stay here," I tell my kids. "I'm going to go get the car and bring it around. And don't let her get up."

Tiffany pops back up and uses what energy she has left to plead, "Oh, no. Please not that."

"Tiffany you're going to the hospital. That's final."

"Fine," she relents. "I'll go to the hospital, but do we have to go in your car? I hate that yucky car."

We're driving down Western Avenue. Tiffany is wearing my sunglasses and has a towel draped over her head like a burka in her effort not to be seen. "My head is, like, pounding," she complains. "All I can hear is, put, put, put, put."

Actually, the sound isn't inside her head. It's a stuttering from

7

beneath the Toyota. I've got a bad muffler that I can't afford to fix. "It'll get better as soon as we get to the hospital," I tell her.

"Why don't you get a new car, Mr. Sherlock? An illegal immigrant wouldn't be caught dead driving over the border in this one."

"I can't get a new car."

"Why not? I get one every year," Tiffany says.

"Because I, unlike you, have children instead of money, Tiffany."

"You can't have both?" Tiffany asks.

"I certainly haven't been able to swing that."

We're about a block from Martha Washington Hospital, but I settle for a Doc in the box on Western Avenue. MWH is a major Northside treatment center, and that means the ER room will have at least a three-day wait.

At the Doc in the box, I get Tiffany and the girls seated before I approach the sour and surly-looking admittance person at the desk. She's dressed in scrubs, but I don't think she's a nurse. She immediately asks if Tiffany has insurance. I could tell her, "When it comes to insurance, not many have as much as Tiffany," but I don't. Instead, I sift through Tiffany's stack of credit cards until I find her insurance card and hand it over. She hands me a clipboard with a pen attached by a metal string. I take it to where the three are seated, which is between a broken arm and bleeding knee, behind a guy who can hardly breathe, and in front of a very bad case of pink eye. I begin to fill out the form. The top part is easy. The bottom part is a little more personal. "Tiffany, do you have any of these diseases?"

Tiffany gives me her "That is, like, totally gross" look.

I rattle off everything from asphyxia to shin splints and Tiffany responds with a resounding, "I better not."

I finish the form, take out my last twenty dollars and clip it under the first page on the clipboard. I return the form to the desk, am told to wait, and in less than ten seconds what I suspect is a real nurse comes out of an opposite door. Every eye in the waiting room, including the pink ones, looks up in hope. The nurse calls out "Miss Richmond."

Moans all around. Money talks. Bullshit walks--or in this case, sits and suffers.

"The doctor will see you now."

The four of us rise.

"You're all Miss Richmond?" the nurse asks.

Three of us sit back down.

Tiffany, who did take off her shoes after my nagging, follows the nurse into the inner sanctum of medicinal repair. Once the door shuts and locks from the inside, Kelly immediately takes off her shoes and puts on Tiffany's. "These are, like, so totally rad."

Kelly gets up and tries to walk. "Watch me, Dad."

"Kelly, sit down," I say. "You're going to break an ankle."

"I was like born to wear Christian Louboutin's."

"Sit down. You don't belong in those shoes."

"What do you mean? They're perfect, they look great … on … me. Whoa-a-a-a …!"

Kelly keels over to her left like a new felled tree, and crashes right into the guy with the broken arm, who screams out in his displeasure, "I think you broke my other arm."

"Sorry, mister," Kelly apologies, "but at least you're in the right place to get that fixed."

I jump up, lift Kelly to her feet, give the guy a quick, "Kids, these days," and deposit my oldest back into her chair. "Take those shoes off right now."

"I will in a second, Dad." Kelly hands her cell phone to Care who snaps shoe shots of her sister for fashion posterity.

I use my cell to call Tiffany's dad, Jamison Wentworth Richmond III. And he, as usual, doesn't take my call. I leave a detailed message. I know he won't call back. His usual custom.

For the next fifteen minutes my kids play with their cell phones. I take a dog-eared magazine off the rack and read an article about President Bush's new tax plan, George H.W., not George W. The other patients continue to moan.

The nurse emerges again from the inner sanctum. The moans stop in anticipation of hearing their names, but only until the nurse says, "Mr. Sherlock." The moans return--louder than before.

"Dad, can we come with you?" Care asks.

"No." I hand Care the magazine I was reading. "Here, brush up on some history."

I hurry through the door held open by the nurse. One foot inside, she admonishes me, "Why didn't you tell us she was Tiffany Richmond?"

"I filled out the form."

"Her father owns this place. And if you don't think we're going to hear about this, you must be in the middle of a brain freeze, mister."

"Sorry."

I am led down a short hallway to an exam room. Tiffany sits on the exam table, one hand holding a mirror, the other one patting blush on her face. An IV line runs into the vein in the crook of her arm. It's dripping a clear liquid into her system.

"I'm Dr. Omagalla Nehru."

At the sound of the voice, I turn to my left and peer down at the balding head of a guy who couldn't be more than 5 foot 3; the perfect Doc for a Doc in the box. His hand is outstretched for me to shake. I take it. "Nice to meet you," he says.

"Is she okay?"

"She's fine."

"What happened?"

"Miss Richmond must have ingested some type of narcotic that had a decided effect on her system."

"What?" I ask.

"I have taken blood, urine, and DNA specimens. We have called the lab, they'll pick it up immediately and they'll have the tests done, STAT. As soon as possible." He raises his index finger to further make his point.

"Good."

The doc added the customary prescription, "Have her drink lots of fluids to allow system flush itself out, and make sure she gets plenty of rest."

"Will do, Doc."

As the nurse removes the IV from Tiffany's arm, Dr. Nehru pulls me toward him and speaks softly so that Tiffany can't hear him. "And please tell the owner of company what good care we take of patient."

"Next time we chat, I'll be sure to mention it."

Tiffany hops off the table, hands the mirror back to the nurse, smiles, and says to me, "They pumped my stomach, Mr. Sherlock."

"Did it hurt? Are you okay?"

"What I wouldn't have done for one of those machines when I was on a purge diet," she tells me.

Outside the clinic, a limo so big it could double as a troop transport vehicle awaits.

"It sure didn't take long for Daddy to go into action," Tiffany says.

"He called you?"

"Of course he called me, he's my daddy."

"I want you to go home, get some rest, and keep drinking fluids, Tiffany."

"Yes, sir, Mr. Sherlock."

"Bye, Tiffany," Care and Kelly say in unison.

"Ta-ta, little dudettes."

The driver holds the rear door waiting for Tiffany to climb inside.

"When do we start, Mr. Sherlock?" she asks me.

"Start what?"

"Finding out who did this to me."

I sigh. "Tiffany, just do what the doctor said."

"Mr. Sherlock, the best revenge is a cocktail served warm."

CHAPTER 2

It's late. The kids finally go to bed. They made me watch this TV show where the world has been taken over by zombies and the only people left are muscle-bound, buffed-up bad actors and well-endowed, equally bad actresses. They all spend their time blowing the heads off the undead dead, while they're busy pairing up with each other in typical soap opera type relationships. Think *All My Children* meets *The Curse of the Living Dead*.

The door buzzer buzzes. Someone downstairs wants to get in. It's probably one of the buddies of the drunk that lives on the second floor who regularly punches the wrong button or all the buttons on the residence doorbell panel.

I get up off the couch, which will soon be my bed, go to my front door, push the respond button, and growl, "Go away."

"Oh, Mr. Sherlock."

"Tiffany ..."

"Buzz me in."

I scream back through the tiny speaker, "You're supposed to be home resting."

"Mr. Sherlock, I got tired of resting. Let me in."

I push the door release button, hear the click, and in the time it takes to climb three flights of stairs, Tiffany enters my apartment.

"Let's go."

"Go where?" I ask.

Care and Kelly pile out of my bedroom. "Can we go too?"

"We're not going anywhere," I tell everyone.

"What should I wear?" Kelly asks.

"We got to get there while the clues are still fresh," Tiffany says.

"Get where?"

"To the club where I got roofied."

"Did you have to wear that?" Tiffany asks.

I have been scolding her all the way down the block to where she parked her Lexus 450. "Don't change the subject. You're supposed to be home recuperating, Tiffany."

"Really, is that jacket the coolest thing you have to wear?"

She is referring to my faux leather jacket.

"It's about as hip as a hip replacement."

"I try to buy clothes that are fashion timeless."

"I would have hated to be around when that thing was in fashion," she tells me.

"Sorry, you didn't give me a lot of time to plan my wardrobe for the evening."

"I'm telling you, Mr. Sherlock, getting you in this club is not going to be easy."

I take a deep breath. These conversations are extremely tiring. "We're supposed to be talking about your health, Tiffany."

"I feel fine," she says pulling out onto the street.

"You don't look fine."

"I don't?" Tiffany jams on the brakes, comes to a stop in the middle of the road, and leans over to see her reflection in the rear view mirror. "Is there something wrong with my make-up?"

"The doctor said you have to let your system clear itself out."

"There's no system in the world faster than mine. I lost four pounds in one weekend by eating only bran cereal," Tiffany says. "That's why I passed out on the bar right away. Most chicks just get woozier and woozier when somebody roofies them. They pass out an hour or two later. My roofie smacked me like an iron skillet to my skull. Boom!"

Why do I even bother trying to reason with her? She doesn't listen.

In a few minutes we're speeding down Lakeshore Drive. I yawn. I'm tired. It's way past my bedtime. "Couldn't we do this tomorrow?" I ask, exasperated.

"Mr. Sherlock, you always tell me that if you don't solve the case in the first seven-point-two hours the case goes into cold case hibernation."

"I never said that."

"Well, you said something like it."

Tiffany cuts over three lanes, and exits the Drive like Dale Earnhardt coming in for a pit stop. She zooms down Wacker Drive, through the Loop, and over the river near Greektown.

The club is named Zanadu, a possible clever misspelling of Xanadu, the palatial home of Charles Foster Kane, but I seriously doubt if any of the revelers have ever heard of *Citizen Kane*. If it's not a video game or

Smart Phone app, the millennial generation has little use for it.

The club is in the West Loop, in a converted warehouse. Twenty years ago this neighborhood was filled with low-life drug addicts and loose women; today it's filled with a much better classes of drug addicts and loose women.

Tiffany pulls the Lexus up in front of the long line of people waiting to get in. Every eye, male and female, watches her flip her keys to the valet. Next, they get a glimpse of yours truly and, no doubt, wonder what a girl who looks like she does could be doing with a guy who looks like me.

I start to walk to the back of the line. Tiffany grabs me by the arm and pulls me back. "Where are you going?"

"End of the line."

"Line? I haven't waited in a line since grammar school."

I follow her as she zips by the "little people".

"Now, don't say anything. Let me do the talking," Tiffany says as we're about to reach two black, bald, humongous slabs of intimidation manning the velvet rope.

"Hi, Arson." Tiffany greets the first man, then the second. "Hi, Sterno."

"Good evening, Tiffany."

Sterno unhooks the rope and Tiffany passes through. The rope is immediately clipped back before I have a chance to enter.

"He's with me," Tiffany tells the pair.

"Tiffany, we can't let your chauffer in." Arson's voice does not match his size.

"He's not my driver."

"Well, we can't let your servant in either," Sterno says.

"He's not my servant."

Close, but no cigar.

"Then what is he?"

"He's with me," Tiffany explains.

"Oh my God," Arson says, as his hands go to his face like the kid in *Home Alone*. "You two are an item?"

Sterno consoles Arson with a hug. It's obvious not only do these two pair up at the door, but they pair up everywhere else.

"Gross," Tiffany says. "He's like old enough to have kids smarter than me."

Arson, whose bicep is the size of my waist, leans over to Tiffany. "We can't let anybody in who dresses like an exterminator from Cleveland."

"You have to let him in."

"We could lose our jobs lettin' some guy in who uses a 2-in-1 shampoo," Sterno adds.

"He's Mr. Sherlock, a detective who is here to find out who roofied me last night," Tiffany tells them in her *I've got more money than God* tone.

"You got roofied last night?" Sterno asks incredulously.

"You didn't hear?" Tiffany replies.

"No," Arson says.

"So, let him in," Tiffany repeats.

"No can do," Sterno says.

"Let Mr. Sherlock in," Tiffany says, "or I'll put on my Facebook Page that the two of you are bald because you can't grow your own hair and you both wear chin straps when you sleep."

The rope comes off its mooring. I step forward, suddenly proud to be a member of such an exclusive group. I fluff up my faux leather jacket and my button down collar shirt and tell the not-so-dynamic duo, "I just want you to know that I don't follow the fashion trends, I set 'em."

As I pass through the portal, I hear a bewildered comment from the waiting peanut gallery behind me, "You letting that guy in?"

I follow Tiffany up a few steps and down a short path to huge metal door, which looks strong enough to keep Attila and his Hun buddies out. A slimy-looking guy in a slimier-looking suit steps forward to block our path. He takes one look at me and says to Tiffany, "Let me guess, you're on a scavenger hunt and you found the Forgotten Nerd?"

Tiffany stares him straight in the eye, "This is Mr. Sherlock, Chicago Police Department, Detective First Class."

Slimy Guy sashays to the left like a matador, "Welcome to Zanadu."

The metal door slides open and a blast of hip-hop music hits me like a tornado hits a trailer park. I step inside and my entire body begins to violently shake to an over-dubbed backbeat mixed with an incessant string of garbled rap lyrics that must be in some other language.

I take a whiff. My hearing might be gone, but my sense of smell still works. The place smells like a perfumed sweat sock. I look around the enormous, nearly unimpeded floor space. People are jammed together like pickles in a jar. The dance floor is packed with bodies twisting and turning like a bucket of snakes. The scene is so intense, so loud, and so overwhelming; the only way you could communicate is by texting, which I don't do because the letters are too small to push on my flip phone. The DJ, who's on a platform above the crowd working two turntables and I can't see how many tape decks, wears a huge pair of earphones, which makes him the only one in the place that doesn't have to listen to the awful music he's playing.

Tiffany pulls me through the throng as if she's walking an unruly St. Bernard. She's screaming something at me, but I can't hear her, or read her lips because the place is vibrating faster than a motel bed with magic fingers. It's probably a blessing I can't hear her. We end up on the other side of the club, in a bar area the size of a basketball court. Thankfully, the area is cordoned off by a glass wall, which makes it somewhat easier to hear.

"This is where you go to have fun?" I ask Tiffany.

"No, this is where you go to be seen having fun," she tells me.

Tiffany leads me to what would be about half court at the bar. She butts in between two guys who have enough mousse in their hair to be a matching oil slick. "This is where I was sitting when I took a sip and my head hit the bar like a tree falling on the moon that you can't hear."

I stop, look up to my left and then to my right. I see exactly what I suspected.

"Then I must have slid off the barstool and landed here on the floor." Tiffany shows me by spreading her hands over the small area.

"How would you know that if you were already passed out?" I ask.

Tiffany ponders my question. "That's a good question, Mr. Sherlock. I just figured that's what happened."

"First rule of life, Tiffany," I tell her. "Assume nothing."

"No," Tiffany says. "The first rule of life is never use soap on your face. It dries out your pores."

Once again, I stand corrected.

I make some mental pictures of the scene, having a photographic memory does have its advantages. Next, I count the bartenders and barbacks behind the bar. In about a sixty-foot space there are eight, six tenders who take orders and mix cocktails with incredible speed and two helpers who keep the ice wells filled and lug the clean and dirty glasses in and out. I lose track of how many waitresses come into the bar station empty and leave with a tray full of cocktails. I'm always amazed how they seldom spill a drop while navigating through the jungle of pulsating flesh.

Whoever owns this Zanadu is going to be able to build his own Xanadu in no time at all. The place is a gold mine.

"Do you remember which bartender served you?" I ask Tiffany.

"Bruno."

"Bruno, the bartender," I say for effect. "Is he here tonight?"

Tiffany looks up and down the bar. "Nope, I don't see him."

"Do you remember where you woke up?"

"In the back."

"Show me."

Tiffany leads me to a break in the bar and down a slight hallway. We go past the men's and women's facilities and stop at a door labeled *No Admittance.* Tiffany knocks. I watch the spy camera above the upper doorjamb switch on. We wait. A buzzer buzzes. I hear a click. Tiffany opens the door and enters. I follow.

It's an office with two desks, one much smaller than the other. There's a couch against the wall to my left between two identical doors, both closed. Behind the smaller desk, a behemoth of a man sits reading a comic book. Seeing Tiffany, he puts *The Fantastic Four* down and I spot a large semi-automatic bulge out of the coat of his ill-fitting suit. He doesn't speak.

But the man seated at the larger desk does, "Tiffany, how are you?" he says.

"I'm good," Tiffany answers with a smile.

The man, who could double as a *GQ* model, rises from his chair and comes out and around to greet us. "You gave us quite a scare last night."

"This is no place for a beauty nap," Tiffany tells him.

The guy takes a look at my jacket, takes a step back as if I have the cooties, and says, "And you are?"

"This is Mr. Sherlock, he's a detective," Tiffany informs the man.

"Chicago PD?"

"So to speak," Tiffany answers before I have the chance.

Mr. GQ eyes me warily, but steps forward and puts out his hand to shake. "Gibby Fearn."

"And what do you do here?" I give as well as I take.

"I'm the Vice President in charge of operations."

I pause when I hear a faint whooshing sound behind one of the doors next to the couch before I speak the inevitable detective opening line, "Tell me what happened."

"We got an alert from the bar last night a little after two. Within three minutes three security men converged on the spot to find Miss Richmond passed out against the bar rail."

"Oh my God," Tiffany says. "I don't want to even imagine what position I was in."

"What did you do?" I ask.

Gibby continues, "I rushed out, thought she was drunk ..."

Tiffany interrupts, "Why would you ever think that?"

"Probably because you were unconscious on the floor next to the bar," I answer for the VP of Operations.

"But that's so not me," Tiffany says.

"Go on, please."

Gibby continues, "It's the policy of the club that when an incident like this occurs, we remove the parties in question from the main floor as soon as possible."

"Bad PR or you just don't want an open spot at the bar?" I ask.

"What do you think?" This guy likes me about as much as he likes my leather jacket.

I hear the *whoosh* again, but this time the sound is accompanied by a *plop*. "Did you bring her in here?"

"What else would we do?" Gibby loves to ask questions. I hate that.

"But you didn't call an ambulance?"

"Why should I? Her breathing was even, her pulse steady, and her color normal."

"Still ..." I say.

"What? People drink, people get drunk," he says. "This is a 3 a.m. club. You don't think this happens all the time?"

"Do you know if anyone took my picture while I was passed out on the floor like an un-chaperoned model at her first after-show party?" Tiffany asks.

"I can assure you nobody from Zanadu did."

"If I find out someone did, this place will never see another dime of my or my daddy's money."

Gibby never retreats to his desk or asks if we want to sit down. I feel about as welcome as I did at Thanksgiving at my ex-in-law's house.

"I let her sleep it off on the couch. She seemed fine by the next morning." End of story.

"You stayed with her?"

"Who else?" Gibby asks with a sarcastic smirk. "I know when to go the extra mile in this business."

"I'd like to speak with Bruno the bartender," I say.

The Behemoth at the small desk speaks up, "Sick."

"Did he pass out like I did?" Tiffany asks.

"Dun't know."

"Could I get his name and phone number?" I ask.

"Dun't know," the Behemoth answers.

I turn to Gibby. "I'll need to see the video tapes from the cameras that cover that area of the bar," I tell him.

"There's a movie of what happened to me?" Tiffany shrieks.

"At least two," I tell her. "Enough to make a documentary called, *Tiffany Gets Tipsy*."

"Oh, my God, I want every copy destroyed."

"You got a card?" Gibby asks. "I'll call you when the tapes are returned from our service."

I give a phony pat to my faux leather jacket pockets, "I left my cards in my other suit. Is it possible to have the tapes here for me by noon tomorrow?"

Gibby gives me a wry smile, as if he's decided not to call my bluff. "What else can I do for you?"

There is one last *whoosh/plop* from behind the door. "I'll let you know," I warn him. Before leaving the office, I ask Gibby Fearn, VP of Operations, one last question, "Would you like to see Tiffany's toxicology report when it arrives?"

"Why would I be interested in her blood alcohol level?"

"What if it isn't alcohol that appears in the report?"

"What if it is?"

Life would be so much easier if people merely answered the questions asked of them instead of asking one of their own.

"Thanks for your time."

I pull Tiffany out the office. Her first comment is "Mr. Sherlock we have to destroy those tapes or at least have my face electronically fuzzied up like they do on those reality TV shows."

I ignore her request. "Come on," I say. "I want to hang out in the bar for a few minutes."

Tiffany says, "Out there? You want to hang out with *me*?" as if she needs each piece of specific information explained in detail.

"If anybody asks, I'll tell them I'm your driver."

"Well, okay, but I wish you had one of those chauffeur hats to wear," she says as we proceed to the bar.

I pick a spot where I can see the entire length of the bar. The place is still packed. Drinks are being poured at a record pace. Waitresses hustle. It's almost two-thirty in the morning and girls are deciding if, and guys are deciding on who, when it comes to who's getting their tickets punched this evening. The two overly-moussed guys are doing about as well as I would in the place.

Tiffany goes to the bar to get me a ginger ale and herself a frilly cocktail. As soon as she returns, she tells me she's going to the ladies room. I stand alone like a wallflower at a high school dance. At exactly 2:32 a.m., Gibby and his muscle come out of their office and make their way down the bar, stopping at each cash register. Gibby inserts a key to the left of the computer pad on the machine, punches in a few numbers, waits for the cash drawer to open, and removes a hefty stack of bills. The money goes into a black canvas bag carried by the Behemoth. It takes less than five minutes to complete all six registers and return to the office.

The moment Tiffany returns, I tell her. "Time to go home."

"But the night is still young."

"But I'm not."

I sleep until nine, quite late for me. Care gets up at ten and Kelly emerges from dreamland around ten-thirty.

"What do you say we take in a class at Sunday school?" I ask as we all stand in the kitchen.

"I go to school five days a week," Kelly says. "That's plenty."

"How about church?" I ask. "We could go as a family."

"I like going to the same church Tiffany goes to," Care says. "The church of St. Mattress."

I give up on their spiritual upbringing and pull my one frying pan out of the cabinet to start breakfast. "Pancakes?"

"You make terrible pancakes, Dad," Kelly says.

"How about bacon?" Care asks.

"Bacon is bad for you," I instruct my children. "It's just a hunk of salty fat, fried up in its own grease."

"But it tastes good," Care says.

"How about French toast?" Kelly suggests.

"French toast it is." I pull bread and eggs out of the refrigerator. Kelly and Care sit at the small table.

"Did ya get lucky at the club last night, Dad?" Kelly asks.

"Kelly, you don't ask your father those kinds of questions."

"Why not?"

"Because that's none of your business, and you're too young to be thinking about things like that."

"Then what should I be thinking about?"

"Anything but that, Kelly."

Care cracks the eggs and Kelly whips them up with a whisk. I add the milk.

"What fun things do you have planned for us to do today, Dad?" Care asks.

"Why is it my job to plan everything?" I counter.

"Because you're the adult."

"You're doing your homework at four," I say reminding them of their usual Sunday scheduled study time.

"What are we going to do until then?" Kelly asks as if this is the last day of her life and she wants to make the most of it.

"How would you like to go to the Zanadu Club downtown?" I ask.

"Cool!"

"What's that awful noise?" Kelly asks as we get on Lakeshore Drive to go downtown.

"The muffler."

"Isn't the muffler supposed to muffle the noise?"

"Not my muffler," I confess. "It has a hole in it."

"How do you know that, Dad?" Care asks, knowing I'm no car mechanic.

"Because I tried to duct tape it shut."

"No wonder Tiffany won't ride in your car," Kelly tells me.

It's not that I don't want to get the muffler fixed, it's just that I'm currently in a major cash flow situation; actually a it's a major *lack of cash flow* situation. I am so broke, I'm almost unfixable. My rent is due, my alimony is always due, and I'm living off my one credit card that is seriously close to being maxed out. I had to search couch cushions to be able to do my laundry. I've recycled everything that can be recycled into cash. My credit rating brings down the national average. Worst of all, I don't know where it all goes. I get a check from Mr. Richmond and it disappears before I can get to the Jewel to buy bananas. My financial situation is on life support, with no one there to help me support it.

We putt-putt to the Zanadu. The valet isn't on duty today. Too bad, it would probably be the only time he'd ever have the chance to park a Toyota Tercel. I park the car and the girls follow me to the metal door. Arson, Sterno, the velvet rope, and the line of people are also absent. I pound on the door a few times, but Slimy Guy also must be off-duty. "Maybe they won't open up because we're not cool enough to get in," I say to my girls.

"Speak for yourself, Dad," Kelly says.

I motion for the girls to follow me around to the east side of the building where I see a services truck parked. The side door is open. We go inside.

"Where are all the people?" Kelly asks, seeing the place is empty except for a cleaning crew. "You said you were taking us to a club."

"I didn't say it was going to be open."

"Dad, that's not fair."

"Kelly, I'm going to teach you to listen to details if it kills me."

"I don't care if anybody is here," Care says. "This place is neat."

My youngest daughter's eyes are as wide as pie plates. She twirls around seeing the numerous video screens, the light boards, the tables, the chairs and the DJ's platform high above her. "Come on," I tell her.

I find my way back to the bar and to the small hallway leading to Gibby Fearn's office. I knock. The spy camera flips on and in seconds the door clicks open. The girls follow me in.

The Behemoth sits in the same chair, in the same suit, and reading the same comic book. He must be an extremely slow reader. "Is Gibby in?" I ask.

"Dun't know."

"Did he leave the tapes?"

The Behemoth reaches over to a grab a manila envelope and hands it to me.

"How about the address and phone number for Bruno the bartender?"

"Dun't know."

I open the envelope to check on the contents. In addition to the DVDs, there's a slip of paper with a name and number written on it. "Thanks," I tell him. I would like to ask if the Behemoth has been home since last night, or if he even has a home, but I don't. I make small talk instead. "Sure is a pretty day out today."

"Dun't know."

I guess that answers the question if he's been home or not.

"By the way," I say in my best small talk voice, "Who's Gibby's boss?"

"Dun't know."

I pause for a few seconds and listen to the quiet. "What happened to the *whoosh/plop* sound?"

"Dun't know."

Enough said. This has been a fascinating conversation. This guy must have scored high on his debate team. I'll bet he really opens up at family reunions. "Thanks," I say.

I turn and the girls follow me out the door. Once we are back in the hallway, I say to my pair, "Now, aren't you glad you have a dad like me, instead of a boring guy like that?"

"No," Kelly says. "With him we wouldn't have to listen to all those life lessons you're always babbling on about."

"When did you ever listen to *any* of them?"

"Dun't know."

Kelly is cruisin' for a bruisin'.

The cleaning crew is now working on the dance floor. Two guys are on their hands and knees scraping off dried gum and gunk while two other guys are huffing and puffing as they maneuver large buff and polish machines over the wood. Theirs is not a fun job.

"You know what that is girls?" I ask as we pass by the work in progress. "That's why you go to college."

Before we climb back into the Toyota, and I hope it starts, I check the time. It's almost 1 p.m., well into the allowable range to call. "Who wants to call Tiffany?"

"I do," Care blurts out first.

"Ask her if we can come over and watch her TV."

Tiffany lives in a penthouse condo on the top floor of a building on Lakeshore Drive between Grand and Chicago Avenues. It has three bedrooms, a maid's quarters, a gourmet kitchen, a full living room, a media room, and spectacular views in all four directions. Compared to my apartment, it's the Taj Mahal. Tiffany considers it a nice starter home.

"Good morning little dudettes," Tiffany greets the girls as we enter.

"It's afternoon, Tiffany," I correct her.

It's the first time Kelly and Care have been here. It's only my second. The best way to keep a residence building ultra-exclusive is not to let people like us inside. Care goes gaga for the second time in the day. She walks around in awe, staring at the art on the walls, the massive TV screen, the computer set-up, and the pure richness of every item in sight.

Kelly tries her best not to be too impressed. She stops at a painting, "Who's this Miro, guy?" she asks.

"Some painter in Europe my designer picked out," Tiffany answers. "I think he was a buddy of that Picasso guy. I got his stuff in the other room."

The art is bolted to the walls. A good idea since they're originals.

"I was just making myself a power shake," Tiffany says. "Want one?"

Kelly and Care both answer simultaneously. "Yes, please."

I decline. Although a shake is probably the only power I'll ever have in this group. We follow Tiffany into the kitchen, where the floor is marble, the counters are granite, and the cabinets are teak.

Tiffany goes to a massive blender on the counter. She adds, pours, measures, chops, blends, and serves. "Yummy," she says, sampling her creation. "So good, and so good for you."

Kelly and Care take their sips. They're not so sure, but they'll down it just to be cool. I wish I could get them to do that with my Chicken ala

Broccoli Supreme.

I survey the counters, observing every appliance and gadget imaginable; all in a color that perfectly matches the decor. "When was the last time you cooked in here, Tiffany?"

"You mean me cooked, or the cook cooked?" She answers my question with a question--which I hate.

"You."

"Me cook, ah no," she explains. "That's why the caterer was invented."

The three women carry their libations to the media room where Kelly puts in one of the DVDs from the envelope left for me at the Zanadu Club. Care mans the remote. "Go ahead, hit *Play*," I say sitting down on one of the two Barcaloungers. The massive TV screen pops on like an IMAX. The picture comes into focus. Thank God there's no sound. I couldn't take any more of that Hip-Hop, Rap, Ska, or whatever is considered music these days.

The shot is from the ceiling camera from the right, with the patrons facing the bar. Tiffany sits dead center, two women to her left, one on her right. There are guys interspersed between the women and a few coming in and out of the picture. The bartender is pouring an expensive looking vodka into three martini glasses.

"Why does the picture look so funny, Dad?" Care asks.

"It's in black and white."

"Yuck, I hate that," Kelly says.

"Did you see that, Mr. Sherlock?" Tiffany yelps out.

"No. What?"

"Stop the tape," Tiffany orders. She jumps up and hurries to the freeze-frame image where she points to the top of a blonde woman's head two barstools down from her. "Look, you can see her black roots."

"That's not really what we're looking for, Tiffany," I say.

"I can't help it," Tiffany says. "When I see a salon fox pac, I'm conditioned to point it out."

I would do all a favor by explaining that Tiffany's *fox pac* is actually a *faux pas*, but nobody would listen; so why bother.

"Watch the drinks, watch the people. We want to see if someone slips anything into your martini."

For the next five minutes or so, we watch the DVD intently. One guy comes up to Tiffany and tries to chat her up, but she shuts him down in seconds. He's replaced by two other guys with the same crushing result. Tiffany sometimes giggles with the girl next to her, waves to someone off camera, and listens to a comment or two from Bruno, whose hands are quicker than a magician's as he mixes one cocktail after another. There is one woman, sitting back-to-back with Tiffany, who gives my assistant a pretty good run for her money in the looks department. I can sense tension between the two. Otherwise, Tiffany's having a pretty good time. The Zanadu Club is her element. Friends come up to say hello, give her an air kiss, or share a laugh. Each carries a glass of whatever, which eventually ends up on the bar. There are so many drinks coming and going, it's difficult to discern whose is whose.

Then it happens. Tiffany shifts slightly to her left, makes a short upward oomph, then collapses onto the bar like a warm glop of Smucker's apple jelly. Luckily, her head doesn't bang onto the wood or take out a row of glasses. Instead her entire body turns into an unmuscled mass of doughy humanity and slowly slumps to the floor, the same way a sugary filling oozes out of a baking pie.

Seeing herself on the screen, Tiffany's entire body tightens with the tautness of a coiled rattlesnake.

"Tiffany, are you okay?" I ask.

She's comatose. Only the pupils of her eyes are moving as she sees herself splayed out on the floor like a TKO'd prizefighter.

It takes a few seconds for the people in the scene to come to her aid, and for me to tell Care, "Turn it off."

The screen goes black. I rush to Tiffany, grab her, and pull her to face me. Her face is ashen; her body barely moving. Clearly, she's in shock. "Tiffany, look at me."

Her eyes finally focus into mine. She speaks, "That was me, but it can't be me. Things like that don't happen to people like me."

"Drink some more power drink," I tell her.

"Here, she can have mine," Care says, handing over her almost full glass.

Tiffany takes a sip, then another. The color returns to her cheeks. She starts to move. "Wow," she says. "I'm giving that movie *no* stars."

"Girls, pick her up and walk her around."

Kelly and Care each take one of Tiffany's arms and lift her out of her seat. "Can we go see your closet?" Kelly asks.

"Great idea," I say. "Go."

After closing the door to the room, I watch the DVD a second time, change discs and watch the same scene from the second ceiling camera twice. There is a third DVD in the envelope, which is a wide-angle, straight-on view from another camera facing the bar. Whoever owns the Zanadu doesn't want to miss a thing. I watch the third DVD twice and remove it from the player. I put all the DVD's back in the envelope, turn off the unit, and go out to find the girls.

"Come out, come out, wherever you are," I call out.

The three emerge out of the hallway. Kelly runs right up to me. She has a look in her eyes of pure wonder and amazement. "Dad," she says, "I've visited heaven."

"We're out of here."

I make sure Tiffany will be fine before leaving. She said her masseuse was on his way over to rub her into reality. We leave.

I get the girls back to the apartment. Talk about a residential letdown. They start their homework at four. We eat at six, or I eat while they complain that my chicken would make Colonel Sanders hurl. On Sunday, they seldom eat at home since they know their mother will take them to McDonald's if they bellyache enough. At eight, I drop them off at my ex-home. I kiss them goodbye, tell them I'll see them Tuesday after school, and that I love them more than life itself.

I go straight back to my apartment, and for the next three hours watch the DVDs over and over and over. And for the life of me still can't see who slipped Tiffany a Mickey.

CHAPTER 3

Bruno Buttaras, aka Bruno the bartender, lives in an impressive looking high-rise facing the Chicago River. Not too shabby for a guy who mixes drinks for a living. Maybe I should get into that line of work. I park my Toyota in the 15 minute zone in front of the building, place an old parking ticket on the windshield, and walk quickly up the driveway. The doorman doesn't open the door. I have to do it myself. Some doorman.

"Can I help you?" the doorman asks. He seems wider than he is tall and is dressed in a blue uniform with gold stripes.

"Does a Bruno Buttaras live here?"

"Who wants to know?" the doorman asks in a snotty tone of voice. Put a couple of epaulets on a guy's shoulders and watch his head swell.

"Richard Sherlock," I pull out my PI's license to impress him.

He takes a long look. "You're a detective named Sherlock? That's pretty funny."

"Funny ha-ha or funny peculiar?"

"You pick," he says.

"Why? I'm not the one laughing."

We stand and stare at each other for a few seconds before I ask, "Is Bruno in?"

"Can't say."

I pull a bill out of my pocket, fold it and slip it in the uniform's breast pocket. "Is he in?"

The doorman takes the bill out, checks the denomination, puffs his big chest out, and puts it back in his uniform's side pocket. "Can't say," he says.

"Then give me my five dollars back."

"Why should I?"

"Because you didn't give me anything on Bruno," I snap back.

"I thought that was my tip for opening the door for you?"

"You didn't open it. I did."

An old lady approaches. He opens the door for her. "Good morning Mrs. Frobisher."

"Good morning, Guido."

I wait for her to go into the inner foyer of the lobby before I say, "You got a lot of nerve making fun of my name when you're a Guido."

"Fine," he says. "Bruno lives on the 41st floor. His code is BB12 on the directory. Call him if you want."

I move to an opposite wall where there's a listing of the building's residents on a screen. I pick up the house phone, punch BB12 on the dial, wait, and listen. I hang up the phone after ten or eleven rings. "He isn't in, or he's asleep," I, for some unexplainable reason, tell the doorman.

"Guess what?" the doorman, enunciating slower than molasses, says. "You … are … right … now …" I hear each word as if a 45 was playing at the 33 speed. "Get … ing … a … tic … ket." He then slowly points his finger to the street.

I turn around, and see the meter maid is pulling up behind my car. I run outside like Snaglepuss making one of his quick exits.

The meter maid is off her three-wheeler and examining the old ticket on my windshield. She is taking out her hand-held computer ticket gizmo when I catch up to her. I could attempt to charm her with my wit and poor excuses. Instead, I scream out "No." I don't bother waiting for her response. I jump into my Toyota, fire it up, and drive off. I thankfully don't get my ticket punched.

I head south to the Harold Washington Library.

I sign in and only have to wait five minutes for a computer terminal. This is where people go if they want to be a nerd in public or can't afford a computer of their own and still want an e-mail address. I sit down and start my homework.

The Zanadu Club is listed under Restaurants and Entertainment services. It's owned by Zanaprise, a Delaware Corporation. The CEO is Jimmy Cappilino. The COO is Frank Buck. Due to it being a privately held entity, there are no yearly figures or gross dollar amounts given.

I Google the CEO and find no listing. I have an odd feeling Jimmy isn't Jimmy's actual first name. There are thousands of listings for Frank Buck. Evidently, he was a big game hunter back in the 1920's who made movies of his adventures in deepest, darkest Africa. There are lots and lots of stories, pictures, reviews, links, and other assorted info on the jungle exploits of Mr. Frank "Bring 'em Back Alive" Buck. I watch a few excerpts from his films of him co-starring with poisonous snakes, charging rhinos, lunging lions, and other assorted beasts who were kind enough to attack while the cameras just happened to be filming. I quickly surmise this is not the Frank Buck I seek. I scroll through another ten pages and find nothing on Zanadu's Frank Buck. I get bored and give up the search. That's the problem with Google; who wants to go through thirty pages of stuff to find what you're looking for?

I try another tactic.

About six months ago, when I had more money than I have now (which is none), I took advantage of a one-time-only offer and shelled out $110 for a yearly subscription to *BackgroundChecker.com*. It's a website for daters who want to find out if the men or the women they meet on *Match.com* or some other dating sites are convicted rapists, thieves, on parole, or wanted in connection for some illegal act. I signed up because my propensity of picking quality women is not one of my better traits. For an additional ten dollars, the site also offers information on the current marital status of individuals who claim they are "single, athletic and toned, love to laugh, enjoy long walks on the beach, and are truly seeking their soul mate." I didn't opt for the add-on service. Personally, a woman being married would be a minor problem compared to some of the problems I have had with the women I've dated.

I discover a number of guys named Cappilino who women shouldn't date because of their assorted criminal records. Or they maybe should date if they like bad boys. None of the Cappilinos listed has the first name of Jimmy or James. When I narrow this down to Cappilinos in Chicago, there are six. I write down the specifics on each; some have addresses, some don't. I next search for Frank Buck, which is a very popular name if you're a criminal, but oddly enough, there are no dastardly Frank Bucks listed in Chicago.

I hit three cherries on my next spin. Bruno the bartender pops up on the screen like one of those cute little rascals in a Whack-A-Mole machine. Bruno has had his share of problems with the law. A stint in juvie at sixteen, busted for shoplifting at twenty-one, got caught passing bad checks at twenty-six, and an aggravated assault charge at twenty-nine. Excellent upwardly mobile career path I must say. He's been out of the joint for three years. Gone straight? I doubt it.

Just for the heck of it, I type in Gibby Fearn and come up with a guy on another upwardly mobile career path. He started out on Rush Street, tending bar in college. He eventually became a manager and hopped around job-wise to a couple of other bars and restaurants. About five years ago, he worked at a big club downtown as its general manager in charge of events, décor and design. An odd job description in my opinion. The listing ended with: *Currently employed at Zanadu as the VP of Operations.*

I get off the website, feeling my money had been well spent. Next, I Google City of Chicago Building Records and add the address of the Zanadu Club. Nothing comes up.

I get up, walk over to the Research Desk, and ask the librarian for assistance. "Excuse me. Could you help me find out something about a building?"

"What do you want to know?" the woman asks.

"I'm not sure."

"It would help to know what you want to know." The woman has a pair of glasses attached to a string of fancy beads, which go around her neck. I'll bet librarians are the only profession known to wear designer lanyards.

"I was in this building the other night and heard this weird *whoosh/plop* sound coming from one of the closets in an office on the second floor.

"Okay."

I continue, "And there has to be some reason for that sound. I thought it might have something to do with the construction."

"Okay."

"So, maybe if I find out what the history of the building is, the *whoosh/plop* sound might make sense."

"Give me the address."

I do as told. The nice librarian types into her computer and in a few minutes reads off some information. "It was built after the Chicago Fire as a meat processing plant and was converted into a fish cannery in 1910 which went broke during the Depression. It was converted again in 1939, this time to build parts for radar systems. After the war it became a warehouse or maybe a distribution center." She stops reading off the screen, takes off her specs, and peers up at me. "Does any of that help?"

"I'm not sure."

"Should I keep going?"

"Please do," I say in earnest. "You're doing great."

She puts the glasses back on. "It pretty much stayed a warehouse until the late 1990's when it was converted to a mini-Merchandise Mart, specifically for the backyard accessories market." She stops.

"What are backyard accessories?" I ask.

"It doesn't say," she says. "But you should know, you're a man."

"Just because I'm a male doesn't make me an expert on backyards," I say to defend my honor. "I happen to live in an apartment."

"I apologize," she says.

"Let's go back to the building."

"Good idea."

"It's the Zanadu Nightclub now," I tell her.

"That has a *whooshing/plopping* sound in its closets." She seems to enjoy adding the obvious sound effects to her sentence. Librarians probably don't get a lot of opportunities to poke fun or take exciting liberties in their day-to-day work.

"Exactly."

"You could go down to the building department in City Hall and search for the original plans, but I doubt if you'd find any *whooshes* or *plops* in the details."

"I just might do that anyway."

The librarian rises from her computer chair.

"Thank you very much," I say sincerely. "I appreciate your help."

"You're welcome."

At that instant Lady Gaga erupts out of my phone. Those kids of mine are always sabotaging my ring tones.

"The sign says to 'turn off all cell phones,'" the lady librarian says to me, her fun personality disappears; replaced with a stern, air of frustration.

I panic. I can't turn it off. Lady Gaga keeps singing; if you want to call what she does singing. "Sorry."

She walks away. I punch the screen of the cell phone and finally answer the call. It's Tiffany. "I can't talk now," I say in my best whisper. "I'm in the library."

"Libraries aren't cool, Mr. Sherlock," she tells me. "Because nobody takes books out of them anymore."

"I'm not very cool either, so I fit right in."

"You got to get an iPad, Mr. Sherlock."

"I'll put it on my shopping list, right after my new car," I assure her. "How are you feeling?"

"Fine," she says. "Have you figured out who roofied me yet?"

"No."

"Seven point two hours is already up."

"Tiffany, we have to go over the DVDs again," I tell her.

"Oh, Mr. Sherlock, I hate that."

"I need names to go along with the faces."

"Can't you just look at the credits?"

I'm able to freeze the picture at different intervals of the DVD, so that Tiffany will not have to see herself sprawled out on the barroom floor like a spent, out-of-water tuna.

"Who's this?" I ask pointing to the woman to the left of Tiffany, a petite brunette, well-dressed, and dripping of old money wealth.

"Marley."

"Marley, who? I need last names."

"Marley Spencer."

"Is she a friend of yours?"

"Kinda," Tiffany says.

"What's a kinda friend?"

"Marley is really nice, but we can't be too friendly with each other."

"Why not?"

"Because we compete for the same men, Mr. Sherlock," Tiffany explains. "There's only so many of our kinda guys to go around."

I point to a guy with an intentional four-day beard, who follows the current *scruffy is cool* fashion sense. "This guy?"

"Hayden. His father owns a company that makes seeds that grow corn that doesn't get worms."

"What do you think of him?"

"He's still in his teenybopper phase.

"Lucky him. This guy?"

"Don't know him."

"This woman?" I point to a very attractive brunette, who sits back-to-back with Tiffany at the bar.

"Bitch."

"How so?"

"Total bitch."

33

"Elaborate, please."

Tiffany gives out a sigh, and says. "Alix Fromound. Her daddy's in steel. Her grandmother had a stateroom on the Mayflower. Their house has more lake frontage than the city of Glencoe. She drives a Tesla. I hate her. She hates me."

"Why?"

"Duh, a guy." Tiffany doesn't wait for me to ask for more. "It was about two years ago." She pauses, now I wait for more.

"I was seeing Radford Wilson, his daddy is the head of some board of trading firm or something, and he owns a nine bedroom house. Raddy was on me like Prada on purse, but I wasn't putting out until I knew he was serious."

"Good for you, Tiffany."

Tiffany points her thumb at herself. "This girl's not going to be a notch on any guy's Ralph Lauren belt." She pauses for a moment before continuing. "Anyway, somehow word got out that Raddy was getting itchy and Alix, who always had a horny twitch for Raddy, went on a birddog attack."

I'm so glad I asked.

"Raddy and I were like on our third date, dancing at a club. I leave to use the ladies room and up comes Little Miss Horny Pants who latches onto Raddy like calories on a donut. She couldn't have been more transparent if she woulda been stark naked coming out of a cake. People told me she was pushing her phony C cups into him like a stripper doing a lap dance."

I cut her off. Way too much information. "Okay," I say. "That's why you hate her. Why does she hate you?"

"Because when we were in high school I did the same thing to her."

Could there be any doubt whatsoever why I hate my job?

An hour later, I had the names of six of Tiffany's friends/foes, but not those of four anonymous talkers, nine passersby, and six guys caught on the wide-angle lens leering in Tiffany's direction.

"When you catch the person who did this to me," Tiffany says. "I want him thrown in one of those prisons where they torture every hour on the hour."

"That might be difficult."

"Why?"

"Because there's no proof that a crime was committed," I tell her.

"You suffered no lasting physical affects, you weren't robbed or molested, and you didn't suffer any emotional hardship."

"What about damaging my reputation?"

"You just admitted you swooped in on Alix just like she did to you."

"But I was just a child; Alix was an adult when she did it to me."

It's late in the afternoon. I'm tired, but before going home, I swing by the building where Bruno the bartender lives and experience phenomenal parking karma. I pull into a legal spot right across from the main entryway. I'm still sitting in the car, enjoying my good fortune, when I see Bruno and a man of similar size and height, exit the front door. I pull up on the front door handle, but the door won't open, yet another device that doesn't work in my life. I have to reach behind me and pull up the locking pin. By the time I get the door open, get out and lock the car, as if someone would ever be dumb enough to steal this thing, the two guys have about a block head start on me. They move east along the river walkway, heading towards Marina City, a sixty-story structure that resembles a very tall stack of flapjacks.

I'm walking faster than most joggers, hopefully not fast enough to be confused with a criminal fleeing on foot. Although both guys are big boys, it's hard to keep them in sight. No matter what you've seen on TV shows, tailing anyone by yourself in a big city is almost an impossible task. There are crowds, stoplights, and construction crews that always get in your way. And if your suspect enters a building with multiple exits, 99% of the time you lose them. When I was a cop we once had six people tailing a guy and we lost him in the first fifteen minutes.

I'm about thirty feet behind Bruno and his buddy. They're about to enter the basement level of Marina City where stores, dry cleaners, restaurants and a myriad of other establishments populate the underground pathways. For the people who work and live there, this place is a confusing labyrinth; it's an unnavigable maze for the unsuspecting. Tourists have been known to get lost in there for days. I know I'm going to lose my quarry once they enter, so I stop, step up on a bench, to get a last clear picture of the two before they disappear into the building.

I take a second to print the photo and add it to the album in my brain. I sit down, render up the not-so-great image in my head, and view it. Bruno looks exactly like he did in the bar, big, firm, muscled, and healthy; all that's missing is a martini shaker. The other guy is maybe six feet, bulky, big, but not fat. His face is impossible to see from the distance, but for some reason he seems familiar. I can't place him.

I check my Timex, pull out my cell phone, and call my girls for our daily conversation. They tell me they didn't learn anything in school, have too much homework, who they sat next to at lunch, and other mindless tidbits of their lives. Kelly goes on and on about the clothes she "just has to have," and Care fills me in on what the Bailouts thought about their last defeat. Not fun to hear. They each ask about Tiffany's well being, but don't inquire about mine. After about five minutes, we're done. I remind them about tomorrow, tell then I love them, and hang up. As pointless, inane, and innocuous as these conversations may be, I enjoy every second.

I walk back to my Toyota. I stand across the street and gaze upon it resting proudly between a Chevy and a BMW. It's such a wonderful sight to behold. A perfectly parked car, in a perfectly legal spot, with no time limit sign, no meter, no orange cones of warning. I take it all in, as if I'm seeing the Grand Canyon for the first time. If you have ever lived in an urban jungle, you know how seldom you come across the perfect, free, unobstructed, parking spot. Yes, for once, all my planets are in alignment, my biorhythms are in sync, and my life finally reaches perfection, if in only a very small way. Why can't cash come my way the same as this parking karma did?

CHAPTER 4

I'm too far west to head all the way back to the Drive, so I take Milwaukee Avenue most of the way home. I find a spot about a half a block from my building--great parking karma seldom lasts. I walk up the block and see a guy standing at the first floor entry door. He's wearing a crumpled black suit and a grey felt fedora. Even I wouldn't wear a felt fedora.

My first thought is that he's a salesman waiting for someone to let him inside so he can peddle an annuity policy that lets you retire when you're ninety with a three hundred dollar a month income. But I'm wrong.

"You Sherlock?" he asks.

"Does Sherlock owe you any money?" I break my own rule about answering a question with a question.

"No."

"Then, yeah, I'm Sherlock."

"Let's take a ride," he says, and motions for me to follow him.

"Let's not," I answer.

He's gruff, billy goat gruff, talking as if he's chewing on tin cans. "Don't argue," he says.

"I'm not arguing," I tell him. "I don't want to take a drive. Traffic is terrible."

"Dat's arguing."

"No, it's not." Now we're arguing.

The man reaches behind his back and pulls out a Glock, a very big Glock. He points it at my nose.

The argument is over. I concede defeat. "Are we taking your car or mine?"

"Git."

The Thug in a fedora leads me down the walkway to a Cadillac parked right in front of my building; evidently it was his turn for good parking karma. He opens the back door. I take the hint, climb inside, take another hint from the barrel of his gun, and scoot over to the far seat. He slips the gun into its holster behind his back and sits next to me.

"This is a real treat," I tell the Thug. "My car doesn't have leather seats."

The driver of the vehicle, who is behind a closed, tinted glass divider, a much better divider than the kind you see in cheap taxicabs, pulls the Caddy into the street. I can only see the back of his head. His hair has been professionally styled to come down into a tear-shaped point, and from that point long strands of hair are braided into a neat little ponytail. Not something I would ever wear, but attractive in its own way. The only other distinguishing aspect of the driver is the dark, aviator glasses he wears. I see them via his reflection in the rear view mirror. He doesn't turn around to wave or motion that he's glad to have me aboard.

"Nice day for a drive," I say to break the ice with Mr. Ponytail.

The driver's voice remains frozen, although I'm pretty sure he heard me, because he immediately glanced into the rear view mirror.

"Can I ask you something?" I ask the fedora wearing Thug sitting beside me, who I'm sure, can hear me.

He doesn't respond.

I ask anyway. "With that gun of yours in the holster behind your back, doesn't it really hurt when you sit down?"

He either doesn't want to talk anymore or he's in too much pain to talk because of the gun pushing into his spine. I have another question, one that might be easier to answer. "Why do you wear your hat while you're in the car? Isn't it customary to take your hat off while inside?"

Again no answer. Thugs aren't known for their knowledge of the Emily Post Rules of Etiquette.

The driver doesn't answer my question, either. Maybe because he's not wearing a hat.

Neither of my captors will ever be successful in the tour bus business.

The Caddy is approaching Western Avenue, "Ya know, if we're goin' back downtown, it's faster to take Western this time of the day," I say to be helpful.

They're not listening. Why should these two guys be any different than anyone else I speak to?

My phone rings. Lady Gaga. Tiffany's calling.

I take the phone out of my pocket, flip it open, and I'm about to say, "Can't talk right now, Tiffany, I'm being taken for a ride in a Cadillac by one Thug in a grey fedora and another one with a ponytail," when Mr. Thug in a Fedora reaches over, grabs my phone, looks at it as if it is a factory second, and breaks it in two.

I hear Tiffany's voice come out of the phone's little speaker, until the guy drops that half on the car's floor and stomps it with the heel of his unpolished wingtip. He hands the other half back to me, the half with the little keypad that is way too small to text with. "Wrong numba," he says in his usual gruff tone.

"Wow," I tell the Thug. "I'll bet you're no fun to sit next to in a movie theater."

For the rest of the trip I sit back and try to enjoy the soft Corinthian leather.

We take Fullerton Avenue to the Drive, all the way through the city, and exit just past the McCormick Place Convention Center. Continuing south and west, we enter into a mostly industrial neighborhood; drive down a back street, and into an alley. The Caddy stops. The Thug opens his door, gets out, and motions for me to do the same.

I figure, what the heck. This is as good a place as any to find out what this is all about.

The Caddy drives off leaving me and the Thug in a fedora standing between two dumpsters. Behind us is a padlocked, eight-foot, chain-link rolling gate with at least a yard of razor along its top. A non-descript, one-story building is about thirty feet away on the other side. There are no signs, no logos and no descriptions of any business on the building. Across the way are a number of junked cars and a sign for *Tub Anew We Do*, a company in the business of refinishing bathtubs. I conclude this after seeing the clever little *before and after* tub rendition on the company's sign.

"Come here often?" I ask.

The Thug says, "Sumbuddy wanna chat." He moves to the end of the gate, takes out one key from his pants pocket, and unlocks the padlock. Pulling the gate instead of pushing, he gets it about halfway open, stops, and motions me to join him. I take two steps forward, and just as I get even with him, a shot rings out from the building in front of us.

I jump almost out of my skin. I hate guns, I hate bullets, and I really hate bullets shot out of guns in my direction. The Thug in a fedora is knocked squarely off his feet. I can see a hole right in the middle of his chest; his cheap, striped tie ruined forever.

I hit the deck and roll to my left, like a kid rolling down a grassy knoll, as another shot rings out. I manage to get behind the dumpster just as I hear the third shot. I do a split-second check of my front body and find no holes. That's something to be thankful for. To my right, I see the grey fedora, sitting, but it has no body or head underneath it. The hat sits on the ground alone like a dropped pacifier on a day-care-center walkway. My head goes back down when the fourth shot pings off the other dumpster like a pinball hitting the free game target.

Being the coward that I am, I cower behind the dumpster, and wait. What else can I do? I punch 911 into the half of the phone that I have left, but discover the cell phone doesn't work without the other half. So much for modern technology.

Two more shots ring out.

I have completely sweated through my clothes. I'm glad I don't have a mirror, because I must be whiter than a Clorox bleached ghost. I have no clue how much time elapses before I hear a siren followed by the sound of screeching rubber as a patrol car speeds into the alley. I'm about to run out and wave my hands for the patrolman to stop, but that could be akin to wearing a pair of antlers on the first day of deer season. Instead, I push the dumpster into the middle of the alley. The cop car doesn't see it in time, and BOOM! The resounding thud is louder than a howitzer. The impact sends the metal square rolling down the alley faster than Ursain Bolt doing the hundred meters. It hits a dilapidated couch waiting for pick-up, flips over, destroys a discarded toilet, flips again, and finally comes to a stop half-way up on the hood of what was once a Ford Taurus before road salt took its toll.

The cop car, with a now heavily-dented front end, stops. The patrolman leaps out, whips out his gun from his holster, takes up a position behind the front door on the driver's side, and aims his weapon straight at me. Being a target twice in one day is not a good thing.

"Freeze!"

Yes, cops actually do yell "Freeze" in these situations.

I hold my hands to the sky. "I'm not the shooter. I'm the guy getting shot at."

"Don't move."

"I'm not planning on it." I watch him relax just a bit and add, "The shots came from that building." With only my index finger moving, I point at the structure behind the open gate. "There was another guy with me," I tell him. "He got shot."

The cop comes out from behind the patrol car door, his gun still aimed at my heart. "Where's he?"

"I don't know."

"You said he got shot," the cop says, approaching me slowly.

"He did."

"Where?"

"In his chest."

"No, where was he when he got shot?"

"Right there, next to the other dumpster." This conversation is lasting way too long. My arms are getting sore; all the blood is running down out of them.

"I don't see any blood." He makes a good point.

Another police car enters the alley.

The cop moves closer; soon he's beside me. "Don't move until I tell you to move."

"No problem."

The back-up blocks the alley from the other direction and that officer comes out with his gun drawn too. The third time's the charm.

"Slowly put your hands behind your back," the first cop orders.

I do as I'm told and feel the cuffs go on. "I'm the shootee, not the shooter," I explain on my way over to the squad car where I am thrown against it belly first, bent over, face pushed down onto the hood, legs spread, and frisked rougher than by an overzealous, TSA agent searching through questionable luggage.

"Ouch."

I feel my wallet come out of my back pocket. I hope they don't take my last six dollars.

"You a PI?" the first cop asks.

"Yes."

"We hate PI's," the back-up informs me.

I can't blame them. I hated PI's when I was a cop. They were always popping up unannounced and always getting in the way. And most of them made more money than the detectives on the force. Since I became a PI, I'm doing my best to reverse the final reason.

I'm placed in the back of the recently dented squad car, where it's very hard to get comfortable with your hands, behind you, bound in carbon steel shackles.

Fifteen minutes or so later, the door on my left opens. "Sherlock, what the hell are you doing here?"

Just my luck, out of the hundreds of detectives in the Chicago Police Department, I get "Wait" Jack Wayt.

Jack Wayt has been a detective in the CPD since Capone was a kid-- actually not that long, but long enough to see a lot of guys, like me, come and go. He's been a detective going on forty years, and has the rings to prove it--rings that are similar to those of a redwood tree, only his are around his protruding stomach. He's worked every precinct, every division, every crime, and every angle. He's solved more cases alone than most squad rooms have with a dozen cops. Murder, larceny, gang crimes, bunco, shoplifting, he's handled them all.

I got to know Jack in my first detective duty as a traffic investigator. This is the spot all detectives start or at least they should. Because traffic investigations have a set time, place, action, suspects, and rules of the road to follow. The incident happened between this street and that street. One car was going this way, the other that way. They collided here. One driver says this. The other says that. Now figure it out.

Jack was a good mentor in my early years. He'd sing my praises when I made the extra effort, thought out-of-the-box, or discovered something that no one else saw. He would also kick me in the rear when I missed the obvious or went off on one of my tangents that made no sense whatsoever. Our paths crossed frequently over the years, as did the paths of almost every other detective on the force. One reason was because Jack had more partners than a porn star. He couldn't work with anyone. He was consistently late, complained about everything, forgot more than most remembered, and would zone out during conversations faster than an Alzheimer's patient. If that wasn't enough frailties, Jack had one more that put him over the top. He had more diseases than the Center of Disease Control. He would complain about having bursitis, rhinitis, phlebitis, ileitis, and colitis. All self-diagnosed, of course. Whenever a drug began advertising, Jack would eventually see the ad, and immediately claim he had the exact symptoms of whatever disease the drug claimed it alleviated or cured. Listening to Jack, you'd swear Stephen Hawking was a picture of health.

"Unlock me, would ya?" I plead with him.

"Wait."

"Why?"

"Sherlock, I think I got COPD."

"What's COPD?"

"I don't know, but I think I got it," he says, sitting down next to me. "Some days it feels like there's an elephant sitting on my chest."

"Have you ever had an elephant sit on your chest?"

"No."

"Then how would you know what it feels like?" I ask.

"Because after I came down with that case of meningitis and my brain swelled up," he says, "my mind's ultra-sensitive to certain stimuli."

"Like elephants sitting on your chest?"

"So to speak," Jack says.

"Get me out of these things, they hurt." I turn my back to him with my hands outstretched.

He unlocks the cuffs. I rub my sore wrists. "Do you want to know what happened?" I ask turning back towards him.

"Not really," he says. "What I want to know is what I can do for my sciatica."

We get out of the squad car. The uniforms are busy stringing up yellow crime scene tape. One tech has picked up the fedora and is admiring it. "That's the guy's hat, the guy who got shot," I tell Jack.

"Where'd he get shot?"

"Right here." I point to the middle of my chest.

"No, I meant where, where."

I take him to the spot between the dumpsters where the gate remains open. "What did he get shot with, a BB gun?" Jack asks.

"No, a real gun with a big bang."

"No blood," Jack says. "Usually when you get shot in the chest with a big gun, there's blood." He pauses, then asks, "Didn't I teach you anything in all those years?"

"Maybe he was wearing a vest."

"Kevlar or the third piece of a suit ensemble?" Jack asks.

"For the sake of argument, let's go with the Kevlar."

For the next hour, I follow Jack walking up and down surveying the scene. He asks me to start at the beginning and tell him everything I remember. I comply. One second before I finish, he says, "Wait."

I pause.

He asks, "What was the license plate of the Cadillac?"

How stupid can I be?

"Do you remember seeing anyone who saw you when you were in the car?"

Damn. He got me again.

"You keep the half of the phone clean, so we can lift a print from the big guy?"

"Whoops."

Jack turns to me, "Sherlock I was going to say that I missed having you on the force, but I've decided to hold off on that comment."

"I was being kidnapped," I retort. "I was under a lot of stress."

"You were under a lot of stress?" he barks back. "Did I ever tell you about the time I came down with Post Traumatic Stress Syndrome?"

"No, but I'm sure you will."

Jack drops me off at a nearby 'L' station and I finally make it through my front door, five hours since I last arrived. I take a long shower, soak my wrists, put a can of soup on the stove to warm, and figure I better return a phone call.

"Mr. Sherlock, I've been calling you forever," Tiffany shrieks into the phone. "I get this weird, annoying noise, then it cuts out, and I can't even leave a message. You've got to get a smart phone."

"I'm not sure I'm smart enough to use a smart phone, Tiffany."

"Well, you got to get rid of that antique thing you use."

"It's already gone," I tell her. "It broke in two."

"See, I told you. It pays to buy quality," she schools me. She pauses for a moment or two. I can almost hear the wheels inside her brain turning. "If your phone broke, how are you calling me?"

"On my landline."

"Get with it, Mr. Sherlock. The only people who have landlines anymore are AARP Members."

I am two years shy of forty and this is the respect I've earned so far in life. Pathetic, truly pathetic.

"Tiffany, what did you call me about the first time you called?"

"I've found a possible break in the case."

"Great. What's broken?"

"I'm not sure," she says. "We have to go see Alix Fromound. I'll pick you up in an hour."

"No. I'm beat. I just got home. I'm hungry. My wrists are killing me.

I want to go to bed. I had a horrible day."

"Oh, Mr. Sherlock, it couldn't have been that bad."

"I got kidnapped, shot at, almost run over by a trash dumpster, held at gunpoint, handcuffed, and roughed up by a couple of cops."

"Okay, if you need a little extra time, fine," she says. I'll pick you up in an hour and a half."

CHAPTER 5

Gibson's is a Rush Street steakhouse which was once, and maybe still is, the most profitable restaurant in the country--if you figured it on the basis of square footage. We're at the bar. Tiffany sips a martini, I, a Shirley Temple, and Alix, a Maker's Mark.

"There was some major, bad mojo workin' that night in Zanadu," Alix says. "Seriously bad."

"I know," Tiffany agrees. "It tossed me right on the carpet."

"I wasn't talkin' about you," Alix qualifies her statement. "That was like the saving grace of the evening."

"Thanks, bioché."

"You're welcome--bitch."

"You two always been close?" I ask.

"Too close," Alix says.

"Way too close," Tiffany ups her one.

"Tell me what was so weird about the evening," I continue in my search for facts instead of insults.

"I'm sittin' at the bar, Monroe Chevelier chattin' me up--" Alix begins.

Tiffany interrupts, "Chevelier was chatting you up? Yeah, right."

"Ahh, yeah."

"As if."

"Tiffany," I interrupt, "would you let her tell me what happened."

Tiffany crosses her arms, gives me a nasty stare, and shuts up.

"As I was saying," Alix brushes back her long, mid-back, jet-black hair with a sweep of her hand and a slight push back of her head. "Chevelier's chattin'me up and this guy I've never seen before comes right up and cock blocks him."

"What?" I say hoping I heard that wrong.

"He puts this major cock block on Monroe Chevelier."

"No way," Tiffany says. "Monroe's daddy's got more money than my daddy."

"Not mine," Alix says.

"Can we rewind," I plead. "What did he do?"

"He cock blocked him."

I heard it right the first time.

"That's when you're talking with some guy and some other guy juts right in between, with his butt to him and his face to you, and starts chattin' you up," Alix explains.

"It's called cock blocking, Mr. Sherlock."

I'm in shock. What has the dating world become?

"It's not so weird when you're getting hit on by some wimp and a good-lookin' stud puts a block on," Alix explains. "But when a dude does it to Monroe, who like wears Armani to the gym and benches presses 400, that's totally bogus."

"So, what happened?"

"Yeah," Tiffany says. "What happened?"

"Monroe's pissed. He gets off the stool, and I think he's gonna go like Jackie Chan on him, when the blocker faces Monroe and all this swearin', and posin', and pushin' goes down."

"And?"

"Little bitch Tiffany goes fallin' off a barstool, and everybody goes scramblin' her way like they're givin' away free Crystal."

"What did you do?" I ask Alix.

"I grab Monroe and pull him towards me."

"Aw, wasn't that nice," Tiffany comments in a sing-song voice.

"Like you wouldn't have done the same?" Alix snaps back at Tiffany.

"Stop, you two," I order. "What did this blocker guy look like?" I can't bring myself to repeat the other word.

"He looked like he knew his way around the gym," Alix says.

"What happened to him?"

"I look up, "Alix says. "And he, like, disappeared."

"And what happened with you and Monroe?" Tiffany asks.

"None of your business."

"I'll find out," Tiffany says.

"Good," Alix says with a devious smile. She takes another sip of her Maker's Mark.

I put the whole scenario into my head, cross reference it with the DVD of Tiffany passing out, and ask, "Alix, how far away from Tiffany were you when all this happened?"

"Few feet."

"What were you drinking?"

"Martini."

"Kumquat?"

"Kettle One, on the rocks."

I throw it all into my head. It makes no sense. I'm not sure the two instances are even related. I try to think it all through while I finish my Shirley Temple, but I can't. My brain is filling up with a pile of loose jigsaw pieces and I don't even have the picture on the box to give me a clue on where to begin.

"Was I right?" Alix asks me.

"About what?"

"About there being some seriously bad mojo hangin' in the Zanadu that night?"

"Correct on all counts," I say.

Alix gives Tiffany an *"I'm smarter than you"* grin.

Tiffany turns up her nose at Alix, and gives her head a snarky shake.

If I don't nip this now, it could get ugly. "It was nice meeting you, Alix."

"I'm sure it was," she tells me.

"Can you take me home now, Tiffany?"

"You don't want to party anymore?"

"I didn't want to party to begin with."

Tiffany and Alix air kiss goodbye, their method of acknowledging mutual enemy admiration. I doubt if these two will ever paint each other's toenails at a sleepover.

I'm lost in thought most of the way up the Drive. Tiffany can't take the silence. "What are you thinking, Mr. Sherlock?"

"I don't know. What are you thinking?"

"Alix and Monroe would never be an item."

"Why not?"

"She's an Aries. He's a Scorpio. Fire and water don't mix."

I'm not into astrology. I let her answer suffice. I'm silent again for a mile or two. "Tiffany, why do you think somebody would roofie you?"

"To have sex with me."

"And who would want to do that?"

"Everybody. I'm totally hot."

"I mean, who would stoop so low as to drug you to do it?"

"Some total psycho dweeb."

I pause. "I'm not so sure."

"No way would a stud muffin do it."

"I'm not so sure," I repeat.

We reach my building. I'm exhausted. "Good night, Tiffany. Be careful driving home."

Before I can get out of the Lexus, she says, "Mr. Sherlock, can I ask you something?"

"You're asking a question to ask a question?"

"Well, you're answering my question with a question," she says. "You told me you hate that."

"Touché, Tiffany. Ask away."

"Mr. Sherlock, you don't think I'm as self-centered, egotistical, spoiled-rotten, and conceited as Alix, do you?"

She catches me off guard. I hesitate. I better be very careful or I'll cause hours of useless, and very expensive, therapy, "Of course not, Tiffany."

"Sure?"

"It's all relative, since your good qualities far outweigh your bad qualities," I say sincerely.

"Thank you, Mr. Sherlock," she says. "That's what I think, too."

"The transition game needs work, Sherlock."

"And I really appreciate your interest in the team, Mrs. Whiner, but what we need to do is get back to basics."

Mrs. Whiner is the only parent who comes to all the games and all the practices. "Exactly right," she yells at me from her seat in the bleachers. "The basics of your transition game."

I smile at the obnoxious woman. She doesn't smile back.

I bring the Bailouts to the center court and have the players sit. Kelly, my oldest daughter, has offered her services as an assistant coach, even though she has never played basketball herself. I accept her offer, any activity that will get her off her cell phone is a plus.

"Team, we're going to go back and start at the beginning." I stand on the center line, ball in hand and my players around me. I present the ball. "This is a basketball."

Kelly stops texting and says, "Slow down, Dad, you're going too fast."

"That's an old joke, Kelly."

"Yeah, but I'm a young kid, so I can use it."

Back to the team. "I want you all to listen up, and remember one word, today, just one," I pause. "Beef. B-E-E-F. Beef."

"My mother won't let me eat meat, Coach," Allison, a mediocre player on a team of less-than-mediocre players, informs me of her dietary restrictions.

"No, it's not about eating beef," I tell her.

"What do you order when you go to McDonald's?" Kaylyn asks Allison.

"We don't go to McDonald's," Allison answers.

"Do you go to Burger King?" Care asks.

"McDonald's is better than Burger King, because it has better fries," Annie, our point guard points out.

"Girls," I attempt to get the conversation back on the game of basketball. "We're not here to talk about fast food."

"Then, why'd you bring it up?" Kelly asks.

"My Mom says we should be working on our transition game," Wilma Whiner, a chip off the old computer motherboard, tells the team.

"Beef. B stands for Balance. The first E for eyes. The second E for elbows. And F is for feet," I explain. "Got that?"

No response, except for Kelly's phone ringing. "Sorry, Dad, I have to take this."

"Stand up everybody." I line up the players across from each other. I pass out balls to the ones on the left, position myself in the middle, and demonstrate. "Whenever you shoot, pass, dribble or whatever, your eyes, elbows and feet have to be in balance. Watch." I use two hands and pass the ball to Kelly, who jumps aside to avoid any contact with the ball.

"Hey, that could hurt," she yelps, as she pulls her precious cell phone close to her torso to protect it.

I might have made a big mistake in my selection of an assistant coach.

Back to the team, "Now, you people try it."

Dribble, dribble, pass, pass, shoot, shoot. The players are a little better than Kelly, but not much. We dribble, pass, shoot; dribble, pass, and shoot some more. I can't remember too many baskets being made in the hour we have the court.

"Okay, on Saturday, I want everyone to think BEEF."
"McDonald's or basketball?" Wilma asks.
Is it any wonder why we haven't won a game?

CHAPTER 6

"Wait."

He says before I have a chance to say "Hello."

"And who are you?"

"Tiffany."

"Tiffany who?"

"Tiffany Richmond, investigator in training."

"Wait" Jack Wayt looks over to me, then back to Tiffany, and asks her, "Do I look a little gaunt to you?"

Tiffany gives him a once over. "You could definitely lose twenty pounds, get a better suit, dye your hair, and get rid of those awful shoes."

"But do I look peaked?"

"I'm not sure, because I don't know what that word means," Tiffany answers and admits.

"I might be coming down with pancreatitis," Jack informs us of his latest self-diagnosis. "I'm almost positive my pancreatic juices aren't flowing properly."

"I have no problem with my flow," Tiffany tells him.

Yet again, too much information.

"Jack, what did you find out about this place?" I ask.

The three of us are standing in the same spot where I was almost killed the other day.

"It's owned by some dummy corporation," Jack says.

"My daddy says a lot of companies are owned by idiots," Tiffany informs us. "That's why they're underinsured."

Tiffany is at the very beginning of her family business' learning curve.

We pace around the outside of the building and try to see something that we didn't see the first time around.

Tiffany would obviously rather be at Saks. She sashays around doing her best not to dirty her fancy shoes in the oil stains, grease, and "yucky" potholes. "Why are we here again?" Tiffany asks. "Because I don't like being in these neighborhoods, especially in this disgusting alley."

"This is where the kidnappers dropped me off and somebody started shooting at me," I tell her.

"You didn't tell me that, Mr. Sherlock."

"Yes, I did. I told you about me getting kidnapped, shot at, almost crushed, and roughed up, the other night when you picked me up."

"Oh, I wasn't listening," Tiffany says.

Why do I bother?

Jack leads us into the back door of the building. "So far we've got zilch."

Inside, the CSI techs are unpacking their hand-held vacuum cleaners. "Don't touch anything, Tiffany," I say as we walk through the junked-up, two room area that's as filthy as a third world slum.

"You might want to tell those guys," Tiffany says pointing to the techs, "they'd be better off hiring a cleaning crew."

Jack leads us to a window facing the rear alley. "This is where someone tried to pop you," he says. "There's powder residue all over."

I move to a chair which sits all alone, no doubt where the shooter took aim.

"Tell you anything?" Jack asks.

"Plenty," I lie.

"Good." Jack knows I'm lying.

We move to the center of the bigger of the two rooms where there's an old table, which was once part of someone's kitchen years ago. It has less dust and grime on its top than the rest of the junk in the place. A CSI tech waits for us before he vacuums. "This the office?" I ask.

"I bet," Jack says.

"What are you two talking about?" Tiffany asks, not wanting to miss out.

"Economics," I answer.

"I hate that," Tiffany says. "The only thing I like about economics is the money."

No surprise there.

We keep searching for clues. Jack points out some things he sees, and I do the same. Tiffany gets real bored--real quick. "Excuse me," she says to get our attention, "but what does all this have to do with me getting 'roofied'?"

"Maybe nothing," I tell her. "Maybe everything."

"Bad answer, Mr. Sherlock. Really bad answer."

In the far back of the building, tucked away around a corner are two doors, both closed. Tiffany moves to the first one and tells us, "I'm gonna hate myself, but two Latte Grandes are calling me home." She opens the first door, steps inside, and yells out, "Oh my God. This is disgusting."

What did she expect, the Ladies Room at the Ritz?

"Help!"

Jack and I immediately run to her aid. She stands in a pool of sticky, dark-red glop. With her right hand she braces herself against the door and lifts her left foot to inspect the effect her "Wrong Way" Corrigan maneuver has had on the sole of her very expensive footwear. The stuff oozes on it like marinara sauce made with too much tomato paste. I look at Jack. Jack looks at me.

"Sure does kill that Kevlar theory," I surmise.

"What is this cruddy gunk?" Tiffany asks.

"You're standing in a pool of blood," Jack tells her

"Blood!" Tiffany screams. "I'm standing in someone's blood?"

"Afraid so, Tiffany."

"In my eight-hundred dollar Steve Maddens!? Oh my God!"

The cheapest cell phones, with the cheapest cell phone plans in the entire Chicagoland area, are found at More4LesMobile. The store, which used to be the Meaner Wiener hot dog stand, and could still be a hot dog stand since More4LesMobile did absolutely no remodeling before setting up shop, is located way west on Belmont Avenue. The More4Les Mobile name implies that you will save big money on your communication needs, but it's more a play on words. The guy who owns the place is named Lester, so every purchase will mean "more for Les." He must be raking it in because every time I drop by, he brags about driving a bigger and fancier car than the one he owned before.

"Richard Sherlock, how are ya?" Les is behind the counter where hot dogs used to lie wrapped around the greasiest fries in town.

"My phone broke, Les."

"Was it under warranty?" Les asks, eyeing Tiffany.

"I didn't know your phones have warranties," I mention to the owner.

"I got guarantees, warranties, protection plans. The whole nine yards. You want it Sherlock, I'll sell it to you."

"Do you have any iPhones?" Tiffany asks.

"Let me see," Les turns around and peers up at what used to be the Meaner Wiener's menu board. According to it, you could chow down on such cholesterol-laden delicacies as the Big Bad Brat, the Devil Dog, and the Ferocious Frank. In their place now are easily removable listings of the phones currently in stock. "No iPhones," he says. "But I did just get a shipment of top of the line ZLE Smartphones."

"What's a ZLE?" Tiffany, my phone consultant asks.

"Only the hottest phone to come out of China since they put up the Great Wall."

"Literally, the hottest?" I ask.

"Bad choice of terms," Les says as he reaches behind the counter, where the food orders used to come up, grabs a phone, and hands it to Tiffany.

"What's this?" Tiffany asks, pointing out a blotch on the screen of the phone.

Lester takes the phone back, scratches the gunk off, and explains, "Relish." He hands it back to her. "This phone's got it all, talking, texting, twittering, it'll even make ice cream cones on a hot day."

"Do you have any Samsungs?" Tiffany asks.

"Tiffany," I interrupt. "I don't need a music service on the phone."

Tiffany looks at me as if I had one of Jack Wayt's diseases.

"Sammys? No, I don't have any right now," Les tells Tiffany. "But I could order one from my supplier and have it here by tomorrow."

"Let me see what else you got," Tiffany tells him.

Les goes back into the kitchen area and returns holding a greasy wire basket filled with loose cell phones. He dumps them on the counter in front of us as if they were sizzling French fries.

"Do all of these come with a set of directions?" I ask.

"No."

Tiffany uses her nail file to pick around the phones so she won't get her nails chipped. "This is all you got?" she asks Les.

"Today."

"These are like TV's without HD," she says of the array of choices.

"Tell me what kind you want," Les tells her. "And I can special order it."

"Are they all used?" Tiffany asks.

"Usually, in more ways than one," Les explains.

Tiffany finally chooses one that has a very tiny keyboard that slides out of the side of the phone; the logical progression from my prior flip phone. Les puts in my old number, and gives me a plug-in charger. I write him a check for seventy bucks and ask him not to cash it for a few days. A new phone, a free charger, and no interest until my check clears. Am I a great shopper or what?

As we're leaving More4LesMobile, Tiffany says, "Ya know, Mr. Sherlock, technology hasn't just passed you by, it's lapped you."

Monroe Chevelier has an office with a television, a wet bar, a 36-inch computer terminal, plus a number of medals, trophies, and awards hanging on its walls. There are no papers on his desk. His wooden in-box is empty, so's his wooden out-box. He sits behind a mahogany desk wearing a perfectly tailored blue blazer that enhances his muscular upper body.

"What can I do for you, Tiff?" he asks as Tiffany and I sit and share the very comfortable leather couch.

"I wanna talk about the night in the Zanadu."

"Which night?"

"The night I got roofied," Tiffany explains.

"I don't have a lot of time left," he informs us.

I wonder if he means he's got some terminal illness, but I don't ask because he's as buffed and brawny as that guy on the paper towel package. "I understand some guy came between you and your date while you were at the bar?" I pose this more as a question than a statement.

"She wasn't my date."

"Told ya," Tiffany says to me.

"What happened?" I ask more simply.

"I was there, minding my own business, talking to Alix Fromound, and this geek comes up and ..."

"Cock blocks you," Tiffany chimes in.

"Yeah, exactly."

"So, what did you do?"

"I stand up, tap him on the shoulder, and I'm just about to crush his windpipe ...," Monroe demonstrates by shaping his right hand into a claw.

"But you didn't?"

"Nope," he says. "Everybody starts going apeshit over something that's going on a couple stools down."

"That was me they were going apeshit over, Mr. Sherlock."

"Yes, I figured that out, Tiffany."

"And when I look back to the guy I'm going to bust," Monroe continues, "he's gone."

"Where'd he go?"

"Who knows?"

"Did you go after him?"

"Nope."

"Why not? You wanted to crush his windpipe, didn't you?"

"Yeah, but all these chicks are screaming, the bartender's climbing over the bar, the security guys are running up. It was like a Super Bowl touchdown in the last minute of regulation."

I sit back, conjure up the DVD scene in my head, and come to no conclusion. When I come back to reality in a few seconds, I ask Monroe, "What do you do here?"

"What does that have to do with anything?"

"Nothing, I just wondered."

"I'm the Executive Vice President of Preferred Accounts." He glances down at his gold Rolex and stands up. "Time to go."

"Big meeting?" I ask.

I turn and see a man in a gym suit approaching us. This guy is equal to, or better than, Monroe in every muscle category on the body. "Ready?" he asks.

"Right with you," Monroe says to the gym rat. Nice to see you again, Tiff." Monroe is well-schooled in the art of giving people the bum's rush. "Sorry, you got roofied."

"Me too," Tiffany says. "I'm used to people going apeshit over me, but not that many people in such a big group."

Monroe Chevelier and the gym rat turn left when they reach the hallway, Tiffany and I turn right. We walk by a number of offices, and a big room with thirty or so cubicles. "What does this CEI do anyway?" CEI being the name of the company.

"I don't know," Tiffany says. "Monroe's dad started it."

I walk slower, trying to listen in on employee conversations.

Nothing. When I reach the reception area, I ask the attractive lady wearing a headphone. "What does this company do?"

"Mergers and acquisitions."

"What does Monroe Chevelier do?" I figure I have nothing to lose by asking what could be considered a very unprofessional question.

"Anything and anybody he wants," she states, nonchalantly.

It's late in the afternoon. Tiffany leaves me to go off to some yoga class where they heat up the room to a hundred and fifty degrees, the instructor bends you into different pretzel shapes, and your entire body sweats like a busted faucet. I do enough sweating over my financial situation, and decline Tiffany's offer to join in the yoga fun.

Instead, I walk over to Bruno's condo to wait and hope for another sighting. While I'm leaning against the concrete railing over the Chicago River, I ask myself a number of questions. The first being: Why am I doing this? As far as I know, I'm not even getting paid. Tiffany isn't hurt and is no longer in any danger. I could chalk the whole incident up to her bad choice of a cocktail. Secondly, why did the Thug in the fedora kidnap me? To scare me, to warn me, to keep me away from something or someone? Thirdly, what was that *whoosh/plop* sound that I can't get out of my head? Fourthly, why does this whole thing intrigue the heck out of me? And, last but not least, will Morrie's Bail Bonds Bailouts team ever win a game?

I stay lost in thought for about an hour, never seeing Bruno. I make my first call on my new phone to my girls, then grab dinner at the first cheap place to eat that I can find. While I devour a turkey sandwich, I read the latest edition of the *Sun Times* that some thoughtful person left on the seat. By the time I leave the restaurant, it's close to 8:30. I decide it would be a good time to go stand in line.

It's not even 9 o'clock, and I'm about the fortieth person in a line that stretches down the block. I can't figure out why anyone would stand in line to get into one specific bar or club, especially if you can walk a block to another one which plays the same music and serves the same watered down drinks. I turn to a pack of female, twenty-somethings in front of me, "Excuse me, but what's so special about this place?"

A girl in a frilly, metallic mini-dress answers, "The people, dude. You gotta party with the right people."

"I can see that," I respond. "But who wants to stand in line to do it?"

"Nobody."

"So, why doesn't this whole line just pick up and move to the club around the corner? Then you'd be partying with the right people and you wouldn't be wasting any time standing here?"

"Doesn't work that way," she tells me.

Her friend, who also is dressed in a metallic mini-dress, points at my outerwear. "Is that one of those Member's Only jackets?" She asks me.

"No."

"I thought you were going for some weird retro look," she says.

"No," I tell her.

"What is it then?"

"Personal flair," I tell her proudly with a smile.

Out of the corner of my eye I see a guy walk by us carrying one of those metallic briefcases. Is this a special "Heavy Metal Night" at Zanadu? When the guy is about twenty feet shy of the velvet rope, I notice the back of his head.

A small queue of braided hair hangs over his shirt collar.

"Girls, save my place in line, would you?" I ask my fashion-conscious new friends and take off without waiting for an answer to catch up with my last limo driver.

I'm about ten steps behind him when Arson unlatches the velvet rope and allows the guy entrance into the inner sanctum. By the time I get there, Arson and his partner, Sterno, form a hip-to-hip impenetrable wall of flesh in front of the rope.

"I've got to get in there," I tell them in no uncertain terms.

"You again," Sterno says.

"Mr. 2-in-1 shampoo," Arson adds sarcastically.

"You've got to let me through," I plead. "That guy you just let in kidnapped me the other day and dropped me off in an alley where I was shot at and almost killed."

"Like we haven't heard that excuse before," Arson says.

"Come on, please?"

"You gotta stand in line," Sterno says.

"I already stood in line."

"That's good," Arson says. "Now you can go back and get some more practice at it."

I'm watching Mr. Ponytail pass through the huge doors into the club, as I ask, "How about if I go in, talk to the kidnapper, and come right back out?"

"No, you gotta wait in line with the rest of the losers." Sterno really knows his job.

"If I wait in line, and finally get up here, are you going to let me in?"

"Not unless you change your clothes in the meantime," Arson tells me.

"Is that one of those Members Only jackets?" Sterno asks.

"No, my ex-wife bought me this jacket only a couple of years ago."

"She probably knew then she was going to dump you," Sterno says.

He might be right about that.

Arson must be hearing instructions through his earpiece, because he pulls the rope back and allows a group of four to enter. I give up. I move to the side and consider my next move. One doesn't immediately come to mind. I turn around and walk away in the opposite direction. I wave when I reach the girls saving my place. They pretend not to notice me. They're too busy chatting away with the two guys who were behind me in line. I'm a matchmaker by default.

I walk the streets in the immediate vicinity of the club, searching for parked limos. I find three on Kinzie Street. One has a driver waiting inside. I rule that one out. Two are parked on opposite sides of the street about one hundred yards apart. I write down their license plate numbers and wait about fifty yards away from each.

Twenty minutes go by. Nothing. I'm getting impatient. I'm standing against a sign advertising *Nightclub Parking* when the limo, which had the guy sitting inside, drives right past me. Riding shotgun is Mr. Ponytail. They go by so fast I can only pick up the first three digits of their plate. This should teach me never to rule anything out based on occupancy.

CHAPTER 7

About a week ago, before Tiffany downed her unfortunate libation, I was wasting my time in the Barnes & Noble on Clybourne Avenue. I love that store. It's huge, has couches, tables, and a Starbucks; all there to enhance my reading pleasure. When I don't have a lot of money, a lot to do, or both, this is one of my favorite stomping grounds. I'm here a lot.

There have been innumerable news stories concerning the demise of the brick and mortar retail bookstores. And in each of these articles, the writer gives umpteen reasons for the collapse of what once was a thriving business. It seems to me the only reason these stores are going out of business is because they let people like me in, allow them to hang around for hours reading whatever they want, and then walk out without spending a dime. If I owned B & N, I'd have floor monitors wander around with stopwatches in hand, relegating each reader to only a couple of pages per book.

One time I was in the Homeopathic Health section and came across *Oh, My Aching Back*. In this heavy on the pictures and light on the words manual, I found a number of ways to improve my bad back. There were exercises, diets, food supplements, vitamins, hot and cold compress solutions, even a chapter on inversions. I read almost half the book, memorized the exercises, replaced the book, not where I found it, but a few shelves away, and went home to try out my new regimen.

It worked! My back hasn't felt this good since Care was crawling. Now, each morning I start my day on the floor, twisting and turning, stretching and straining, curling and coiling. As soon as I have the time, I'm going back to B & N and read the rest that miracle worker.

I'm in the middle of the Flounder Fetal Position when the phone rings. It's Jamison Wentworth Richmond the Third. Well, actually not him, he never speaks to me; it's only one of his assistants. She informs me that there has been a serious blip on their Paid Out computer screen and I have to investigate a certain pharmacy in Evanston, which is suddenly doing a land-office business on some of the most pricey pain killers on the market. Lortab, Oxycontin and Percodan are moving off the shelves faster than anything at Walmart on Black Friday. The bulk of the cost of these little magic bullets is being billed to Medicare, but since it pains Mr. Richmond to pay out even the measly amount the government doesn't cover, he calls me. Unfortunately, since I borrowed money from him to pay off my divorce, I have to drop everything and get on the case.

Is it any wonder I hate my job?

The drug store is located on the north side of Howard Street, which is the southern border of Evanston, and the northern border of Chicago. Pretty much a lower-middle-class workers' neighborhood--which most workers would like to move out of. It used to be the territory of the Insane Unknowns street gang, but with the shifting population trends it's now ruled by the Latin Kings. I sincerely doubt if the change in street gang affiliation has changed the property values in the area. The large sign across the front of the store reads Evanscago Drugs. Beneath Evanscago it lists drugs, liquor, and sundries as its main stock in trade. I've often wondered what sundries are. I never hear people say, "I have to go to the store to pick up some sundries," or "Honey, we're all out of sundries," or "There's a sale on sundries this week at Osco." Maybe I'll investigate sundries while I'm investigating the store.

I find a parking spot about a half block away; no parking karma today. I sit and watch. Between nine and ten a.m. only two customers enter the store. By their attire, their demeanor, and their inability to walk a straight line, it's a good bet they're buying the second item listed on the Evanscago sign.

There's a very small parking lot adjacent to the store, room for maybe six cars. Two of the spots are filled, one by a Lexus and one by a Mercedes. Each was there before I arrived. At a few minutes before eleven, a third Lexus enters the lot and parks. The customer gets out and enters the store. I can't believe it. What the heck is Tiffany doing, shopping here?

I get out of my Toyota, walk up Howard Street and wait two doors down. When she emerges, I call out, "Tiffany..."

"Oh, Mr. Sherlock," she says and hurries over.

"What are you doing here, buying some sundries?"

"What are sundries?"

"I don't know," I tell her.

"Then why'd you ask me?" She pulls me aside. "I had to see you," she tells me.

"How'd you know I was here?"

"Daddy told me."

"You were in his office this morning bothering him?"

"How'd you know?"

"I'm a detective."

"Mr. Sherlock, there's something we have to talk about," she tells me.

I look up the block and see four or five customers enter the drug store. "Tiffany, I can't talk right now, I'm working."

"Doing what?"

"I'm on a stakeout."

"Oh, I've done those," she says with a downward wave of her hand. The only thing stakeouts are good for is a snappy-nap."

"We have to get off the sidewalk," I tell her, leading her to my car.

"Oh, no, I can't get into your car. I might get a rash."

"We can't stay out here," I tell her. "I don't want to be seen."

"If I were you," she says, "I'd rather be seen out here than in that crummy car of yours."

"I don't have a choice. I'm incognito."

She looks at me with her *You're telling me something I don't want to know* look. "Are you wearing Depends?" she asks.

"No, Tiffany, I'm incognito, not incontinent."

"Oh, that's right," she says. "Incontinent sounds very *Parisian*."

"If you say so, Tiffany."

America's private educational system is failing its youth almost as badly as the public one is.

"Tell you what," she says. "Since I'm already here, I'll go undercover into the store. What do you want me to do?"

There's no getting rid of her. "Buy some sundries."

I get back in my car. Tiffany goes shopping. Three minutes later, a mid-sized bus with markings I can't read pulls up in front of the store. I count at least thirty Asian individuals as one by one they slowly file out of it; all of them clearly senior citizens, none of them especially healthy. They enter the store very orderly and methodically, just as if they have done this many times before. No sooner has the last one entered than Tiffany comes bounding out and sprints my way--a difficult task with four-inch clogs on your feet.

"It's like Pearl Harbor déjà vu, Mr. Sherlock," Tiffany says excitedly as she reaches my car. "They must have busted through one of those immigration fences on our Chinese border."

Tiffany's ignorance of geography is as bad as her vocabulary. Or it was a really, really long bus ride for the group. "What were they doing in there?" I ask.

"I don't know. They were all clumped together, making sounds like silverware bouncing off marble tile." She's talking a mile a minute. "My first thought was they all had yellow fever."

"Do you know the symptoms of yellow fever?"

"No."

I'll ask Jack Wayt next time I see him. He'll know.

"It was, like, really freaky," she says. She wipes down the front of her dress as if she's ridding herself of a horde of unwelcome ants. "It was like I was a minority person."

"I'm sorry you had to go through all that."

Tiffany becomes quite emphatic, "There's only one thing to do."

"What's that, Tiffany?"

"Exfoliate."

Although she hates my car, Tiffany makes me drive her to her Lexus, which is parked less than a hundred feet away. "What's that noise? She asks.

"There's a hole in my muffler."

She gives me a quizzical look. "You're not wearing a muffler."

"The car's muffler."

"It's not that cold," she says. "But anything that covers this car is an improvement."

We arrive at her car. "Mr. Sherlock, I have to talk to you."

"I can't now, Tiffany. I'm working."

"All right, but soon, okay?"

After Tiffany takes off, I take her parking spot, get out of my car, and go inside Evanscago Drugs. Enough of this going incognito.

It's a madhouse inside. Thirty or so Asian senior citizens are milling around eating rice cakes. All unhappily wait for their names to be called by the pharmacist who can't speak Mandarin or any Asian language for that matter. The craziness is compounded by the fact that some of them can't hear very well or they're totally deaf, some can't walk and they just stumble along, and some are just whacked out to begin with, probably because they can't find the sundries section. I've seen enough. Case closed. I'm out of here.

Outside, I call Mr. Richmond. He must see my name on his phone screen because he bounces me straight to his voice mail. I'm succinct in explaining a pretty common Medicare Insurance scam and add that Tiffany was instrumental in helping me crack the case. Next, I call the Evanston Police Department and ask to speak to Bruce Lansky, a detective I used to know back in the day when I was in the CPD. We have a nice chat, catch up on crimes, and I tell him of the scam going down at Evanscago Drugs. He tells me "I owe you a lunch, Sherlock."

I ask him instead just to give me the cash he'd spend on our lunch. He laughs. I don't. I wasn't kidding.

It's a nice, cool fall day. The air is clean and crisp, the sun is shining, a good day for a walk along the lakefront. I start out at Evanston's Clark Street Beach and walk north through the Northwestern University campus. Fall is, by far, the best season in Chicago.

I make the mistake of taking my cell phone with me. "Wait" Jack Wayt calls to inform me that he has contracted a toenail fungus, which could be deadly since his fungi closely resembles the photo of a fungus featured on his favorite website *Diseases 'R Us*. After we discuss possible cures and remedies, including amputation, Jack goes over what he found in the area of my almost demise. "Traces of coke, meth, oxy, some seeds. I'm telling you, Sherlock, once these new medical pot dispensaries are up and running it's really going to cut into weed sales on the streets," he says.

"And that's a good thing?" I ask.

"One less bell to answer," he sings, poorly.

In California and other states, if you want to smoke dope legally, all you gotta do is go into your neighborhood cannabis clinic and tell the "Doctor" you've got an "anxiety problem." He'll ask you what you're so anxious about and you tell him: "Because I don't have any pot." So, he'll write you a prescription for medical marijuana which you can purchase in the front of the store. Suddenly you're cured.

"Did you find out who owned the place?" I ask.

"The usual off-shore corporation that's more time and effort to uncover than it's worth."

"Has the building been used recently?" I keep the questions coming.

"As far as we know, no."

"Did anything come up on the three digits I got off that limo license plate?" I'm referring to Mr. Ponytail's vehicle.

"No," Jack says. "It's a lot easier to trace a car if you get the entire plate number."

"If I add that the guy driving the limo had a little ponytail, would that help?" I ask.

"I doubt it."

We talk for a few more minutes on what we don't know about the case. Jack then tells me he has to go "soak in a tub of Epsom Salts," and hangs up.

I walk another hundred yards and my phone rings again. I'm supposed to look at the screen before I answer, but I always forget to do that. "Hello."

"This is a courtesy call," the voice says.

I interrupt, "Before you start, let me tell you I don't buy anything from anybody who calls me on the phone or sends me anything in the mail."

"I ain't selling nothing."

I interrupt him again, "I don't do phone surveys either."

"Listen bud."

"And I'd like to help all the charities that call, but I'm a charity case myself."

"Listen," he raises his guttural voice, "you keep your nose outta where it don't belong or you ain't gonna have no nose to stick in no place." He hangs up.

I hate telemarketers. Whatever happened to the No Call List?

I fumble around with the phone, somehow getting to the "Calls" screen and see Private Caller at the top of the list. I manage to find my way back to the main screen, hit *69 and get a busy signal. Private Caller comes back on the screen. I'll have to stop by More4LesMobile and inquire about having Private Caller installed on my phone.

I'm approaching the Northwestern campus athletic fields. I'm willing to bet that most people around here don't know that the ground they're walking on used to be Lake Michigan. The terra firma beneath them is nothing more than an honest-to-goodness landfill, or in this case "lakefill." Northwestern is probably the only university in the country that manufactures its own land for its own expansion. I turn around and start back south and my phone rings for the third time. In life, some say everything comes in threes.

"Hello."

"Gibby Fearn."

"How are you?"

"A person here wants to speak with you," Gibby says, putting all pleasantries aside.

"Put him on the phone."

"He's not here."

"If he wants to speak with me, why didn't you just wait until he was around, and then call me?" Seems logical to me.

"Why don't you be here at nine," Gibby asks/orders.

"Where?"

"Where else? Zanadu."

I seem to be in the middle of a streak of bad-mannered phone callers.

"Who should I ask for?" I ask.

"Who do you think?" Gibby says. "I'll make the introductions."

"Should I bring anything?" I'd hate to show up, discover it's pot luck, and not have a dish.

"Nine." *Click*.

I'm almost back to my car when the rule of three plus one kicks in. *Ring*.

"Hello."

"Mr. Sherlock."

"Tiffany, where are you?"

"I'm getting a peel."

"I wish I was."

"We have to talk," she says.

"We are talking," I remind her.

"Not about that. It's personal what we have to talk about."

"Okay."

"So, when can we talk?"

"How about tonight?" I ask. "I have to be at Zanadu at nine. Want to join me?"

"Like on a date?" she asks in a tone that suggests she is going to be exposed to a deadly bacteria.

"No."

"Oh, Mr. Sherlock, that's a relief," she says breathing a little easier. "I thought you were asking me out. That would be, like, totally creepy."

Arson and Sterno wear matching pink, shiny, silk jumpsuits. They resemble two mountains of coal wrapped in breast cancer ribbons.

Sterno opens the rope wide for Tiffany to enter, but again slams the door on me.

"Look on your list," I tell them. "Richard Sherlock."

Arson runs his finger down the first page on his clipboard and stops suddenly. "How'd you get on the list?" he asks.

"I told you, I don't follow the trends, I set 'em."

The rope comes off its mooring and I pass by, "Nice to see you boys. Love the new look."

The second door is wide open. No Slimy Guy to recheck the people who have already been checked. We walk right in. The god-awful rap music is still blaring away, but the place isn't yet cooking. It's a little easier to make yourself heard. "I need you to go find Bruno," I tell Tiffany.

"I'll start my surveillance at the bar," she says.

"And, if he's not working, find out why."

"Where are you going?"

"Gibby wants to introduce me to somebody."

"Isn't that nice," Tiffany says sweetly. "Why?"

"I haven't the faintest idea."

We walk through the dance floor, but split when we come to the bar. Tiffany goes right, I go left. I arrive at the door marked *No Admittance*, knock, and wait. The door automatically opens and I walk in. The Behemoth sits in the same chair, reading the same *Fantastic Four* comic book; talk about a slow reader. The guy has on an ill-fitting blue suit this time, but it's the same brand and style as the one he had on before; no doubt the product of a 2 for 1 sale. Gibby quickly removes a bill counting apparatus, placing it into the lower drawer of his desk, before he comes around the desk to greet me.

I hear the *whoosh/plop* sound. "What's that noise?"

"What noise?" Gibby asks.

"That *whoosh/plop* noise."

"Dun't know," the Behemoth speaks without lifting his eyes from the *Fantastic Four*. The plot must be quite intriguing.

"Every time I come in here," I tell the pair. "I hear the same weird noise."

"Do you hear it now?" Gibby asks.

I pause to listen. "No."

"I dun't neither," the Behemoth adds.

Gibby heads for the door and motions for me to follow. "Why don't you come with me?"

Before leaving the room, I turn to the Behemoth. "You know the Fantastic Four save the world in the end of that comic book."

The Behemoth peers up from the page and gives me a big brute sneer. I think I hit a nerve.

Gibby leads me down a narrow hallway that parallels the back side of the bar. We reach an unmarked door. He punches a code onto the small keyboard and the door unlocks. We go through and find ourselves in a back stairwell. I follow him up one flight to another door. He knocks. A light goes on above us, the camera turns on, and the lock on the door clicks. Gibby pushes it open.

The office is more suited for the top floor of a Wall Street brokerage firm than a nightclub with disco balls. The only thing missing is a downtown view. Tasteful art on the walls, Oriental rugs, ultra-modern furniture, a wet bar, and a very large desk three oak trees gave their lives for. I feel about as out of place as a plaid suit at a funeral. A black guy, maybe mid-forties, impeccably dressed, comes forward.

"Mr. DeWitt," the stern, business-like Gibby, says. "This is Mr. Sherlock. Mr. Sherlock, Mr. D'Wayne DeWitt."

DeWitt looks me up and looks me down.

"You can call me, Richard," I say extending my hand to shake.

DeWitt ignores my outstretched hand. "You can call me, Mr. DeWitt."

And so I shall.

DeWitt motions for Gibby to leave the room. He does so without hesitation. Mr. DeWitt moves to the corner and pulls the drawstrings on a set of curtains on the left. Once open, the Zanadu Club lies beneath us like an IMAX movie being played with no sound and lousy plot. "Sit," he says motioning me towards a couch. "Drink?"

"No, thank you."

He pours himself a glass of ice water from a Waterford pitcher on the coffee table, and sits across from me. "Miss being on the force?" he asks.

"Some days," I tell him. "Mostly, I miss my paychecks."

Mr. DeWitt folds his hands above his lap. He wears diamonds on two fingers and in one ear lobe. "I have a problem, Mr. Sherlock."

I immediately think, "Just one?" I got a whole slew of them, my kids, my ex-wife, the rent, the electric bill, gas prices, car, etc., etc., etc.

"Are you available for hire?" he asks.

Is a rabbi Jewish? Is the Pope Catholic? Is Buddha a Buddhist?

"I better ask what the problem is," I tell him.

"Someone is trying to destroy my business."

I look out on the dance floor packed to the gills with well-dressed partiers. "Whoever it is, Mr. DeWitt, it doesn't look like they're doing a very good job."

"Trust me. Poisonous seeds have been planted and they are ready to take root."

"A few spiked drinks aren't going to kill your vibe. They might even help it."

"Success breeds envy. Envy breeds ideas. Ideas breed ill-conceived actions."

I lean forward a bit. "What exactly do you think they're going to do," I ask, "that could put a dent into what you've got going here?"

"Kill me."

I pause to contemplate his answer. "That certainly wouldn't help your bottom line."

"No, I wouldn't say so."

He sits straight as an honest judge, staring right into me, with absolutely no emotion of his face.

"Did someone try to slip a Mickey into your drink?" I ask attempting to link two crimes into one investigation.

"I don't drink."

"Well, what exactly did he, or she, or they, try to do?"

"Nothing yet."

D'Wayne DeWitt is not being very helpful to the cause of his new employee. "Then why do you suspect someone is attempting to kill you?"

"I know," he says. "And that's all you need to know."

D'Wayne DeWitt might be better off spending an hour with Miss Freeda, Palm Reader, Tarot Master, and Seer to the Stars. "From what I have seen, you already employ enough muscle to keep the Taliban at bay."

Mr. DeWitt shifts in his chair ever so slightly. "All I want you to do is find out what is going on. You don't have to stop them, confront them, or come up with a plan to solve the problem. All I want to know is who and what."

"And then what?" I ask.

"I'll be happy and you'll be paid."

Something is wrong with this picture; actually there are many things wrong with this picture.

"Four hundred dollars an hour, plus expenses," he says.

But that isn't one of them.

He pulls a gold money clip out of his pocket, counts out a number of hundreds, and offers them to me. "On account," he says.

Once I lay my hands on the money, I know my fate is sealed. I contemplate it for less than a nanosecond and grab the cash. Boy, do I need this cash. "I'll start tomorrow."

Mr. DeWitt rises from his chair. "You'll start tonight."

Well, it's clear who will be the head ramrod on this wagon train. "What do you want me to do?"

"I don't know," he says. "You're the detective."

"I'll get right on it." I rise. With the wad of money in my pocket, pressing against my leg, I feel as if I have risen from years in a financial coma. The dawn has broken. Spring has sprung. Unplug me from life support. I'm alive. I'm alive.

I am almost to the door when I turn around and ask, "By the way, do you have a guy working for you, kinda short, wears aviator glasses, and has a little ponytail running down the back of his neck?"

"No."

I believe I just found my starting place.

"I'll be in touch."

I make my way down the flight of stairs. At the stairwell door which leads back into the club, I insert one of my business cards against the locking catch. I test the door to make sure it will open next time around, close it gently, and make my way back down the narrow hallway. When I reach the bar, I find Tiffany having a grand old time. She's sipping a martini, while three or four guys are chatting her up. Alix Fromound is back-to-back with her; the same as they were the night Tiffany took a header off the barstool. Alix has only one guy talking to her. Tiffany is definitely ahead in tonight's popularity contest. A number of other well-dressed friends are yipping and yapping, playing with their cell phones, or bouncing to the music; a splendid time is guaranteed for all.

"Oh, Mr. Sherlock," Tiffany says seeing me approach.

"What'd you find out?" I ask.

She pulls me close to her, "Monroe is no longer seeing Alix," she says in all her glory. "He dumped her ass."

"I meant about Bruno the bartender."

"I haven't seen him."

"Did you ask?"

"They said he hasn't been here all week," Tiffany says. "But it's okay, this new guy makes a much better Cosmo."

Good to know my assistant has done such a thorough job in her assignment. "I need you to help me," I have to yell since the music has been pumped up to its highest decibel level.

"You see someone you like? I can run interference for you if you want."

"No. thanks. I need you to watch a door for me."

"It's not the men's room door is it?" she asks.

"No."

I tell the current Tiffany fans she will return in a few minutes and pull her off the barstool. "Come with me."

I lead her down the way I came until we reach the narrow hallway leading to the door I just jimmied. "All you have to do is stand here and if anybody goes in that door you call me on your cell phone. Can you do that?"

Tiffany has to think it over, "Probably."

Not the answer I wanted, but it will have to suffice. I leave her at the head of the hallway, walk to the stairwell door, open it, remove the card, and close the door gently. I walk down the stairs until I reach the bottom floor.

With my penlight flashlight, which all good detectives carry at all times, I slowly proceed down a dark, dank, moldy basement hallway. I listen carefully, but all I hear is myself. I come to an old pump in the center of a large room. It's attached to a four-foot high pipe, which comes down from the floor above and runs the entire length of the building. I remember what the nice lady librarian told me. Some of it is starting to make sense.

I backtrack, find the stairway, and climb up one flight. On this floor I don't have to use the flashlight. There are a number of hanging light bulbs, the old kind, not the new LEDs, to illuminate my way. The hallway is somewhat clean, as if people use it just often enough to keep it that way. I step gingerly. A *whoosh* zips by my head faster than an arrow from Robin Hood's bow. I stop. A few seconds later, I hear a faint *plop* somewhere in the distance. I reach up, lay my hand on a horizontal iron pipe running a foot off the ceiling, and wait. It takes maybe a minute before I feel the vibration. I hear another *whoosh* and feel something shooting down the pipe at a breakneck speed. I follow the pipe down the hallway until it branches off and disappears into the interior of the building. I keep walking and come to a heavy metal door. It's the kind they used to use in speakeasies with a metal slide right at eye level. Another *whoosh* is followed quickly by another *plop*.

The doorknob has no dust. I consider entering, but everything changes when the next thing I hear is my cell phone ringing. I get it out of my pocket by the third ring. It's so nice not having to listen to Lady Gaga or Taylor Swift or whatever ringtone my kids put in when I'm not around.

"Is somebody coming?" I ask right away.

"No, Mr. Sherlock," Tiffany says.

"Then why did you call me?"

"Because I'm, like, really bored doing this," she says. "Can I go back to the bar and party now?"

The doorknob twists on the speakeasy door. I take off running down the hallway. Somehow I find the button to break the phone connection. I hear the door creak open. I take the first left, find an unlocked room, go inside, and stop breathing. I hear footsteps go up the hallway then come back down the hallway at a slower pace. I wait until I hear another creak, wait a little longer, and find my way back to the stairway. I go up the stairs to the floor where I began.

Tiffany's back on the barstool having her usual great time. When she sees me, her first comment is, "You didn't have to hang up on me. It was a simple question. You could have just said 'no'."

"Sorry, Tiffany," I apologize. "Three ninjas were coming after me with Samurai swords to cut me up into human sushi when you called."

"There's never a good excuse for being rude, Mr. Sherlock.'"

No one listens to me.

I survey the bar scene and feel as out of place as a fat girl in a bulimia ward. "By the way, Tiffany, what did you want to talk to me about?" I finally say.

"Oh," she says, "that can wait. I'm having too much fun right now."

I make my way out of the bar area, through the dancing mob, out the first door, and back to my buddies manning Zanadu's eye of the needle. "Arson," I ask the big guy, "remember that guy a couple of hours ago, carrying a metal briefcase? He was short and had a little ponytail hanging down the back of his neck."

"Yeah."

"Who was he?"

"I don't know."

"You know him, Sterno?"

"Some supplier."

"What does he supply?"

"Supplies."

"He's not very friendly," Arson tells me as he unhooks the rope and allows two hot girls to go inside.

Well, it's nice to know his rudeness wasn't merely for my benefit. "You know his name?"

"No."

"How long does he stay?"

"Not very long," Sterno says.

"How long?"

"Fifteen minutes, maybe."

"You know what's in his case?" I ask the two.

"Maybe limes," Arson says. "Or something like limes."

"That would certainly make for an interesting twist in the case."

The boys don't get my humor.

"Does he always have the case with him when he leaves?" I ask.

"Yeah."

The guy's got to be a bag man, one of those guys who collects the cash derived from an illegal enterprise—like selling hard drugs—and giving it to his superiors.

I don't go back inside Zanadu. I can only take so much techno rap music or whatever it is they're playing. Instead, I walk around the outside perimeter of the building. On the west side there's a loading dock, with three spaces for semi-trailer trucks. The three roll-up doors look like they haven't been opened since the British invasion, the one the Beatles started, not King George III. The rear of the building backs right up to the Chicago River; there are no entry or exit points here. I quickly realize the need for the basement pump and the plumbing line running from it.

There's no way I can work my way around the building from here, so I have to backtrack. I walk back across the front entrance, around the line of waiting customers, and get to the east side of the building. This is the side used for the workings of the club, where I entered the day we came to pick up the security DVDs. There's a door marked *Employees Only*, two loading dock doors, both open and obviously both used frequently. There's also a separate door leading to an open maintenance room and a wide hallway, which leads to a large walk-in freezer on the left and the same size refrigerator on the right. I stand across the way, maybe fifty feet back. With the two loading doors open, the action inside the hallway is easy to see. Cases of beer and liquor are transferred, trash is deposited into dumpsters, and plastic trashcans of empty glass bottles are dumped, quite loudly, into huge separate containers. I'm so happy the Zanadu recycles, but they really should swap out those light bulbs in the basement for some more efficient LEDs.

One person I recognize. He's young, Hispanic, and wheeling a cart full of ice from the freezer. It's Bruno's barback. His face looks like someone who had just gone three rounds with Mike Tyson. "Hey," I yell walking towards him. "What happened to you?"

"*No hablo Inglés.*"

Yeah, right.

I'm less than a few feet from him. "You didn't look like that the other night."

"*Nada, señor,*" he says. "Nothing. No, nothing." And the iceman goeth.

I would have chased him, but a Non-Brink's, Brink's truck pulls up and backs into the last loading dock spot. There's no company name or logo on its side panels. Out of the hallway comes Mr. DeWitt, the Behemoth without his comic book, and Slimy Guy, the ultimate arbiter of who enters the hallowed halls of Zanadu. He's rolling a cart full of two-foot high metal boxes in front of him.

As they approach the truck, a guard exits the passenger side door with his gun drawn. He walks to the back of the truck and unlocks the rear door. Three metal boxes are loaded into the truck. The guard marks his manifest. Mr. DeWitt signs the sheet and takes a copy. The driver locks the door, holsters his gun, climbs back into the front seat, and off he goes. As if on cue, as soon as the armored vehicle leaves, a limo takes its place.

The Behemoth and Slimy Guy wheel the cart back into the building. A few seconds elapse while Mr. DeWitt waits on the open dock. Satisfied with what he sees or doesn't see, he bids goodnight to a worker passing by with a slight wave, walks down the steps, and enters the back of the limo, opening the door for himself.

This is the signal that it's time for Sherlock to go home and go beddy-bye.

I go back to the front entrance, cut into the front of the line. "Name's on the list," I remind Arson and Sterno, who hate my sudden capability of going to and fro, and re-enter the club. I find Tiffany at the bar. She's smack in the middle of three guys vying for her attention. "Tiffany, I'm going home."

"Bye."

I wave.

"Oh, Mr. Sherlock," I hear before I'm out of earshot.

"I forgot to ask you something," Tiffany says, loud enough to be heard over the musical clatter.

I walk back to her and lean in. "What?"

"Do I look thinner to you?"

"Is that what you wanted to talk about?" I break the rule of answering a question with a question, but since this is Tiffany, I give myself a lot of leeway.

Tiffany tosses her long hair back, one of her better flirting moves to keep the boys around her interested. "This afternoon they must've scrubbed off at least a pound of exfoliated skin and I just wondered if I looked thinner to you?"

I have to be careful answering this question. "It's hard to tell, Tiffany, when they only take a little off the top."

CHAPTER 8

"Wait."

"What for?"

"I'm having trouble breathing."

"Why?"

"I think I'm coming down with asthma."

"I don't think so, Jack," I tell my detective friend. "It's a condition you only get when you're a kid."

"I'm a late bloomer, Sherlock."

We sit in a dumpy restaurant, not far from a Westside station. There're a number of swarthy, slovenly, mean guys in the place; each of which Jack seems to know well. I'm hoping Jack will buy me breakfast. I need every dollar Mr. DeWitt gave me. "We had another O.K. Corral shootout last night," he tells me between bites of his grits. "Four down, two critical, three wounded. A sleeping kid took one in the leg from a stray bullet into his apartment"

There's a major drug war going on in Chicago. It's so rampant and widespread that the Mayor is seriously considering calling out the National Guard.

"I heard a good idea the other day," Jack says. He talks to decompress from his very stressful job. "Every bullet you buy should cost a thousand dollars."

"And what would that accomplish?" I ask.

"No more innocent bystanders."

I eat my scrambled eggs, while Jack runs at the mouth a few more minutes. When he takes a break, I ask, "You ever hear of a guy named D'Wayne DeWitt?"

"DW 2."

"Who?"

"DW 2," Jack says. "That's what we called him."

"He hired me last night."

"Are you that hard up, Sherlock?"

"I'm in pretty bad shape."

"You might want to reconsider your client base."

"Who is he?"

Jack pushes his empty plate away and sips his coffee. "Usual story started out running a corner. As his contemporaries or competition got busted, shot up, or killed, D'Wayne moved up the ladder. In a business of dumb guys, he's smarter than most. He got to the point where he was pulling in some pretty heavy coin. But a couple of rocks got waylaid, some narc buries a tracer in one, and while DW 2 is out driving his silver Escalade, whammo, he's pulled over, rousted, and busted."

"They bust a guy that big over a couple of crummy rocks of cocaine?"

Jack burps. "Didn't make much sense to me either. They gave him three years and he was out in eighteen months."

"D'Wayne's running a nightclub now. He's gone straight."

"Nobody who runs a nightclub has gone straight, Sherlock."

"He says somebody is trying to kill him."

"If that's a surprise to you," Jack says, "you should find another line of work."

"I've been trying to find another line of work," I admit, "but I can't do anything else."

"From what you're telling me, you're not too good at this either." Jack pushes himself away from the table. "You got any money?"

He doesn't give me enough time to lie.

"Use some of it to buy the breakfast."

As we walk out of the place, I mention, "You know you're not wheezing anymore. Maybe the time you spent with me cured you of your asthma?"

Jack stops. He pulls the front of his shirt out of his pants, pushes his belt down, and reveals his very fleshy muffin top. "Okay, then Doc," he says using both hands to point his navel out at me like it was a Cyclops's eyeball, "does this look like melanoma to you?"

"No, dirty lint."

"Remember the other day when I asked you if you thought I was as self-centered, selfish, spoiled rotten, and egotistical as Alix Fromound?" Tiffany asks as we sit in her Lexus.

"Yes."

"And you said it was all relative."

"Yes."

"Is that like aunt or uncle relative?" she asks.

"No, Tiffany," I explain. "I used relative as a term of comparison.

Compared to Alix, you're not self-centered."

"Not even a little bit?"

"Tiffany, what's this all about?"

I see a meter maid pull up behind us and stop. "We have to move," I tell my assistant.

Tiffany puts the Lexus into drive and we cease being double-parked across the street from Zanadu's valet station. An empty limo is parked at the stand. "Go around the block," I tell her. I turn around to keep an eye on the limo until Tiffany turns at the corner.

"Mr. Sherlock, I've been doing a lot of thinking."

This is frightening on more than one level.

"What about, Tiffany?"

"About my life, my aura, my place in the universe."

"And ..."

"I'm not sure I'm where I want to be."

"Neither are most people in life," I try to reassure her as we pull back into the double-parked spot we just left.

"How about your aura, Mr. Sherlock. Do you know where you are?"

"My life is such a mess, Tiffany. I wouldn't know my aura if it hit me up side of the head."

"So, it's all relative? She asks.

"There he is," I interrupt the conversation when I see Mr. Ponytail, with metal case in hand, coming out of the club and getting back into his limo. "Get ready."

The limo pulls out. "Let him get a head start," I tell Tiffany. "Stay back. Don't get too close."

We follow our fine-coiffed friend to where he gets on the Eisenhower Expressway and heads west. "This is kinda fun," Tiffany says as we cruise along.

We travel about ten minutes. "He's getting off up here," I warn her.

We're out of the city and in Oak Park. The limo exits on Harlem Avenue, and goes right. It continues to Madison Street and takes a left. Less than a mile later we're in Forest Park. A lot of parks in this area of Chicagoland. A mile or two later, he takes a right, goes three doors down, and pulls into a driveway in River Forest. "Stop right here, Tiffany." She pulls up a half a block away and cuts the motor off.

Mr. Ponytail gets out of the limo and locks it electronically. He picks at his fingernails as he walks down the driveway and steps into the back door of an old wood frame house.

"That doesn't make any sense," I remark.

"What doesn't?" Tiffany asks.

"He didn't take the case in the house with him."

"I don't get it," Tiffany says.

"Neither do I."

We sit in the car for a few moments while I contemplate what I don't understand. Tiffany's patience wears out quickly. "Where to next?"

"Back to the club."

"That's the spirit, Mr. Sherlock. Party, party, party."

After Tiffany tosses her keys to the valet, she proceeds past the loser line, heading straight for Arson and Sterno. At some point, she realizes I'm not behind her. She stops, does a one-eighty, and sees me heading for the east side of the building. "Mr. Sherlock, where are you going?"

"This way, Tiffany."

She catches up to me and immediately asks, "What are you doing? We're special, we get to walk past all those people, make them feel jealous, and get right in."

"We need to do something else first."

I lead her to a spot about twenty feet from the employee entrance and the loading area. "What can we possibly be doing over here? This is like where the hired help goes."

"I need your expertise, Tiffany."

"Oh, which one?"

"Housekeeper Spanish."

"No problem. I can do that," she assures me.

We only have to wait a few minutes. The Hispanic barback comes out of the building, meets an in-kind buddy, and sits. The buddy smokes, our guy doesn't; smart guy.

"See that guy over there?" I say to Tiffany, pointing to the barback. "Go find out how he got beat up."

"Him? He's hardly my kind."

"I'm not asking you to make-out with him, just find out how he got beat up. Use some of your fabulous aura."

"Mr. Sherlock, I told you, my aura's not in a good shade right now."

"Well, this'll give you a chance to help get it back in shape."

"Okay."

Tiffany walks over to the barback. I wait in the shadows. If I go along, the guy will clam up faster than my daughter Kelly when I ask her about boys. Tiffany makes contact, spends a few minutes chatting away, and returns to where I'm standing.

"What did he say?"

"Yo, no say *mucho*."

"What does that mean?"

"Not much."

I start again, "What did you ask him?"

"I asked him if he uses bleach on his whites."

"Why did you ask that?"

"Because it's bad for the fabric and you can smell it on the clothes when you're wearing them," Tiffany explains. "It's a pet peeve of mine."

"That's not what I want to know."

"But when you're talking housekeeper Spanish, that's always very important."

"Tiffany, did you ask why he got beat up?"

"Yes."

"And what did he say?"

"I'm not sure." Tiffany sees the displeasure on my face. "He started yapping faster than Speedy Gonzales on speed and he lost me."

"Did you pick up on anything he said?"

"He might have said something about not doing windows."

So much for my assistant's expertise.

We walk back to the front of the club. "Tiffany, you go inside and see if Bruno's working. If he is, come out and get me."

"Why don't I just text you?" she asks.

"Because, I don't text."

"Mr. Sherlock, we're going to have to sit down and have a long talk one of these days."

Tiffany leaves me standing at the valet stand. I'm not sure what to do. A lot more people are coming to the place than going. The line gets longer. I still don't understand why anyone would wait to get into this place. Do they have some secret desire to spend all their money, sweat through their best clothes, and have their eardrums damaged?

A black SUV, bigger than my apartment, pulls up. The windows are so heavily tinted I can't see inside. I move to the side so as not to be confused with the guy who parks the cars and wait. The back doors of the land yacht open. Four babes and three guys pile out, each wearing more gold bling than the sundries section of Fort Knox gift shop. I'm almost blinded as their outfits reflect the lights coming off the front of the club. This group doesn't wait in line either. And not many of those standing in the line seem to care.

I come around to the side to get a clear view of the group of seven approaching Arson and Sterno. They don't speak, but they do exchange a few head bobs, shucks, and jives. Each of the men gets a pat down. The girls don't have enough on to hide anything under, but their purses get the once-over. The velvet rope is opened and the gang of seven proceeds inside. The SUV drives off from the valet stand. Somebody drew the short straw and has to watch the car. Life's tough.

It's probably a good idea to go inside and check-in with Mr. DeWitt, since I'm in his employ and want to show him I'm busy on the job, but I can't get through the door to the stairway that leads to his top floor office. Instead, I head for Gibby Fearn's office.

"Was I right about the Fantastic Four saving the world?" I ask the Behemoth, who sits in his usual spot.

"Dun't know."

"Good answer."

"What do you want," Gibby asks me, not rising from his desk which is festooned with all sorts of pictures of him with rappers, athletes, and other celebrities I don't recognize.

"I'd like to see Mr. DeWitt."

Gibby shrugs his shoulders in response.

"Is this his bowling night?"

"Dun't know," the Behemoth speaks.

"Anything I can help you with?" Gibby asks.

I'm about to say "no," but come up with a thought. "How well do you know Jimmy Cappilino?"

"Who?"

"Jimmy Cappilino," I repeat. I figure a guy like Gibby would have to know the CEO of the corporation that owns this high-tech dance hall.

"Who?" Gibby repeats.

I look over at the Behemoth.

"Dun't know."

This guy would not be your first choice as study group partner.

I tell Gibby, "The CEO of the company that owns this joint."

"Sorry, name doesn't ring a bell," Gibby says.

"Sure?"

"He dun't know," the Behemoth says.

I wonder if Gibby enjoys having the Behemoth speak for him, but this does not seem to be the time to ask.

I bid farewell to the pair and go out to find Tiffany at the bar. Monroe Chevelier is hovering over her like an umbrella. It doesn't bother Tiffany in the least. I watch the courting ritual for a while; maybe I can learn something.

Monroe has the presence bit down to an art form. He's obviously not there to make idle conversation. He wants to encapsulate Tiffany. He moves around her, shifting his muscular body in a constant display of power. He leans forward towards the object of his desire, just close enough to let Tiffany play her part in the game. Her hand on his wrist. A gentle tug on his lapel. Smoothing her fingers down his tie to feel the silk. She's perfected the art of the hair flip; a casual brush-back, using two fingers to sweep the strands from her face then raising her head slightly, opening her blue eyes wide, and adding a slight smile as the pièce de résistance.

I can't watch the ritual any longer, I feel like an ornithologist studying the mating rituals of a couple of sapsuckers. I step up to them. "Excuse me," I say politely.

"Oh, Mr. Sherlock," Tiffany says. "You remember Monroe?"

"Of course."

He doesn't offer his hand to shake, so neither do I; that'll show him. "Tiffany, what about Bruno?"

"Fired him."

"Who fired him?"

"His boss."

"Why?"

"The new guy said he hasn't made a shift this week."

"Tough to find good help," I conclude.

"But you know who I did see here tonight?"

"The posse of drug dealers that just came in?" I make an educated guess.

"No, the two guys with too much mousse who were in the video the night I got roofied," Tiffany says. Monroe adds a nod to second the fact.

"Are they still here?"

Tiffany rises from the barstool and looks around at the crowd. "Nope, I don't see 'em."

"They probably struck out and went home," Monroe remarks in a less than positive tone.

"Well, that's what I'm going to do too, but I'm not going to bother with the striking out part."

"You mean you want to go now?" Tiffany asks, as if it's the one question she fears.

I allay her worst fears, "I'm a big boy. I can get home by myself."

She quickly opens her purse, pulls out two twenties, and hands them to me. "The cab's on me."

"Thanks, but I got it," I tell her, refusing the money.

She pushes the bills at me anyway. "I insist."

"Okay, you convinced me." I take the money. "Nice to see you again, Monroe."

"You too, dude," he says. He gives me a quick fist pump. This guy must be great closing a high stakes negotiation.

"Night, Tiffany. Careful what you drink," I say before leaving the happy, almost couple.

"I'll have Monroe be my taste tester," she says and repeats the hair flip.

Instead of a cab, I take the 'L' home and pocket a profit of $38. Every little bit helps.

CHAPTER 9

As a rule, Tuesday is my kid day. I pick my daughters up from school and they spend the night with me. They use this important time with their dad to complain about my cooking, having to sleep in the same bed together, the basic cable TV package, my dial-up Internet connection, and the absence of sugary snacks in the house. These are the times I really feel I'm building a vital and long-lasting bond with my children.

However, today is Thursday and it's today that I'm picking up the girls from school. For some unknown and unexplained reason, my ex-wife has been flipping my weekday with the kids around more often than Tiffany changes shoes. I lodge complaints to her about the sudden shifts, explaining that I have been working non-stop, but I always get the same reply, "If you're working so hard, you should be able to pay more child support." The one time somebody finally listens to me and this is the response I get. I can't win.

"Dad," Kelly says getting in the car, "do I have to go to Care's dumb basketball practice?"

"Yes, Kelly, I made you the assistant coach. Don't you remember?"

"You didn't tell me it was going to be boring," Kelly answers.

"It's boring because you don't make the best out of the situation."

"No, Dad," she says. "It's boring because the team sucks."

"Don't say *sucks*."

"That's not swearing."

"I don't care, I hate that word."

"Okay," Kelly says. The team is sucky and terrible."

I raise my voice one decibel level. "Well, then together it will be our job to make the team better."

"Oh yeah, like that's gonna happen."

Care, whose grammar school is adjacent to Kelly's middle school, joins us a few minutes later. "Hi, Dad."

"Hi, Care. Did you learn anything in school today?"

"No."

"Don't forget our school motto girls," I repeat for the umpteenth time, "Learn something new every day."

"Oh, Dad," Kelly says. "You can be so lame."

I drive around to the back of the school and park close to the entrance of the gym. Morrie's Bail Bonds Bailouts are already on the court playing with their cell phones instead of the basketball. I see Mrs. Whiner of "transition game" fame and give her a slight smile. She rises from her seat in the bleachers, walks down, and presents me with six one-page diagrams of plays she believes will work in our next game. "What you should do is post-up the center on offense."

My team couldn't tell the difference between a post-*up center* and a Post-*it note*.

"Mrs. Whiner," I tell the woman. "If there's ever a contest for School Parent of the Month, you'll get my vote."

She's not sure if I'm kidding or not, which is good.

I turn to my team, "Okay girls, pretend you're in a movie theater, and silence your cell phones."

Reluctantly, they follow my orders, except Kelly, who can't go three minutes without scrolling. "Today, we're going to work on our defense."

"We hate defense," Annie, our point guard, speaks for the team. "We want to shoot."

I ignore the request, even after I hear Mrs. Whiner scream out, "Practice the pick and roll play I gave you."

"All in good time," I call out for all to hear. "All in good time."

I arrange the girls on the sideline in two lines. "All right, everybody put your hands up in the air."

"What is this Dad," Kelly asks, "basketball or the Hokey Pokey?"

"I want you to run all the way to the end of the court and back. And don't drop your hands down. Keep them up." I blow my whistle and the team takes off running. They look as if they're auditioning to play trees in a kindergarten play.

As soon as the girls are on their way, I move to the opposite side of the court, as far away from Mrs. Whiner as possible. And from this point on, every time I move, she moves all the way around the court to sit behind me. As soon as she does, I move to the other side. If you can't beat 'em, avoid 'em.

Three of my players don't make it to the end of the court before they rest their arms. A couple others start to complain immediately, one isn't coordinated enough to run and raise her hands at the same time. Another says she's "too pooped to pop." And our best player, Shemika, waves her arms back and forth like an overtly gay Dorothy Gale impersonator, skipping merrily down the Yellow Brick Road.

"God, they look like a bunch of deranged wannabe ballerinas," Kelly tells me.

We try two more *Hands Up* defense drills that I found in a *Basketball for Dummies* book I read at Barnes & Noble. They work about as well as the first one. After hearing: "This hurts," "My fingers are numb," and "this could cause permanent damage," I let the girls shoot baskets for the remainder of the practice hour.

I blow the whistle a final time. "Okay, team, we'll see you all Saturday when we really take it to Charlie's Chilidogs."

"Yeah, like that's gonna happen," my soon-to-be ex-assistant coach comments.

I fix a new turkey meatloaf recipe that I found on the back of the ground turkey package for dinner. The kids hate it, so I boil some water, toss in some pasta, and serve it up with butter and parmesan cheese. I eat the meatloaf, sans real meat. It's not bad, but it does need a little kick.

"Don't you have any Ragu?" Care asks.

"Mom always has Ragu," Kelly adds.

"Those bottled sauces are filled with preservatives. They're not good for you," I tell them.

"Couldn't be any worse than this turkey meatloaf," Kelly says stabbing my gourmet delicacy with her fork as if she's Tony Perkins in *Psycho*.

After dinner, after homework, and after showers, we usually sit in the front room and argue about what to watch on TV. I always lose.

"What's going on with Tiffany, Dad," Care asks. "Is she better?"

"I am happy to say that Tiffany is back to normal."

"Tiffany's not normal, Dad," Kelly says. "Tiffany's rich."

"Well, whatever she is, she's back to it."

"What happened to her?" Care asks.

"Somebody slipped something into her drink."

"What?" Kelly asks.

"Something that made her sick," I answer.

"One time at lunch Ricky Starr blew a load of snot into Billy Merrit's Mountain Dew can when he wasn't looking," Care informs us.

"That happens all the time in my school," Kelly adds.

"Well, let that be a lesson to you," I tell them.

"What?"

"Don't drink Mountain Dew or anything else out of a can."

"What happens if we're out in the desert and the only thing we have to drink is out of a can?" Care asks.

"It'll be on your conscious, Dad, if we drop dead of thirst," Kelly warns me.

"I'll drown myself in guilt with a 12-pack of Mountain Dew. Would that make you happy, Kelly?"

"No, but a Diet Coke right now would."

"Did you find the guy who did that to Tiffany?" Care asks.

"I'm working on it."

"We're available if you need some help."

"I'll call if I need back-up."

They go to bed. I go to bed. In the morning, I get up. They get up. I take them to school. Kiss them goodbye. End of joint custody for another week.

I'm across the street, in front of Bruno's condo building, when Tiffany shows up her usual half-hour late. She doesn't look too chipper.

"You okay, Tiffany?"

"I'm not sleeping well."

"Is that your fault or someone else's?"

"Are you asking me if I'm doing someone and *they're* keeping me up all night?"

"Not in so many words," I answer.

"The answer is 'No,' but I do wish that was the reason."

"How about you and Monroe?"

"I got him hooked," Tiffany says, "but I'm waiting to reel him in."

"Why?"

"I'm not sure, that's why I'd better wait."

"Good choice, Tiffany."

We have a few seconds of silence before Tiffany asks, "What are we doing here, anyway?"

"We have to go see Bruno. This is where he lives."

"His parents must have money," Tiffany says, reviewing the building.

"See that doorman?" I ask pointing out my buddy.

"How could I miss him? That outfit is atrocious," Tiffany critiques. "Nobody wears epaulets anymore."

"Doormen do."

"Why do you think doormen wear uniforms, Mr. Sherlock?"

"Because they're in the service," I answer.

"You go in the army to be a doorman?" Tiffany continues her line of questioning.

"No, they're in the service business."

"I think it would be a good idea if all people in service businesses wore uniforms," she says. "It would take the guess work out of who I could order around."

Tiffany's comments of this nature should never be responded to and die a very sudden death.

"Right now, Tiffany, all we have to be concerned about is getting past that doorman and into the building."

"That's easy," she says nonchalantly.

"Really?"

"In the back there has to be a ramp to the underground parking. Go down to the first floor door there and wait for me to open it up."

"Really?"

"No problem."

I make my way to the back of the building, find the ramp, head down one level, and find the door which requires an electronic pass card to open. I do my best to stay on the back side of the mounted security camera while I wait. Three minutes later Tiffany opens the door.

"How'd you do that?"

"When you grow up in a penthouse condo, you learn all the tricks."

We find the elevator and take it to the 41st floor. As soon as the doors open, my senses tell me something isn't right.

Down the hall we stop at 4112. I knock. No answer. I knock harder. Again, no answer. My senses are kicking in big time. "You smell that?"

Tiffany sniffs the air. "Public restroom?"

I get down on my hands and knees and smell the space between the door and the carpet. Not good.

"I hope you don't expect me to do that," Tiffany says.

I try the door. It's locked.

A couple of years ago, one of the better second-story jewel thieves in town by the name of Shervy Reckless passed along to me his favorite lock pick set in an attempt to convince me he'd given up the business. Two weeks later a diamond the size of my little toe was stolen from a woman who lived on the sixty-fourth floor of a building on Lakeshore Drive. I couldn't bust Shervy for the theft, but I did get a nice lock pick set out of the experience.

I go to work on the door. It takes less than a minute to unlock the knob lock. It takes me about five to get the deadbolt open. I open the door a crack, but stop Tiffany as she moves forward to enter. "Wait," I pull my handkerchief out of my back pocket and hand it to her, "you're going to need this."

"Are you going to give me a cold and I'm going to start sniffling?" she asks.

"No, but trust me, you're going to need it."

I open the door, we step inside, and the stench almost dyes our hair.

No matter what any cop, criminal, soldier, hit man, or mass murderer tells you, nobody likes the odor of a decomposing corpse. The stench is unimaginable and extremely unbearable. Combine the worst farts of a cow, a rhinoceros, an elephant, a family dog, and fat Uncle Louie, and you won't match the noxious aroma of a decaying body.

"Don't touch anything, Tiffany," I order her as I make my way to the patio door and open it all the way. Windy City air blows in and we get a bit of relief.

Tiffany follows my path and meets me on the patio. "That smells worse than three dollar perfume."

I retrieve my handkerchief. "I'm going back in," I tell her.

"I'll wait out here. I don't want the smell to get on my new exfoliated skin."

I find Bruno, or what was once Bruno, face down on the floor of the bedroom. I'm going to break my rule never to assume and assume that someone took an iron rod to his head because his skull is bashed in and a fireplace poker covered in dried blood is lying not too far away. There's also a large splatter pattern on the wall behind the bed, hardly artistic. I don't get too close.

And to add to my last bit of murder trivia facts, it's also true, no matter what anyone says, nobody likes discovering the body of a murder victim. It's disgusting. The image stays with you forever. Your stomach churns, your teeth clench, and your sphincter tightens. Today is no exception.

I back out of the room, return to the outside deck, and call "Wait" Jack Wayt.

Before I can say a word, Jack says "Wait."

"What?"

"Sherlock, do you know if you can get shingles if you haven't had chicken pox?" he asks.

"I don't know, Jack," I confess. "You'll have to ask your doctor."

"It's hard to get a hold of that guy. They always tell me he's in surgery when I call."

"Is he a surgeon?"

"I didn't think so."

"Jack, I don't want to tell you how I found this, but I got something for you."

"A cure for my psoriasis?"

"No, a murder."

"Sherlock, I'm on drugs," he snaps back in an exasperated tone, "not murder."

"This one may be related."

"In my condition, I really don't need any more aggravation," Jack tells me. "I could have a bipolar relapse."

"What do you want me to do, Jack?"

"I'll take care of it, but if my stress level gets any higher and that tick I used to have over my left eye kicks back in, you're to blame."

I give him the address, the floor, the condo number, and tell him the doorman on duty is a jerk.

Tiffany sits on one of the four outdoor dining chairs close to the state of the art barbeque. I don't understand why people spend so much money on gas-fired, outdoor cooking extravaganzas. It's the same gas that the kitchen stove uses when you broil indoors. The only difference I can see is one grill you clean, the other you don't. So, people shell out thousands of dollars for gas-fired outdoor grills for the sheer taste that a filthy grill gives their steaks and burgers.

I look over at Tiffany; she seems lost in thought, which is a pretty tough thing for her. "Are you okay?"

"Not really."

"The smell still getting to you?"

"That and my current state of mental health."

"Want to talk about it?"

"Not really," she says. "It's hard to talk about stuff when there's a dead body close by."

"Good point."

I cover my face and go back through the unit to the front door. Once there, I notice the dead bolt on the side of the inner door. It's new, but the door is old. I turn back to rejoin Tiffany and see that one fireplace piece is missing from the set in front of the fake marble fireplace. Why anyone would want a fake fireplace in their home is beyond me. A fireplace without wood burning capability is like a car with no engine, a snake without fangs, or a daughter of mine without an attitude.

I pause as I pass by the decorative unit and give the mantel an odd glance; something's not kosher. The bottom edge of the wood mantle is worn in a weird way. With one hand holding the handkerchief against my face, I use my other hand to reach up inside the opening at the weird spot and feel around. If I were a physician, this is where I'd say "Cough." Satisfied with my diagnosis, I hurry back to the deck, hang my head over the railing to get the freshest air, and breathe deeply.

Three minutes later, the first person to come through the door is detective Neula "No-No" Noonan. What did I do to deserve this?

"No, no," is her reaction to seeing me. "What are you doing here, Sherlock?"

"I just happened to be in the neighborhood ..."

"No, no, save it Sherlock," she cuts me off. "I've been lied to by enough men in my life, don't add yourself to the total."

"The body is in the bedroom."

"No-No" Noonan reaches into her purse and takes out a pair of latex gloves and mesh booties. She pulls the gloves on first and has to hold onto a chair to balance to get the booties over her shoes. Considering her size, this isn't the easiest of tasks. Before she heads into the bedroom, she gives me one final order, "Don't move." She disappears into the room and dashes out three minutes later with a face that's a lighter shade of pale.

"No-No" joins Tiffany and me on the deck. "No, no," she says between gasps of breath. "This is not my idea of a good way to start my day." She hits one number on her cell phone and says, "Come on up, we got a ripe one."

"No-No" sits down in the chair next to Tiffany. "What are you, about ninety pounds?"

"One-oh-two this morning," Tiffany tells her.

"I got thighs that weigh more than that," she admits.

"No-No" relaxes a bit to catch her breath, as much from the stench as from the sight.

"You want to know how much I weigh?" I ask.

"No, no, I don't."

Neula "No-No" Noonan has been a CPD detective for over twenty years, each year of service adds to her pension--and her girth; it's a toss-up which addition is greater. Svelte she's not, but she has become somewhat of a legend and not entirely due to her size. "No-No" Noonan one time figured out, after three previous detectives had failed, that the body of a man found dead in the middle of a field with absolutely no discernible clues (no footprints, no tire tracks, no nothing) was not a murder victim at all but a guy stowed away in the belly of a jetliner who fell out when the landing gear opened up coming into O'Hare. Another time, she deduced that a jealous wife had used a turkey baster to extract her husband's man juice from her own female parts and inject it into her husband's mistress' female portal, after she bludgeoned the much younger woman to death with a tire iron. Neula "No-No" Noonan has a knack for the bizarre; to be a great murder detective, it helps.

The homicide team enters the condo wearing gloves, hairnets, booties, and breathing apparatus; some people really know how to dress for the occasion. "Let me get them going, Sherlock, then I'll be back," she informs me.

Tiffany and I wait on the patio.

"I'm worried about my life, Mr. Sherlock," Tiffany tells me right out of the blue.

"Why?"

"Because I no longer see my life as being positive."

"Really?"

"Afraid so."

The next question is quite obvious. "When did you last see your life as positive?"

"I'm not sure, but it was sometime before last Friday night," she tells me in a somewhat concerned voice.

I'm about to ask another question, but she beats me to the punch. "I had a vision."

"A vision?"

"When I was roofied and passed out on the floor of the bar," she says in all seriousness. "I had a vision."

"What did you see?"

"My life flashed before my eyes."

"Really?"

"I was in an old pair of ratty jeans, Keds, and a red T-shirt that had *Bioche and Proud of It* written on the front in big purple letters."

I'm not really sure how to respond, "Okay."

"The jeans and the Keds were bad enough, but the worst part was the T-shirt," she pauses. "I never wear red. Red is for losers. And red with purple is a real fashion fox pac."

"I didn't know that."

"The vision was telling me, my whole life, my whole fashion sense, has been an ultimate failure. A sham, a shame; squandered in a sea of senseless senselessness."

"Did you make that up?"

"No, I read it in *People* Magazine," Tiffany admits. "It might have been a quote from Lindsey Lohan."

Tiffany takes a breath. This is hard for her. "Every time I think I can forget the vision, it comes to me in a recurring dream."

"What?"

"The same dream, over and over, like a Seinfeld re-run. It's a constant awful reminder of my failure to have a positive aura."

"I'm really sorry to hear that Tiffany."

"No-No" Noonan returns. We have to table our discussion.

"All right, Sherlock," she says making me get up from the chair. "Tell me everything and no bullshit."

"Wait."

"Wait" Jack Wayt comes onto the patio deck.

"No, no. Not you too," "No-No" says seeing Jack.

"Does anybody know what the symptoms of muscular dystrophy are?" Jack asks.

"Yeah," a weakening of the commitment muscle," "No-No" says.

Did I mention that "Wait" Jack Wayt and Neula "No-No" Noonan had a past and now have issues concerning their past?

"There always seems to be a little more Neula, every time I see you, Noonan," Jack says taking a good-sized pinch of her upper arm fat.

"I'm surprised you could even remember with the onset of dementia you must be experiencing right now," she shoots back at him.

I cut this off before it gets ugly. "As I was saying, Tiffany here …"

"That's me," Tiffany qualifies.

"… gets a roofie slipped to her last Friday night in the Zanadu Club."

"I know that place," "No-No" says.

"How?" Jack questions. "They don't have a buffet there."

"Don't push me, "Wait" Jack Wayt."

"Don't worry, I'm not that strong."

"In mind or body," she qualifies for him.

I continue, "Bruno, the guy in the other room, was a bartender at Zanadu."

"No, no, don't tell me," "No-No" interrupts. "You just happened to stop by today to pick up his recipe for *mojitos*."

"No," I say. "I haven't been able to find him. I've been looking for him all week."

"Mystery solved," "No-No" says. "Case closed. Go home, Sherlock."

"Tell her about the kidnapping and getting shot at," Jack says.

I go through pretty much the rest of the sordid tale, leaving out the parts about my working for D'Wayne DeWitt and my problems with Mrs. Whiner and the girls' basketball team. I end with, "It's all connected somehow."

"So were we," "No-No" Noonan says looking over at "Wait" Jack Wayt.

One of the CSI techs comes out of the bedroom, lifts his breather, and yells out, "You can come in now."

Three of us rise. Tiffany stays put. "I'm good," she says.

The CSI techs are kind enough to delay covering the body so the three of us can feast our eyes upon the disgusting mess. A small amount of darkened blood escaped from the wounds when the techs turned the body over for a more intimate look, adding a brighter sheen to the remains. There was one blow to the back of the head, and one to his left side, just above the temple. By the craters in Bruno's head, it seems obvious that whoever killed him was able to freely swing for the fences. There are no signs of a struggle. It was obviously wham, bam, and thank you, Bruno. There are pieces of skull on both wounds. What could be brain tissue, but probably isn't, has oozed out. Rigor mortis has set in. Bruno is as stiff as the fireplace poker that killed him. The carpet is soaked with the blood from his head wound. If these floors are cheap, and gravity has its way, the unit beneath is going to have one revolting stain on its ceiling.

"He comes in first," "No-No" says walking through a scenario, "gets whacked from behind, and gets spun around." She points to the wall. "That's the first splatter."

Jack picks up the story. "He gets hit again before he goes down. Right here." Jack steps over the blood puddle.

"Right handed batter," I add.

"When?" "No-No" asks the CSI tech.

"A few days at least," the CSI tech says. "For a bartender, he's fermented quite well."

"Wrap him up," she says to the boys.

While the CSI techs are wrapping Bruno up for take out, I snag a pair of latex gloves, put them on, and start opening drawers. It doesn't take long. "Bingo."

The two detectives join me at Bruno's chest of drawers. One of them pulls out two tins that used to hold crackers or cookies, but now hold an assortment of the most popular thrill pills.

"Zanax, Oxy, Roofie, Seconal, Depacote..." Jack knows his business. "I like the way he kept them in their own little sections."

"There's no stack of cash," I point out.

"He's a bartender, he'd have cash," "No-No" says. "But this doesn't scream robbery to me."

"A crime of passion?" Jack wonders out loud.

"What would you know about passion?" "No-No" asks Jack.

"I know it takes two to have some," Jack replies.

Tiffany's voice interrupts the verbal post-relationship tête-à-tête. "Mr. Sherlock, I'm going downstairs. This is all, like, making me sick."

The comments or the situation? I wonder.

"I'll meet you at the Starbucks," she says.

"Which one?" There's a Starbucks on every corner in downtown Chicago.

"I don't know," she says. "Just keep Starbucking along until you find me."

"Okay," I yell back. "And don't look this way when you leave the condo.

I wait a few seconds, and hear, "Oh, gross!"

Nobody listens to me.

CHAPTER 10

I find Tiffany in the third Starbucks I visit.

"Tiffany, why don't you go home and take a beauty rest?" I suggest. "Or whatever will make you feel better."

"My vision was a life-changing event, Mr. Sherlock."

"I wouldn't be so sure."

"My entire existence passed before my eyes," she reminds me.

"Maybe not, Tiffany. Drugs can do funny things to your system. They could have flipped some switch in your brain and caused a hallucination."

"No way," she says, "The powers of the universe are telling me I have to change."

"How?"

"I'm not sure."

I try to think this through, although there's not much here to think through. "So, you might want to become less selfish and self-centered?"

Her face snaps toward me, as she asks, "You think I'm selfish and self-centered?"

"No."

"Then what made you say that?"

"I was just repeating what you told me before, Tiffany."

"That's not what it sounded like to me," she quips quickly. "You think I'm as bad as Alix Fromound."

"No, I don't."

"Yes, you do," she says. "You just said it."

"No, I didn't." I can't win here. I should quit while I'm only this far behind.

"You're not helping, Mr. Sherlock."

"But I'm trying."

Tiffany grips her head with both hands, gives a poor rendition of Edvard Munch's *The Scream*, and cries out, "The pain, the pain in my brain is almost unbearable."

"Calm down," I plead with her. "You have to calm down."

Tiffany is almost in tears. "Mr. Sherlock, this is awful. Every time I look in a full-length mirror I see myself in red. I hate that color!"

"Tiffany, relax."

"I can't."

"Have another latte," I suggest. A truly stupid suggestion once I think about it.

Tiffany takes a deep breath.

"Why don't you go visit your spa? You can get a massage, have your nails done, your hair cut, get a facial, order a nice dinner, see a movie, take two aspirin, and call me in the morning."

"I don't get up in the morning," she reminds me.

"Call me whenever. I just want you to feel better," I assure her.

"Well, okay," she says. "You talked me into it."

I walk over to the Zanadu Club. I figure I better start earning my keep.

Gibby Fearn, who is busy supervising the added decorations being put up over the dance floor, sees me enter. "What do you want?" he calls out. He's a little surlier than the last time we met.

"Big night tonight?" I ask coming up to where he stands directing traffic.

"Record release party."

"Hip-Hop, rap, or regular?" I ask.

"Who cares, as long as they drink a lot of booze," Gibby tells me.

Two workers are hoisting a banner with a picture of some SRW (singer/rapper/whatever), I've never heard of. The guy flashes an ear-to-ear smile with a set of diamond-encrusted braces on his teeth.

"Is Mr. DeWitt in?" I ask.

"No."

"Do you know where I can find him?"

"No."

"Do you know where he lives?"

"No."

This is the longest string of responses from Gibby that aren't questions in return to my questions.

"You don't know where your boss lives?" I repeat, in case he didn't hear me the first time.

"Who said he was my boss?" Damn, he breaks his streak.

"Then what is he?"

"Who knows?"

"Are you always this helpful?"

"What difference would it make?"

I'd hate to see Gibby when he's being evasive.

Before I can come up with my next query, Gibby asks me, "What have you learned so far?"

"That people are their own worst enemies," I answer without hesitation.

"I meant about Mr. DeWitt," he says, but the way he says it, I get the idea he's fishing.

"He seems like a nice enough fellow who has lots of friends, is a good dancer, and cleans the lint trap after each load in the dryer."

Gibby stares me down with his cold, beady eyes. "What about his problem?" he clarifies.

"That's what I need to discuss with him," I tell the VP of Operations.

"I know," Gibby says. "What?"

"Gibby, has anyone ever mentioned you can be difficult to converse with?"

"Who'd want to do that?"

"Well, let me tell you," I tell him. "In any good conversation, you have to give a little to get a little back."

"That goes for you, too?" he asks.

This is a perfect example of what I'm complaining about. "Yes," I say exasperated.

"Fine," he says.

"Bruno the bartender."

"What about Bruno the bartender?" Gibby throws it right back to me.

"No, now it's your turn, Gibby. Tell me about Bruno."

"I fired him."

"Why?"

"He quit showing up."

"When?"

"Week ago."

"Did you fire him in person?" I ask.

"No."

"You fired him over the phone?"

"Yes."

"What did he say when you fired him?"

"Nothing."

I want to interject into our conversation what an excellent job he's doing answering my questions, but I figure I better not risk it.

"You said, 'You're fired,' and he just hung up?" I ask

"I didn't *talk* to him," Gibby says. "I texted him."

"What?" I'm aghast at even the thought of it. "You can't fire somebody with a text."

"Why not?"

"Because you just can't," I argue. "Getting fired is personal. You have to bring him in, sit him down, and 'let him go,' face to face. It's the American way."

"No," Gibby says. "Texting's much easier."

I can't believe this. What is the business world coming to?

"Okay," Gibby says, "I answered a lot of questions. Now, it's your turn. What's Bruno got to do with Mr. DeWitt?"

"Bruno didn't take his firing very well." I'm making good on my half of the bargain.

"How do you know?"

"Because he's dead."

"Dead?"

"Yes, dead."

"He's dead because he got fired?"

"I'm not sure about that," I admit.

Gibby is quiet for a few moments while he processes what I hope is new information. "I wonder if I have to still pay him two week's severance?" Gibby's a consummate manager.

"I can assure you he won't be lining up at the bank to cash his check."

The workers hoist a huge, overflowing treasure chest of what I suspect is fake bling onto the temporary stage set up for tonight's event. The chest will be a good place to put the SRW's diamond braces after his teeth straighten out.

"How'd he die?" Gibby asks, as if he's now making small talk.

"A headache," I tell him. "A really bad headache."

"Too bad," Gibby says. "He brought in a lot of business." Gibby offers his suggestion for the epitaph on Bruno's tombstone.

A new set of workers come in, wheeling two carts filled with hundreds of small gift bags, Gibby directs them to a table adjacent to the stage.

"What's in the bags?" I ask.

"Swag," Gibby answers.

I have no clue. "They're bags of swag?"

"Yeah."

"What's swag?"

"Stuff."

"Swag stuff?"

"Yeah."

I'll ask Tiffany. She'll know.

Gibby gets busier, as more and more people show up to put on the finishing touches for the upcoming festivities.

"You like your job?" I ask him.

"Most of it," he says. "The Zanadu wouldn't be the Zanadu if it wasn't for me."

"What would it be without you?" I ask.

"Certainly not as profitable." Gibby directs a few more workers then turns back towards me. "You like your job?"

"No, I hate it."

"So, you're one of the mass of men who leads a quiet life of desperation?" Henry David Thoreau. Apparently Gibby is well-read.

"No, I tell everyone I hate my job," I say. "The problem is nobody ever listens."

As I speak, a group of party set-up people comes over for more direction and I doubt if Gibby hears my final sentence.

As Gibby is engulfed with management duties, I get lost in the shuffle and make myself scarce. I wander over to the back of the bar, find the hallway behind it, and make my way to the stairwell door. For some reason, it's propped open. This must be a sign. Fate tells me to go right on through. I do so, down a couple of flights of stairs to the floor with the old light bulbs. I listen carefully for a *whoosh/plop* sound, but nothing. I proceed down the same dusty hallway to the speakeasy door. I very carefully grip the knob, but it won't move. I listen for sounds from inside then take out my lock pick set and have the door open in two minutes.

The room is maybe 15x15, with a long table, three chairs, and a small refrigerator off to the left side. On the table are two, top-of-the-line adding machines, the ones a CPA would use. Running above my head is the metal tube that I saw out in the hallway. It ends in this room. There is a slide opening at the cap end of the pipe. I open it and see two round six-inch containers. I reach in and pull one of them out. It screws open, just like a thermos.

I will no longer be up nights wondering what the *whoosh/plop* was all about.

The only other item of note is a small potbelly stove on the back wall of the room. Its stack runs up to the ceiling, then straight across, and up and out to the east side of the room. No way in hell this venting system would ever pass any Chicago building codes. There's no woodpile, but an old metal trashcan sits to the left, half-full of grey ashes. I've seen enough. I remind myself that this is the bar business, and what I've seen isn't anything abnormal in this milieu.

I re-lock the door on my way out, another trick I learned from my burglar friend Shervy Reckless. I've always been surprised by the fact that more thieves don't lock up after they leave a job. It makes sense if you ask me, but nobody ever asks me.

Upstairs, on the main floor, the party is ready to begin. All that's missing is the crowd. I walk to the edge of the floor and position myself to see the windows of the penthouse office of Mr. D'Wayne DeWitt. The curtains are open and the lights are on. Gibby was either lying or DW 2 just arrived. Whatever. It's time to visit the boss.

I push the door open as soon as it buzzes and enter the office. Mr. DeWitt is behind his desk. On the couch are two twenty-something girls, barely dressed in micro-mini skirts, high black leather boots with four-inch heels, and dripping with gold jewelry. I wonder if they got their bling from the bag of swag.

I gulp when I see the pair. "Did I come at a bad time?"

"No." Mr. DeWitt motions me to come towards him.

"One of your employees has been murdered," I tell him. "I thought you might want to know."

"Who?" he asks, not moving a muscle past his lips.

"Bruno Buttaras, the bartender."

"That Mudda," one of the blingsters on the couch comments. "He never fills his martinis all the way to the top."

"Thank you," I turn and tell her. "That was a motive I didn't consider."

Mr. DeWitt picks up the desk phone, pushes one button, and says, "Who is our PR person?" He waits for a moment. "Get her on the phone."

"You're not sending out a press release, are you?" I ask.

"Not yet," he says in all seriousness. "Who's the cop on the case?"

"Detective Neula Noonan."

"Fat?"

"Yeah, that's her," I answer.

One look to the couch would tell you the boss isn't into plus size women.

The phone on Mr. DeWitt's desk rings. He picks it up, "DeWitt." He listens for two seconds, and asks, "Did you hear one of our bartenders got iced?" He listens for one second and says, "Keep it that way." And he hangs up. Being a fly on the wall during a conversation between Mr. DeWitt and Gibby would be a waste of time.

"Mr. DeWitt," I sit in the chair across from him, to make this meeting more businesslike. "In order for me to investigate who may be attempting to harm you, it would help if I knew a few things."

"What for instance?"

I press on. "Like, where you live, where you hang out, what you like to do in your spare time, and has anyone ever tried to kill you in the past?"

"Why?"

"Knowledge is power."

"Not always," he says.

Both girls on the couch light up cigarettes. I'm amazed how many young people smoke. I would have thought that after thousands of news stories about the health hazards of tobacco, the warning labels on the packs, and all those the PSA's that star people with holes in their throats, the message would have gotten through. Apparently not, the girls puff away like chimneys.

I'm not really sure what to say next and the silence becomes uncomfortable. So, I tell him sincerely, "I'm only trying to do the job you hired me to do."

He puts his fist to his chin, rubs the flesh on his upper neck, and says, "I live in a condo, I hang out here," He points at the girls. "I do them in my spare time, and if someone did try to kill me, they missed."

My four questions have been answered, but I don't feel any more knowledgeable, and certainly no more powerful.

"You should be able to find out everything you need to know right here," Mr. DeWitt says in the manner of closing our conversation. He pulls out his money clip, peels off another hunk of bills, and hands them my way. It's difficult, but I hold myself back from jumping for joy.

"Could I get the run of the place?" I ask. "So far, the people around here have made me feel about as welcome as a Muslim at a Tea Party Rally."

"Talk to Fearn."

I am about to ask, "Do I have to?" But I don't, not wanting to upset my best customer ever. I walk to the door, passing the girls on the couch. "You really shouldn't smoke. It's not good for you," I tell them in fatherly tones.

"You smoke when youse was twenty-two?" the blingster on the left asks me.

"Yeah, but only when I wanted to look older."

The one on the right looks me up and down. "And youse sayin' that we dumb?"

Point well taken.

Downstairs, the partiers are starting to trickle in. It's early, around dinnertime. I don't want to go home, because it's best I do some investigating around the club tonight. Investigating what and who, I don't know. All I know is I have a few hours to kill. I call "Wait" Jack Wayt.

"Want dinner?" I ask before Jack can tell me his latest ailment.

"As long as it's gluten free."

"Wait."

"What, Jack?"

"You know anything about irritable bowel syndrome?"

"No. And I don't want to."

Jack shifts uncomfortably in his chair. We sit. He has a cocktail. The waiter takes our orders. We chat until the food arrives.

"Anything on Bruno?" I ask.

"Small time hood. He did a couple of stints. Once for assault and once for pushing weed and a few pills," Jack says. "Probably carried his old business into his new career."

"You know," I tell Jack. "It used to be you went to a bartender to find out the best place to eat, now you go to him to score some weed."

"You smoke enough weed, you don't care where you eat as long as you get to pig-out on a lot of food." Jack slices a hunk of rib-eye, bathes it in its own juices, shoves it in his mouth, and masticates the meat like a cow chewing her cud. "It wouldn't surprise me one bit if the fast-food industry is behind the legalization of pot."

"Did Bruno have any connection to DeWitt, when DeWitt was working the street?" I ask.

"Not that we found."

"It's all connected somehow," I say to Jack, as I nibble on my free-range chicken breast. "From Tiffany, to Bruno, to Mr. DeWitt, to the guy with the pony tail."

Jack puts another slice of steak in his mouth before he swallows the one he popped in before it. "You know in eighty percent of doping cases, the bartender has something to do with it?"

"I didn't know that."

"If you're going to be in the business, Sherlock, you got to keep up." Once a mentor, always a mentor.

"They do it for their own benefit or for the benefit of somebody else?" I ask.

"Both."

"A dumb crime if you ask me," I speak my piece. "For a couple hundred bucks a guy risks his job drugging some woman so some other idiot can have sex with her while she's comatose?"

"It's not like he's a brain surgeon putting his medical practice on the line," Jack tells me between chews.

"There's something more here," I tell him. "I can feel it."

"I can feel something too," Jack says gripping his gut. "It might be gastroenteritis."

The pain can't be too bad, because he finishes every morsel of his steak.

We spend the rest of the meal talking about people we know, people we knew, and people we don't want to know anymore. Jack is a good guy. I enjoy his company.

"You might as well know," he says finishing his coffee. "We got a lot going down in the next ten days. City Hall is screaming about all the kids killing each other."

"Shouldn't they be happy the gangs are thinning out their own herds?"

"Politicians are never satisfied," Jack says. "If we wiped out every crime ever committed, they'd complain we used too many cops to do it."

I pick up the tab for dinner. After this C-Note disappears, and I pay next month's alimony, child support, and rent; plus put a very small dent in the overdue balance on my one credit card, I'll be back to almost being broke, a situation in which I have had entirely too much practice.

The party at the Zanadu was for Bobo Bling, a rap artist whose latest CD, *Bang Dat Big Black Booty*, would be available to download starting tomorrow. I did learn from overhearing a conversation that the diamond-laden braces on his teeth are known as *his grill* and considered the epitome of bling. I consider it the epitome of stupidity.

I'm off to the side of the club listening, or having no choice but to listen, to Bobo sing of bashing butts and bling. I quickly tire of hearing the MF word put into his alleged lyrics so many times, the words almost lose their disgusting flavor. And the music is so loud, the people couldn't hear an air raid siren if one went off. I'm in the middle of a society I have no business even being near. I feel like an abacus in a roomful of computers.

But the sociology of Zanadu fascinates me. The patrons are between the ages of 25 and 35. White, Black, a few Hispanics, but no Asians. Most are straight, well-dressed, carry expensive cell phones, and text one another constantly. The Blacks hang in groups at the edge of the dance floor or up against the stage if someone is performing. The Whites inhabit the bar area. Everyone shares the dance floor.

The Black girls are the best dancers, followed by the Black dudes, followed by the White chicks. The worst dancers are the White guys, no question. White girls will dance with other White girls and Black girls will dance with other Black girls, but guys never dance with each other. Way too gay.

Blacks share their bottles of the bubbly. Whites order individual drinks. The Hispanics drink imported Mexican beer, a show of loyalty no doubt. No White guys have Black girls on their arms, but a number of

Black guys hang with White girls. It's quite obvious that Black girls don't like White girls with Black guys. America has come a long way in solving its racial problems in the past fifty years, but watching how we now self-segregate ourselves is interesting. Maybe I should go back to school and become a sociologist. Anything would be better than being an on-call private eye.

Before tinnitus sets in, a malady I'm sure "Wait" Jack Wayt has endured, I end my sociology study. Plus, I can no longer endure one more misogynistic song from Bobo Bling. I go outside and stand across from the line of idiots waiting to get past Arson and Sterno. A few minutes pass and the Non-Brink's Brink's truck drives up and parks at the loading dock area of the club. The passenger, the same guy as before, exits the vehicle and waits by its rear doors. A minute or two goes by and Mr. DeWitt, the Behemoth, and the cart full of two-foot high metal boxes arrive via the *Employee Only* door. Slimy guy is nowhere to be seen. I guess he's manning the front door to keep out the riffraff. I walk quickly in their direction to get a better view. I'm just past the valet, when a familiar Lexus pulls up.

"Tiffany, what are you doing here?" I ask as she exits her car and flips her car keys to the attendant. "You're supposed to be home recuperating."

"I took your advice, Mr. Sherlock," she tells me. "I got a massage, a facial, a trim, and a mini-wax. And I was looking so hot I didn't want to waste it by going home. So I came here, where I figured guys would trip all over themselves to hit on me. And, you know, nothing makes me feel better than that."

I look over at the Non-Brink's truck. The cash boxes are loaded. DeWitt signs the manifest sheet and I make a decision. "Tiffany, get your keys back from the valet. We need to tail someone."

"Oh, boy! I love this stuff."

I make Tiffany lay off the gas pedal and stay at least a block behind the much slower truck. We follow it east for three blocks. Thankfully, it's nighttime, and there's very little traffic; tailing a vehicle downtown during the day would be near impossible. The Non-Brink's armored truck makes its way over to Wacker Drive, heading into the Loop. It takes a circuitous route to Lower Wacker Drive and proceeds southwest.

If you didn't know, the downtown area of Chicago, known as the

Loop, is built on stilts. Back in the 1800's, after numerous floods and typhoid outbreaks, the city fathers decided to reverse the flow of the Chicago River to send its sewage, industrial waste, and other disgusting filth down to their neighbors in St. Louis. The feat was an architectural marvel of engineering. And while they were reversing the river, they also raised all the buildings above the waterline to assure a flood-free city. Not a bad idea. Today, Chicago is the envy of many cities because the skyscrapers in the Loop all have one full floor on a level below ground for loading, unloading, trash pickups, and countless other necessary uses. No wonder Chicago is still called the City that Works.

"Turn right," I order Tiffany, as the truck drives down a building ramp and disappears into an underground garage.

"Want me to drive in?" Tiffany asks.

"No." I see the address and memorize it. "Go up top."

We have to take a few turns to find a ramp that gets us back to street level. We backtrack to South Wacker Drive. "That's the building," I say, seeing the address.

There's a Northern Trust on the first floor and at least thirty stories above it. Tiffany pulls up and parks in a taxi zone. "I didn't know banks took deposits this late at night," I say, knowing something is really wrong with this picture.

"Maybe there is a huge ATM in the basement and you have to use real long pin numbers to access your account," Tiffany suggests.

"No, I don't think that's it."

"I could ask Monroe," Tiffany says. "He'd know."

"Why would he know?"

"Because he works here," Tiffany answers as if I already knew this fact.

"He does?"

"We were here the other day," she tells me.

She's right. I didn't recognize the building.

"And I thought *I* was losing it, Mr. Sherlock."

CHAPTER 11

"What were you doing in Bruno's condo?" Neula "No-No" Noonan asks me.

But before I have a chance to lie, answer truthfully, or even be horribly evasive, the waitress takes our orders. "I'll have the Reuben on rye, potato salad, chips, and a diet Dr. Pepper."

"Turkey on wheat, no mayo, no mustard."

Guess which one of us is watching their weight.

"I'm totally getting off those sugary sodas," "No-No" tells me proudly.

"The longest diet starts with the first bite, or the first sip in your case, Neula."

The waitress marks her pad and leaves us alone.

"So, Sherlock, what were you doing there?" "No-No" asks. "You do know I can put you in some serious trouble, right?"

Threats to my well-being are never appreciated, but they do tend to work quite well eliminating any lies or evasions from my explanations. "Bruno was the bartender the night my associate, Tiffany Richmond, had a Mickey slipped into her drink at the Zanadu Club."

"*The* Tiffany Richmond of Richmond Insurance?"

"She be the one."

"Bad choice," "No-No" concludes correctly.

"Quite."

"No-No" returns to topic. "You sure Bruno did the slipping?"

"No, but he's the logical choice."

"Logic and murder do not always make good bedfellows," "No-No" tells me.

"Nobody uses the term 'bedfellows' anymore, Neula."

"I do."

"Why?"

"Because I like it." "No-No" seems to be in a particularly bad mood.

"I've been on Bruno's tail all week, but when he didn't show up for work, I figured something wasn't quite kosher."

"You're not Jewish," she reminds me.

"It's personal flair, just like you using 'bedfellows.'" Touché.

"So, you broke into his apartment?" She says more than she asks.

"Only after I smelled the unmistakable odor or rotting flesh coming out from under his door," I explain.

"No-No" happily discovers she's sitting upon a pack of old crackers in the back of her booth seat. She retrieves the small square, tears the plastic open with her teeth, pours the cracked cracker crumbs into her hand, and pops it all into her mouth. "There were prints all over the place." Little bits of Saltine shoot out onto the table as she speaks. "Nobody in the system came up as a match."

"Bruno knew the person who killed him," I say without a doubt.

"No-No" searches for another pack of stray sustenance, but comes up empty. "By the angle and the force of the blow, it was a guy."

"I don't know," I say. "Could be a buffed up, lady basketball player."

"No, no." She ignores my thought. "It was a guy."

"Assume nothing," I tell her. "That's my first rule of life."

"Let's consider motive," she says. "If it was a drug deal gone wrong, they would have taken the pills in the drawer."

"It could have been a robbery," I suggest. "I'm sure there had to be a stack of cash in that drawer. Bruno was a bartender."

"No, no," "No-No" says. "I checked that out. All the tips go into a pot and are divided up among the servers, the bartenders and the barbacks. They each get a check every two weeks for their share."

"That still doesn't mean he couldn't have been skimming a few bills off the top of the pile," I make my point. "We *are* talking about the bar business."

"No, no, we're talking about a lot more than what you can make in tips," "No-No" says. "We found another ten grand in the condo."

"Behind the phony fireplace?" As soon as I utter the words, I regret I said them.

"How would you know the money was hidden behind the mantel in the fireplace?"

I've just given "No-No" the goods for another threat against my well-being. "Come on, Sherlock, out with it."

"I'm a real good guesser." A lousy answer, but the best I can come up with at the moment.

"No," she says.

"It came to me in a dream."

"No, no."

"I went to a psychic and she read it off her Tarot cards?" My excuses started poorly and I've gone downhill ever since.

"I don't buy that either."

I come clean. "I saw that phony fireplace and said, to myself why would anyone want something so big, that doesn't work, and serves no purpose, junking up their apartment. So, I reached inside and felt around."

"No-No" shoots me a stern look of disapproval.

"Hey, I was born curious."

"Take any for yourself?"

"No," I state emphatically. And repeat it just to make sure "No-No" gets the message.

"Motive, Sherlock, motive?" she asks.

"We only have six," I remind her. "And we've already eliminated one."

Most people believe that there are hundreds of reasons to murder somebody, but in actuality there are only six: Anger, Fear, Greed, Jealousy, Desire, and Revenge. There is no such thing as a motiveless, first-degree murder.

The waitress brings the food and "No-No" attacks it like a starving wildebeest. Her Reuben squeals from the hurt she's putting on it.

"No, no Sherlock," she says while she bites. "We're working a combination here. This is more than just greed or anger. Whoever did the deed didn't walk into the place planning to kill Bruno. Something went down that touched him off."

"I'm not sure I buy that, Neula."

"There's something else I don't understand," she says.

"What's that?"

"What are you getting out of this, Sherlock?"

"I can assure you my motive isn't greed because I'm not even sure I'm getting paid," I admit. "You want me out of the picture?"

"Nope," she says. "I need you to do something for me."

"What?"

"Find out if "Wait" Jack Wayt still has any feelings for me."

"Oh, my God, Neula, do I have to?"

"Yes, or I'm going to come down on you like stink on a rotting corpse."

"You wouldn't."

"Sure I would."

"No-No" orders a slice of "lo-cal" apple pie â la Mode for dessert. I pass. When her dessert arrives, she asks for a slice of cheddar cheese. I don't know how putting cheese on apple pie ever got started, but it makes absolutely no taste bud sense to me.

Thankfully, my new phone rings just as "No-No" inhales the *low* calories in front of her. I would normally look on the phone's screen to see who is calling, but I haven't figured out how to get that feature to work. "Hello."

"We have to talk, Mr. Sherlock."

"Meet me outside the Zanadu Club."

I bid Neula "No-No" Noonan a sincere goodbye and she returns my cordiality with a burp.

It takes me fifteen minutes to walk through the Loop and across the river. It takes Tiffany a half hour to drive half that same distance. She parks illegally. Tiffany doesn't need parking karma; her Daddy pays her parking tickets. She gets out of her car, dressed in a breezy floral print shift; her hair and face are perfect. She walks up to me with an "I've got a new lease on life" attitude.

"What got into you?" I ask in a very positive tone.

"Mr. Sherlock, I've decided to make a major change in my life," she announces as if she's a repentant sinner seeing a celestial light from above.

"That's great, Tiffany. What?"

"I've decided to hire a life coach."

"A what?"

"A life coach, Mr. Sherlock. It's the latest thing."

"What's a life coach?"

"That's a person that tells you how to make you life better," Tiffany informs me.

"Tiffany, you're life can't get any better."

"I'm having my first session with her today," she tells me. "And I'm feeling really great about it already."

I'm skeptical, to say the least. "Who is this person?"

"Dr. R. Bosley Radcliff."

"How did you find her?"

"The Internet."

"And how do you know she's any good?"

"She's certified."

"Certified in what?" I question. She could be a certified nut case.

"No, Dr. R. Bosley has a CLCC after her name."

"What's CLCC stand for?"

"Certified Life Coach Counselor."

"Who certified her?"

My question stumps my young assistant. "I don't know. Maybe the Head Certified Life Coach Coach's Counselor?"

"Tiffany, I don't know if this is a good idea. How much is she charging?"

"Three hundred an hour."

"Three hundred dollars?" I can't believe this. "Tiffany, I'll give you advice for half that."

"You mean that same stuff you unload on Kelly and Care?" Tiffany says. "Nobody listens to that kind of advice."

She's correct there.

"Just promise me one thing." I pause for her to nod. "If she asks you to invest any money, in any business, just smile and say in your politest voice: 'I'll have to get back to you on that.' Can you do that? Please."

"Mr. Sherlock, I didn't just fall off a Brink's truck."

Speaking of Brink's trucks, one passes by us, turns into the service driveway of the Zanadu, and parks at the loading dock.

"This is odd," I mention.

"Are we going to tail this one, too?" Tiffany asks.

"I'm not sure." I watch a guy exit the passenger side of the truck and wait at the edge of the loading dock. A few minutes pass, then Gibby, the Behemoth, and the money cart come out the *Employee Only* door. Slimy Guy is conspicuously absent. The exact same exchange takes place as the other ones that I saw before at night with the Non-Brink's Brink's truck, except this time Gibby's in charge and not Mr. DeWitt.

"Get in the car, Tiffany. We're going for a re-run."

We follow the Brink's truck to three more stops, one drugstore, one market, and one OTB parlor. "This is boring, Mr. Sherlock."

"I know," I tell Tiffany. "But it should be."

"Can we go now?" she asks. "I don't want to be late for my first appointment with my new Life Coach."

"What time is your appointment?"

"Three."

"It's three-fifteen now," I tell her.

"So?"

My ears can't take another night at the Zanadu. I'm heading home.

I took the 'L' downtown, so I take the 'L' back. Once in my apartment, I get both my girls on the phone. "Kelly, you don't have to come with us to the game tomorrow, if you don't want to," I tell my oldest.

"I'll go," she says. "It's kinda fun watching Care and the Bailout Bunglers get humiliated."

"I'm so glad you enjoy it so much."

I talk to my youngest next. "I got a new idea for approaching the game tomorrow, Care."

"Does it have anything to do with Mrs. Whiner?" she asks.

"No, our transition game is not our major problem," I say. "It's more of an attitude adjustment we have to make."

"Whatever you say, coach."

We talk for a few more minutes, say a lot, but provide little information, news, or anything of substance. Kids are like that. Actually, most adults are too.

I conclude with, "Love, ya, kids. Love ya."

I eat the leftover turkey meatloaf for dinner. Some meals are better the second time around. My turkey meatloaf isn't one of them. The rest of the night I sit at the computer.

In four hours of Googling, clicking, searching, and surfing, here is what I learn:

    1. After you finish reading a section, don't click on the "X" in the upper right-hand corner because you'll cancel out of the stuff you were reading and have to start your search all over again. It took me six or seven times to figure this out.

    2. Bruno Buttaras was once a promising high school varsity baseball pitcher who registered 93 mph on the radar gun. He rejected a college scholarship in favor of the minor

leagues, but he lasted only two seasons; the reasons for his departure were not given.

3.   Although privately held, with no public records to back up the stories, the company Monroe Chevelier's daddy started, Chevelier Environmental Investments, is said to be one of the fastest growing hedge funds in the country. It's rumored that its assets top the billion-dollar mark.

4.   The pneumatic tube, the *whoosh/plop* thing, which I found in the room at the Zanadu with the speakeasy door, reached its peak use as an in-factory communication device in the late 19th and early 20th centuries. The US Postal Service was one of the biggest users of the invention.

5.   There's no medical listing for a Dr. R. Bosley Radcliff. There's also no address, regular or Internet, for an Association of Life Coaching Counselors. There are a number of schools, institutions, and Internet sites where you can become a certified life coach by taking a stay at home study course that can "enrich your life and the lives of others."

6.   The Internet has surpassed the local tavern as the place where a man 35-40 years of age will most likely find a wife.

The first five searches concerned the case: the last one was personal.

I turn the computer off and find my very non-tech pocket notebook and a pen. Since it's not my weekend with the kids, once the game is over on Saturday I will have plenty of time to burn shoe leather on the case. I open the notebook to a clean page and begin to make a list of all I have to do. After the first page is filled in, I stop listing. I know I'm never even going to accomplish all the items listed, so why bother to list any more?

I'm tired. I have a big weekend ahead of me. I go to bed.

"Listen up team. The problem is that we're setting our sights too high," I tell my young hoopsters seated before me. "We have to walk before we can run."

"You don't want us to run, Mr. Sherlock?" Annie the point guard asks. "Because if we don't run, we really won't have a chance."

"No, Annie," I explain. "That was a figure of speech. What I'm saying is we have to take things one step at a time, not put ourselves under too much pressure, accomplish the little goals before we take on the bigger ones."

"We're really tired of losing Mr. Sherlock," Kaylyn, the most sensitive girl on the team, tells me.

"We can't focus on losing. We have to focus on playing our game," I preach.

"But we play terribly," Allison says.

"My Mom says we should be playing more of a triangle offense," Wilma Whiner relays one of the many comments her mother had her memorize.

"What we need is to get a little confidence under our belts," I continue.

"They're not wearing belts, Dad," my on-thin-ice assistant coach informs me. "Basketball uniforms are unflattering enough without adding accessories, especially ones with Morrie's Bail Bonds written on the back of the shirts."

"Maybe what the team needs is a nickname," Marta, our oh-so-very-forward forward suggests. "Like the Girlgoyles, the Lady Vampires, or the Ladypaploozers?"

"The last name's the best," Kelly says. "It's got 'Losers' already in it."

"Listen team," I load up on the sincerity. "Our goal today is simple. All we want to do is avoid the Slaughter Rule. We can't win if we don't get to the second half. So, let's get there and see what happens."

"You actually think they can win?" Kelly asks. "Dad, you're losing it."

I can't take it any longer. I turn away from my team and look directly at my assistant coach. "Kelly, you're fired. Your coaching career is over. Go sit in the bleachers and play with your cell phone."

"Wow," she says before she climbs up the bleacher benches. "Talk about a being a 'sore loser'."

The whistle blows for us to take the court. Before they go out, I bring the team around me, put down my hand, and the others stack theirs over mine. "All right now let's hear a big cheer. On three, 'Team'." I count. "One, two, three …"

The team yells out, "On three, Team."

Boy, do we need a lot of practice.

I do not consider myself a racist, and have never been accused of being a racist, but I have to say I do not believe it's fair or equitable when the opposing team has four physically fit Black girls in their starting line-up. These girls are taller, quicker, more agile, and have more court savvy to burn than any of my Bailouts. And the one white girl they start must be at least nine feet tall. Our team only has one Black girl, Shemika, who would rather be attacking a rebus than catching a rebound. And she's our best player.

One minute into the game I realize my hopes of us having second half play are futile. It's a slaughter waiting for the rule to kick in. One girl can hit consistently from twenty feet out. One drives the lane like she owns it. And one girl is a swifter thief than most of the pickpockets I've arrested. We're hopelessly outplayed, outgunned, and outmanned, or in this case outwomanned, in every phase of the game.

The only aspect of the game where we are in any way equal is the amount of noise being generated by our fans. They have five or six cheering parents, but we have Mrs. Whiner screaming loud enough to give everyone in the gym a coronary.

The clock hits 00:00 to end the first half and I feel a tidal wave of relief. First, for the end of the humiliating beating the team has taken and second, for the end of Mrs. Whiner's diatribe of criticism, "Sherlock, you wouldn't know a zone defense if one rebounded off your empty coaching head."

It's impossible to ignore her less than helpful critique of my coaching capabilities.

"Okay, girls, go give them a high five and tell them 'we'll get you next time,'" I tell the Bailouts.

The girls are as heartbroken and disappointed as I. Kaylyn's crying, Allison has a tear in her eye, Care wears a hang-dog expression, but they're feeling less than a quarter of the misery Mrs. Whiner is expressing at the moment. She's carrying on like a second grade version of a Tiffany clone who didn't get the biggest Prada purse for her birthday.

After the ceremonial handshakes, my players leave our bench and, in unison, immediately pick up their cell phones and start punching away on the screens. It's not if you win or lose that counts, what's important is the messages you received while you were away from your phone for the last twenty minutes.

It's almost noon, time to get the girls back to their mother's house. I have to yell to get Kelly's nose out of her cell phone, "Kelly, we're leaving."

By the time we make it to the Toyota, Care has pretty much forgotten the game; I wish I could say the same.

"Oh, Dad," Kelly says to me as I unlock the car doors. "Mom wanted me to give you this before you took us back." Kelly hands me an envelope. *Richard Sherlock* is written on the front in my ex-wife's handwriting. Her use of my last name speaks volumes.

Since my divorce, my ex has taken to writing instead of speaking to me. She has the girls deliver me notes concerning money owed, late payments, weekly schedules, etc., etc., etc. It's so important to have a positive, free-flowing, conversational relationship with your ex-spouse, especially when you're raising your kids in separate households.

I wish we had one.

"What's this?" I ask Kelly.

Kelly shrugs her shoulders. "You got me," she says and gives me that little crooked smile of hers.

"Yeah, right, Kelly."

The note is short, sweet, and to the point. "What?" I drop the note to my side. "I can't take you kids this weekend; it's your mother's weekend." I'm not screaming, but I am pretty loud. "Where is your mother?"

"She's on the lake," Care says.

"On the lake? What lake?"

"Michigan, I guess," Kelly explains.

"She went sailing," Care says.

"Sailing? Your mother hates water almost as much as she hates me."

"She's with the Commodore," Care says.

"Commodore? What's a commodore?"

"Mom's new boyfriend," Care says. "He's got a boat."

Kelly explains, "He said we could go with them, but when we found out there was no place to charge our cell phones on the boat we didn't want to go."

"What?" I can't believe this. "I have to work all weekend. I'm on a case."

"We can help," Care says.

"No, you can't. It's too dangerous."

"Or you can take us to the mall, give us a lot of money, and we can shop while you go off and investigate," Kelly suggests.

"Why didn't your mother tell me this two days ago?"

"Maybe it slipped her mind," Care says.

"I don't think so."

My ex-wife has stuck it to me again. I feel like a well-used voodoo doll.

"Get in the car."

"Dad," Care says climbing into the front passenger seat. "Can we go to McDonald's? I'm really hungry after all that exercise."

"No."

"Can we go to Taco Bell?"

"No. How many times do I have to tell you? Fast food is bad for you."

"Evidently, a lot more," Kelly says.

"You'll eat what I have at home to eat." I lay down the law.

"Oh God," Kelly says. "Not that turkey meatloaf. If we eat that we could die."

"You know, Kelly," I'm almost screaming again. "I already fired you once today. One more negative comment and you'll have one foot in the orphanage."

It's quiet for a few moments while I pull out of the school gym's parking area. I'm steaming and the kids know I'm steaming. My mood bothers Care a lot more than Kelly. "I thought you said you wanted to spend more time with us," Care says sheepishly.

"It's not that I don't want to see you more," I try to remain calm. "It's just that I have to work and make a living to pay for everything. And my schedule is hardly nine to five."

Kelly says, "Ya know, if Mom marries the Commodore, you won't have to pay alimony anymore."

"How would you know that, Kelly?" I ask.

"I'm smart. I pick up things."

"If your mother ever does marry again, I'm sure she'll set the date for the day after my final alimony check clears."

CHAPTER 12

I'm usually pretty good about noticing anything out of the ordinary, but my ex-wife has got me so ticked off I am completely oblivious to who else is parked near my building. The three of us get out of the car, the girls are still bitching about the lunch offerings inside, and I'm met one on one with a familiar face.

"Memba me?" the Thug asks.

"Oh jeesh," I say and quickly look to my left to see Mr. Ponytail in the driver's seat of the infamous Cadillac limo. "What are you doing here?"

"Time ta take a nother ride." Thug's got that same ugly black suit on. Who wears a suit on Saturday except maybe attendees of formal funerals? His head is bare.

"Didn't have time to get another hat?" I ask.

"No, but tanks for askin'. Now, get in da car. Time ta go."

"No," I tell him emphatically. "It's time for lunch."

"Who's your friend, Dad?" Care asks.

"He's not my friend."

"Aren't you going to introduce us?" Kelly asks.

"No."

I move towards the front door of my building, but I'm stopped by a bulk of thug.

"Sumbuddy wanna chat wit you, Sherlock," the Thug says.

"I'm not in a very talkative mood."

"Den get inta one." The Thug bumps me with his belly.

"No, thank you."

"Youse goin' wit us."

"No, I'm not. I'm busy being a parent right now."

The Thug turns slightly to the right and lifts his coat to reveal he still wears a Glock behind his back.

I try to whisper. "The last time we did this I got shot at. I will not put my kids in that situation."

"No," he says. "I got shot at. Youse was a innocent bystander."

"I didn't feel too innocent."

"Dat was an unfortunate, but dat won't happen again," he assures me.

"What's going on, Dad?" Care asks, sensing something is wrong.

"We's goin' for a ride," the Thug tells Care and Kelly.

I have no choice. I best do my best not to alarm the kids. "You've always wanted to ride in a limo, haven't you?" I ask my daughters in the calmest tone I can muster.

"Ah, duh," Kelly says.

The girls walk down the path to the street where the Caddy awaits. The Thug opens the rear door and motions for them to get in first. Before I get in, he says to me, "It's yer fault. Youse wasn't spossed to have yer kids dis weekend."

"Tell me about it."

Mr. Ponytail pulls the limo into traffic. The glass partition remains in the *Up* position. Kelly stretches her legs out and luxuriates in the rear seat, "Now this is more like it. We should travel like this all the time."

"Where are we going?" Care asks.

"We's goin fer a ride," the Thug answers.

Kelly takes out her cell phone and begins to text. "My friends aren't going to believe this."

The Thug reaches over and grabs Kelly's phone out of her hands.

Kelly's face turns bright red. She starts to shake. This could be worse than someone reaching into her chest and pulling her heart out. "What are you doing? That's my life in your hands!" she screams.

"Just wanna borrow it," the Thug says.

"You can't."

I pat Kelly to calm her down. "He's not going to hurt it," I tell her.

The Thug looks at Care, "Youse got one too?"

"Everybody has one," Care informs him.

"Youse too," he says to me.

I hand my new phone to him and Care follows suit. I warn him, "You do anything to hurt those phones and you'll have a riot on your hands."

The Thug tells the girls, "You'se can hav'em back when da ride's ova."

I can see the girls don't trust our host. "It's okay, girls," I say to add a layer of calm. "You'll get your phones back. I promise."

"Now, how bout sumthin to drink, ladies?" Our host and tour guide asks. "Look in da fridge."

Kelly dives down to the unit to check the items. Care tells our host, "We're hungry."

"Hungry?" the Thug asks, as Kelly surveys the quality of liquor in the cabinet.

"Can I have a martini?" Kelly asks.

"No."

"I need something to calm my nerves, Dad."

"When did you start drinking martinis?"

"I haven't, but this could be a real good time to start," Kelly says.

"Please," Care continues. "Can we stop and get something to eat? I'm starving."

The Thug glances over at me with a look of *dun't you feed yer kids* on his face.

"Welcome to my world," I tell him.

"Well," the Thug says. "I could eat." He pushes a button on the console where he sits and relays to Mr. Ponytail at the wheel, "Stop at McDonald's."

"Yeah," the kids yell.

"We're not stopping at McDonald's," I protest.

"Why not?" the Thug asks. "I like dem Big Mac's."

"That food is terrible for you," I tell him in no uncertain terms. "Do you have any idea of what the fat content of a Big Mac is?"

"Who cares," he says. "It tastes gud."

Not only am I and my entire family getting kidnapped, we're also being taken against my will to a McDonald's for unhealthy fast food. Talk about adding injury to insult.

Ten minutes later we are through the drive-up window and the back seat of the limo is filled with bags of burgers, fries, and apple turnovers. The pungent aroma of the grease each of them was cooked in permeates the air. The girls both clutch extra large chocolate shakes. The sugar content in those drinks will have them bouncing off the ceiling tonight like a couple of atoms in a super-collider. I'm the only one refraining from the feast.

"Ya know, Dad," Kelly says with her mouth full of fries. "You could have had a filet of fish sandwich. That would have been good for you."

"Kelly, I heard the fish they use to make those sandwiches comes from the goldfish people flush down their toilets." I will stop at nothing to scare my kids away from the evils of fast food, although my comment is a little late to stop today's gastrointestinal carnage.

Twenty minutes later, the limo stops at a gorgeous, Greek Revival converted "two-flat" on Howe Street, just off Armitage Avenue in Lincoln Park. "We's arrived," the Thug announces. "Git out, Sherlock."

I sit tight.

"Git."

"Come on, kids," I motion for my daughters to leave their collection of greasy food wrappers, cardboard, and napkins in the car and follow me.

"No," the Thug says. "Just you."

I make no move to get out the open door. "I go, my kids go with me."

"Dey ain't finish'd eatin'."

"They're kids, they're never finished eating."

We all climb out of the back seat.

Mr. Ponytail waits in the car while the rest of us trudge up the concrete stairs, past the two lion statues that vigilantly guard the entrance, and through a leaded glass door that's probably worth more than most people's IRA's. It's worth a lot more than mine; since I don't have an IRA. We stand in the foyer dominated by a fireplace and a tall Grandfather Clock. "Wait here," the Thug tells us before he exits.

"Ya know, Dad," Kelly says. "This is the way we should be living. Riding around in a limo, going to McDonald's, and having a crib like this to call home."

"I have to go to the bathroom," Care says.

The Thug returns with an impeccably dressed, dark-haired man of about forty. Kelly immediately scopes out his Rolex watch, his expensive designer suit, and his diamond cufflinks. "Please, come in," he says.

"I love your look," Kelly tells him.

We are ushered into a front room of Persian rugs, mahogany bookcases, and meticulously designed wood trim. The walls are lined with impressive original paintings. I recognize the Picasso. This is Tiffany territory.

"I understood this wasn't your weekend with your children," he tells me.

"I'll mention it to my ex-wife so she can cc you on all of her last minute scheduling changes."

"Dad," Care reminds me.

"Can she use the bathroom?" I ask.

The man motions for the Thug to escort my youngest down a short hallway. Kelly goes along—the power of suggestion no doubt.

He sits. I sit. He adjusts the ring on his right hand. "Mr. Sherlock, I would like to hire you."

"What?"

"I said I would like to hire you," he repeats. "Are you available?"

"You kidnapped me and my family to interview me for a job?"

"I wouldn't put it exactly like that," he says.

"How would you put it?"

"My schedule is somewhat inflexible and my needs are immediate. I wanted to speak with you as quickly as possible."

"Is that the same reason I got nabbed the first time around too?"

"That was a little bit different, and I apologize for the inconvenience." His manner of speaking is very reserved and a little too nonchalant for me.

"Next time, just call, okay?"

He takes his time, crosses one leg over the other, and glances around the room. "Nice place isn't it?" he says. "A business associate of mine owns it. He lets me use it while I'm in town."

"If you ever need a place that's downscale, I got one for rent."

The dark-haired gentleman politely ignores my remark. He folds his hands like a praying child and rests them in his lap. "I have an internal problem with one of my businesses and I need some assistance in defining the scope and depth of the situation."

"Let me guess," I say. "The Zanadu Club."

"You're very perceptive, Mr. Sherlock."

"Thank you, Mr. Cappilino."

He gives me a slight, knowing smile. "I'm not Jimmy Cappilino."

"Then who are you?"

"A reasonable facsimile," he says, "since Jimmy Cappilino does not exist."

"I'll take him off my Christmas card list."

"You do that, you'll save yourself a stamp, Mr. Sherlock."

I try my best to size this guy up. "Was I referred to you by someone, Mr. ---?" I ask.

"You can call me Rogers."

"Mister Rogers, you mean like the guy who wears the sweaters on TV?"

"Or like the naval officer Henry Fonda played in the movie or

126

Hammerstein's partner." He leans slightly forward. "There's a certain amount of chicanery going on within the walls of my business and it bothers me greatly. I would like you to find out what it is and report back to me."

There's no doubt in my mind that Mr. Rogers knows I'm working for more than one master at the Zanadu, but I see no reason to bring this up in our present conversation.

"All I ask is we have a similar working relationship as an attorney and his client," he specifies.

"That can be difficult in my business," I tell him.

"I will make it worth your while." He reaches into his breast pocket, pulls out a leather wallet, opens it, counts out ten one hundred dollar bills, and hands them to me. I can't remember a time when I found it so easy to get paid. With Mr. Richmond, ninety days is his starting point.

He stands up. "I have had my associate put a number into your phone, so you can reach me."

Considering my current state of uneasiness, I decide it's best not to mention that I don't know how to operate my cell phone.

"Don't call unless you have something to report," he lays down one law. "I'm not one for small talk."

The Thug and the girls return as if on cue.

"Goodbye, Mr. Sherlock," the dark-haired man says politely and turns away to admire the Picasso.

We are escorted out the door. Once outside, the Thug returns our cell phones. My kids are relieved beyond belief. Kelly grips hers as if it is a winning lottery ticket. "Oh my God," she says, "I've missed you."

Mr. Ponytail looks up at us from behind the wheel of the Caddy.

"We'll find our own way home," I tell our host.

"Sure?" The Thug asks.

"Positive," I tell him and add, "Why don't you use the time to go buy yourself a new fedora?"

"I might do dat."

I take a hand of each of my daughters and lead them down the street towards Armitage.

"You got some really weird friends, Dad," Kelly tells me.

"They are hardly my friends."

"I din't tink dat," Care says.

"And if I ever hear either of you talking like that idiot back there, neither of you will see another Fruit Roll Up until you're twenty-one."

We walk over to an Italian ice place on Armitage, just a little past Sheffield Avenue. It's fall, but the ice tastes great anyway. We kill a half-hour waiting for Tiffany, whom the girls called, to pick us up. When she arrives, she double-parks, and hops out of the Lexus; excited as a kid going into a candy store. "Hi, little dudettes."

"Hi, Tiffany," they say almost in unison.

Tiffany can't wait to give me the news. "Mr. Sherlock, you won't believe what my new life coach wants me to do."

"You're right. I won't."

"She says I should be channeling out of my inner Sword of Damocles which has overtaken my aura and put that energy into new positions of power and prestige." She's so excited, she can't stop. "I didn't even know I had a Sword of Damocles. I thought the best I had was the diamond stickpin Grandmama Moomah gave me."

"Don't feel bad, Tiffany," I tell her. "Most people don't even know Damocles had a sword."

"Tiffany," Kelly says, "that's sounds so totally cool."

"Yeah, doesn't it?" Tiffany says with a smile.

"Tiffany, do you have any idea what your life coach is talking about?" I ask.

"She says I have to begin putting out positive vibes in my momentums to attract the positive ions in the universe waiting to be tapped into action."

"And how did Dr. R. Bosley Radcliff suggest you do that?"

"The doc said I should find ways of bringing out a new 'Nice' Tiffany to replace the old "Not So Nice" Tiffany."

"Did she give you any ways to become 'Nice'?"

"She's leaving it up to me," Tiffany tells us. "I'm going to come up with ideas and we'll discuss them in our next session."

"Another three-hundred dollar session?"

"And worth every penny, Mr. Sherlock, although I hate pennies."

"Well," I admit, "I'm glad to see you're feeling better." Maybe three hundred dollars is a small price to pay for Tiffany's happiness; I just wish I were the one getting paid.

My phone rings, but before I can answer it, Kelly says, "Dad, you need some new ringtones."

"Forget it, Kelly." I answer the phone. It's "Wait" Jack Wayt.

"Wait," he says in greeting. "It's Saturday, Sherlock. You know what happens on Saturday?"

"No."

"I start to feel the effects of my Adult ADHD."

"Is that why you're calling me?"

"No," he says. "I'm at Bruno's condo. You better get over here."

"Do I have a choice?"

"No."

I can't figure out how to end the call so I turn off my cell phone. "I've got to go."

"Where, Dad?"

"Crime scene."

"Bruno's?" Tiffany asks.

"That's the place."

"Can we come?" Kelly asks.

Tiffany tells the girls, "You don't want to go there. That place stinks worse than the perfume section at Target."

The girls have already been taken against their/my will, which is plenty for one day. A blood-soaked murder scene will not add anything positive to their upbringing. The problem is what do I do with them?

"Tiffany, are you busy?" I ask.

"I'm always busy."

"Doing what, may I ask?"

"Nothing really," she says. "I'm just naturally busy."

"Would you mind taking Kelly and Care to Water Tower Place?"

"Ah, YES!" erupts from my pair of spendthrift offspring.

"I can't," Tiffany says. "I just remembered I got a date."

Damn.

"With Monroe," Tiffany says with an odd smile on her lips. "This might be the night."

"Are you sure?" I ask.

"Pretty sure."

"Where is he taking you?" Care asks.

"I don't know, but it better be someplace expensive."

"So, can we come with you to the murder scene?" Kelly asks me again.

"No."

"Why not?"

"Because it's not good parenting for a father to have his kids visit a condo where a guy got bludgeoned to death."

"Why not?" Care asks.

"We see that on TV every day," Kelly says.

"Why don't I drop you off at the library," I suggest. "And you can spend a couple hours getting smarter."

"That's totally lame. If we can't go see all that blood, we want to go shopping."

"How about a movie?"

"There's nothing we want to see except new clothes." Kelly doesn't stop there. "You said we could go to Water Tower Place if Tiffany was with us."

I had to open my big mouth. Now, I'm stuck. "Tiffany, will you give them a ride?"

"No problem."

I pull out my wallet. "Here's four hundred dollars," I give them each two bills. "Spend it wisely."

Kelly grips the bills tighter than Moses did the Ten Commandments. Her eyes widen as she stares at them as if they were tickets to heaven. Care rolls the money up and stuffs it into her front pocket. I couldn't have had two more different kids.

I have Tiffany drop me off in front of Bruno's building. Before getting out of her car, I turn to my girls. "I'll see you at the bottom of the escalators at four o'clock. Don't be late."

"Thanks, Dad."

"Have a good time."

"Oh, Mr. Sherlock," Tiffany says pointing to the building. "Your buddy is working."

I see Guido, the jerk doorman, opening the door for some old lady.

"You know," Tiffany says. "He looks familiar."

"How?"

"I don't know."

"You do run into a lot of doormen," I remind her. "And they're all in uniform."

"Oh, yeah, I didn't think of that."

"And you prefer to group all service people into one easy to identify category."

"That saves me a lot of effort on my part, so I can put that time into attracting more positive ions to the new 'Nice' me."

"Good luck with that, Tiffany."

I exit the car, repeating to the girls, "Remember, four o'clock."

The Lexus speeds away. I walk up the driveway and through the revolving outer door.

"You, again," Guido greets me.

"Open the door for me."

"Why should I?"

"Because I'm here on official police business."

"I got reamed big time after you got in here the last time," he tells me. "How'd you do that?"

"I'm not sure."

He's not sure how to respond, so he doesn't.

"I'm sorry if I put a black mark on your career path, Guido." I apologize and dig him in one sentence.

"This is hardly my career," he says sourly.

Guido opens the inner door. I pass through, go straight to the elevator bank, and take the second car to the 41st floor.

"Wait" Jack Wayt sits on a couch in Bruno's apartment. "Wait," he says before I can say "Hello."

"What?"

"Sherlock, I think I'm feeling a touch of gout in my little toe." He lifts his left foot.

"Maybe you tied your shoe too tight," I suggest.

Jack reaches down, unties the knot, loosens the laces, and reties his shoe. "That's better," he says. "You ever consider going into medicine?"

"I've considered everything to keep from doing what I'm doing."

The crime lab had a field day in Bruno's place. Big swaths of the carpet have been cut out as well as the drywall with the blood splatter. There are two big holes in the bedroom wall. All the drawers are open and their surfaces are covered with dust from fingerprint kits. The fireplace mantle has been pulled off the wall. Some hard-driving real estate agent is going to have a lot of refurbishing to do to before he puts this unit on the market.

"Come on," Jack says. "I want you to see something."

I follow Jack to the hallway between the front room and the bedroom. He opens the linen closet door, pulls out two stacks of towels, reaches in, and removes a piece of drywall from the far end that at first glance looks like regular wall. "The crime boys were so busy ripping the place apart, they forgot to check the obvious." He moves to the side so I can see.

Stacks of boxes, bottles, and vials of prescription drugs fill a foot of cabinet space in the rear of a hidden cupboard. "What are they?" I ask.

"Steroids."

"This wasn't what was in the drawer I found," I say reminding myself as well as Jack.

"You've got enough steroids and growth hormones here to put a major league locker room to shame," Jack says.

This doesn't make sense. "Bruno was in a much different business than I thought."

"You know, Sherlock," Jack says. "If I owned the Cubs, I'd make every player on the team bulk up. Even if they got caught, who'd care? At least the fans wouldn't have had to wait until next year."

"Wouldn't work, they're the Cubs," I tell him. I pause before I ask, "You talk to anyone at the Zanadu who said Bruno was pushing muscle meds?"

"No, but there wasn't much doubt he was pushing everything else," Jack says.

I peer back into the stash in the linen closet, "Could these be for personal use?"

"Only if he was trying to become the Incredible Hulk," Jack says.

Jack replaces the false front to the cupboard, and we return to the front room where I first found him. He sits on the couch. I sit in a chair.

"Anything else you find that I should know about?" I ask him.

"No, not about this," he says.

"There is something we have to talk about, Jack."

"What?"

I swallow hard and take a deep breath. I'm sure Jack is not going to like what comes out of my mouth next. "Jack, "No-No" wants to know if you still have feelings for her."

"Damn it, Sherlock," he snaps back at me. "I invite you over here to help you out, and you turn into Cupid."

"I had to ask you, Jack. I didn't have a choice. "No-No" was going to charge me with breaking and entering if I didn't."

"She was bluffing. How naïve about women are you?"

"Really, really naïve," I tell him.

Jack's dander is way up. "Let me tell you two things about women, Sherlock."

"Okay."

"You can't live with 'em," he pauses for effect. "And you can't live with 'em."

I can only wonder: where was my mentor when I met my ex-wife?

"Jack," I say as calmly as I'm able. "You haven't answered my question."

"And you can't make me, Sherlock."

I give it a minute or two for the subject to dissipate then get up to leave.

"Where're you going?" he asks.

"I got to pick up my kids. Thanks for letting me in on the new wrinkles."

"That's not why I brought you over here. Sit down." Jack opens his tattered briefcase, pulls out a stack of money, and tosses it on the table my way. "I need you to do something."

"What?"

"Buy me some drugs."

"Why? I already cured your gout."

"Not that kind of drugs. I need some cocaine."

"Jack ..."

"Here's the address," he hands me a slip of paper. "Make sure you use the top ten bills."

I look down at the wad of cash. I only wish.

CHAPTER 13

The girls come down the escalator at eight minutes before five, both loaded down with rope-handled bags from some well-known expensive stores. "I thought I told you four o'clock."

"You did," Care admits.

"But we wanted to make sure we spent all the money you gave us so we wouldn't have to waste any of it going home on the 'L'," Kelly says.

"How did you afford all that?" I ask, pointing to their stashes.

"Shopping," Kelly says. "It's an art."

We walk to the Chicago Avenue station and catch a train heading north. It's dinnertime by the time we get into our neighborhood, so I decide we stop at a local spot and eat. They have burgers. I have fish. They tell me of their shopping forays and describe each item they purchased. They are truly happy. It's amazing what having a little money in your pocket can do for you and your family. I even feel pretty good about it.

We walk to our apartment, and, once in the door, I tell them, "I have to run an errand tonight. I don't want you fighting over the TV remote."

Neither listen. They're both playing with their cell phones.

I go into my bedroom, change into jeans and a sweatshirt, and return to the girls who have taken their purchases, spread them out over the furniture, and are taking pictures with their cell phones to send to their Facebook friends.

"Keep the doors locked and don't let anybody in," I say this extra loud. "If anybody knocks, call me on your phone and I'll tell you what to do."

I hope they're listening; sometimes all I can do is hope.

The address "Wait" Jack Wayt gave me is on the Westside. The one-story brick building is on a street off Madison Street, a particularly crummy neighborhood that's a mile or so west of the United Center. The entrance to the building, which was previously a retail operation selling retread tires to owners of cars like my Toyota, is off the rear alley. It's a perfect retail location—if you're in the drug business.

If you've ever considered delving into the sale of illegal substances, you might want to reconsider. It's not a great line of work. It has a business model that is structured like a pyramid. The enormous base is made up of uneducated street kids who have flunked out of school and have very few other employment options available to them. The drug lords at the top of the pyramid realize these dumb, impressionable punks are ripe for picking, so they hire them at a minuscule wage with no fringe benefits and make them salesmen. The middle section of the pyramid is composed of the drug distributors. Although they're paid much better than the sellers on the street, often in 18-Carat bling instead of cold cash, these Johnny-come-lately entrepreneurs run the greatest risk of all. If they get busted, they wind up in the slammer for a very long time.

I think you should know there's a great disconnect between the distributors in the middle and the chieftains at the top. The exclusive few who import the dope and supply it to the distributors seldom get busted because they keep their distance from the down and dirty aspects of the trade. For them it's quite simple. If anything goes wrong they merely walk away, go back to the massive labor pool at their disposal, and start over.

These kingpins are just like a lot of America's respected corporate CEO's who sit in their ivory towers, sip 12-year-old scotch, and order their MBA generals to use cheap, foreign, sweatshop labor to reduce costs. So what if a fire breaks out in a Bangladesh factory making battery acid and hundreds of workers are killed. They simply blame it on the locals in charge and move the operation to some other factory in Katmandu.

It works the same way in the drug business. In order to keep their distance, the big bosses establish phony corporations and rent abandoned buildings to use as retail "outlets." It works out great because it's easy to keep watch on the operations at a safe distance, maintain quality control of the products, supervise the employees, offer an easy access to the product for their customers, and most importantly, it allows them to totally control the enormous amount of the cash generated by the transactions. If one of these "outlets" gets busted, the supplier merely picks up, moves to another building and sets up shop there.

Transporting the cash from the "outlets" to the "bank" works in almost the same way it does in the "legitimate" business world—only with a great deal more caution. Under the cover of night and when the coast is clear, somebody drives up to the "outlet," picks up the money, and drives off.

The last thing a major drug supplier wants is to be in any way involved when a turf war breaks out, where kids are shooting each other at will, and innocent people are getting caught in the crossfire. He wants complete deniability. And he often says with a straight face, "Hey, they're independent contractors. It isn't our fault." If you look at the business from the top, it's a moneymaking machine. If you look at it from the bottom, it's a nightmare on any level—business or otherwise.

I pull up in my Toyota and wait with the engine running. The building is similar to the one where the felt fedora Thug took one in his Kevlar vest. Less than a minute later, a kid not much older than sixteen comes up to my open window. "Yo," he greets me.

I show him the ten bills "Wait" Jack Wayt gave me to use and say, "Blow."

The kid takes my money, runs inside the building, and two minutes later runs back out to my car. He drops a baggie of white powder in my lap, and walks away. He doesn't even bother to say "Thanks." And people wonder why customers have so little retail loyalty.

I drive directly to the precinct station in Cabrini-Green, where "Wait" Jack Wayt is waiting.

"Wait, he says.

"What?"

"The toe on my other foot is hurting."

"Did you loosen that shoe?" I ask.

He doesn't answer. I hand him the recently purchased baggie and pull out what's left of the wad he gave me in Bruno's apartment.

"Will you let me know where the trace ends up?" I ask.

"If it ends up anywhere," he tells me.

I hold out the cash for him to take.

"Keep it."

"Thanks."

"Don't mention it," He's not merely being polite, but merely playing the game. In reality, this is a small price to pay for the services I rendered.

"Don't worry," I assure him. "I won't."

Jack knows that I know the unwritten rules of this game.

I feel the thickness of the stack of bills, try not to smile, but in my head all I hear is ... *Cha-ching, cha-ching, cha-ching.*

I'm home. The kids are asleep. Personal shopping can be exhausting, although I wouldn't know since I do so little of it. I pull the wad of money out of my pocket and add it to the bills Mr. Rogers gave me. The total is $1,700. This is more cash in hand than I've had since my divorce two years ago. Feeling those bills between my fingers, seeing how green, and how comforting they are; it's a feeling I haven't had in a long, long time. It'll buy me a new muffler, new winter boots and new jeans, and a full refrigerator. It'll also pay off my credit card debt. No more pink statements in my mailbox. Hallelujah!

I fold the bills in half, wrap two rubber bands around them, and place them in the bottom of a small tin recipe box I keep in the upper kitchen cupboard. The money from Mr. D'Wayne DeWitt is already there. Now the total is well over $2,500.

While I'm at it, I take out a stack of blank 3x5 recipe cards, find a pen that works, and retire to the living room, which doubles as my bedroom when the kids are with me. I fix the couch up with a sheet and blanket. I do a couple of back exercises before lying down. I feel pretty good. I have one last thought of the stack of money safely tucked away in my kitchen cupboard and fall asleep with a grin on my face.

The Original Carlo, a particularly bad painting I bought years ago at an outdoor art sale for eight dollars, hangs on my living room's biggest wall. It's a rendition of a dilapidated barn with four red mailboxes in front of it, all set against a lemon yellow background or maybe it's a lemon yellow sky. Why the sky is yellow, or why a barn would ever need one, much less four, mailboxes, only adds to its artistic allure. I consider the work so bad, it's good.

When I'm on a case, *The Original Carlo* serves another purpose. It becomes a bulletin board for my handwritten index cards. It helps me to keep everything I know about a case in one convenient place and see it at a glance. I add row upon row of easily movable 3x5 cards which I stick on the picture with push pins. It's easy to add, subtract, mix and match, whatever. Hardly high tech, in no way artistic, and the process makes *The Original Carlo* look like it has shingles. But hey, it works for me.

Sunday morning, a little after nine, the kids are snoring away, and I go to work. I start scribbling away on the recipe cards. I write one item on each card—a thought, a fact, a suspicion, an instance, a happening, a question, or a conclusion. When I have prepared about fifty cards, I begin push pinning them into *The Original Carlo.* All with the purpose to make some sense of the case at hand.

Tiffany is at the top of my first column. Beneath her name, I have the when, where, how, and what concerning her drug induced state. I have a card for each person either around her or close to the situation when she took a header off the barstool at the Zanadu—Alix, Bruno, Monroe, and the blocker. I left the "C" word off so my impressionable daughters won't see it and ask me any embarrassing questions.

My next column is headed *Gibby Fearn.* Beneath his name is a card for the Behemoth, his comic book-reading comrade-in-arms. I have cards listing what Gibby does and what he doesn't do. I also list the times of his inside and outside money pick-ups and drops. I'm not sure why I do this, but for some reason it seems to make sense.

The third column is headed *D'Wayne DeWitt.* I list his rap sheet, his two girls, his job, and his digs at the Zanadu on separate cards. I also have a number of cards for what I don't know about him—where he lives, his finances, his hangouts, his friends, and his business associates. There's also a card with the amount of money I have received from him so far, $1,900. I usually don't use *The Original Carlo* as a spread sheet, but the money is coming in so fast and furious it's kinda fun to have it up there to see my finances flourishing for once.

I make two more columns. One for *Bruno Buttaras,* which lists everything I know about him and his murder. His is the longest list by far. The second is for *Mr. Rogers,* the shortest of the listings. I have very little to report on my latest client except for the $1,000 he gave me.

Lastly, I put up random cards on which I've written aspects of the case for which I have no clue where they fit in. These include my two kidnappings, the Non-Brink's Brinks truck, the Brink's truck and each of their destinations; Monroe's CEI company, the shooting at the first retail dope location, the blood on that floor, the gang/turf war currently in progress, Neula "No-No" Noonan's suspicion of a male murderer, "Wait" Jack Wayt's steroid find, and the baggie of blow I picked up for him in that crummy neighborhood off Madison Street on the Westside.

I consider adding a final column that will chart the relationship status of "Wait" Jack Wayt and Neula "No-No" Noonan, but I decide against mixing business info with personal info.

I sit for about an hour staring at the partially covered painting before me. What I have is Tiffany getting roofied, a murder, money being laundered through the Zanadu, a shooting, a drug buy, a potential murder scene, two new employers who pay me in advance, the Behemoth, a Thug who used to wear a fedora, Mr. Ponytail, the absence of a Mr. Capellino, and Bobo Bling's horrible MF rap CD. I know in some way, shape, or form it's all connected, but there's not yet a thread stitched between any two. I don't get far in figuring any of it out because I'm interrupted by a just risen Care.

"Good morning."

"What are you doing, Dad?"

"Trying to make some sense of nonsense.

"Why?"

"Because that's my job."

"Care wipes the sleep from her eyes, looks up at the first column on *The Original Carlo*. "Are you going to find out who did that to Tiffany?"

"I certainly hope so."

Care takes another long look, "You know something, Dad?" She pauses dramatically and I await the bombshell. "You have really horrible handwriting."

I sigh. "Thanks for the compliment."

Kelly emerges from the bedroom and plops down on the couch; she's still half-asleep. "Aren't you going to say 'Good morning,' Kelly?" I ask.

"I wasn't planning on it," she answers.

"Do you know what I think would be a great idea?" I say with a zing in my tone.

"Nope," Kelly says negating any of my zing with her droll response.

"Why don't we all get dressed up and take in a service at one of the neighborhood churches?"

Care turns her nose up at the idea. Kelly is vocal, "Bad idea," she says.

"I think it's a great idea. It would do you girls good to listen to a good sermon."

"You go, Dad," Kelly says. "And bring home some loaves and fishes."

"Sermons aren't like take-out, Kelly," I inform her. "You have to be there to experience it."

"Then why are so many sermons on TV?" Kelly asks.

"Those shows are for people who are shut-ins and can't attend a regular church service in person."

"We're shut in right now," Care says.

"I'll TiVo one and watch it later," Kelly promises.

"I can't afford TiVo," I tell them what they already know.

"Mom has TiVo," Kelly says, knowing it makes me crazy when she plays the "Mom has that at her house" card.

"I'll tell you what, Dad," Care assures me. "I'll tape one at Mom's and make sure Kelly watches it with me."

"Yeah, I don't think that's going to happen."

"Why don't we go out and spend some more of your money?" Kelly suggests.

"I let you do that yesterday or have you already forgotten?"

"No," Kelly says. "I'm considering yesterday was a practice day and today you'd give us some more money so we could go out and put to use what we learned about shopping yesterday."

"As I said before, Kelly, 'Yeah, I don't think that's going to happen.'"

My phone rings. Care picks it up and punches the screen. "Care, don't answer my phone."

"Hello," she says.

"Well, Dad," Kelly says, "if we can't go shopping maybe we can use the time to put some new ringtones on your phone?"

"Don't you dare."

"It's Tiffany," Care says, handing me my phone."

It's Sunday, long before noon. If Tiffany is calling, something isn't right. "Hello."

Her message is clear. I hang up. "Get showered and dressed, girls. Tiffany is taking us to brunch."

140

The Ritz, the Four Seasons, the Park Hyatt, and the Drake all have Sunday Brunch Bacchanalias. This is where they open up their ballrooms, pull out their best dinner china and silverware, and spread out enough food to feed a refugee camp on tables that circle the room. Their breakfast fare has everything gastronomically imaginable—and even unimaginable: fruit, cereal, toast, pancakes, scones, bagels, bacon, sausages of all sizes and varieties, white eggs, brown eggs, even green eggs and ham. You can order custom-made omelets in more flavors than Baskin-Robbins and Ben & Jerry's combined. If you can stomach looking into the glassy eyes of a just caught salmon, you can scoop out some of its smoked flesh and enjoy devouring it. There's French toast made from every type of bread including French. There's biscuits and gravy for those from the heartland, grits for the Southern folk, enough shrimp to satisfy Moby Dick's cravings, and a pastry display that would be the envy of that cupcake chef on TV who Care watches all the time. It's enough to make anyone run for an antacid. And I won't even go into the libations available, but the bar provides everything from Bloody Marys to Virgin Moonshine. Sunday Brunch is America's answer to a Roman Orgy; all that's missing is the adjacent barfatorium.

Here's the kicker, these exorbitant smorgasbords come with a hefty price tag that usually starts at around fifty bucks a head. So a family of three will spend more on a Sunday Brunch than I will spend at the Jewel-Osco in a month. Ridiculous.

"Hi, little dudettes." Tiffany spots us in the lobby of the Four Seasons Hotel.

"Tiffany," I say as the girls ceremoniously group hug, "why don't we just go to some local breakfast place. We don't need all this food."

Tiffany, who is dressed in tweed skirt and a yellow cashmere sweater, the standard fall attire for the fashion conscious girl of Chicago, says, "Nobody can really see you in a one of those overcrowded breakfast nooks, Mr. Sherlock. And if they did see me there, I'd be horrified."

"Whatever."

There's something not quite right about Tiffany. Maybe her Sword of Damocles is poking her in the rear. I can't tell what the problem is by looking at her, but I'm a bit surprised that she called me instead of her new life coach, Dr. R. Bosley Radcliff. Maybe the doctor doesn't give advice on Sundays.

We are led by the Maitre d' to one of the better tables. The waiter arrives the moment our butts touch down. Tiffany orders a mimosa. I order three orange juices. Kelly and Care are straining their necks at the epicurean potpourri surrounding us like a wagon train of food trucks. I tell my girls, "Here's what you do. Walk around the entire room, see all the stuff they have to eat, and then decide where you want to start. Pick and choose carefully. Don't get filled up on one thing. You can go back as many times as you want, so make variety the spice of your breakfast life."

The kids get up and make a dash for the breakfast dessert table. Nobody listens to me.

I turn to Tiffany who is gulping the mimosa. "What's the matter?"

Tiffany downs half of the drink before answering. "Something happened to me last night that's never happened to me before."

"What?"

"It's kinda hard to talk about."

"What is it?"

"Do you promise you'll never repeat this, post it on Facebook, or tweet it to anyone?" She's serious, very, very serious.

"Yes."

She hesitates.

"Want me to cut my finger and swear to you in my own blood?" I ask to reassure her.

"Maybe later."

"Okay, tell me."

"Mr. Sherlock, I got shut down last night," she whispers, as if she's confessing that she once committed a horrendous crime against humanity.

"What?"

"This probably happens to you and maybe everybody else all the time, but it's never, ever happened to me." She puts her head into her hands to hide her shame.

"What?"

"I got shut down." Tiffany's wrist goes to her forehead. She rubs her temples to ease the pain. She sniffles as if she's about to break into tears.

I still have no clue what she is referring to.

Tiffany lifts one hand from her face and whispers to me. "I wanted to do it and he didn't."

"Do what?"

Tiffany drops both hands and gives me her *no one can be this stupid look.* "It, Mr. Sherlock," she cries out. "IT."

The explanation dawns on me like a fireplace poker to my skull. "Monroe?"

Tiffany nods and returns to the whispering mode. "After our date, I invited him up to my penthouse. I made it very clear what was going to happen next, and when I get his clothes off, do you know what he does?"

Even though I have a real good idea, I say, "No."

"He starts posing and flexing."

"Posing and flexing what?" I have to ask.

"His muscles.

"How many?"

"Mr. Sherlock. I'm standing there in nothing but my best lace chemise and a smile, and he's there going through this Arnold Schwarzenegger, flex-a-thon routine in front of my mirrors. It was nauseating. And he's oiled up enough to be in the Gay Pride Parade."

"You think Monroe's gay?"

"No," Tiffany says. "I know for a fact he's not gay."

I don't ask for an explanation.

"It was like he was more interested in looking at himself in the mirror than looking at me. Can you believe that?"

"No, Tiffany, I can't." I pause for a moment. "What did you do?"

"Well, I just stood there and watched him go from one pose to another, from one mirror to another …"

I interrupt her, "And you've got a lot of mirrors."

"Lots."

Hardly surprising.

"I asked him what he was doing," Tiffany says. "And he tells me he's 'counting his cuts.'"

"What's that?"

"I thought it was one of those diseases like bulimia. But I couldn't see any scars," Tiffany says.

I wonder how I'm going to put all this on an index card for *The Original Carlo.* "Maybe it was a good thing you didn't do it, Tiffany. You sure wouldn't want to pick up something."

"Plus, think what all that slimy stuff on his body would do to one thousand count satin sheets," she adds.

"I wouldn't lose any sleep over this. It's him, not you," I reassure her. "And there is no way he's ever going to put this on Facebook."

Tiffany gives it a second to sink in then peers up at me. "Thanks, Mr. Sherlock. I feel better already."

I should charge her three hundred dollars for this, but I won't.

Kelly and Care return to the table. Each carries two plates heaping with enough food to feed Napoleon's army. I see pancakes, crab legs, scones, croissants, bacon, and lots of sweets, lots and lots of sweets.

"This place puts Hometown Buffet to shame," Kelly says as she sits down.

"You take them to Hometown Buffet?" A shocked Tiffany asks.

"Once," I lie.

"That is so not cool."

Tiffany doesn't line up in buffet line, possibly because she refuses to stand in any line. Instead, she nibbles off Kelly and Care's breakfast abondanza. There's plenty for the three of them plus the entire roster of Morrie's Bail Bonds Bailouts—including Mrs. Whiner.

I rise and join the rest of the brunchers. Why not? When at a Roman Bacchanal, do as the Romans do. I have a cheese omelet, two slices of wheat toast, and a fruit cup. Dumb choices for a fifty-dollar meal, but I have no great interest in sampling the Chef's Special Lobster Thermador or his prime rib au jus. Call me plebian.

As we are leaving the hotel, Tiffany asks me, "Have you found out who roofied me yet, Mr. Sherlock?"

"No, I've got a lot on my plate right now." No pun intended.

"Why not?"

"I'm working on it."

"You better get moving," Tiffany says. "The effects of a crime like that can wear off quickly."

I, for one, certainly hope so.

CHAPTER 14

The kids ate so much at the brunch, I almost have to roll them onto the 'L' to get them back to my apartment. By the time we get home, it's late afternoon. They have homework to do, but no books to do it with because instead of me picking them up for the weekend they were more or less dropped in my lap with a note from Mom. I disturb their digestion process as they lounge in front of the TV set like a couple of couch potatoes. "We better get going."

"Can we take our new clothes with us to Mom's?" Kelly asks.

"If you do," I argue, "you won't have anything to wear when you're here with me."

"That'll give us a reason for you to take us shopping during our visitation time with you," is Kelly's retort.

"Visitation time?" I repeat her phrase. "Is that something else you 'picked up', Kelly?"

"It does have a nice ring to it," Kelly says. "So, can we, Dad?"

What am I going to say, "No?" I sigh out a breath to reveal my displeasure and tell them. "Go ahead, get your stuff, and put it in the car. Hurry up. We've got one stop to make along the way.

A different faux nurse mans the front desk at the Doc in the Box health center where Tiffany was treated last week. Different nurse, same attitude, "Yeah, what's your problem?" she asks, as the kids and I approach her desk.

"Is Dr. Nehru in?"

"He's with a patient."

"I only need to see him for a few minutes."

"That's what they all say," she tells me. She picks up a clipboard with a pen attached and hands it to me. "Sit over there, fill this out, and bring it back with your insurance card," she growls. "I hope you have one, 'cause if you don't, the county hospital's right down the street."

I take the clipboard, loosen the latch on its top, pull out the first page, and write on the back a short note in big letters and hand it back to the helpful hospital worker.

She reads quickly. "Tiffany Richmond? As in Richmond Insurance,

Richmond?"

"She'd be the one."

Immediate attitude adjustment. "Please have a seat," she says cordially, jumping from her chair. "The doctor will be with you shortly."

I take the girls by their hands and lead them to the waiting area. We sit as far away from the sneezers, the bleeders, and the scratchers as possible. It seems to be a particularly bad day for nasal ailments.

Five minutes later Dr. Omagalla Nehru comes out to greet us. "Richard Sherlock, so nice to see you once again."

He ushers me to enter into his inner sanctum. "Wait here," I tell the girls. "And try not to get infected."

Neither is listening. They are both playing with their cell phones.

"Hey, Doc."

"I have the results right here," he tells me holding a few pages in his left hand. "Did I mention I had them done 'stat'?"

"What's the word, Doc?"

"No Flunitrazepan."

"English, Doc."

"No hypnotic sedative present."

"I still don't get it."

"No Rohypnol."

I stand there stumped again.

"She wasn't roofied." He surprises the heck out of me.

"If Tiffany wasn't roofied, what was she?"

"She was given a mixture of testosterone, human growth hormones, and an adrenaline producing compound." He pauses, sensing my inability to understand. "You might say Miss Tiffany was 'Super-Red Bullied.'"

"You mean she was hopped up like Barry Bonds?"

"Lucky she wasn't tested by the IOC, because she would have been banned from the Olympics for life." The Doc laughs at his own joke.

The only person I can immediately suspect of doping Tiffany would be Alix Fromound. She slips Tiffany a Mickey, causing her svelte figure to inflate to something resembling the Michelin Man and Alix wins the next *Slim Is In* competition.

"Mr. Sherlock, I hope you can find a way to drop into your conversation with Mr. Jamison Richmond the Third what top notch, A-one, professional procedures were performed on his lovely, daughter,Tiffany; within the appropriate, cost-conscious guidelines of the Richmond Medical Organization."

It would be fair and truthful to tell Dr. Omagalla Nehru that Mr. Jamison never speaks, never has spoken, and probably never will speak to me, but I don't. I'll never know when I might need a little medical help myself, so instead I say, "The next time Jamison and I are out having a few cool ones, I'll make sure to mention it to him."

"Many thanks, Mr. Sherlock. Many thanks."

I return to the waiting area to find my girls wearing surgical masks and latex gloves, with see-through booties on their cell phones. Before I can ask, the desk nurse explains, "It's not only my job to heal the sick, but also to keep the healthy, healthy."

"Gee thanks."

There's a yacht the size of a Carnival cruise ship parked in front of what used to be my house.

"Jeesh," I say to the kids, "Captain Jack Sparrow doesn't have a boat this big."

"Mom told us the Commodore is getting an airplane, too" Care informs me.

"Is he going to trade in his yacht for an aircraft carrier?"

"Want me to ask him?" Care asks me.

"No, I'd rather be left in suspense."

"Are you jealous, Dad?" Kelly asks me.

"No."

"You look jealous."

"How do you 'look jealous,' Kelly?"

"I don't know," she says. "You just do."

"Grab your stuff, get into the house, and do your homework," I order them.

"Bye, Dad."

"And tell your mother no more notes. If she wants to change the schedule or tell me something, she can call me."

"Sure, Dad."

They're not going to say anything. I'd be better off writing a note to their mother about no more notes.

I give them each a big kiss, tell them how much I love them, and watch them walk up the path and into the front door. No matter how many times I do this, I always feel sad when that door shuts behind them.

Back at the ranch, I put up a few new cards on *The Original Carlo*. I sit and stare at the accumulation of 3x5 scribbling for an hour or so and end up more confused than I was when I stared at it this morning. To make myself feel better, I go into the kitchen, retrieve the recipe box from the upper cupboard, open it, take out the money, and count it two or three times. Now, I'll sleep like a baby.

Tiffany picks me up at my apartment, at 11a.m. This is the hour she considers bright and early. "Mr. Sherlock, I've decided not to let what happened, or actually what didn't happen, between me and Monroe to not bother me anymore."

She has used a double, double negative, but correcting Tiffany's grammar would be a similar task to trying to stop the guy who pushes that boulder up the hill all the time only to have it roll back down before he reaches the top. "Good for you, Tiffany."

"It's much, much more important that I follow through on the plan of action I've laid out for myself." She is driving way too fast as she cuts in and out of the lanes on the Drive.

After all the trips we've made together, you'd think I'd be used to her driving, but no. It still scares the heck out of me. "Could you please slow down? I'd like to see my children as adults some day."

"I can't slow down, Mr. Sherlock, my life coach told me I have to strike out when I'm really hot."

I say a silent prayer to the God of Airbags, then say, "What have you decided to do?"

"I've decided to launch a three-way plan of action to attract good karma and bring out the 'Nice' Tiffany in me."

This should be good. "That's a wonderful idea."

"First, I'm going to set up a charity to provide women on purge diets with free stomach pumps." She gets off the Drive and takes Ohio Street, heading west. "Any dieter who's ever had to stick their head in a toilet is going to love it. Plus, it'll be good for the environment and public health. Consider all the flushing that won't be happening and it is a much cleaner and more efficient way to rid yourself of unwanted calories."

"Wow."

"Next, I'm going to establish a free service to help teenage girls make better fashion choices," Tiffany explains number two on her to do list. "I'm so tired of being appalled at what I see walking on Michigan Avenue: like girls wearing stripes with checks, exposing their butt cracks, letting their muffin tops spill out. And, some of those tattoo choices. I tell you, Mr. Sherlock, something's gotta be done. So, what I'm going to do is publish a *Rules of the Road to Proper Fashion*."

"I can't think of anyone more qualified to take on that task," I tell her.

"And this is my best idea, Mr. Sherlock."

I can hardly wait.

"I want to open up a help line, kinda like the kind people call when they're committing suicide, but this one's for people with relationship issues," Tiffany says. Before I can respond, she keeps going. "The uniqueness of this service is that it'll be restricted to women who are *attractively challenged*."

"Do you mean ugly?"

"So to speak."

Tiffany rolls through a stop sign, honks at a truck, and keeps talking. "I was thinking about it, and I thought to myself, since I've had guys chasing me since middle school, I've probably gone through every relationship issue there is, but someone not so hot, hasn't."

"Why not?" I ask.

"Because no guys are chasing them because—" She pauses.

"They're not as hot?" I answer.

"Exactly," Tiffany says. "I'll be opening up my entire world of dating experiences to give these 'not-so-attractively fortunate' women the answers they need to get the man they want."

"Well, Tiffany, you certainly picked needs to fill that I would have never considered. I can't wait to hear what Dr. R. Bosley Radcliff has to say about your plan of action."

"She's going to love it. I just know it."

"I'll bet she'll want to discuss the details for hours."

"Mr. Sherlock, I'm already starting to feel niceness coming up through my pores."

"Good for you, Tiffany. Good for you."

Tiffany double-parks her Lexus in front of Bruno's condo building.

The doorman comes out. I'm surprised to see it's not my old buddy Guido. "You can't park there," he says.

Tiffany hands him a twenty-dollar bill.

"But there are exceptions to every rule," the doorman smiles and says.

"Where's Guido?" I ask the new guy.

"He got fired."

I don't feel an overwhelming abundance of remorse upon hearing the news. "Was it because people were sneaking by him into the building?" I ask to qualify, and quantify, any guilt I may or may not have.

"I'm not really sure."

The new man is much smaller in size and height to his predecessor. The uniform he's wearing fits him like a wet blanket.

"The Condo Board said people were complaining." His answer immediately erases any guilt I should have had.

Tiffany asks the new guy, "Are you wearing the same uniform he wore?" Why she would want to know this is anyone's guess.

"Probably."

Tiffany steps back to eye the guy as if she were a critic at a fashion show. "A little big in the shoulders, isn't it?"

"Lady, I would've worn a monkey suit if they would have asked me to. I'm just glad to be working," he says in abrupt honesty.

"The least they could have done was have it dry-cleaned." She points to the blotches on his sleeve. "Wearing your own stains is disgusting enough, but wearing someone else's is totally gross."

"We're here on police business," I tell the doorman. "Detectives Wayt and Noonan are expecting us in 4112."

The doorman graciously opens the door. We enter and head directly for the elevator bank. "Well, that explains a lot," Tiffany says once the doorman is out of audio range.

"About what?"

"Why doormen look so geeky. They have to wear *One Size Fits All* uniforms."

"Tiffany, your powers of deduction never cease to amaze me."

As we enter Bruno's condo, "Wait" Jack Wayt is on the couch and Neula "No-No" Noonan is in the chair facing him. I wait to hear "Wait" from Wayt, but there's only a tense silence hanging in the air, as thick as an odor from a dead body in the other room.

"Is something the matter?" I ask.

"Yeah," Jack says. "Emotional Stress-Related Anxiety Disorder."

"No-No" snaps back, "You get that by coming into contact with someone infected with Bad Boyfriend Bacteria."

"Uh-oh," Tiffany says to me, "I'm sensing a case of really bad mojo here."

Jack glares at "No-No". She scrunches up her nose and glares back at him. This is a fun party to be at.

"Why don't you both take a deep breath, think positive thoughts, face the other person, and say the first nice thing that comes into your mind," Tiffany, in her new role as a relationship expert, suggests.

"I'll go first," "Wait" Jack Wayt says. "Neula, you have very attractive small feet for someone your size."

"No-No" doesn't wait for Tiffany to tell her it's her turn. "Well, if you connect all your liver spots with a pen, you'd have a beautiful work of body art."

"Before I forget, Neula, let me congratulate you on your winning the Food Taster of the Year award."

"And kudos to you Jack, for being the Hypochondriac of the Millennium."

"Can we call a truce here?" I jump in to suggest.

"No, Mr. Sherlock," Tiffany tells me. "We're making progress. They're talking." Tiffany sits on the coffee table between the combatants. "Now, next we're going to tell the other person the emotion that first drew the two of you together."

"A free dinner," "No-No" says.

"I heard she was easy," Jack says.

"From who?" "No-No" asks.

"Everybody," Jack says shooting eye darts at "No-No." She glares back at him like the noonday sun. If this goes on any longer, the two of them are going to go at it like a couple of starving Sumo wrestlers in a Winner Takes All the Lunch competition.

"Tiffany, I don't think this is working very well."

"Sure it is," Tiffany assures me. "We just have to get them over their anger hump."

A very bad choice of terms.

"Next, I want each of you to tell the other person exactly what you're feeling about them at this exact moment."

"I feel a week's worth of indigestion ready to explode," Jack pauses. "Watch out, Neula. Fire in the hole!"

"You let loose, Jack, and I'll call Homeland Security and have you arrested for launching a sarin gas attack."

"I have some news concerning the case," I drop into the conversation. "It might be fun to discuss it."

There's a pause from the combatants. Thank God.

"Wait," Jack says. "So do I."

"Me too," "No-No" takes the lead. "Bruno died from two blows to his skull from the fireplace poker. By the angle of the attack, it was done by a right handed, six-footer who weighed at least 200 pounds."

"I checked every gym in Chicago and not one bulked-up body builder identified Bruno from his picture," Jack says.

"It happened in the late afternoon. There was no struggle. Bruno never saw it coming," "No-No" counters.

"The blood found in the building where you got shot at Sherlock was matched to a gangbanger who died that night at the Cook County ER."

"And Tiffany here wasn't roofied, she was slipped a mixture of HGH, testosterone, and adrenaline," I add to break up the tit-for-tat between the detectives.

"What?" Tiffany exclaims.

"Evidently the upper had a downer effect on your system, Tiffany."

"Oh my God! This doesn't mean I'm going to start growing hair in weird places and want to join a roller derby league, does it?" she asks.

"Remember, the doc pumped most of it out of your system."

Tiffany lets out a "Whew," then says, "I'm telling you, that stomach pump machine is going to be the next electric light bulb."

"Nobody in the apartments next door, or on this floor, heard anything that day," "No-No" says, getting back to the demise of poor Bruno.

"And there isn't a print in this place that's worth a damn," Jack sums up.

"You think Bruno was dealing steroids from the bar?" "No-No" asks me.

"Jack thinks so, I'm not so sure," I answer.

"Who cares what Jack thinks," "No-No" tosses in.

"Zanadu is crawling with drug dealers," Jack makes his point.

"If the killer was in business with Bruno, he would've taken the drugs with him after he whacked him," "No-No" says.

"I know. That part doesn't make any sense," I answer.

"Maybe they were fighting about taking drugs and not selling drugs?" Jack throws out.

"Bruno was a seller, not a user." "No-No" adds. "There were no traces of narcotics in his system from the autopsy."

"Then why would he have a bunch of little party favors stashed away in those tin boxes?" I question back.

"He was a bartender," Jack says. "To him, it could've been like having a well-stocked liquor cabinet for visiting guests."

"Or the killer was a user and Bruno was cutting him off?" "No-No" twists it around.

Tiffany raises her hand high, as if she's had a brainstorm. "I've got it," she says excitedly. "It's a crime of passion. Don't you see? They're gay."

"Who's gay?"

"Bruno and his killer."

"What?" Jack says.

"It's like this. Bruno's gay lover can't get the ape off his back. They have a spat. Bruno smoothes things over and thinks everything is hunky-dory. But on their way to the bedroom for some smokin' hot make-up sex, roid rage kicks in and then wham, Bruno takes a couple of whacks to his skull."

I'm not buying any of this so I tell the group, "I'm not buying any of this."

"Oops, I just remembered something," Tiffany blurts out. "I'm totally wrong."

"How's that?"

"Bruno wasn't gay!"

"How do you know that?" "No-No" questions her.

"I've got gaydar. If Bruno was gay, I would've known it."

"You're sure about that?"

"Absolutely! Nobody's got gaydar like I've got gaydar," Tiffany says as if this is a trait people would be proud of having. "I can spot a gay guy at sixty paces, even if he's wearing a Larry, the Cable Guy T-shirt."

"You still believe Bruno's death, Tiffany's Mickey, and the Zanadu are all connected?" Jack asks me.

"I did," I tell him, "now I'm not so sure."

"I'm going to stay on the dealer angle," Jack says.

"I'll go back over Bruno's rap sheet," "No-No" says. "Maybe there's something in it I missed. He was a low-level hood before he started mixing spirits."

"I'll be at the Zanadu," I say. "Suspects never fall far from the crime tree."

Tiffany gets up off the coffee table. "I gotta go. I have an appointment with my new Life Coach twenty minutes ago."

"Let's go," I tell her. "I'd hate for you to be later than your usual late."

As Tiffany and I reach the front door, Jack asks, "By the way, was the deadbolt locked when you broke in and found the body, Sherlock?"

I hesitate before I answer. "I don't remember."

"What do you mean 'you don't remember'?" "No-No" asks.

Neula already holds a B and E charge against me on her *You owe me Sherlock* list. I certainly don't want to add my illegal lock picking set to her collection. "I thought you had a memory like a Polaroid," she says.

"Not anymore," I tell her, which is actually the truth since Polaroid went out of business.

"Let's just work on the angle that Sherlock found some way to get around a locked deadbolt," Jack says. He knows I picked the lock, because he would have done exactly the same thing.

"Bruno couldn't have locked the door after he was dead," I conclude.

"His keys were on the kitchen counter," "No-No" adds.

"Buildings have rules about having personal deadbolts." Jack takes another step in this process.

"So," "No-No" says, "all we gotta do is find an extra set of keys and we have our killer."

"Maybe, maybe not," Jack says.

"Maybe Bruno had a significant other, who he gave a set of keys, because he trusted and cherished their relationship," Tiffany says to the detective pair. "Just like you two used to have."

Every high-rise condo building employs a maintenance engineer. He's the guy responsible for keeping the heat, the air conditioning, and the electricity on, the water running, the facility neat, and the tenants happy. In Bruno's building, that guy is named Clyde. I cleverly discovered this fact by reading *Clyde* on the patch above the pocket on the front of his blue uniform overalls.

"You wouldn't happen to know how I could get a hold of Guido, would you?" I ask him.

The older gentleman removes an ancient Rolodex from the bottom drawer of a well-battered and bruised desk. He spins it slowly being careful not to allow the address cards to shoot out like lottery tickets from the machine on the 7-11 counter. He finally finds the right card, and tells me. "I got a cell phone number."

"By the way," I continue, "you didn't notice anybody odd coming and going in the building the day Bruno got bonked, did you?"

"People come and go all day around here," he says. "But I can't remember anybody any weirder than the usual weirdos."

"What's the rule on personal deadbolts?"

"We don't like 'em, but as long as the building has a duplicate key, we look the other way."

"You have a duplicate key for 4112?"

He gets up from his cluttered desk, selects a key from the forty-odd ones that he has on his chain, and goes to a four-foot by four-foot metal box bolted to the wall. He unlocks and opens the box, revealing sixty rows of hooks, the majority of which have keys hanging on them. "Yeah, I got it right here." He holds the key out for me to see.

"Thank you." "No-No" is not going to want to hear about this.

Outside, after Tiffany retrieves her car keys from the doorman and he removes the phony ticket off her windshield, he tells her, "Drop by anytime."

Before we climb into the Lexus, I ask Tiffany how she got into the condo building the day she smuggled me in.

"All you have to do is wait for the doorman to leave his little desk for a minute or two, then you go in the outer door, duck into the little mail room each building has, take out your set of keys, pretend you're getting your mail, and hang out. Then you wait for another tenant to get his mail and go in with him, or you stand by the inner door with your keys out and someone coming in from the garage, who you smile and wave to, opens the door for you."

"But what happens if the doorman comes back and sees you standing by the inner door or in the mail room?" I ask.

"I don't know," she says, "that's never happened."

I punch the number that Clyde gave me into my cell phone.

"Hello."

"Is this Guido?"

"Yeah, who's this?" The voice sounds groggy. Maybe he's hungover. Maybe he's depressed. Maybe he's both.

"It's Richard Sherlock."

"You're the son of a bitch who helped me lose my job," he says.

"If that was the case, I apologize, but Guido—"

"What, asshole?"

"Do you remember anyone going in to see Bruno that afternoon?"

"I already told the cops everything, ask them."

"Do you remember if you got buzzed that afternoon to let someone in the rear door and, when you got there, no one was waiting to get in?"

"How stupid do you think I am, Sherlock?"

I don't answer, instead I tell him sincerely. "Guido, if you need a reference for a new job, I'd be more than happy to—"

"Go to hell."

Click. Buzz.

I try to help someone out and this is the thanks I get.

Tiffany fires up the Lexus and informs me, "I have to go, Mr. Sherlock. Now I'm really late being late for my appointment."

"I have to do some surveillance work later. Do you have plans for this evening?"

"Nobody makes plans for a Monday. Mondays are for revitalizing your skin and your system so you'll look your best by the weekend."

How can I be so stupid?

Tiffany drops me off in front of the *Sun-Times* building. I bid her farewell and wish her a memorable hour with her new Life Coach. I go inside, take the elevator to the bottom floor, and say hello to my old buddy, Theobald.

"Sherlock, what brings you down here, besides the elevator?"

Theobald is the master embalmer of the Chicago *Sun-Times'* Morgue. He's been preserving the written word of this newspaper since Mrs. O'Leary's cow kicked over that lantern way back in the day. He looks about two hundred years old and it's been at least that long since he's seen the sun. His skin is whiter than a bleached hospital sheet.

"D'Wayne DeWitt, ever heard of him?" I ask him.

"Haven't seen that name since George Bush."

"Which one?"

"Can't remember."

"It doesn't matter. Can you check the files?"

"Sure. You want George H.W. or George W.?"

"Neither. I'm looking for D'Wayne DeWitt." I write the name down on a piece of scrap paper so I won't have to constantly spell it for him.

We start with the computerized files and work our way back in time. D'Wayne was born in 1970 at Cook County Hospital, 7 lb. 3 oz. Mother, Darlene DeWitt. Father not listed. There were no records for time served until he was nineteen, when he did a nine-month stretch in County for possession, his third offense. He was called as a witness in a drug trial when he was twenty-six, but info on this is pretty sketchy. Next time he pops up is in Joliet, where he gets a five-year sentence in 1999 for dealing. Darlene must have taught D'Wayne how to behave because he gets out in two. Then nothing. D'Wayne either avoids capture, gets smarter, or goes legit; the last is a long shot in my book.

We then search every article on the Zanadu Club. There is a ton of them. I have to wade through every event, party, gala, and bash held at the venue—boring to say the least. There's little on the construction, ownership, management, or corporate affiliations of the business. A good PR firm knows how to avoid publicity as well as get publicity. My eyes are going blurry. I've had enough for one day. I thank Theobald, and tell him they now have sun block up to 100 SPF.

He tells me, "Don't need sun block, Sherlock. I tan naturally."

I need time to ponder all possibilities. I go home. On the 'L' I call "Wait" Jack Wayt and ask him to find D'Wayne DeWitt's home address. It takes him less than ten minutes to call me back. Besides the address, he warns me, "Stay out of the ghetto tonight, something big is going down."

CHAPTER 15

While Tiffany forks out at least another three hundred dollars for her new life coach, I decide to go it alone. I take one last look at all that is missing on *The Original Carlo*, grab my keys, and head for my car, which is down the block. It fires up on the third try. Lucky me.

I take the short drive towards Lake Michigan, get on the Drive going south and get off at Belmont. I park in the park, across the street from a condo building facing Belmont Harbor. From here I have a clear view of everyone's comings and goings. I don't have to wait long to find out if "Wait" Jack Wayt was right about the address. A limo pulls up at four. D'Wayne DeWitt walks out the front door, climbs inside, and off he goes. I strain my eyes to see the driver, but no luck. The windows are tinted darker than a moonless night.

Tailing someone is never easy, but I take chase anyway. Putt-putting along in my Toyota, I stay a few car lengths back until the limo heads into the Loop. I lose them on Randolph Street, but I figure out where they are headed. A few minutes later I catch up with them at the Northern Trust Bank on Wacker Drive. It's the same branch Tiffany, the Non-Brinks Brink's truck, and I visited the other evening. Mr. DeWitt goes inside. The limo pulls out. I park in the cabstand, leave the car running, and wait. Cabs honk. I get out of my car, lift up the Toyota's hood, and mouth a few swear words. The honks cease.

Fifteen minutes later, Mr. DeWitt emerges. This was no quick ATM visit. The limo comes around the corner, stops, and picks up its passenger. I rush to close the hood and follow. Next stop is a non-descript building off 15th street on the near South Side. Mr. DeWitt's visit is less than ten minutes. The third stop is a similar building eight or ten minutes away, close to the Robert Taylor Homes public housing project. He stays only five minutes. I can't blame him. You can easily get mugged, robbed, or shot in this neighborhood. If the locals are looking for action, I can only hope they have the good sense to target the guy in the limo and not the one in the crummy Toyota. The final stop is at Rory's Rib Tips. The limo pulls up to the drive-thru window, and cold, hard cash is exchanged for what looks like the *DeLuxe Bucket of Bones, with greens, mashed potatoes, and cornbread*. I make a note to tell Mr. DeWitt that it's not a person attempting to kill him, but cholesterol.

The last leg of the journey takes us to the Zanadu Club where Mr.

DeWitt is deposited at the employee entrance. The limo exits the scene. I go off to find a free place to park, which happens to be about six blocks away.

It's Monday night. The Zanadu is open, but has all the appearances of being closed. There's no Arson, Sterno, velvet rope, or loser line. Monday would be perfect for a Seniors Only Night. They could play Big Band tunes, serve easily chewable food, and play bingo in the bar area. I'll suggest this to Gibby Fearn.

I enter. The dance floor is empty, no people and no music. In the bar area, there are about nine people sipping beers or drinks, watching a baseball playoff game on three HDTV screens; neither the Cubs nor the White Sox are involved. No surprise there. The bartender who replaced Bruno is on duty, paying his dues for being the last one hired. "Excuse me," I say to the new man on the job. "Is Mr. DeWitt in?"

"Who?" the bartender replies. Evidently he's a lot newer to the job than I thought.

I walk down the rear hallway to the *No Admittance* door and knock, wait for the camera to click on, and the door to open. Neither happens. At the stairway, the door is locked. I walk back out past the bar area to the edge of the dance floor where I can look up to see if the lights are on in Mr. DeWitt's penthouse office. The curtains are closed. I can't see a thing.

I need to see my client and ask him a few questions, most notably what was he doing visiting suspected retail drug outlets? But the first order of business is getting through that door and up the stairs to get that all important employee/client face-to-face time. I am so close, yet so far away. I thoughtfully contemplate the situation and realize that there're only four choices opened to me. I could scream. I could pound on the stairway door. I could pick the lock, walk up the stairs, and drop on in. Or I could go to the bar, buy a couple bags of Beer Nuts, and toss a handful against his windows like a groom wanting to elope. It is always good to have choices in life, even if all them are pretty lousy. Screaming is obnoxious, pounding is childish, picking locks is illegal, and tossing Beer Nuts is just plain stupid; plus the Zanadu doesn't sell Beer Nuts. I eliminate them all and contemplate some new and better ideas, but not for long.

BOOM!

The silence of a Monday night nightclub is shattered by an

explosion from D'Wayne DeWitt's penthouse office. Two panels of glass windows are blown out like an Iraqi IED exploded. The force of the blast knocks me back into a wall and down on the floor. I grab a table and use it to cover up my face and upper torso as shards of glass hit all around me harder than metal confetti. Smoke billows out of the two open windows as if multiple tear gas canisters were tossed inside. There must have been screams from the bar area, but I hear nothing. My hearing goes into temporary hiatus as my eardrums try to recover from the initial blast.

I look up to see the DJ's platform swaying like a circus trapeze. Next, I focus on the bar area where six of the patrons have hit the deck and the other three remain glued to their stools watching the TVs. It must be a real good game. I get to my feet, find a shaky balance, and run to the new bartender who is busy shutting off beer taps that evidently were opened by the force of the blast. Two of the patrons reach over with their mugs and help themselves.

"You got a key to the stairway door?" I scream at the barkeep, but have no idea how loud since I'm temporarily deaf.

He says something, but I can't read lips. I run to the hallway and, as I am headed to the door, I'm met by Gibby's comic book reading Behemoth. "What happened?"

"Dun't know," he mouths then pulls out a set of keys and unlocks the door.

The two of us run up the stairs, me leading the way. The door to Mr. DeWitt's office is wide open with heavy black smoke as thick as a refinery fire pouring out. I take a deep breath, pull my handkerchief out of my pocket and push it against my nose and mouth, squint my eyes, and charge inside. Three steps in, I ram my shin into either the coffee table or some other low-lying piece of furniture. Ouch. Now, I'm limping. "Mr. DeWitt, D'Wayne, where are you?" I attempt to scream through the cloth which is really stupid since, if I'm temporarily deaf, wouldn't he be too? And if he did answer my call, I couldn't hear him anyway.

I get down on my hands and knees to grab any remaining good air in the room and to search for survivors. I head for what I hope is the back of the room where Mr. DeWitt had his desk, but my journey is interrupted by a swift kick to my rear, and a body falling over me like a giant domino. The Behemoth splays out onto the space in front of me and rolls around like an out of control Pilate's ball. I take a detour around him and push my way through the debris. Luckily, there are no flames. The smoke is beginning to dissipate. I see some motion to the right of me, crawl toward the movement, and find a shoe with a foot inside. I straighten up slightly and hit my head on the top of the desk. Ouch. I feel upward to the leg attached, and continue until I have the entire body in my grasp. It's D'Wayne DeWitt. He's covered in soot. His brown suit is now charcoal.

I hear sirens in the distance, which is a double positive for me. One, I know the Fire Department is on its way and two, I can hear again. I cannot immediately tell if D'Wayne is breathing or not. I pinch his nostrils shut with my thumb and forefinger. I'm just about to lock lips with his and blow my breath into his lungs when he starts to cough. This is a relief because that kind of activity during the cold and flu season is just asking for trouble.

The Behemoth has managed to work his way beside me. "You get his feet." I tell the Behemoth. A leader always emerges during a time of crisis.

"Huh?"

"You got a better idea?" I ask.

"Dun't know."

We manage to pull Mr. DeWitt out from under his desk. With the Behemoth at the bottom and myself at the top, we pull and push the stretched out D'Wayne DeWitt through the smoke and debris and back through the door to his office. Once we're on the stairway level, I kick the door shut. I order the Behemoth to keep going down. A half flight of stairs later the smoke has dissipated. We rest the unconscious DeWitt against the railing. He's breathing, but not real well.

"Didn't you ever take CPR training?" I ask, but don't wait for his standard "Dun't know" response. I position myself behind D'Wayne and begin a semi-Heimlich maneuver. I wrap my arms around his waist and push up repeatedly on his diaphragm. He's breathing fairly well by the time the paramedics come and slap an oxygen mask over his face.

They offer me a mask and I accept believing that a few shots of pure oxygen can't be a bad idea. The Behemoth declines, "Dun't like notin' on my nose."

To each his own.

Four or five of Chicago's finest rush by us, run up the stairs and into the smoke-filled office. They let loose with a spray of fire retardant that would put an overly aggressive crop duster to shame. The walls, the furniture, the artwork, and all the accompanying design touches are covered with thick, white foam. The original motif of the room is history replaced with a winter wonderland of white, gooey, cotton candy fluff. A glittering, wintry, sci-fi, Currier & Ives take on the traditional work space.

"D'Wayne can you hear me?" I ask, figuring a loss of hearing would be a common occurrence in these circumstances.

He coughs.

A paramedic removes D'Wayne's oxygen mask, lifts a bottle of water to his lips, and pours. D'Wayne spits it out onto the Behemoth's bad suit.

"Dat wasn't gud."

D'Wayne coughs some more, comes to, and grabs the bottle from the paramedic. He takes a quick swig and spits that out too. This time the Behemoth dodges the stream.

"Fool me once …," I compliment him.

The paramedic takes a cloth, wets it, and wipes D'Wayne's face the same way he'd bathe an infant.

"What'd I tell you, Sherlock?" These are the first words out of the victim's mouth; not ones I would have expected, or personally have used in this situation.

I hurry to think of what he told me and the first item that crosses my mind is the hourly amount he's paying me: twice my regular rate, and three times what Mr. Jamison Wentworth Richmond III divvies out.

"I told you someone was trying to kill me," he says.

"That seems to be pretty much a given at this point."

"Where's Fearn?" Mr. DeWitt asks the Behemoth.

"Dun't know." Standard answer.

"You think Gibby Fearn did this?" I ask.

"Dun't know."

I point my head at Mr. DeWitt. "I'm asking him, not you."

"Still dun't know."

I bet the Behemoth is a real riot when he plays charades.

The paramedic is working on Mr. DeWitt, getting more fluids into him, sitting him up straighter, and placing a wet compress against his forehead.

"Why would Gibby want to kill you?"

"Isn't that what I hired you to find out?"

The chances of using Mr. D'Wayne DeWitt as a reference for future employment are becoming bleaker by the moment.

"Well, yeah, but …," I hesitate for a moment. "What motive would he have, besides taking another step up the corporate ladder?"

"Ask him."

A seat stretcher arrives, the kind that allows the victim to be transported in a seated position down stairs, or across difficult terrain. Mr. DeWitt is carried away like a king on a throne by two firemen-porters. I turn to the Behemoth. "Why would Gibby want to kill Mr. DeWitt?" I question incredulously.

"Dun't know."

Why do I bother?

I climb up the half flight of steps to return to the scene of the crime and wade around in the sticky goo on the floor. Now with the smoke mostly gone, I see where I found Mr. DeWitt on the floor, in the back of the room, behind where his desk used to sit. I reach down and retrieve a smart phone lying in the corner. Lucky for me the inspecting fireman's back is turned away from me. The phone is hot to the touch. I wrap my handkerchief around it and push some of its buttons hoping to get the screen to come alive, but no luck. It's either totally ruined or merely no longer brainy. I slip it in my pocket for future reference. I walk back over to the blasted out windows where another fireman stands holding a cylindrical metal object in his hand.

"Souvenir?" I ask.

"Fourth of July leftover," he tells me.

"Amateur?"

"Looks like it."

"Why didn't the whole place go up in flames?" I ask.

"Fireworks are not incendiary devices as a rule," the fireman says showing me the metal tube, which is closed at one end.

"This one certainly had a smoking addiction," I add.

"Yeah, it sure did."

I leave the fireman to finish his job. I call "Wait" Jack Wayt and tell him the story. He's hardly thrilled and says he'll be over within a half hour. I call Neula "No-No" Noonan and repeat what I told Jack, but before she responds to my information she asks, "Is Jack coming over?"

Back downstairs I knock on the *No Admittance* door and, this time, it buzzes open. Inside, I find the Behemoth on the phone. He hangs up almost immediately.

"That Gibby?"

I'm sure he wants to say "Dun't know," but he looks up and says nothing. He rises from his chair.

"The cops are coming," I tell him. "You better wait at the bar."

"Dun't drink."

"Don't start."

The Behemoth leaves the room.

Alone at last. The first thing I do is go to the two doors on the opposite side of the room. One is a closet. The other is the size of a closet, but there are no shelves or any racks to hang coats. However, there is the beginning, or the end, of the cylindrical tube that runs to the accounting room in the basement. I open the slide at end of the cylinder and find it empty, but I can feel the suction of air pressure. I close the door and examine the contents of the smaller desk where the Behemoth sat. I find eight *Fantastic Four*, three *Superman*, and two *Batman* comic books. There's also an empty shoulder holster large enough to carry a very damaging handgun, a box of bullets, a stapler, two pens, and an unopened packet of mints. I take the mints as evidence and close the drawer. I'm about to examine Gibby Fearn's desk, but there's something I have to take care of first. I insert one of my business cards against the locking catch before heading down the hall to the men's room. When nature calls, I must answer.

I stand at the urinal, doing my business, looking up at the Tribune's sports pages inside a glass case attached to the wall. There are articles on the Bulls and the Bears. The Cubs are considering a blockbuster trade. A lot of good that'll do. In the lower corner of the last sports page, there's a picture of a guy I've seen somewhere before. This is where it's great to have a photographic memory. He's not a sports figure any Chicago fan would recognize, but I do. The accompanying short article reports that Oscar Odie, an ex-athlete, now a personal trainer, has been busted for dealing steroids in local locker rooms. He's the gym rat I saw in Monroe Chevelier's office. It's always nice to see a familiar face in the paper.

"Wait."

I stop the moment I step out of the men's room.

"Sherlock, you ever use a stool softener?"

"No, Jack."

"Damn," Jack says and snaps his fingers. "All right, what happened?" he asks as we walk down the hallway to the stairway.

I give Jack the lowdown. He listens without comment. "Mr. DeWitt thinks it might be Gibby Fearn, the manager of the Zanadu," I end with.

"Why?"

"He told me to ask him."

"And Fearn's going to say, 'Hey, of course I tried to blow him up'?" Jack says.

"I didn't say that was what I was going to do," I say in full retreat mode. "That's just what he told me to do."

"Well, that's dumb." Jack has a way with words.

The two of us are outside Mr. DeWitt's office when "No-No" arrives. Before saying "Hello," she hands Jack a small bottle of Pepto Bismol. "I know how you get if your food doesn't digest properly," she says with a slight smile.

"Thanks." Jack opens the bottle and takes a healthy pink swig.

I wait for Jack to ask "No-No" the same softener question he did to me, but Jack must consider certain ailments *guys only* stuff.

"The fireman said it was the work of amateurs," I tell my cohorts.

"No, no, I don't think so," "No-No" comments.

"Why not?"

"Too much smoke." "No-No" has a good point.

"I followed Mr. DeWitt this afternoon," I inform them. "He did a tour of his own special kind of drug stores before stopping for a bucket of ribs."

"Where?"

The question comes from "No-No". I answer, "Rory's Rib Tips."

"The drug stops, Sherlock, not the take-out place," Jack snaps back.

"One off 15th Street and one near the Robert Taylor Homes," I qualify my information. "I got the addresses in the car."

"Rory's has great cornbread," "No-No" can't help but add.

I continue, "Mr. DeWitt also stopped off at the Northern Trust over on Wacker. He's probably checking on the money being skimmed off the top of the Zanadu coffers."

"You sure about that, Sherlock?"

"A truck pulls up every night and carts off the cash," I tell them.

"I've seen it."

"That means we gotta call in the IRS," "No-No" says.

"This case is growing faster than the Asian Flu," Jack says. "I don't need this, Sherlock."

"Well, I also suspect a little private cash is being lifted too," I add. "A little guy with a ponytail takes a briefcase full of it out every night."

"As if I don't have enough wrinkles," Jack laments. "You gotta add another one."

"I think your lines make you look distinguished," "No-No" says. Her new tactic of recapturing her lost love is now fully evident. Best of luck, "No-No."

We plod around in the goo and muck long enough to ruin a good pair of shoes. We find nothing of interest. "Let's go down to the manager's office," I suggest.

I get no argument.

"Why's the door propped open?" is Jack's question before we enter Gibby Fearn's office.

"Beats me," I comment as I remove my business card from the lock. "One of you should make a note of that."

"No, no. I don't think so."

Inside, Jack goes straight for the two doors and opens the one on the left. "What's in here?"

"Closet."

He opens the one on the right. "What's in here?"

"A pneumatic tube."

"It looks pretty old to me," Jack says.

"Not *new* as in a new car," "No-No" tells Jack. "It's pronounced the same way, but it's spelled differently. It means something operated by air or gas under pressure."

"Kinda like my stomach."

"It's how they moved the money from this floor to an office in the basement where they fudged two sets of books," I explain.

I walk over to Gibby's desk. "No-No" lumbers over to the Behemoth's desk. Jack sits down and takes another swig of Pepto Bismol. "Some days I can almost count the drip, drip, drip of my stomach acids," he says.

"Oh, honey," "No-No" says. "I'm so sorry you're feeling poorly."

Jack burps up a little pink, but re-swallows it immediately.

Gibby Fearn is a very organized manager. His files are perfectly lined up and alphabetized with a handwritten tab attached to each one. The papers inside them are in perfect order, organized by date with the newest on the top. The largest files are labeled: *Personnel*, *Music*, *Repair*, *OSHA*, *Health Insurance*, *Payroll*, and *Maintenance*.

"Where's the computers?" Jack asks.

"If you have a computer, you have records," "No-No" answers. "If you have records, you have evidence."

"And if you have evidence, you got problems," Jack sums up.

"I'm telling you, they're lifting a slew of money out of this place," I say. It's no wonder why Mr. D'Wayne DeWitt hasn't quibbled about my hourly rate.

I open the middle drawer in Gibby's desk, take one look, and ask. "Either of you got a pair of latex gloves handy?"

"No-No" dons her gloves as I pull the drawer all the way out. Jack joins us to see the array of evidence: a coil of thin wire, a blasting cap, and a small clock, all resting on a thin layer of black powder.

"This guy is either the dumbest criminal on the face of the earth or this is the worst job of implicating someone since Judas tried to blame everything on Mary Magdalene."

Jack evidently never went to Sunday school. Years from now my daughters could be making the same types of comments. Heaven forbid.

"No, no. I don't think so. No criminal is this stupid," "No-No" says.

"I don't know," I say, "I've known some pretty stupid crooks."

"What are you doing?" The voice comes from the other side of the room.

The three of us look up to see Gibby Fearn coming through the door.

"This your office?" "No-No" asks.

"Yes."

"This your desk?"

"Yes."

"This your stuff?"

Gibby joins us at his desk to see the contents of the drawer. "No," he answers the question.

"Sure?"

"Positive."

"You're under arrest for attempted murder," "No-No" tells him.

"What?"

Jack fumbles around searching for his handcuffs. He turns to the two of us. "I hope one of you thought to bring along a set of bracelets."

"Don't worry, honey," "No-No" says giving him a sexy little smile as she pulls out a pair from behind her, "I always carry a pair."

CHAPTER 16

"I've taken on my first attractively-challenged relationship charity case, Mr. Sherlock."

"Good for you, Tiffany."

"You want to know who it is?"

"Neula "No-No" Noonan."

"How'd you know that?"

"I'm a detective, remember?"

"Wow, you're awesome.

We arrive at the Cook County Jail, the biggest jail in the United States. If that doesn't say something about Chicago, I don't know what does.

"They have valet service?" Tiffany asks.

"No," I answer. "This is the kind of place you want to lock your car and take your keys with you."

"I hate that."

There is really no dress code for visitors at the Cook County Jail, but if there were, Tiffany's corduroy mini-skirt, hooker-hose, high heels, and form-fitting, black turtleneck sweater would be listed as *Riot Worthy*.

The first portal we pass through is similar to the security one at O'Hare. You place all your personals in a plastic container: shoes, belt, phone, money, etc. then, proceed to the scanner where you lift up both arms and the x-rays sweep across your body to determine if you're concealing anything. One bored cop watches me, yawns, and waves me through, but the entire contingent of six officers come over to make sure Tiffany isn't hiding anything underneath a sweater already so tight you could see the perforated edges of a postage stamp underneath. The officers argue about whether rank outweighs tenure in order to determine who is the most qualified to frisk Tiffany for hidden contraband. Before my assistant is asked to, "Put your hands on the counter and spread 'em wide," I intervene.

"Let's not overdo our duties gentlemen, especially on someone with a daddy who has some very good friends in some very high places."

One of the cops asks, "Who?"

I whisper to him.

"You're good to go, Miss," he says, as he waves Tiffany through. "And please enjoy your visit to the Cook County Jail."

As we head for the next security checkpoint, Tiffany asks, "Does that scanner pick up tan lines, Mr. Sherlock?"

"On you, it probably does."

"Hey, Sherlock," Sergeant Dirk McKee remembers me from my days on the force. "Your hand ever heal up after you punched that idiot captain of yours in the nose?" he asks as we pass through the checkpoint. "You know I got that on disc and when I need an attitude pick-me-up I watch it over and over."

"So happy you enjoy it, Dirk," I tell my old buddy with a smirk on my face.

Wouldn't you know it, the one time I get mad, not only do I punch my supervisor, but I do it on local television, which makes its way to the Internet, which becomes a *Most Watched* on You Tube. Lucky me.

"You really cracked that jerk a good one, Sherlock," Dirk says with an air of respect. "You shudda punched the DA too."

"Next time."

"Who you wanta see?" Dirk asks.

"Gibby Fearn."

"Oh, yeah, the new guy," Dirk says. "Wait in there, I'll bring him in."

Tiffany and I enter a square box room. It's decorated with a table, three chairs, and nothing else. Tiffany sits down and immediately notices her chair is bolted to the floor. "This room could use a lot of *feng shui*," she remarks.

I sit.

"You know, Mr. Sherlock," Tiffany says, "you always seem to know so many people no matter where we go. I can't imagine a better person to visit disgusting places with than you."

"Coming from you, Tiffany, that means so much."

Dirk leads a shackled Gibby into the room and sits him in the chair across from us. "You want me to keep the bracelets on him?" Dirk asks.

"Not necessary," I answer. "This one's harmless."

Dirk unshackles Gibby and stands in the back of the room, his Taser at the ready.

"Is this bullshit or what?" is Gibby's first question.

"Agreed, but it might be good bullshit, if there is such a thing," I say.

Gibby stares at me with very angry eyes.

"Hi, Mr. Fearn. Remember me? Tiffany Richmond?"

Gibby is the only male in the entire jail who will see Tiffany today and not salivate; well, at least the only straight male. He doesn't answer my protégé's question. "What are you doin' here?" he asks.

"We came to chat."

"Why would I talk to you?" He asks, as is his custom. "The only person I'm talking to is my lawyer."

"Don't."

"You got a better way of getting me out of here?"

"Not now."

"What else do I got, except to blow the lid off the Zanadu scam?"

"That's a bad choice of words, Gibby."

"Who else knows what I know?"

"I don't know," I say emphatically. "But if I were you, I'd seriously consider the consequences of explaining how the laundry got dirty."

"What, and rot away in this hellhole twenty-four-seven?"

"Gibby, it would be kind of dumb of you to spill the beans, and end up dead as a result."

"Right," Tiffany adds, "that would be totally dumb."

"Take my advice, Gibby, don't say a word to anyone, in here, out there, to a lawyer, to a cop, to anybody. Just sit tight and wait."

Gibby peers up at the two of us. "I was only doing my job."

"And that could be the worst thing you could say." I'm as sincere as I can be. "Trust me, Gibby. Wait, please wait."

Gibby doesn't respond.

"Dirk," I say to my old buddy, "we're done here."

Gibby is re-shackled and led out of the room. He doesn't even say "goodbye." You would think a guy in the hospitality industry would be a little more polite.

Tiffany turns to me and asks, "You think he's going to keep his mouth shut, Mr. Sherlock?"

"I doubt it."

"Why?"

"No one ever listens to me. Why should he?"

"Coming in for an upgrade, Sherlock?" Les asks as soon as he sees the two of us enter his store.

171

The Meaner Wiener board behind him lists a number of new phones that weren't listed before. "Got some real beauties in this morning."

I pull out the cooked phone I found in the remains of Mr. DeWitt's office and hand it to Les.

"I don't do trade-ins," Les tells me.

"Can you get it to work?"

Les fondles the phone. "What did you do to it? Drop it in a barbecue pit?"

"Pretty close."

As Les fiddles with the phone, Tiffany asks, "What's the best plan you have?"

"Get rich and move to Costa Rica," Les says without hesitation.

"I meant monthly cell phone plan?"

"I have a one-time only, flat rate, pay me, go away, and talk and text to your heart's content plan."

"How much does it cost?"

"How much you got?"

"I don't know," Tiffany says. "I wouldn't know where to start counting my money."

"Do you like older men?"

"Older or as old as you?" Tiffany asks.

I better get the conversation back on track. "Les, can you get the phone to work?"

Les quits finagling with it. "It's roasted and toasted, dead as the Betamax, never to speak again," he tells me, holding up the phone. "But for less than a buck and a half, I can replace it with a Samsung 4G with all the bells and whistles. I'll even throw in an app for locating the North Star so you can find your way home no matter where you are on the face of the earth."

"All I need to know is the last call made on it," I say.

"Why didn't you just ask me," Tiffany takes the phone in hand, flips off the back panel, removes the SIM Card, and asks Les, "You got a phone that works?"

"Hopefully." He hands her the fryer basket.

Tiffany picks out a cell phone, opens its back, exchanges the SIM card, turns the phone on, waits, punches a few keys, and points the screen towards me. "It's not a number, Tiffany says. "It's a password."

"I hate those things," Les says.

The screen shows a 2, 4, @, S, and a W. "It's not a password," I tell them.

"How would you know, Mr. Sherlock?" Tiffany asks. "You're so tech-challenged, you're like behind Edison before he invented the telephone."

"It's a remote code."

"So, the last time he used it, he was ordering up a movie?" Tiffany asks.

"You know," Les tells Tiffany. "If you're interested in a cheap Netflix package, I can do that."

"No thanks," Tiffany says. "I'm already well bundled."

"You certainly are," he says.

I place Mr. D'Wayne DeWitt's SIM card in my wallet for safekeeping. "So long, Les."

"Call me if you'd like to chat," Les says to Tiffany.

"By the way, do you need any relationship advice?" she asks him.

"I might. Why do you ask?"

"I'm doing a non-profit relationship service for a certain type of people and you look exactly like one of them," Tiffany explains.

"For you, I'm always available."

As we leave the former hot dog stand, I conjure up *The Original Carlo* in my head and plug in my new bits of information. Wide-open spaces are finally starting to fill in.

Back in her Lexus, Tiffany asks, "Where to next?"

"The IRS."

"Are you getting audited?"

"Tiffany, the only reason I would ever get audited is because they can't figure out how I can exist making next to nothing."

"My Daddy says IRS stands for Irrational Recovery Service."

"For most people it stands for I Regret Swindling."

The appointment is for 1:30. When we enter the conference room on the 59th floor of the Kluczynski Building, we hear, "Wait."

"What?"

"Remember that problem I was having with my feet?" "Wait" Jack Wayt asks me.

"You had your shoes tied too tight."

"It might have been a touch of gout."

"Try wearing loafers, Jack."

Tiffany jumps into the conversation with, "Detective Wayt, don't you think Neula's looking good since she went on her new diet?"

"Neula's been on more diets than Oprah, Kirstie Alley, and all the Biggest Loser contestants combined."

"She's already lost four pounds," Tiffany informs Jack.

"Neula losing four pounds is like a suitcase falling out of a 747."

"She's doing it for you," Tiffany snaps back at Jack. "The least you can do is show some appreciation for what she's going through."

I can only hope and pray "No-No" hasn't received a free stomach pump.

"Yeah," Jack reluctantly tells Tiffany. "I'll see what I can do."

The door opens and a man who looks a frail seventy, moves slower than a cripple at eighty, and has the demeanor of a curmudgeon at ninety, enters the room. "I'm Holler."

Jack and I both stand and offer our hands to shake.

"Lloyd Holler," he says. "That's two L's in Lloyd and two L's in Holler. Lloyd Holler."

"I'm Jack."

"I'm Sherlock."

"I'm Tiffany, and that's two F's in Tiffany."

"Who are you?"

"Detective in training," Tiffany proudly tells him.

"Stick around, little lady, I've been around these blocks more than a mailman," Lloyd informs her.

Lloyd sits at the head of the far end of the table, four or five chairs from us. He exchanges one pair of coke-bottle glasses for an even thicker pair of the same, and coughs up some phlegm. He wipes the disgusting liquid into an already multi-stained handkerchief. "One of you got paper and pen?"

Jack hands over a pad and cheap pen, but only after putting on a pair of latex gloves.

"The cheat, who is he?" Lloyd asks, spewing a spray of spittle in our direction. "I'll break him in two."

"D'Wayne DeWitt," I answer.

"Spell it."

"It has two D's, just like your name," Tiffany makes the connection.

I spell the name slowly, voicing the apostrophe and giving a slight melody in my rendition. My efforts are not appreciated.

"Got a Social Security Number?" Lloyd barks.

"No."

"I got to do everything?" Lloyd Holler hollers at us.

"He works at the Zanadu," I tell Agent Codger.

"What the hell's a Zanadu?"

"It's like only the hottest club in the city," Tiffany, with two F's, energetically informs him.

"A disco?"

"Kinda," Tiffany explains.

"I used to disco," Lloyd admits.

I try not to imagine what Mr. Holler did on a dance floor with that handkerchief.

"What was your fave busta-move to bust?" Tiffany asks.

"This is America, little lady, speak English," Lloyd admonishes Tiffany, who has no clue what he's referring to.

I attempt to get the conversation back on track. "This D'Wayne—"

"Is he a big case?" Lloyd spits out an interruption. "Because I only got six months, two weeks, and three days to wrap it up." Lloyd's nose is running faster than Tennyson's *Brook*.

"What happens then?" Tiffany asks. "Are you scheduled to die or something?"

"No, retire."

"Then what are you going to do?"

"Anything I want."

I tell Lloyd, with two L's, Holler, with two L's, everything I know about Mr. D'Wayne DeWitt, including the Non-Brink's Brink's truck, the account at Northern Trust, even the addresses of the places Mr. DeWitt visited the day I tailed him. Holler takes notes, not very many, but a few.

"That's all you got?" Lloyd loudly spits out again. If this keeps up, there'll be a puddle of snot on the table big enough to float the Commodore's yacht.

"That's it."

"So, now I got to go out and bust my butt to nail this guy? Don't you flatfoots ever bring in anybody ready to get scorched?"

"Sorry."

Lloyd hocks up a goober which, fortunately, he catches in his handy handkerchief before it gets anywhere near us. He exchanges his reading glasses for his walking glasses, gives us a departing scowl, and rises slowly from his chair. "If you ask me, they should have never done away with debtor's prisons." He leaves the room without further comment.

"I'll bet he's a lot of fun in the carpool to work," Jack remarks, depositing his gloves in the trash.

"Agent two L's doesn't impress me as a guy with a lot of hobbies," I mention. "I sure hope he takes up some before he retires."

"Snake charming might be a good fit," Jack says.

"Or maybe a handkerchief tester," Tiffany suggests.

"Let's get out of here before I get infected with some two L bacteria," Jack says.

As we head for the exit, Tiffany says, "My Daddy is right again."

Jack and I gaze at Tiffany, waiting for the inevitable big "payoff."

"He told me IRS guys are meaner than a cripple with no insurance."

For once I couldn't agree more.

Tiffany is already late for an appointment to waste another three hundred bucks with her life coach, so I have her drop me off at the 'L'. Before climbing out of her car, she asks, "What do you think of the 'Nice' me, Mr. Sherlock?"

The question takes me a bit by surprise. "Well, it's not really important what I think, Tiffany, it's what you think that's important."

She's lost in thought for a few seconds, which is a lot for Tiffany. "Well, being free of seeing myself wearing red is certainly a big relief. I can't tell you the pain that it caused me. And I like that I'm like doing so many good deeds now, especially my relationship advice for the attractively challenged, but …" she hesitates. "I'm just not feeling it."

"In what way? What's missing?" I ask.

"I'm not sure."

"Tiffany, you had a traumatic experience back at the Zanadu. You saw your whole life pass before your eyes," I tell her. "I'm glad you're rebounding from that experience in a positive way, but sometimes you have to give things a little time to let life sort itself out."

"You think I might be moving too fast?" she asks.

"You have to let water seek its own level."

"What does water have to do with me?"

"It's an expression, Tiffany," I explain. "After a flood, water needs time to run off and get back to the level where it's supposed to be."

"You want me to run off?"

"No, Tiffany. I want you to take your time, be introspective, really think your life through, and then make decisions on what to do next."

"Mr. Sherlock, I hate thinking. That's why I hired a life coach."

I'm sitting in the bleachers, waiting for the Bailouts to take the floor for their final practice of the year. The game on Saturday is our one last chance for a perfect record of 0-8, all lost by virtue of the Slaughter Rule. What an accomplishment for a first year coach.

Mrs. Whiner is seated next to me. She has a stack of paper in her hands from which she reads aloud, describing in extensive detail how to post-up, split the defense, use the fast break, and spread the floor. I have no clue what she's talking about, because I'm not listening. And it feels really good not to listen, to be on the other side of the fence for a change, so to speak.

I've tuned her out while I'm having an epiphany of my own. The obvious has dawned on me like the sun coming up over Lake Michigan. All of a sudden things are as clear as Tiffany's diamond earrings. I feel a great sense of relief and it feels wonderful.

"Thank you, Mrs. Whiner," I say to the obnoxious woman, having no clue if she's even finished with her diatribe. My team enters the gym. They hardly seem happy to be here. "Okay, Bailouts, let's take the court."

Kelly arrives, playing with her cell phone. The item has become almost an extension of her hand. I interrupt her thumb sweeping the screen. "Can you get music on that thing?"

"Ah, duh, Dad."

"Good," I tell her. "Find some dance music and be ready to play it when I tell you."

"Hip Hop?"

"Well, certainly not the Bunny Hop."

"What's the Bunny Hop?"

I order the girls to line up at half court. "Our last game Saturday is going to be different, girls," I announce.

"We can't lose any worse than we've lost before," little Annie says.

"What's the point of practicing, if we're going to get slaughtered anyway?" Allison asks.

"Are they going to call the Slaughter Rule halfway through the first half?" Kaylyn asks.

The "Little" Whiner informs the team, "My Mom says we should be using more pick and rolls."

"On Saturday, we're going to pick our roles a lot more carefully."

"What are we going to do, Dad?" Care asks.

"What's right, for a change."

The first drill I have the team do is my new Dribbling Dance Drill. "Every time you bounce the ball, you've got to bounce your booty along with it," I explain.

The team looks at me as if I've got all my screws loose.

"I want to see more moves than a can of worms on steroids."

I signal Kelly to start the music, grab a ball and give the team an example of what I want. I shuck, jive, jute and boogie as I bounce the ball before me. I must look like an idiot, but in seconds the girls join in and we have a basketball dance-a-thon. It's so much fun, even Kelly steps up and in. The girls are throwing one arm up, while dribbling with the other. They swing their hips, tap their toes, and whirl their dervishes to the beat of the song and the bouncing ball. At the end of the awful music, every member of the team is laughing hysterically.

The next drill, which I create on the spot, is the Backboard Bounce Back. I line the girls up a few feet left of the free throw line and tell them to dribble up, toss the ball onto the backboard so that the person behind them can catch the rebound and throw it back onto the board to keep the process going. Each time the ball hits the board, I have the girls count out the number aloud. Kelly gives us a few upbeat tunes and we begin to bounce. It takes a while to get the idea, but we get the number up to six in about five minutes. By the time everyone is winded, we have a record of ten consecutive bounces. Good for us.

Next, we do a singing drill, starting with *Old McDonald Had a Farm*. Every time you are passed the ball, you have to continue singing the song. I call out when to pass. The team loves the *E, I, E, I, O* part the best. To further encourage them, I allow requests: songs by Katy Perry,

Taylor Swift, One Direction, and several other acts I've never heard of blast out of Kelly's cell phone. The girls, even Wilma Whiner, love it.

By the end of the practice hour, the girls are exhausted, from the bouncing, the singing, and mostly laughing at what they've been doing. But there is no one more spent than Mrs. Whiner who has watched the new drills in absolute horror. I see her sitting back in the bleachers absolutely aghast in what she has witnessed. All she can do is fan herself with her multiple pages of unsolicited basketball strategies to keep from fainting dead away.

"See you Saturday, Bailouts."

And they cheer back in positive expectation.

This was fun.

"Was it Bruno who doped Tiffany's drink, Dad?"

Homework's done. Dinner was another complaint fest. And now the three of us sit in front of *The Original Carlo*. "I may never know for sure," I answer Care's question.

"Why not?"

"Somebody bashed his head in." As soon as I say this, I regret it.

"Cool," Kelly says.

"You're not supposed to say it's 'cool' when you hear about a murder, Kelly," I admonish my elder daughter. "And don't tell your mother you sit around here and discuss my murder investigations, either."

"Who do you think iced him, Dad?" Kelly continues, not listening to a word I just said.

"I wish I knew." For some dumb reason I continue the morbid conversation, "To be honest, I haven't a clue."

"I bet it was D'Wayne DeWitt," Care says.

"Why?"

"Because he's probably got a lot of pent-up anger, having the name D'Wayne."

"Gibby did it," Kelly says. "He's a vigilante trying to clean up his own nightclub."

"Where'd you ever pick up the word *vigilante*, Kelly?"

"I don't know. I'm telling you, Dad, my mind's like a sponge. I absorb stuff without even knowing I'm sucking it up."

"Well, absorb this: quit spending so much time on that phone of yours. Every time I see you, you have that thing pushed up against your ear."

"It's not there now," Kelly snaps back.

"Is it recharging?" I ask.

"How'd you know?" Kelly asks.

"Your father's a detective."

"Want us to move the cards around on *The Original Carlo*, Dad?" Care asks.

"It wouldn't do any good," I tell her. "The problem is I can't find the connection between the crimes."

"Maybe it's a woman?" Kelly suggests.

"I don't think so."

"Dad," Kelly says, "I'm trying to think outside the box."

"How about money?" Care tries again.

"It's always about money," I tell her, "because life is always about money."

"I thought you told us life was about choices, Dad," Kelly says.

"It is, but if you don't have any money, you won't have a lot of choices."

"So, the Commodore can choose anything he wants while you have maybe one or two picks on a good day?" Kelly asks me.

I hate arguing with any teenager, especially one who is my daughter. "Well, maybe you should ask the Commodore if he'd be interested in adopting you, Kelly?"

"That's not a bad idea."

"Does he have kids now?" I ask.

"No."

"Well, that explains why he's got so much money."

"I don't want to get adopted, Dad," Care reassures me.

"Thank you, Care."

"You will when you get older," Kelly tells her sister, "and your closet is as empty as Dad's refrigerator."

I look at the clock. "Time for showers, then time for bed."

Care doesn't argue, she yawns.

Kelly says, "Already?"

"Git."

They shower, get dressed for bed, and, as I come in to kiss them goodnight, Kelly hands me a note. It is addressed *Richard Sherlock*.

"Not again," I moan.

I read it. "What do you mean you don't have school next Wednesday?" I ask Kelly.

"It's one of those teacher service days."

"Why can't your mother watch you?"

"She's busy."

"What? She has a job interview with a Mr. Salmon on Lake Michigan?"

"She didn't say."

"Yeah, right."

CHAPTER 17

"This is for dragging my ass outta there," Mr. DeWitt informs me from his hospital bed. His doctor is holding him over to the side to clean out the gunk in his lungs. Another stack of Hamilton's is laid across my palm.

"I don't think Gibby Fearn was the one who tried to blow you to kingdom come, Mr. DeWitt," I tell him honestly.

"Then who the hell do you think it is?"

I really wish I had an answer, a good answer for him, but I don't. "I'm working on it."

"Maybe if you spent more time searching for the bomber, and less time following me around you might get somewhere."

"What do you mean?" I play dumb.

"I can hear that crappy piece of shit car of yours putt-putting behind me."

I've got to get that muffler fixed.

"Gibby had no motive to smoke you," I say.

"What do you mean?" Mr. DeWitt yells back. "The only person stopping him from running the Zanadu is me. He's a corporate climbing little weasel who would stop at nothing to get what he wants."

"So, why didn't you just fire him?" I ask the obvious question.

"Because it's complicated at the top."

By the way he makes this comment, I realize I shouldn't ask the obvious question of who's in charge.

"So, what do you want me to do, Mr. DeWitt?"

"Get out of my sight."

"I can do that."

"You're fired."

Evidently, it isn't all that complicated to fire me. "I'm sorry I couldn't be of more service to you, Mr. DeWitt. If there's anything I discover from this point on, I will report it to you."

"Don't bother."

I decide to wait for a better time to ask him if I can use his name as a reference. I leave the room. Once outside his door, I pull the stack out of my pocket. It would have been really tacky of me to count it in front of him, but now I rifle though the bills like a gambler in a hurry to place a big bet. Eleven hundred bucks.

Cha-ching, cha-ching, cha-ching.

"No, no, I do love you, Jack. I was just tired that night."

"Jack," Tiffany says, "Neula is telling you how she feels."

"Well, let me tell you how I feel," Jack says. "This gout of mine might actually be a case of phlebitis."

Although I'm sitting at a table in a very nice restaurant, I feel like I'm in the front row at a taping of a bad *Doctor Phil* episode.

"No-No" says, "No, no, Jack, can't you give me another chance?"

"I might not be able to because a blood clot might break loose, go all the way to my head, and leave me brain dead."

"Neula," Tiffany says instructing her pupil, "tell Jack you'd be more than happy to stay at his side if he falls into a coma."

"I'll be there for you."

"Jack, your turn—"

I interrupt Tiffany. "Can we order?" I flag the waiter over to our table.

"She and I will have a salad with no dressing, a broiled chicken breast with no sauce or butter, and iced tea, lemon, no sugar," Tiffany announces.

"Really?" "No-No" questions. "Couldn't I get mine with fries at least?"

"No," Tiffany lays down the dieting law.

"I might be the one in a coma, if I don't get some real food into me," "No-No" laments.

"And you, sir?"

"Fettuccini Alfredo, cream of whatever you got soup, and lots of bread slathered with butter and garlic." Evidently, Jack is playing hard to get via the menu.

Tiffany glares at Jack. "Ordering the Heart Attack Special, that's totally rude."

"Okay, forget the butter," Jack says.

"I'll have the turkey sandwich," I tell the waiter. He exits quickly. I can't blame him. "I need a favor," I tell the detectives.

"What?"

"I need you to pull some guy over tonight, get him out, and search his car."

"No, no, we can't do that," "No-No" says without hesitation.

"Sure we can," Jack says.

"No no, we can't. We need a search warrant."

"Oh, come on," Jack says.

"A warrant or at least a good reason," "No-No" tells Jack.

"How about a briefcase full of dirty money?" I ask.

"Sounds reason enough for me," Jack says. "Who is it, Sherlock?"

"I'll point him out to you tonight."

I'm not wild about gyms and I've never liked health clubs. They don't make any sense to me. Why would anyone consider a place healthy when all the members leave their sweat on the equipment for the next guy, spit on the floor, and leave their dirty towels all over the place? The shower stalls always have the latest species of athlete's foot bacteria, plus the sinks and vanities all sport a full assortment of hair follicles, used razor blades, dried toothpaste spittle, and dirty Q-Tips. Most confusing to me is why so many of the people working out wear ear buds to either listen to music or talk on the phone while they grunt and groan on torture devices with overly impressive monikers like the Hip Abductor and Thigh Eradicator?

Monroe's health club is no exception, except for the fact that here all the work-outers aren't only just filthy and sweaty, but filthy, sweaty, and filthy rich.

As Tiffany and I enter the workout area, it's a bit difficult not to raise eyebrows. I'm in my usual pair of slacks and a polo shirt. Tiffany is dressed ready to pose for an *Elle* photo shoot in a racy little blue tube top and black yoga pants combination.

"Do you see what I see, Mr. Sherlock?"

"Bacteria multiplying?"

"No. It's that no good, self-centered, egotistical, conceited, bitch, Alix Fromound." Tiffany has locked her eyes on her nemesis like a pointer rigidly aiming at a soon-to-be-dead duck.

"She's here working out, Tiffany."

"She's working *it* out alright," she says. "And *right* in front of Monroe."

"From what you've told me, it's not like you and Monroe are becoming Antony and Cleopatra."

"Who?"

What would be the point of a history lesson here? She wouldn't listen.

"Just because I don't want him," Tiffany says, "doesn't mean I want her to have him."

"That doesn't sound like the new 'Nice' Tiffany to me."

"When it comes to Alix Fromound, the 'Nice' Tiffany is history."

Tiffany marches right up to where Alix pumps iron on a machine designed to tighten and tone the areas underneath surgically enhanced breasts, of which Alix has two.

"What are you doing here?" Tiffany barks at Alix, who wears a black spandex body suit so tight it looks like it was sprayed on.

"Exercising."

"What, your libido?"

"Mine doesn't need any exercise," Alix snaps back. "But I hear yours does."

I can see Tiffany's brain go into overdrive, wondering what Alix knows or doesn't know. "Who'd you hear that from?"

"I have my sources."

Tiffany stares her down.

Alix stares right back.

"You're here because Monroe's here," Tiffany accuses.

"Maybe he's here because I'm here."

"No way."

"Yes, way."

Tiffany digs in. "You don't belong here."

"I'm a member. Are you?" Alix responds with a question.

"I wouldn't be a member of any club that has you as a member," Tiffany states emphatically.

"That doesn't leave you many choices then, does it? Because I'm a member just about everywhere."

"Eastbank?" Tiffany throws out a club just west of Michigan Avenue.

"Of course." Alix says tossing her nose into the air.

"Oh, where the more *mature* woman goes and *pretends* to exercise?"

In seconds they each may run off searching for a pair of designer boxing gloves. "I'd love to hang around and referee, ladies," I tell them, "but I've got work to do. Enjoy your time together."

Neither hears a word I say. I leave the two, hoping there's no blood on the floor when I return.

To my left is a boxing ring where Monroe and his workout partner are semi-sparring. I make my way in that direction until I reach the edge of the ring. Monroe wears a pair of half-gloves, and is punching away at what looks like over-sized oven mitts worn by Oscar Odie, his much ballyhooed and newly-indicted trainer. I have to admit that shirtless Monroe is quite the physical specimen with his rippling pecs, dancing deltoids, and six pack abs. As he throws his jabs, hooks, and haymakers, his entire body glistens as a mass of coordinated muscles. I'm impressed.

I read somewhere, probably at my favorite Barnes & Noble, that boxing is the latest workout craze. I don't understand how boxing could be good for you, since it would seem getting hit in the head repeatedly would be the antithesis of improving your health and well-being. The only exercise I can imagine being any worse for your body is Mixed Martial Arts where you add kicking, gouging, and head butting to the aforementioned boxing punishments. Gee, I feel healthier just thinking about it.

The buzzer sounds and Monroe ceases his onslaught. They probably save the bell for the real fights. He comes over and stands well above me, his whole body dripping beads of sweat. "What are you doing here?"

"I was in the neighborhood, thought I'd drop by and see what it would cost to get my own locker."

Monroe squats down, now he's only twice my level. "What do you want?"

I give Oscar, who's standing in the opposite corner, a half-hearted glance. "I heard your trainer got caught dealing steroids," I say.

"It's a bullshit charge."

"You the one who put up his bail?" I ask.

"It's tough to find a good trainer," Monroe says.

"I can only imagine."

I change tactics. "The night Tiffany went down in the Zanadu, could you describe the guy who came between you and Alix?"

"I already told the cops. Ask them."

Monroe has a point. I concede and move on. "What were you drinking?"

"What difference would that make?" He asks a question to my question—which I hate.

"Humor me," I plead.

"What I always drink. Stoli on the rocks, two olives."

"No Gatorade?"

"It's a bar, not a gym."

"You never saw the guy before?"

"What guy?" I'm pretty sure right now Monroe wouldn't mind giving me a punch or two.

"The guy who stepped between you and Alix."

"No," he says. "How many times do I have to tell you?"

I see out of the corner of my eye that Oscar shifts closer to us, listening to our conversation. "I just thought I'd ask again," I say to Monroe. "Sometimes your memory kicks in after you give it time to work on its own electrical impulses."

This is one of my theories concerning the power of the brain. You think real hard on a problem or a remembrance and then you totally put it out of your mind for a while. This allows your brain's electrical synapses to go to work and figure it out for you.

"That's bullshit."

Evidently, Monroe doesn't adhere to my theory.

"Was there anything else about that night that seemed odd or out of place?" I ask.

"Listen, buddy," he says firmly, "I didn't have anything to do with anything that night. I've told you. I've told the cops. That's enough. Get out of here. I've got work to do."

I back up a couple of paces, signaling the end of my questioning. All I can think is what he's said is bullshit too.

Oscar comes over to Monroe. The buzzer sounds. The punching begins. I wonder if Oscar ever gets to punch Monroe.

I retreat to Alix and Tiffany, now at the Gluteus Maximizer machine. No blood on the floor. Whew.

"I'll tell you something else, Alix," Tiffany says.

"What?"

"What I want, I get," Tiffany tells her in no uncertain terms.

"And what you want, I already have," Alix returns.

"I trust you two ladies had a nice visit," I say in closing.

"Idiot."

"Me?"

"Yes, you."

Jack, "No-No" and I are back at the IRS. Lloyd Holler Mr. "two L's and two L's" is snorting snot like Ferdinand the Bull. "I busted my butt to crack that D'Wayne DeWitt."

"And?" I ask.

"From what you told me, I thought I could put this s.o.b. on a skewer, slow roast him over hot coals, and eat him for lunch," Lloyd says. "And all I discover is that he's as clean as a Chicago blizzard."

"He's a drug dealer," I tell Lloyd.

"Not according to his financials."

"I watched him pay a call on his retail outlets."

"Properties that he owns or rents, with all property taxes paid up to date."

"How about the money he's getting from the Zanadu?"

"He's a paid consultant," Holler hollers at me. "They paid him sixty grand last year. Perfectly legal."

"He rides around in a big ass limo and lives in a penthouse."

"All inherited."

"Inherited? From who? The guy grew up in the ghetto."

"All perfectly legal, you bonehead."

"I'm telling you," I plead my case. "I can't be wrong about this guy."

"Yes, you can, because you're an idiot. Don't bother me again, unless you got a guy I can fry at high heat." Lloyd makes one last swipe at his dripping nose with his well-soaked handkerchief and leaves the room.

"Way to go, Sherlock," "No-No" says.

"Yeah," Jack adds, "now we're all going to get audited next year."

"If you think we're letting your friends in," Sterno tells me, "you're smokin' some really nasty weed."

We're at the Zanadu. I'm at the head of the line. Thankfully, Jack and "No-No" are out of earshot.

"Those two look like bookends at a fat farm reading group," Arson adds, seeing my detective buddies standing by their car.

"Don't get your Calvins in a bunch, boys," I tell them. "Has the guy with the ponytail arrived yet?"

"Yeah, ten minutes ago."

I walk over to my detective friends. "He's here."

Jack gets into the driver's seat, "No-No" rides shotgun, and I slip in the back of a standard-issue black Chevy Impala. I've always wondered why police departments all buy the same cars for undercover work; same make, same model, same color. Do they actually consider that "good" cover?

"I was wondering if you'd like to stop by on Sunday for dinner, Jack?" "No-No" asks as we sit and wait.

"You're not having that rabbit food that Tiffany's been making you eat?"

"No, I'm taking Sunday off. No diets on the Sabbath."

"Well, I'll have to see how I'm feeling," Jack tells her. "Last Sunday, I came down with what I thought was the beginning of a brain tumor."

"How would you know something like that?" I ask.

"I was feeling an odd growth on my cerebellum."

"Jeesh," I can't help myself and say from the back seat.

I look up and see Mr. Ponytail coming out of the Zanadu with his metal briefcase in hand. "That's our boy. He's going to get into that limo, so get ready."

"No, no," "No-No" says. "I still don't think this is a good idea."

Jack ignores her advice and puts the Chevy in gear. He carefully follows Mr. Ponytail until he gets off the expressway at Harlem and turns north. The flashers go on, and the limo pulls over. Jack and "No-No" get out. Jack goes to the driver's side window. "No-No" stands to the right with her hand on the butt of her gun.

From where I sit, I can't hear what Jack has to say at the window, but when Mr. Ponytail exits the car, it's obvious he's not a happy camper. Jack motions to "No-No" to start searching the car from the passenger's side as he and the victim watch.

The entire process takes about fifteen minutes.

"No-No" climbs into the Chevy first, followed by Jack. There is a pause before both doors slam shut simultaneously.

Jack makes the first comment. "You IDIOT!"

"I told you this was a bad idea," "No-No" adds.

"He says he's going to press charges, Sherlock," Jack tells me, his voice echoing in the closed car.

"No, no, I said. This is a dumb idea," "No-No" says.

"If the Chief finds out about this one," Jack says. "He'll have us both back walking a beat."

No cop walks a beat anymore, but this is probably not a good time to correct my friends.

"No-No" adds, "There was even a decal on limo's front window that said he 'supports our brave police and firemen.'"

"You didn't find anything?" I ask, incredulous at the results.

"No, we didn't, Sherlock." Jack slams his fists onto the steering wheel. "I can feel my heart starting to palpitate. If I drop dead, Sherlock, it's your fault."

Jack holds a hand to his chest, as "No-No" rubs his shoulder to make it all better.

"Did you open the briefcase?" I have to ask.

"Of course we opened the briefcase," Jack screams again.

"And it was as empty as your empty head," "No-No" finishes the thought.

"I can't believe it," I tell them. "I've watched that guy carry money out of the Zanadu every night I've been there. Did you find out who he was?"

"He's an independent limo driver, with his license and insurance paid up in full."

"He hasn't had a parking ticket in three years," "No-No" finishes the crime report.

"You screwed up with the IRS and now you've screwed up with us," Jack informs me.

"That's two strikes, Sherlock," "No-No" says.

"Well," I say, to make it all better, "at least you two are now agreeing on something."

CHAPTER 18

My back is killing me.

I wake up this morning and I'm tighter than a shrink-wrapped Slinky. My lumbar vertebrae ache worse than a jilted lover. It must be a delayed reaction to the hit I took when I was thrown backwards after the explosion in D'Wayne DeWitt's office. It takes me ten minutes just to reach out and grab the bottle of ibuprofen only to find one pill remaining inside which slips through my fingers before I can get it into my mouth.

I take a breather and squiggle my body to the edge of the bed and do my best to lower myself to the floor. Of course this doesn't work either and I flop to the carpet like a dying salmon. Ouch! The pain is riveting through my body like lightning through thunderclouds. I'm angry, not only at my body, but for not finishing *Oh, My Aching Back* the last time I was in the Barnes & Noble.

It must take me twenty minutes just to get up onto all fours and another twenty minutes to inch my way to the bathroom. I turn on the shower and crawl into the small space. If you've never taken a shower on all fours, I can assure you, you're not missing much. By the time the hot water heater's water runs out and turns cold, I am semi-standing. I get a robe around me and walk out of the bathroom, slumped over worse than a stoop-shouldered octogenarian.

I lay on the floor in the front room, lift my feet to the couch and stare at *The Original Carlo,* which is the only item in the room that could possibly make me feel worse than I already feel. So far, all that's gone right in this case is safely tucked away in a recipe box in a cupboard in my kitchen.

There are more unanswered questions, plot holes, and unconnected dots gazing down upon me than bullets of pain shooting into my back.

Everything is wrong, really wrong. My IRS visit and subsequent *hollering* from Lloyd, with two L's, Holler, with two L's, was a disaster. Mr. Ponytail's empty briefcase makes absolutely no sense. I'm investigating the chicanery that's going on in an upscale nightclub where maybe the only profit they make is from the money they steal from themselves. But I can't find any dirty money anywhere. How lousy of a detective can I be? I know Mr. DeWitt is as dirty as one of Monroe's

T-shirts after a workout and, yet, he miraculously acquired all of his assets by inheriting them. Huh? Why is there a Brink's and a Non-Brink's truck in competition? Bruno had a profitable sideline dealing drugs out of the Zanadu and used some of his profits to bulk himself up, but how could he be so stupid as to let someone waste him in his own condo, which by the way was a place he shouldn't have been able to afford? And where does Mr. Rogers or Jimmy Cappilino fit into all of this? I have no clue. What started out with something as simple as Tiffany getting roofied, has turned into a maze with more dead ends than a poorly planned housing project.

I lie in a prone position for over two hours and come up with nothing except more emotional, mental, and physical pain. What a way to start the day.

Around eleven, I get to the phone and call Tiffany. It rings about nine times before it kicks to her voice mail. I leave a message for her to meet me at the Zanadu.

I force myself to eat a couple of pieces of toast. The bread should slow down the four, ancient ibuprofen I found in the bottom of the junk drawer in the kitchen. This cure is currently eating a hole through the lining of my stomach. I get dressed, take about a month of Sundays to get down the three flights of stairs, and walk the block and a half to my car. Getting in is an excruciating experience, which I know will only be topped in severity when I have to get out. Whether the Toyota will start is always a mystery, but it does on the first try; something is finally going right.

As I putt-putt down the street, I happen to glance in the rear view mirror to see sparks flying off the back of my car like Fourth of July sparklers gone wild. Whatever went right has now reversed itself. I stop the car, get out (painfully, exactly as I suspected), and somehow manage to get down on my hands and knees to see the muffler resting on the street pavement, its back end severed from the tail pipe like a rusted out plumbing trap from the early 1800's.

Ten minutes later I pull into AAAAA Auto, obviously a business wanting to be first in the Yellow Pages. I'm the only customer in the shop.

"How much to …?"

"We don't junk cars here," Albert, the owner, service manager, and mechanic tells me before I can finish my sentence.

"... fix the muffler?"

"You want to fix something on this car?" he asks. "Why?"

"Because it's broken."

"The whole car's broken."

"You want to fix it or not?" I ask, standing humped over worse than that Notre Dame bell-ringer.

"I'll feel like a mortician applying make-up to a 90-year-old corpse," Albert admits.

"You want to fix the muffler or not?"

"Sure," he says. "But I'll have to order the part. Maybe I can find one on eBay."

"That's it," I reach the end of my short rope. "I'm taking my business to Quadruple 'A' Auto."

"Oh, come on, buddy," Albert says. "Can't you take a joke?"

"Not today."

"That's surprising, because you sure have no trouble driving one."

"Just fix the muffler."

"Go in; make yourself at home," Albert says, pointing me to his customer waiting area.

I hobble into the filthy room, which has more grease stains than Albert's coveralls. I attempt to sit in the cheap plastic patio chair, but it's too painful. I find four paper floor mats that read *You're AAAAA-OKAY at AAAAA* and line them up on the stained, cheap carpet. I lie down upon them and put my feet up on the chair. A few minutes later I manage to get out my cell phone and call Tiffany.

"Oh, Mister Sherlock," she answers.

"Tiffany, why didn't you call me back?" I have no problem making my voice sound disgruntled.

"I wasn't supposed to call you back."

"I left you a voice mail," I continue.

"Nobody does voice mail anymore," she informs me. "We text or we do Facebook."

"Tiffany, I need your help."

"I know. There are so many places we can begin."

"You have to come here and get me," I tell her. "My car broke down."

"And that's a surprise?"

I give her the address of where I currently lie.

"Mr. Sherlock, I have some very disturbing news."

"Does it have anything to do with your life coach?"

"Kinda, maybe, but not really."

Lying on the floor of a greasy auto repair shop is depressing enough, "Can it wait, Tiffany?" I ask. "I'm not doing real well right now."

"It's pretty devastating," she says.

"I don't think I could handle any more devastation at the moment. Could you please just get in your car and get up here?" I plead.

"No problem, Mr. Sherlock."

At midday it's about a twenty-minute ride from Tiffany's penthouse to where my feet rest on a plastic chair. Tiffany arrives an hour and a half later.

"Where have you been?"

"I came right away."

"No, you didn't."

"Yes, I did," she argues. "I hung up the phone, put on my make-up, did my hair, found something to wear, fixed myself a power shake, answered a couple text messages, checked my Facebook page, got in the car, stopped for a latté, and drove right here. It's not like I dilly-dallied around or anything."

I shake my head. "No, I guess not."

"Why are you on the floor, Mr. Sherlock?" she asks as she peers down upon me.

"My back went out."

"Went out where?"

"At the Zanadu when Mr. DeWitt's office exploded."

"You left your back at the Zanadu?"

"So to speak," I tell her. "Help me up."

Tiffany gets me to my feet. On the way to her Lexus I tell Albert, "I'll be back to get my car later."

"No way, buddy," he says, coming over to us as he wipes the grease off his hands onto an already overly greasy rag. "You ain't sticking me with that clunker."

"You think I would just leave and never some back?" I ask.

"That's what I'd do."

"Me, too, Mr. Sherlock, I hate your car."

I give him a down payment of two hundred dollars. "This enough assurance that I'll be back?"

"Make it three hundred."

I test Tiffany's patience as I carefully slide into her car. Not much of a test because after about thirty seconds she remarks, "Mr. Sherlock, could you please hurry up? I need another latté."

"I'm sorry my suffering is holding you up."

When I'm finally settled in the front seat, she asks, "Where to?"

"Zanadu."

"Are we going to look for your back?"

"No, we're going to find a checkbook."

"A checkbook," Tiffany says. "I love checkbooks."

Tiffany pulls out of AAAAA Auto like a NASCAR driver out of a pit stop.

The Lexus might have ergonomic seats, but no amount of ergo can make my back feel any better. Every time Tiffany does one of her sudden lane changes, I go into convulsive end-of-life spasms.

"Mr. Sherlock, you want to hear my devastating news?"

"Oh, sure. Why not?"

"I found out that the PNBBA competition is being held in three weeks."

"What?"

"When I heard the news and put two and one together, I was devastated."

"Tiffany, what's a PNBBA?"

"The Professional Natural Body Building Association."

I sit speechless.

"It's their annual Posedown in Pittsburgh," Tiffany tells me as if this is as common knowledge as the best spa for a facial in Chicago.

"You've totally lost me," I tell her between shots of pain to my vertebrae. "Is this something you want to attend?"

"I'm not going. I wouldn't be caught dead there."

"Why not? It sounds like a swell time."

Tiffany makes a lane change that slams my body into the door, as if I need any more pain and suffering.

"It's a contest to see which bulked up, over-muscled, six packed, abs-bulging, bicepted weightlifter has the ugliest muscles on his body."

"Did your life coach tell you to go?"

"No."

"Then why are you telling me this?

"Guess who's posing at the Posedown?"

"Arnold Schwarzenegger."

"Maybe in the eighty and over category, but in the thirty-somethings' category, guess whose striking a pose?"

"Just tell me."

"Monroe."

"Monroe Chevelier?"

"Is that totally gross or what?" Tiffany says.

I let this sink into my brain for a minute or two.

"He'll be all oiled up in one of those speedo thongs, primping like a centerfold in some gay porno magazine."

"Have you ever seen a centerfold in a gay porno magazine?"

"No, but I've got a good imagination, Mr. Sherlock."

This is interesting. "So, that night in your bedroom, Monroe was practicing for the upcoming event?"

"Or he was trying to impress me," Tiffany says. "A lot of guys do that."

A connection, finally a connection.

Tiffany parks in front of one of the bays at Zanadu's loading dock, making a beer truck driver very angry. "We'll just be a minute," she yells at the guy as she helps lift me out of the car. "We just have to go in and get his back, back."

Tiffany walks, I stagger up the ramp and into the club. There are a number of workers busy setting up for a big night, including Bruno's bruised barback. It suddenly dawns on me the reason for his bruises. "Excuse me," I say to the young man. "Could I see your Green Card?"

"*No hablo Inglés*," he says, moving quickly away from us.

"He said he doesn't speak American," Tiffany translates. "You know, I just realized something. Hispanic people have green cards and white people like me have platinum cards. Isn't it interesting how the world divides itself by colors?"

"Fascinating, truly fascinating," I agree.

It takes us a while, but we finally make it to the door labeled *No Admittance*. I knock, the camera turns on, and the door clicks open. Inside, the Behemoth is reading *The Fantastic Four*.

"You haven't finished that yet?"

"Dun't know."

"Hello, Tiffany," says the Slimy Guy, the same guy who I encountered at the inner door to the Zanadu the first night I was here. He's obviously the new VP of Operations. All of Gibby's pictures, flare, and knick-knacks are nowhere to be seen.

"How are you?" he says to Tiffany.

They exchange air kisses. I'm in no shape for kissing, air or otherwise. I put out my hand to shake. "You know, I never got your name."

"It's Massey."

"Something Massey or Massey Something?" I ask.

"Just Massey."

"Are you like one of those rock stars who only have one name?" Tiffany asks, "like Sting or Bono?"

"Isn't Bono's first name, Sonny?" I ask.

"Dun't know," the Behemoth answers.

Massey returns to his new desk, which has only half the number of framed pictures as Gibby had. "Mr. DeWitt has informed me that you are no longer in his employ."

"That's correct," I tell him. "But I still work for Mr. Rogers."

"Who?"

"Mr. Jimmy Cappilino?"

"Who?" Massey sounds like an owl.

"The owner of the corporation that owns the Zanadu."

Massey doesn't answer, but the Behemoth does, "Dun't know."

"I need to see the financials," I say.

"No can do," Massey speaks.

"I can get a warrant," I tell him.

"How? You're not a cop," Massey says in response.

"He used to be," Tiffany says.

"That doesn't count."

"You've had a doping incident, an explosion, and a fire," I remind him in my sternest detective voice. "I can have this place shut down in an hour."

"No, you can't," Massey shoots right back at me. "You can barely stand up."

I guess my voice doesn't match my present physical demeanor.

"Can we see your checkbook?" Tiffany asks him.

"No."

"Why not?"

"Show me yours first." Massey's right back at Tiffany.

"No can do."

"Why not?"

"I pay my bills by credit card or on-line," Tiffany explains.

Massey sits back as smug as a kid with a secret. "Show me yours and I'll show you mine."

"I'll show you mine," I enter the conversation.

"I'm sure there's not much to see there," Massey says.

This has been a real fun visit. We'll have to come back and do it again real soon.

"Anything else I can help you with?" Massey asks.

I try one last intimidation. "If your clientele find out the place was bombed, I doubt that it would be good for business."

"Actually, they already know and so far it's been pretty good for our street cred." He smiles a sickly, smug smile. I hate when people do that.

Tiffany and I leave the office. On our way back to the loading dock, I see Arson and Sterno playing grab ass in the corner. I give some quick instructions to Tiffany. She walks over to the boys, chats then up, and returns a few minutes later. "Harris Bank," she tells me.

That's all I needed to know.

"Are we going there next?" Tiffany asks.

"No, we're going back to jail."

I would have thought the thrill would have been gone, or at least diminished, but no. The boys in the jailhouse line up like fans along the red carpet at the Academy Awards to watch Tiffany go through the metal detector.

We sit in the same room as before. Gibby is escorted in by Dirk McGee. Mr. Fearn's attitude has not improved.

"You here to give me more advice?" he asks.

"Did you take the last advice I gave you?"

"What difference would it make?"

I'll take that as a "no."

"Want to get out of here, Gibby?"

"What do you think?"

So far we've had five exchanges, all questions with no distinct answers. At this rate, we won't get anywhere in our conversation.

"I can get you out of here," I tell him breaking the cycle.

"What do I have to do?"

"To start with, quit asking me questions."

Gibby gives me a dirty look.

"Mr. Sherlock hates when you answer one of his questions with a question," Tiffany informs him.

"I've got an attorney," Gibby says. "You wanna know what he said?"

Another question; nobody listens to me.

"Sure, why not."

"He told me not to talk to you." Gibby leans forward. "For all I know, you could be recording this conversation and I could be incriminating myself."

"No way," Tiffany says. "Mr. Sherlock is terrible with anything electronic. He doesn't even know how to text."

I look over at Dirk standing at the back of the room. The look on his face tells me *Oftentimes, life is easier behind bars.*

I cut to the chase. "I need to know who really owns the Zanadu."

"Why would I want to tell you that?" Gibby snaps back at me. "Everybody tells me not to tell anybody anything, including you."

"But I'm on your side."

"How the hell do I know that?"

"You can trust Mr. Sherlock," Tiffany assures him.

"Doesn't he work for DeWitt?" Gibby is back to the questions.

"Nope. He got fired," Tiffany says.

"If I tell him anything," Gibby says to Tiffany, "what do I have left to bargain with."

"You're going to have to trust somebody," I tell him.

"How about this? You tell us something without actually telling us?" Tiffany suggests.

I must have reached the point of no return with Tiffany because I know exactly what she means. I explain for Gibby, "We'll paint the picture and you merely nod your head 'yes' or 'no'?"

"You can't nod 'no,' Mr. Sherlock," Tiffany informs me. "You can only nod 'yes.' You can shake 'no,' but you can't shake 'yes'."

"Thank you for clearing that up, Tiffany."

Gibby wrinkles his brow. I sense he may be amenable to Tiffany's idea.

I begin, "The Zanadu is phenomenally profitable, with piles of cash being generated each night?"

"And who do they have to thank for that?" Gibby asks. This has not begun well.

"You're just supposed to shake yes or no," Tiffany reminds him.

"And all the money is funneled into the basement where they use two accounting systems?" I continue.

Gibby is about to speak, but instead shrugs his shoulders.

"That was neither a 'no,' nor a 'yes'," Tiffany translates.

"The receipts, credit cards and whatever money can be traced, goes to the Harris branch on State?" I continue.

"Where are you going with this?" Gibby, the one with the questions, asks.

"The cash goes to an account at Northern Trust over on South Wacker Drive, right?"

Gibby shakes his head.

"No?"

"A shake is a 'no,' a nod is a 'yes,' Mr. Sherlock."

I can't believe this. "The Non-Brink's Brink's truck doesn't leave the Zanadu and drop off at the bank on Wacker?"

Gibby shakes.

"You sure?"

Gibby nods.

"He's positive," Tiffany says.

This doesn't make sense. "And that guy with a ponytail doesn't carry out a briefcase of cash every night?"

Gibby shakes his head a number of times, then says, "I made a mistake."

"About the guy with ponytail or the account at Northern Trust?"

Gibby shakes like a metronome.

"That's a 'no, no, no,' on that one," Tiffany says.

"My mistake is thinking you had some clue about what the hell is going on." Gibby pauses. "We're ending this now, before I say something I'm going to regret for a long, long time."

Dirk McGee walks forward to Gibby's side. "This has certainly been enlightening."

"Next time we visit we'll play charades," I tell him.

"Great," Tiffany says, "I love charades."

Gibby Fearn is re-shackled and escorted out of the room. I'm getting more and more depressed by the moment.

"What's the matter, Mr. Sherlock?" Tiffany asks me as we walk out of the Cook County Jail.

"I broke my first rule of life."

"You bought some cheap make-up?"

"No, I made an assumption."

"You assumed the make-up was good before reading the label?"

"No, Tiffany," I say, creaking in pain, "I assumed the money from the Zanadu was going out the door faster than my ex-wife wastes my alimony payments."

"It wasn't?"

"I figured Mr. DeWitt was taking his cut every night with a pack of cash. The guy with the ponytail is picking up a share for somebody, the guy I met on Armitage gets his, and the Non-Brink's truck is delivering a skim to a no-named account at Northern Trust. And that's not all. There's someone doing a nightly accounting in the basement of the place, a Mr. Jimmy Cappilino who doesn't exist, but probably gets paid too; and let's not forget the usual stealing by the bartenders, hostesses, waitresses, barbacks, and whoever else gets to handle cash in the place. The place is a thief's goldmine."

"You think Gibby is in on the take."

"He's the only guy I think who's not."

"But everybody else is."

"Yes."

"So, if everyone is getting a cut, why'd they screw it up by killing poor Bruno?" Tiffany asks.

"Greed."

"You know what's really great about being phenomenally rich, Mr. Sherlock?"

"No."

"People like me could care less about greed."

This is a fact I will never realize on a personal basis.

Tiffany pulls out of the parking structure. "You think one of the people at the club killed Bruno?" she asks.

"Yes."

"You think Bruno tried to blow up that guy Mr. DeWitt?"

"Bruno was already dead when the bomb went off."

"Could have been on a timer," Tiffany says. "He had the newest iPhone."

"Or Bruno had a partner trying to get even."

"I already told you Bruno wasn't gay," Tiffany corrects me.

I think out loud. "Maybe Bruno was trying to extort the Zanadu for a bigger piece of the pie? They killed him to make a statement to anyone else who had that idea."

"You don't think he was killed because he roofied me?"

"You weren't roofied."

"Oh, yeah," Tiffany says, and takes a few seconds to consider the possibilities.

"I know who did it," Tiffany says. "It was that no good, rotten, self-centered, egotistical, Alix Fromound. I can't stand that evil bitch."

I ignore her invective and we're both quiet for a few minutes. "Turn left, Tiffany."

Tiffany heads back towards the Loop. "Where to?" she asks.

"I'm not sure," I answer, then reconsider. "Drive by Bruno's building."

"You want to see if the new doorman got his uniform tailored yet?"

"Yeah, that's it."

CHAPTER 19

When in doubt on a case, perform two tasks. "Wait" Jack Wayt taught me this years ago. Retrace all the steps you've taken. Maybe you missed something. Maybe you didn't combine two aspects. Maybe seeing it all in a different light will give you a new perspective. Next, retrace the money. In this case I can't—because I didn't find any money.

We sit across the street from Bruno's building and watch the new doorman in action. He's definitely much better at his job than Guido was. He opens the door for everyone, smiles politely when he does it, and says "thank you" when he gets a tip. I'm impressed.

I have a thought. "Come on," I say to Tiffany. I start to get out of the car, but a bolt of pain hits me like a rubber bullet in a street riot. I can barely stifle a cry of pain.

Tiffany is out of the car, standing at my window. "Aren't we getting out?"

"Go talk to the guy," I tell her. "Three things I want you to find out."

I give her detailed instructions on three questions to ask. She marches right up to the new guy and chats him up as if he were her new BFF. He seems to answer every question without question. If all detectives were as gorgeous as Tiffany there would be a lot more questions answered. And time saved and cases solved.

She returns to the car in five minutes.

"What did he say?" I ask.

"One, yes, he can get into the lock box of unit keys in the back. Two, Guido got fired because a lot of tenants complained about him. Three, I forgot the question, so I didn't get an answer. And four, they told him he's stuck wearing that oversized coat until they have some money in the budget for a new one."

"Two out of three isn't bad, Tiffany, but why are you so interested in the doorman's attire?" I ask.

"It's part of the new 'Nice' me, Mr. Sherlock; finding fashion fox pacs and pointing them out to people. It's another way I'm helping society."

"By the way, how is the 'Nice' you doing?"

"Parts of it I really like, like my aura improving, like not seeing myself in red, like helping the attractively challenged; but there's some parts I'm not too wild about."

"Like what?" I ask and immediately begin to worry that I'm starting to sound like Tiffany.

"Parts. I'm not sure which part, but parts."

"Well, you know what they say, Tiffany, 'Parts is parts.'"

"Whatever."

Our next stop is Lincoln Park. I have Tiffany pull up in front of the Greek Revival "two-flat" on Howe Street which the kids and I once visited via a Thug escort.

"Who lives here? Tiffany asks.

I write down the address. "I don't know. That's what we have to find out."

I have her continue down the street and park. I call Bruce Lansky, my detective friend in Evanston, a much better choice than Jack or "No-No" for obvious reasons. "Hey, instead of buying me lunch could you pull the owner of a residence for me?"

"Sure."

I provide the address. Two minutes later he says, "Wendell C. Bartlett."

"Any record?"

"None."

"Say where he works?"

"Nope."

"We can still get together for lunch, but we'll go Dutch," I tell Bruce and hang up.

I do my best to turn towards Tiffany. "Can you Google on that cell phone of yours?"

"Mr. Sherlock, you are so far behind when it comes to techie stuff, you're like living in the Stone Age without a hammer."

Tiffany finds Wendell C. Bartlett. He's the head of Equalization Inc., a financial services firm specializing in accounting systems for stock and commodities trading operations. As soon as I get home, Wendell C. Bartlett is going to have his own recipe card on *The Original Carlo*.

"Where to next?"

"Northern Trust on South Wacker Drive."

"Oh, good, I love visiting my money."

It's now late afternoon and traffic in the Loop is horrible. We inch our way towards the 31-story building. "Tiffany, how much money do you have in this bank?"

"I have no clue."

"If you can still count it, it means you don't have enough?"

"That's one way of putting it, Mr. Sherlock."

"Do you know anyone at Northern Trust whose name you could use to get a favor?"

"Don't have to," she says. "It's their job to know me."

Tiffany finds an illegal spot to park. I give her directions on what to find out. She leaves the keys in the ignition. "Now, if a cop comes, please move the car, Mr. Sherlock. My dad's getting a little pissy about my parking tickets."

"Do you blame him?"

"It's not like I've had a hundred."

"How many have you had?"

"Ninety-three."

As she gets out of the car, so do I. I figure if a cop does come and I'm not behind the wheel, by the time I do get out of my seat and into the driver's seat and drive away, that could be enough time for the car to be towed away.

Tiffany's gone for about fifteen minutes. On her return, she asks, "What are you doing in my seat?"

I give her a brief explanation before I take a long time to get out and then back in. "You didn't move my mirrors, did you?" she asks. "I hate when anybody fools with my mirrors."

"What did you find out, Tiffany?"

"The first person wouldn't tell me."

"Did you tell him who you were?"

"Yes."

"And?"

"He still wouldn't tell me."

"So, you didn't find out?"

"Of course I found out," she says. "I told the manager if he didn't tell me, I'd have my dad pull all his money out."

"What did he say?"

Tiffany pauses.

"You didn't forget, did you?"

"Let me think."

I pause.

"Oh, yeah. He said the Zanadu doesn't have an account there."

"No?"

"Then he asked me ..."

I cut her off, "He asked why you were asking?"

"No. He asked me if I wanted to go to lunch with him. I told him I already had lunch."

Tiffany turns on the ignition. "Now, where're we going?"

"I better go pick up my car."

"Oh, leave it, Mr. Sherlock. I hate that car."

My car remains the only car at AAAAA Auto. The Yellow Pages just doesn't get the results it used to. Blame the Internet.

"Three hundred eighty-six bucks."

"You're kidding?"

"Hey, shouda had this done before the warranty ran out," Albert tells me, wiping his hands on the same greasy rag as before.

"The muffler wasn't broken in 1993."

"I know," Albert says. "I was just funnin' ya."

"Seems like an awful lot of money for a muffler," I tell him.

"Especially when you consider you're spending over three hundred bucks on a car that's worth maybe five hundred."

Enough. I peel off a hundred dollar bill and hand it to him.

"Don't you have anything smaller?"

I take the hundred back and hand him a fifty. "Take it or leave it."

"The car or the money?"

Everybody's a comedian.

Back home I call the girls. Care had an especially trying day at school attempting to explain to her friends why a boat the size of Panama is now parked in the driveway of the house I used to own. I can't help her. Kelly tells me of yet another designer outfit "she just has to have" to keep up with her fellow middle school *fashionistas*. I also tell her I can't help her.

"You figure out who tried to poison Tiffany, yet, Dad?" Kelly asks.

"I'm working on it."

"Figure out who bombed the Zanadu?"

"I'm working on that too."

"How about who killed the bartender?"

"Kelly ..."

"Are you thinking outside the box, Dad?" she asks. "You should go back and, whatever you thought before, reverse it."

"Is this something you learned from me?" I ask.

"No, I saw it on a TV show."

"Thanks for the advice."

"You're welcome."

"Are you coming with us to the game on Saturday?"

"Of course, Dad," she says. "It will be the last time I get to witness total humiliation until my sister picks another sport to fail miserably at."

"See you Saturday." I end the conversation a bit differently than usual. "I sometimes wonder why, but I do love ya."

"Love ya, too."

I find an old heating pad, plug it in, and wrap it around my lumbar region. Only the right side of the pad heats up. I really wonder why I save items that only partially work. I lay down in front of *The Original Carlo* with my feet up on the coffee table, and contemplate. I can't come up with anything new because my back is killing me, even the heated side. It takes about twenty minutes to feel somewhat painless there, then the phone rings. I have to get up and answer it. It's one of those telemarketers trying to sell me a home improvement package. I hang up. Whatever happened to the No Call List? Now, I'm hurting on both sides again.

The only activity I can do to help make me feel better is to go into the kitchen, retrieve my recipe box, take out the cash, and count it. Thirty-five hundred bucks! I feel better already. Maybe I should put a down payment on a new car, or cut down my credit card debt, or take the girls someplace during my week at Christmas, or start an IRA? Or maybe pay for a back transplant, if such a procedure exists.

I return to the front room to stare again at the cards tacked up on the ugly painting. As soon as I get comfortable, the doorbell rings. Up again. I painfully hobble to the intercom box. If it's that drunk who lives below me, his drunken friend, or a door-to-door salesman, I'm going to unlock my gun and start shooting. I push the button. "Who is it?"

"It's me, Tiffany. Hurry up and buzz me in. I hate where you live."

By the time I get to my front door and unlock it, Tiffany has already walked up the three flights of stairs and is waiting impatiently to be admitted. "That is the ugliest belt I have ever seen," she says as she stares at me in dismay.

"It's not a belt. It's a heating pad."

She touches the back of the pad. "Shouldn't it be hot?"

"It doesn't work very well."

"Neither do I because I hate work," she admits as she comes in and sits on the couch. "Mr. Sherlock, I have a problem."

"Join the club." I lay back down on the floor.

"My new life coach is taking me in a direction I don't want to go."

"Which direction is that?"

"Her direction."

"Not good."

"She wants me to help spread her theory about her program to harness the power of your own smile."

And this is surprising? "How exactly does she want you to spread her theory?"

"First, she wants to use my perfect teeth in her brochure. Second, she wants me to give her a list of all my friends. And third, she wants to use my place for something like a Life Coach Tupperware Party." Tiffany hesitates. "Mr. Sherlock, it's very difficult talking to you about my problem when you're the one lying down," she tells me.

"I'm in a lot of pain, Tiffany."

"So am I. What should I do?"

"Smile."

"I'm not kidding, Mr. Sherlock."

"Whenever she asks you for something, just smile. You'll kill her with kindness."

"I've never been any good at kindness," Tiffany admits. "This is the part of the new 'Nice' me that I'm having a problem with."

"Just promise me one thing, Tiffany," I plead. "If she asks you for money, just smile, and don't give her a penny."

"I would never give anyone a penny," she says. "I hate pennies."

The phone rings. "Would you get that for me, please?"

"Sure," she says, getting up. "It's not every day I get to talk on a landline."

I listen to the one sided conversation.

"No, this is Tiffany." Pause. "Have you asked Neula out yet?"

It has to be "Wait" Jack Wayt.

"I don't care about your dumb diseases. Quit being such a jerk and ask her out." Pause. "I'll let you talk to him if you promise to take her someplace expensive." Long pause. "And wear a suit with shoes without gummy bottoms." Pause. "I know, so quit being a jerk and I won't have to tell you again."

Tiffany carries the phone over to me.

"Here. It's Detective Wayt," she says with a half-hearted smile.

"I would have never guessed."

Jack doesn't immediately complain about being sick. This must be important. I listen and hang up.

"Help me up," I plead with Tiffany. "We have to go."

"I'm not going anywhere with you if you're going to wear that atrocious-looking belt."

The place hadn't changed much since my first visit. The only real difference being I'm arriving after the shooting instead of being there during one.

Jack is commanding a team of cops, CSI techs, and a clean-up crew.

"Wait."

"What Jack?"

"I'm feeling a little lightheaded."

I survey the scene and say, "I can see why."

There're pools of blood all over the place: On the pavement where the sliding chain-link gate is open, on one side of the dumpster where I previously hid, and by the doorway which leads into the small non-descript building. I look around for a fedora, but don't see one.

"No-No," who has come along for the ride, chats with Tiffany who hops around the red puddles like a frog going from lily pad to lily pad.

"What happened?" I ask Jack.

"Shootout."

"Who won?"

"I don't suspect there were too many winners in this contest." Jack hands me a pair of plastic booties and a pair of latex gloves. "You're going to need these."

Once I'm booted up and slip on the gloves, I follow him inside the building. "You had dinner?" he asks.

"Not yet."

He opens the front door. "I doubt if you're going to want any after this."

In the front room, I count six victims, each lying in a pool of blood, some covered by plastic, and some not. There are hundreds of bullet holes in the walls. You're bound to kill somebody if you just keep firing. The place reeks with a pungent mixture of dried blood and sulfur fumes. The table and chairs, which were here before have been blasted into the corners; automatic weapons destroy furniture as well as people. A few blood splatters still trickle down the walls. The scene is reminiscent of another day long ago in Chicago—February 14, 1929, St. Valentine's Day.

"You know, Sherlock," Jack says, "with all the megabucks generated by the drug trade in this town, you'd think there would be enough to go around for everybody."

"It's greed, Jack, helped along with a double dose of stupidity."

We walk around the front room, and go into the back room where we find more of the same.

"You got any brand names to go along with the bodies?" I ask.

"I'm pretty sure one side was the Latin Kings. I'm not sure about the other."

"Find any drugs?"

"Whoever won took what was for sale, also the guns and any bling they could rip off a neck or pull off a finger," Jack informs me.

"Souvenirs."

"It's always nice to take a memento with you to remember the fun times." Jack stops at one of the victims, a woman. "I can't wait to hear what the mayor has to say about this one."

"Maybe you can make an argument about thinning the herd?" I ask, trying to come up with something positive in this disaster.

"Not when the herd keeps getting bigger and bigger."

I stop.

Jack stops. "What?"

I lean over the body. Small, young, fragile. The cigarette she was smoking is burned down to the filter, but it remains between her fingers. That's about the only part of her that isn't red. She must have been shot ten times. She sure doesn't look as good as she did the day I met her in D'Wayne DeWitt's office.

CHAPTER 20

I'm exhausted by the time I return home. I grab the blanket off the bed and spread half of it on the floor then lie down, put my feet up on the couch, and wrap the other half of the blanket over me. I fall asleep immediately. Two hours later, I'm awake, after a full color version of the massacre I visited a few hours earlier came to me in a dream.

No matter what you read, see on TV, or what anyone tells you, each time you witness the aftermath of a murder, the horrible sight is indelibly implanted into your psyche. The latest incident is always worse than the previous one because you constantly try to convince yourself that people just can't be that mercilessly brutal. No normal mind has the capability of fathoming the extent of devastation human beings can bestow upon one another. Each time you witness a scene of wanton killing, a little piece of your soul dies.

It's a little past 2 a.m. I try to get back to sleep by counting sheep or by self-hypnosis. I imagine myself floating on a cloud, and moving to every possible position to ease my aching back, but nothing works. I'm as wide-awake as a rooster cock-a-doodle-dooing.

I rise and flip on the light on the side table. *The Original Carlo* stares down at me like Miss Tamblyn, my sixth grade teacher, did when she caught me passing love notes to Mary Ellen Webster. I sit for a while then stand up and move the cards around. I mix and match pairs of suspects like a Yenta arranging an odd assortment of marriages, but because there are so few females in the mix a lot of the relationships have to be same-sex. Monroe Chevelier and Oscar the Trainer go together, but how about Monroe and Bruno, Bruno and Oscar, or Bruno and Gibby Fearn? Wendell Bartlett has got to be hooked up with CEI, the Zanadu, or both. Does Mr. Ponytail work for Mr. D'Wayne DeWitt or Mr. Rogers? Does the Behemoth know the Thug; maybe they're in the Brotherhood of Enforcers Union together? The only two which I'm positive are an inseparable pair are Arson and Sterno. I mix and match every possible combination, including Alix and Tiffany as co-conspirators. Talk about a match made in criminal heaven.

And I come up with a big fat zero.

It's close to 5 a.m. and I'm still at it. I've gotten nowhere with the folks. I might as well consider the monetary aspect of the case. What else is there to do?

If everyone is getting a piece of the Zanadu action, how much can be left? The place obviously rakes in a ton of money via its high-priced drinks. But maybe the club takes a cut from guys like Bruno who deal drugs on the premises. Or maybe there are other illegal operations going on that I've been too busy (or not smart enough) to uncover. The question is: is all that cash flow large enough to pay the bills with a lot left over to allow all the principles to enjoy their lavish lifestyles?

I think back to the case of the infamous Studio 54 nightclub in New York City. In the late-70's, the owners were raking in money hand over fist, none of which they had any intention of paying taxes on. But how do you to remove all of that moolah from the club without anybody noticing? They couldn't just carry the stuff out in their pants pockets; after all pockets are only so big, even on rich guy's pants. The solution: store the cash in the club's basement—in garbage bags and carry it out like it was the trash. Who would question trash bags being carted away? But the IRS got wise. When they busted the place they found over two million disco dollars stuffed in ump-teen Hefty trash bags.

And all I have is a tiny recipe box in a kitchen cupboard for my stash.

Money is the key to this whole mess. I'm sure of it. I know from previous cases how clubs like this are structured. The owners form limited liability partnerships with as many as thirty-four partners in the mix. They pump a ton of money into decorating the place and get the best PR firm money can buy to promote the hell out it as the "newest, hip, happening place." They pay some high-profile celebrities to party with the crowd, so that the place is packed night after night and watch the money roll in.

Cha-ching. Cha-ching. Cha-ching.

After the newness and the thrill start to wear a bit thin, the partners realize another hot spot is bound to come in soon and knock them off their throne. So, they cut back on the PR, can the celebs, water down the drinks, and milk every dime out of the place. The cash from the till becomes dividends and they chalk up hefty tax write-offs to use against previous profits—thus making profits from their losses. Soon the place is in arrears. They end up selling the building for almost as much as they put into it, start searching for another location, and create another "hip, happening place."

And I can't get to first base uncovering who owns, or who runs, or who controls the Zanadu. I've tried Google, business records, city licenses, everything except the IRS because I'm scared of asking Lloyd Holler for another favor.

The only persons I haven't had the pleasure of meeting are the guys who count the money. The guys, or maybe there're girls or maybe there're a mixture of both, who sit in the basement, count the cash from the pneumatic tube, and disperse it to whomever or wherever. I've asked around, but learned zilch. Are they trolls who live under the Kinzie Street Bridge and only come out at night to perform acts of accounting chicanery? Who do they work for? How much do they make? Do they get vacation benefits? Do they have to contribute to their own health insurance? Most importantly, how do they keep the operation secret from the rest of Chicago? Loose lips sink ships. I have to find these guys and see who's willing to talk.

I'm still sitting at 7 a.m., staring up at the cards on the *Carlo*. I hear the neighborhood coming alive outside. Cars leaving parking spots, kids on their way to school, the street sweeper sweeping away, and neighbors walking their dogs to their neighbor's lawns.

And it hits me like a cream pie right in the face.

How could I have missed this? How could I have been so stupid? It's all there, right in front of me. Why didn't I see it before? If I could move my feet like a normal person, I'd kick myself in the butt. I sit in awe of my own stupidity. It's all so simple, so clear, and so logical.

They're not carting money out of the Zanadu; they're carting it in!

Excited, I put in a call to "Wait" Jack Wayt. He doesn't pick up. I call "No-No". She doesn't pick up. I wonder if they aren't picking up together? I call Tiffany. Of course I don't expect her to pick up. She's got to be sound asleep.

"Oh, Mr. Sherlock."

"You're awake?"

"Couldn't sleep."

"Why not?"

"I had a dream about the dream I had when I got roofied at the Zanadu."

"Were you wearing red?"

"No, thank God."

"What happened in the dream?" I ask.

"I was sitting there seeing myself *see* myself, but I couldn't see

214

what it was all about."

"What was what all about?" I ask for an explanation, but I suspect her answer will be more confusing than her previous statement.

"What *me* was all about," she answers, as if this is a perfectly logical conversation.

I contemplate that for a moment then ask, "So, you couldn't sleep because what *you* are all about is what's bothering *you*?"

"Exactly."

I'm certainly glad that's all squared away.

"Tiffany, I need to use your big TV set."

"You want me to DVR a show for you?"

"No, I need to go over the DVDs from the Zanadu again."

"I can't watch that stuff ever again, Mr. Sherlock. It's too devastating. That's what started this whole mess."

"I know, but there's something I have to see. Please?" I plead nicely.

"Sure", she says with a sigh, "come on over. But take a cab. Just knowing that car of yours is parked in my building makes my stomach spaz out."

The 'L' ride downtown is hardly good therapy for a bad back, especially when you have to stand, sharing a pole grip with eight or nine other riders during rush hour. The pain subsides a bit because my mind is racing. I discover two other aspects I've missed, and how to quickly alleviate both missteps.

I hobble into Tiffany's penthouse a little after 10 a.m.

"Tiffany, you don't look good," I tell her on first sight.

"I don't?" she questions. "I should. I'm supposed to always look good. It's my mantra."

"Isn't a mantra something you repeat over and over?"

"No, that's something you say to convince yourself of something you're not sure of, like 'Blondes aren't dumb, blondes aren't dumb.'"

"Tiffany, we have to go over these tapes."

"Do I really have to look at them again?"

"Yes, because I need your help," I say as we go into her media room.

I ignore the first disc and place the second one in the machine, return to the couch, and sit next to Tiffany, who shields her eyes with her hands. "Mr. Sherlock, I hope you realize how hard it is watching the moment in time that my life changed forever."

"Bear with me. I promise this won't take long."

I fast-forward to the spot on the disc where Monroe Chevelier is chatting up Alix, Tiffany sits warding off the two overly-moussed guys, and Bruno is mixing drinks and placing the finished products on the bar already filled with cocktails. I hit *Pause* and the picture freezes in place. "Tiffany, look."

Tiffany slightly parts the fingers covering her eyes. I zoom in. "Is that a kumquat martini or a regular martini you're drinking?"

"It can't be a kumquat. Kumquats only come in martini glasses."

"Your drink has ice and olives in it."

"It must be Grey Goose or Kettle One. I drink those, too."

I hit the *Play* button and the scene continues. Tiffany covers her eyes again. I find the spot and slow the shot into slow motion. "Look at this, Tiffany."

"I don't want to see myself drop."

"No, just look way to the left. Watch the guy come between Alix and Monroe."

She parts fingers again. "Hey, that's the cock blocker."

It's too bad we can't see the guy's face, but what we can see is the guy step right between the two. "See anything weird about this?" I ask my protégé.

"No, the guy's doing Monroe a big favor."

I back up the disc and we watch it again. "See, he never faces Alix. He never speaks to her."

Tiffany drops her hands from her face. "So, you're saying this was a *no-cock*, cock block?" she asks, incredulous at the thought.

I hate that term.

"Play it again," Tiffany says, now intrigued.

"The guy didn't have any interest in Alix ..." I say as the scene slo-mo's past.

"Can you blame him?" Tiffany interrupts. "Alix is a total bitch."

"He's got something going on with Monroe."

Unfortunately, the two men go out of frame, and we see Tiffany take one more sip of the martini, start to sway, and ...

"Stop the tape! Stop the tape!" Tiffany yells as she throws her hands over her eyes.

I hit the *Power* button and the TV goes black. I wait a moment. "Tiffany, you can come out now."

Tiffany slowly lowers her hands, making sure the screen is dark.

"You may have been a victim of circumstances," I tell her.

"What does that mean?"

"I'm not sure, but I am sure your drink didn't get spiked because someone wanted to have sex with you."

"That's hard to believe because just about every guy I meet wants to deposit my dollar sign in his checking account."

"Can you blame them?"

"No," she says. "If I were a guy, I'd want to jump my bones too."

I let that comment pass—without comment. I sit for a few seconds, adjust my back into a different position, and picture in my head one more recipe card on *The Original Carlo* falling into place. I come up with a plan. I'm not sure it's a good plan, but any plan is better than the plan I had before, which was no plan.

"Tiffany, I know you're feeling a bit down today, but I have a problem only a person of your rank and status can help me with."

"You need a sponsor to get into the University Club?"

"No."

"Kemper Lakes?"

"No."

"That's a relief because with your wardrobe it wouldn't be easy getting you into the parking lot of those clubs."

"I don't dress that badly, Tiffany."

"*That* is a matter of opinion, Mr. Sherlock."

"Whose opinion?"

"Mine."

I better move on. "What I need you to do is ..."

"Fix you up with a rich woman who doesn't care that you have kids and wear Member's Only jackets?"

"That isn't a Member's Only jacket."

"Then it's gotta be a Member's Only knockoff."

"Tiffany, I need you to help me throw a very exclusive private party this evening."

"Mr. Sherlock, you've got the right girl for the job."

Like a warrior smells the blood on his weakening opponent, I sense the end of the case is near. Things are in position to fall into place. I just have to make sure that the right square pegs land in the right square holes.

Our first stop of the day is at the Northern Trust Building on South Wacker Drive. While she's driving in her usual "pedal to the metal" fashion, I give Tiffany specific directions. "Go in, surprise Monroe, and tell him he's invited to the party you're giving tonight at the Zanadu."

"Does the party have a theme, Mr. Sherlock?" Tiffany questions. "A good party needs a good theme."

"How about one of those murder mystery things?"

"Oh, yeah. Those are totally fun."

"Just don't tell anyone this one is for real."

"Why not?"

"It might spoil the surprise."

"Oh, this could be the party of the year." She's excited. Her eyes light up like a Zanadu strobe light.

We step out of the elevator and walk towards the receptionist. I add one final piece of info. "Be sure to tell Monroe to bring his friend Oscar with him."

"Does Oscar have a lot of money?" Tiffany wants everyone to have the proper monetary qualifications before she puts them on her list.

"No, but his parents do," I lie.

"Close enough."

I stop as we reach the receptionist, but Tiffany walks straight down the hall towards Monroe's office.

"Where's she going?" the receptionist asks me.

"To see Monroe Chevelier I guess."

"She can't just barge in like that," she shouts.

"God knows Monroe's not busy."

The woman relaxes. I've said what she's always thinking.

I give her a few seconds to answer an in-coming call, and say, "I'd like to see Wendell Bartlett."

"He doesn't have an office here," she informs me. I notice that she's the same receptionist who was here before. The turnover must be light.

"But he comes here all the time, doesn't he?"

"Yes."

"I was told he was coming in today," I lie again.

"He very well may be," she says. "But I don't keep his schedule."

I see Tiffany coming back towards me. I have what I need. Time to go. "Thank you, anyway," I tell the woman.

"If I see Mr. Bartlett, who should I say was here?" the receptionist asks before I can get away.

"Richard Sherlock."

"Richard Sherlock," she pauses for a moment, "you're not any relation to the famous detective, are you?"

"No. Why would you ever think that?"

The receptionist turns back to her work. I take Tiffany by the arm. We pick up the pace and get to the elevator just as it is opening. "Are Monroe and Oscar coming tonight?"

Tiffany turns to me and says, "Mr. Sherlock, nobody ever turns down an invitation to one of my parties."

I make two more phone calls from Tiffany's Lexus. Neither recipient picks up. Now, I'm worried.

"What's wrong?" Tiffany asks.

"I can't reach Jack or 'No-No'."

"Maybe because they're busy reaching for each other."

"I need their help to pull this off tonight."

"You don't want them at the party, do you?"

"Yes, they have to be there," I tell her.

"Mr. Sherlock, do you realize they're going to bring the party way down in the looks department?"

"I'll tell them to stand in the back."

Tiffany considers the situation. "I was going to hire a photographer, but not anymore."

We arrive in front of Bruno's condo building. "This won't take a minute," I tell Tiffany as I struggle to get out of the car. She gets out anyway and walks toward the front door with me. "What are we doing here?" she asks.

"I thought you might need a doorman for the party this evening," I inform her.

"I already had someone else in mind."

The new doorman comes out to greet us with a smile. "Hello," he says politely. "You know, you're here more than some of the residents," he says, still swimming around in the same dirty, stained, oversized coat.

"Could you do me a favor?" I ask, hobbling towards him like a camel on its last legs.

"Get you a wheelchair?"

"No. Tell me something," I begin. "Why did the tenants complain about Guido?"

"He used to have his buddies come over and hang out in the lobby."

"You ever see them?"

"Some of them still drop by."

"Do they share anything in common?"

"Like what?"

"Are they heavyset, stocky, big guys who kind of lumber instead of walk?"

"Come to think of it, yeah, they are."

I smile. "Thanks." I hand him a ten-dollar bill. It's nice to have money to spend on incidentals. "Let's go, Tiffany." I turn and escort her back towards the car.

"I thought you said we were here to hire a doorman for tonight?" Tiffany's more confused than she usually is.

"We are, but I got a better guy in mind."

As we get back into her car, she asks, "Mr. Sherlock, I thought you put me in charge of the party?" Tiffany is a bit miffed after hearing my second decision on the party planning. "This is something I do best."

"You are in charge, Tiffany, but it's important we have the right mix of guests."

"I wholeheartedly agree," she says firing up the Lexus. "I have about twenty-six people on my list and all of them are really hot."

"They can come, but not until later. A select few of us are going to have kind of a little get-together at the club first."

"Kind of like a pre-party party?"

"So to speak."

Tiffany smiles, happy to be back in charge. "Where to?"

"The police station, I have to find "No-No" and Jack."

"Actually, that's really good," Tiffany says. "I can tell them what to wear."

"A little late, aren't you?" the desk sergeant asks seeing me. "The ceremony is almost over."

"What ceremony?"

"Jack Wayt's award ceremony."

Tiffany and I make our way to the large squad room to see Jack, in full uniform, standing next to the Chief of Police who is at the lectern. "No-No" stands to the right of Jack with a wide smile of pride on her face. There must be thirty cops sitting in attendance.

"Jack Wayt," the Chief continues, "I want to congratulate you for not only being one of Chicago's finest detectives, with a service record unsurpassed in professionalism and proficiency, but also for breaking a long-standing record in the history of our police force. Few thought it could ever be broken. So, Jack, for thirty-nine years, seven months, and eight days of continuous service, I hereby bestow upon you The City of Chicago's Service Medal for the employee with the longest work record without a sick day taken or requested."

The applause begins and continues as the Chief drapes a medal around Jack's neck then shakes his hand vigorously. "Congratulations, Jack."

I wait until Jack shakes every hand in the room and makes his way over to Tiffany and me. Before I can speak he says, "Wait."

"What?"

"My fibromyalgia is acting up again."

"I thought only women get that disease?"

"I've come across a special strain."

"Why didn't you call in sick?"

"I will if it gets worse."

I speak sincerely. After my last request went south, I want him to grant me one more favor. "A lot of the pieces are falling into place, Jack. If I can get all the suspects in the same room, someone is going to screw up, and we'll have our murderer."

"What do you want me to do?" he asks.

I tell him.

"I can't do that."

"Of course you can, Jack. Wear that medal and you can do anything."

It takes a few more minutes to convince Jack, but I do. The next person won't be so easy.

"No, no. No way."

"You have to get him there," I tell "No-No."

"It'll be financial suicide if it doesn't work out," she says.

"Make him an offer he can't refuse."

"Like what?"

"I don't know," I admit.

"Tell him it's my party," Tiffany says to help the cause. "And my parties are famous in this town."

"It won't matter to him."

"He's got to be there," I plead with "No-No". "You've got to find a way."

We sit in her Lexus on Oak Street, just north of the Loop and less than two blocks from Lake Michigan. Tiffany refuses to get out.

"I can't do it."

"Yes, you can."

"No, I can't."

"She has to be there."

"But I can't stand being in the same room with her."

"Tiffany, get in there, go right up to her, and invite Alix to the party tonight," I say to her. "The 'Nice' you can do this."

"I think that's what I hate about the 'Nice' me," Tiffany says. "Being nice."

"She has to be there. It's important. Please," I beg nicely.

"Do I have to?"

"Yes."

"This isn't going to be easy," she says, walking slowly away.

I wait in the car, as Tiffany trudges into a swanky day spa. She re-emerges five minutes later. "She said she'd have to see if she could clear her schedule."

"Does that mean she's going to show?"

"Nothing will stop that conceited little bioché from being there."

Tiffany drives me to the Cook County Jail. "Wait" Jack Wayt should already be inside.

"See ya tonight," Tiffany says as she peels out. She'll spend the rest of the day confirming the invitees and interfacing with the caterers, the decorators, maybe even a DJ or two; and a put together a killer ensemble to die for. It'll be a hot time in the old nightclub tonight.

"Where's the babe, Sherlock?" The question is asked by a trio of guards as I go through the metal detector.

"She's busy, but she sends you her best," I tell the disappointed officers.

Jack is already waiting in the interview room when I arrive.

"Wait."

He says as I offer my hand to shake.

"I think I broke a blood vessel in one of my metatarsals when the Captain was pumping my hand like he was trying to get water from a dry well."

"I think you'll live, Jack."

"As if I had a choice," Jack says rubbing his right hand.

I fill Jack in on more of my discoveries and theories as we wait. "Most of what you've told me, you have no way of proving," Jack tells me.

"Once I figure it all out, proving it will be a mere formality," I assure him.

"Easy for you to say, Sherlock."

Dirk McGee leads Gibby Fearn into the room and immediately removes the shackles.

"Getting tired of the hotel accommodations?" I ask him.

"What do you think?"

"You have to admit, the room service is prompt."

Gibby looks at Jack. "Who are you?"

"This is Detective Jack Wayt."

It's probably good they don't shake hands.

"What's the medal for?" Gibby asks.

"Longevity," Jack answers.

"What do you want?" Gibby asks.

Questions, questions, and more questions. Having a conversation with Gibby is like over-dosing on the rules of *Jeopardy*.

I take a seat at the table to relax my back. "Gibby, I know you didn't try to blow D'Wayne DeWitt to kingdom come. I also know you weren't in on the skimming going on at the Zanadu, although you watched it go down night after night. And I'm pretty sure you'd love to get out of here. So, I'm going to ask you one last question, but you have to give me an answer and not another question."

For once, he doesn't question me.

"Would you like to go to a private party tonight at the Zanadu? I promise you will get the door prize, which is immunity for anything you say, but we will expect you to speak up when it's your turn. There'll be food, free drinks, and lots of fun people. So, if you're not busy tonight what do you say?"

"Can I bring a date?" he asks.

"Gibby, I said no questions."

"You can bring a date," Jack tells him, "as long as it's not your lawyer."

Gibby gives us a good long stare. "Sure," he says. "I could use a night out."

Jack drops me off in front of the Zanadu at five o'clock. Tiffany is supposed to meet me here now, but of course she's late. I use the time to make a phone call.

"Guido, it's Richard Sherlock."

"Yeah."

"I'm feeling pretty crummy about you being out of work, and I've taken the liberty of setting up an interview for you."

"Yeah, where?"

"The Zanadu."

A pause, a pause of interest on his part.

"I've told them all about you. They have a position open, and the VP of Operations wants to meet you."

"What's the job?"

"Floor manager."

He hesitates for a moment before answering. "What time should I be there?"

"Nine."

"Okay," he says and hangs up.

Doesn't anybody say thank you anymore?

I wait another fifteen minutes and Tiffany finally shows up. "Where have you been?"

"I had to get something new to wear tonight."

I should have known.

We go inside where the Zanadu is setting up for another night of Hip Hop bacchanalia. Bruno's replacement is behind the bar stocking vodka. His barback is loading clean glasses onto shelves. I stop in the middle of the dance floor to peer up at D'Wayne DeWitt's skybox. There's plywood in the last two panels where the glass was blown out in the explosion.

We proceed past the bar area, through the back hallway to the door marked *No Admittance*. I knock. The door lock clicks open and we step inside.

"How's the new job treating you?" I ask Massey seated at his desk.

Massey covers up the work in front of him. "Just fine."

"How are you?" Tiffany asks the Behemoth.

"Dun't know."

"Mr. DeWitt told me to tell you we have no reason to admit you into the club," Massey says.

"Speaking of Mr. DeWitt, do you know if he's in?"

"I'm not sure."

I look over to my comic book reading buddy and he tells me, "Dun't know, either."

"Let's say we all take a trip upstairs and see for ourselves?"

I don't give them a chance to argue and hurry as best I can out the door. I'm pretty close to the stairway door when Massey catches up.

"Mr. DeWitt doesn't want to see you," he informs me.

"I need to reserve a room for a private party."

"I'm throwing a very exclusive event this evening," Tiffany adds.

"I can help you with that."

I tell him. "It's going to be a coming-out party for the person who blew a hole in Mr. DeWitt's private suite."

Massey stops, gives me a long look, and punches in the code to open the stairway door.

We make our way up the flight of stairs, which for me is excruciating.

"Hello, Mr. DeWitt," I say as I enter the somewhat refurbished suite.

"What are you doing here?"

"I need to borrow your digs for a little get-together this evening."

"Not possible," he tells me.

"I'm inviting the person who tried to waste you, the person who murdered your bartender, a couple of drug dealers, a real life hoodlum or two, plus some other folks who really know how to party."

"You are?" a very flummoxed and surprised Tiffany asks

I assure Mr. DeWitt, "You're not going to want to miss it."

"Want me to escort these people out?" Massey asks Mr. DeWitt, as the Behemoth licks his lips in anticipation.

"Oh," I say to Massey, "you and your large friend are also invited. The party just wouldn't be the same without you two."

"Mr. DeWitt," Massey repeats.

Mr. DeWitt comes from behind his desk, waves Massey off, and approaches me. "This some kind of a joke, Sherlock?"

"Maybe, although I'm not sure exactly who the joke is going to be on yet."

Mr. DeWitt is about to speak, but holds his thought.

"Parties are always more fun when there is an element of surprise, don't you think?" I ask everyone.

The Behemoth is the only one who answers, "Dun't know."

"I love a good party," I tell the group.

Massey looks to his boss for the next move, but Mr. DeWitt backs off. "What if I'm busy and can't attend?" he says.

"Then someone will come and escort you," I inform him. "Trust me, Mr. DeWitt, you're not going to want to miss this one."

The man gives me one last look, and walks back behind his desk. His motion is as good as a checking the *yes* box on an RSVP invitation.

"The festivities should start around nine," I say.

"I'll have my people come and set up at around eight," Tiffany adds. "Any special dietary things I should know about?" Tiffany inquires. I think that's very thoughtful of her.

"Dun't know." Again, the Behemoth is the only one to answer.

Before we exit the Zanadu, I scribble down a list of my attendees and hand it to Tiffany. "You better give this to Arson and Sterno."

She reads the list. "Mr. Sherlock, I can't have these people at one of my parties."

"Why not?"

"They're way out of my social network, hardly my kind, and once

Alix sees this, she'll post them on Facebook and my name will be Ms. *Persona Non Party.*"

"When this party is over, that list is going to be on a lot more places than Facebook."

"Twitter?"

I go home, call the girls and remind them I'll pick them up tomorrow at ten to go to Care's basketball game.

"I want to thank you, Kelly," I tell my oldest.

"What did I do?"

"You helped me figure out the motive behind the Zanadu case."

"I did?"

"You certainly did. I couldn't have done it without you."

Kelly has no clue what she did, which I find quite amusing.

"So, you figured out who tried to poison Tiffany?"

"No, not yet."

"You figured out who iced the bartender?" she asks, getting more confused by the minute.

"No, I haven't figured that out either."

"So, Dad, what did I do?"

"You opened my mind to possibilities, just like I try to do for you, daughter dear."

"Oh my God, now I'm the one giving out life lessons."

"Like father, like daughter."

I tell my daughters I love them, remind them again to be ready on time tomorrow, and hang up.

I keep my new phone in my hand and start punching buttons to find the list of phone numbers saved. Once I find the right page it will be easy to find the right number, because, as far as I know, it's the only number that has been saved. It takes me about five minutes, but finally the number pops up. I write it down, turn the phone off, wait, turn the phone back on, and dial the number.

He picks up on the second ring.

Looking up at *The Original Carlo,* it's easy to go through the entire case step by step with him. I tell him what I know for certain, what I suspect, how I believe it was all done, and what's going to happen this evening.

He says very little, asks no questions, and gives no directions. But he does say he will be in contact with me one more time and calmly hangs up the phone.

I lie down on the floor, put my feet up, and fall asleep. Sleep, oh blessed sleep.

I awake a little before eight. I load up with another four ibuprofen, take a very hot shower, find my best pair of slacks, a shirt still in the cleaner's plastic covering, and get dressed. Just to be sure, I make a trip into the kitchen, take down the recipe box in the cupboard, and open it. I count the money, smile, and return it to its hiding place. Just before I leave, I grab my faux leather jacket from the hall closet.

It's time to party.

CHAPTER 21

"You wore that!" is Tiffany's opening comment upon meeting me in front of the Zanadu.

"I like this jacket," I tell her. "It makes me feel good."

She looks gorgeous in a tight blue mini-dress, matching 4-inch heels, and a luminous gold choker around her neck. Her blonde hair shimmers in the neon light. "How could something so atrocious make you feel good?" she asks.

"Because when I put it on, it proves I'm no slave to fashion."

We walk past the long line waiting to get in. "Are we set up inside?"

"I went with the canapés, the ramaki, and avocadoes wrapped in bacon and shaped like a heart."

"Bacon isn't good for you, Tiffany."

"I was going to go with the shrimp, but I never know what to do with the little tail after I eat one," she admits.

"Life can be difficult."

We reach Arson and Sterno.

"You wore that? Again?" Sterno says to me.

"Considerin' some of the outfits your other friends are wearin', we've had to tell people the private event is a costume party," Arson adds.

"Who's here so far?" I ask.

Arson shows me the list. I scan it quickly then I show the pair a photo. "This guy show up yet?"

"He came about ten minutes ago."

"Still here?"

"Yeah."

I turn to Tiffany. "Go get Jack Wayt, and tell him to get down here right now."

"No problem," she says and hustles off.

I point to another name on the list. "When this guy arrives, tell him how to get to Mr. DeWitt's suite."

A tap comes on my shoulder. I turn.

"My orange jumpsuit would have looked better than the jacket you've got on, Sherlock."

Before I can answer, Sterno's hand pushes past me. "Mr. Fearn, we really miss you."

"How's business boys?" Gibby asks.

"Not as good as when you were here."

I whisper into Gibby's ear, "Don't forget to join the party when it gets going."

"Would I have it any other way?" Gibby nods at me. "Later, you guys," he says to Arson and Sterno with a wave of his arm as he enters his former place of employment.

Jack arrives. "Wait."

"What Jack?"

He holds his hands to his ample stomach, "I feel a bit of food poisoning setting in."

"How many of those avocado bacon wraps did you eat?"

"Let's just say more than two."

I remind him of his prey for the evening. "Invite him up as soon as you see him, okay?"

"You sure you know what you're doing, Sherlock?"

"Of course I do," I lie. Since Jack knows I'm lying, I don't really consider it a lie.

Arson parts the rope and I amble up the path towards the main door of the club. I hear a voice from the line yell out, "You're letting that guy in wearing that?"

"He's in a scavenger hunt," Sterno answers the critic.

My back is feeling a little looser. I'm able to walk and stand upright, although the flight of stairs to Mr. DeWitt's skybox is a bit painful.

The moment I walk in the door, I see Tiffany has had her designer place taped outlines of dead bodies on the floor to give the party its murder mystery theme. There are streamers made of yellow crime tape hanging down, with canisters of gelled light illuminating an eerie film noir lighting scheme. The candies in the Waterford bowls are chocolates in the shape of bullets. There is a large poster on the back wall, which is actually a blow-up of the box cover of the *Clue* board game. Tiffany certainly knows how to set the party mood. But at this instant, Tiffany is hardly in a good mood. She and Alix are going at it like a couple of designer pit bulls.

"This party blows, big time," Alix barks at Tiffany. "This group looks weirder than a Star Wars convention."

"You go to Star Wars conventions?" Tiffany snaps back at her.

"No, but I've seen pictures."

"Give the party time," Tiffany suggests.

"An extra decade wouldn't help this get together."

"I'm telling you, it's gonna be great," Tiffany says. "Just you wait."

"Sure, why not?" Alix says. "It's not every day I get invited to the Ugly Bug Ball."

Tiffany looks over at me with more blame in her eyes than George Winston has jewelry.

I survey the situation. D'Wayne DeWitt sits behind his desk as if it's a barrier to keep him safe from social predators. Monroe and Oscar stand over against the wall, sipping Stoli and counting each other's cuts which are easily seen since each wears a designer T-shirt two sizes too small. Massey stands with his arms folded across his chest. The Behemoth is next to him, his suit fitting much nicer since either Jack or "No-No" enforced my rule of having to check your Glock at the door before entering the party zone. Gibby Fearn sits across the room, sipping a cocktail and tossing darts with his eyes at Mr. DeWitt. The most outlandishly dressed of the evening has to be Lloyd Holler, who wears checkered, bell-bottoms, a tie-dyed T-shirt, and two strands of love beads; all that's missing is an Afro wig. I guess the only way "No-No" could get him to come was to promise he could relive his days as a disco dervish. Guido chows down at the buffet table, not what I would do at a job interview. There's an older man in a three-piece suit who I've never met, plus two dumpy, middle-aged guys who wear square-bottomed shirts outside their pants that end at their belt line. I wouldn't be caught dead in one of those. I look over at "No-No," who nods her head, telling me "these are the guys."

I work my way over to the battling females. Tiffany grabs me by the arm, pulls me aside, and says in my ear. "What are you trying to do to me? This is the worst party ever." She puts particular emphasis on *ever*.

"Relax, Tiffany. It may not look good now, but I promise you it's going to get hotter very soon."

"It better, Mr. Sherlock. My total reputation is on the line."

"What's he doing here?" Alix says to me, as she turns towards the other attendees.

"Who?"

"Him." She points.

"Guido, the doorman?"

"Better keep him away from Monroe."

"Why?" I ask.

"It could get rough," Alix spits out.

"Why?"

"He's the cock blocker."

"What?"

"That's him, no doubt about it."

"You're sure?"

"I'm always sure," she says. "And I'm also sure this party blows, big time."

I take a long look at Guido. One round peg fills a very big round hole. In my head, another recipe card fits into place on *The Original Carlo*.

"I think I'll go over and squeeze one of Monroe's muscles," Alix says. She cocks her head towards Tiffany. "Watch me make it bigger." Alix walks away, smug as a gold bug in a Persian rug.

Tiffany starts to lunge at Alix, but I manage to hold her back. It's all she can do to contain herself. "You got to do something, Mr. Sherlock. No amount of 'Nice' Tiffany being nice is going to save this party."

Luckily, the Hispanic barback enters the room to pick up dirty dishes and glasses, just as Jack escorts Mr. Ponytail inside. Once all three are in the room, I signal Jack to stand guard at the door to deter any guest wanting to leave early.

I walk to the center of the room where I can easily see everyone. And it's time to start the festivities.

"If you'd all like to get a drink or a snack and find a seat, we can get going," I announce to the assembled.

"What the hell is this all about?" Mr. DeWitt asks from the other side of the room.

"It's going to be a game of show and tell," I say to Mr. DeWitt as well as the other guests. "I'm going to start off by doing the telling and then hopefully you all will join in with the showing."

Mr. DeWitt stays at his desk. Massey and the Behemoth pull up chairs next to him. Alix, Monroe, and Oscar take the couch. Guido grabs a chair in front of the boarded up panel, with Tiffany not too far from him. Lloyd Holler sits smack dab in the middle of the room so no one can miss him. Gibby sits on the couch that faces Mr. DeWitt. "No-No" stands next to Jack, making a formidable barrier to anyone or anything coming in or out. Mr. Ponytail positions himself close to the buffet, obviously very hungry. The barback finds the farthest corner in the room and sits on the floor. The others find a place to sit or they lean against a wall, not really knowing what the heck they are doing here.

"Thank you all for joining us. I thought that since this whole, silly magilla began in a party atmosphere, it is only right to have it end in one too." I pause to smile, but get none in return. "It all started innocently enough when my young assistant Tiffany fell off a barstool."

"I didn't fall off, Mr. Sherlock," Tiffany is quick to correct me.

"Why don't we let all my Facebook friends be the judge of that," Alix says to Tiffany. "I have pictures."

"You wouldn't dare," Tiffany screams back at her nemesis.

"Girls, girls. Let's not squabble," I say. "No, Tiffany didn't fall off in the traditional sense. She sipped a cocktail which didn't agree with her and she dropped to the floor like a sack of flour from a kitchen counter."

"See," Tiffany says to Alix.

"We can consider this action the inciting incident to our story," I continue. "Tiffany's unfortunate consumption of the wrong martini becomes the fly in the ointment, the bad cog in the gearshift, or the spanner in the works so to speak." I pause to let this all sink in. "What happens to Tiffany screws up everything for everybody else. If any of you wants to blame anyone for the mess they're in, she sits before you."

"Oh, Mr. Sherlock, how can you say such a thing?"

"Bear with me, Tiffany. The story is just beginning." I pace around the room and all eyes follow me. "When I arrived that night to investigate, nerves were already beginning to fray. I snoop around, watch the tapes, and talk to witnesses. I must have been learning more than I should because someone tried to scare me off by kidnapping me, driving me way across town to some dilapidated building that functions as the neighborhood pharmacy, and either by bad timing or perfect staging, I find myself in the middle of a shoot-out worthy of a Bruce Willis epic.

"I usually scare pretty easily, but I know that Tiffany's dad either gets an answer to who drugged his daughter or yours truly is out of a job; even though getting fired may be a blessing, since I hate what I have to do to make a living."

I pause to turn to Massey. "By the way, Massey, for future

reference, you might want to inform Arson and Sterno the worst person they can allow through their velvet rope is a nosy detective."

"I'll make a note of it," Massey says without writing anything down, his way of not listening to me.

"So, as I wade through the case, getting absolutely nowhere, another unforeseen upending of an apple cart takes place. Somebody bashes in the skull of the bartender who was voted most likely to have spiked Tiffany's drink. Unfortunately, I'm the one who finds the body, which is hardly something I like to do. Poor Bruno the bartender, who was living a palatial lifestyle off a mixologist's usually skimpy salary, is dead. And from what we find in Bruno's apartment, it's pretty clear he had a lot more items on sale at his bar station than just kumquat martinis."

I move over to stand behind Guido. "The doorman at the building where Bruno lived, my man Guido here, knows all about Bruno's second income and would give his eye teeth to get a job at the Zanadu and pick up where Bruno left off." I take my hands from the guy's broad shoulders and point over to Massey. "That's the guy you want to talk to about a position—if you get the chance." I move away slightly. "Guido and Bruno have something else in common, but I'll get around to that in a minute." I pause. "Let's go back to the Zanadu."

"Let's not and say we did," Mr. DeWitt says from his desk.

I walk toward him. "Mr. DeWitt, did you know that the guy who invented the pneumatic tube was also the guy who invented the first tricycle and underwater paint? It was some Scotsman named William Murdoch. A pretty smart guy. His tube invention caught on big time in the 1800's. Hundreds of high-pressure tubes were used to messenger stuff from one part of a factory to another. I'll bet that most of you don't know that this very building used to be a factory and that it had a pneumatic tube installed in it. It's still in place and it still works really well. Doesn't it?"

"Incredibly well," Gibby says.

I point out Gibby before continuing. "For those of you who haven't met Gibby Fearn, he's the one responsible for making the Zanadu the most popular club in the city." I clap my hands for effect. "His tireless dedication to throwing the biggest bashes, hangin' with the hippest hip-hoppers, and bringing in people with the right street cred has made the place more profitable than two dozen McDonald's. Gibby did all the work, but someone else took all the credit."

"Exactly," Gibby agrees. He shoots a cold stare at Mr. DeWitt.

"Every two hours, Gibby and his buddy here," I say as I move over towards the Behemoth, "go around and collect the cash and receipts from the registers. Back in the office, Gibby separates the cash from the credit cards, puts the cash in a cylindrical container, and shoots it through the tube, down to the basement where these two gentlemen …" I interrupt myself to point at the two guys in the decidedly frumpy shirts. "… count it, divide it, and prepare it for its next journey. Am I close, Gibby?"

"Very. I had no control of the money once it left my desk," he speaks as promised.

"But they did treat you well, didn't they?" I ask Gibby. "And they provided you with a bodyguard."

Gibby points at the Behemoth. "Except, he wasn't there to protect me. He was there to watch me," Gibby says.

"That's what I thought." I smile at the Behemoth.

The ogre doesn't smile in return, but says, "Dun' know."

I move next to the two guys "No-No" had brought upstairs to join the party. "And these are the gentlemen who had the enviable job of sitting in a dark, dank basement like King Midas counting his gold."

"We's plumbers, jus' here to fix a leak," the guy on the left says.

"Certainly dressed for it," I say and compliment facetiously, "I love those shirts."

I see Tiffany's eyebrows rise. She never knows when I'm kidding.

"If you're plumbers, where are your tools?" "No-No" asks them.

"In da truck."

"Where's the truck?"

"Da valet's got it."

"You don't valet a plumbing truck," "No-No" says.

"Your job, boys," I continue, "was to create a second set of books for the Zanadu, record the skim for the owners, and make sure any profit was IRS-proof."

"What?" Lloyd Holler hollers from his seat.

"It gets better, Lloyd. Just hold on."

"Oh, no," Lloyd argues. "It doesn't get any better than this."

"Wrong, Sherlock," Mr. DeWitt says from the other side of the room. "Check the returns, you'll see almost a half-million dollars in profits from the Zanadu last year, all of which we paid taxes on."

"Maybe so, Mr. DeWitt," I say directly to him, "but you know and I know that the Zanadu was more than just a profitable nightclub. The Zanadu was like a funnel. Cash came in, not just from the drunks at the bar, but from the outside as well." I come back across the room to the buffet table where Mr. Ponytail eats. "At least once a night, a suitcase full of cash arrives via this gentleman, after he makes the rounds to a number of other retail establishments owned and operated by you and your Zanadu partners."

"You must have me mistaken for another guy," Mr. Ponytail speaks. "I'm an independent limo driver. If anyone ever needs a limo to the airport, e-mail or text *Fly Me to O'Hare.com*," he says to the group and pulls out a stack of business cards to pass out.

I stop him before he can use my party to advertise his services. How tacky.

"There's no better place to launder cash than a nightclub that takes in a ton of it." I say with authority. "The Zanadu was the answer to the problem of what you do when you have too much cash on your dirty hands."

"You can't prove that," Mr. DeWitt says.

"No, but I don't have to," I tell him. "All I'm interested in is finding out who spiked Tiffany's drink, which brings me back to that fateful night."

I look around the room. Alix seems quite fascinated at my show and tell. Monroe and Oscar are a bit pale, I'm sure they will hit the tanning booth before the big Posedown in Pittsburgh. Mr. DeWitt is pissed. Gibby Fearn shows a bit of smugness, while Lloyd Holler can't wait to hear more. Massey takes on a nervous twitch. Tiffany loves every minute of it. Her party is now destined to become a classic in the Chicago social scene. Jack and "No-No" hold hands as they guard the door.

"Bruno had an okay business dealing the usual cocaine, oxy, uppers, and downers over the counter at the bar. But he wanted more. Bruno was branching out into the very lucrative business of sports medicine. He had seen the real drug pros at work from his spot at the Zanadu, and figured there was a niche for him in the better muscles through chemistry field. Instead of pushing pills to party brats, Bruno was going to be a real drug kingpin. And, to keep his distance from the street hoi polloi, like a real drug dealer, he employs a partner in his sports venture as his salesman and distributor."

I pause, turn toward the physical trainer in the room and say, "Any of this ring any bells, Oscar?"

"I didn't even know the guy existed," Oscar announces to the group.

"Oscar is sick of being a personal trainer, dealing a few pills here and there. He wants to make some real money filling the prescriptions on a regular basis. Who would be better to do that than a guy who hangs around gyms every day?" I point at Oscar. "You knew all the players. You knew what they wanted. Look what you've done with Monroe; proof positive that steroids are an athlete's best friend. The only problem is you don't have any money to get started, and you don't have the connections Bruno has."

"You got the wrong guy," Oscar pleads his innocence.

I digress for a few moments to hopefully make things a little easier to understand in the future. "When a regular business has competition, it fights on price or selection. It offers discounts, advertises, whatever it takes to maintain its market share. In the illegal drug business, you kill the competition—by killing the competition. Al Capone did it on St. Valentine's Day. And unfortunately the same type of competition has been evident in Chicago over the past few months."

I turn to face Oscar. "So, Oscar, you decide the best way to break into the business, is to horn in on Bruno's action. You go to your benefactor Monroe, state your case, and come up with a plan."

"I did not," Oscar says.

I turn to face the guests. "Monroe is full of money and not just from his daddy. Monroe has a short list of clients who pour hundreds of thousands of dollars into the CEI hedge fund where he works. He is quite persuasive in acquiring investors and getting them to part with their money, because every night an unmarked armored truck drives into his building and drops off loads of cash which will be invested in the fund." I pause to allow the info to sink in. "And the best thing about Monroe's job is that it allows him lots of free time to bulk up and compete in body building events, like the Posedown in Pittsburgh in a couple of weeks. Let me be the first to wish you good luck in the competition, Monroe."

"If anyone's taking drugs, it's you Sherlock," Monroe says.

"Mr. Walter C. Bartlett over there, whom I haven't had the pleasure of meeting personally, figured out a way to launder the cash into the fund without ringing any bank disclosure bells. Correct, Mr. Bartlett?"

"Incorrect."

"You are the Walter C. Bartlett who lives in a mansion on Howe just north of Armitage?" I ask, already sure of his answer.

"No."

"No?" This can't be right. Or he's lying.

"I sold the place three months ago," he emphatically states. "You want to see the paperwork? I got it."

I hate being wrong, and I really hate being wrong right now. "Who'd you sell it to?"

"Some no-name corporation that paid over my asking price in cash."

I hesitate and look over at Jack who knows I've screwed up. I try to fake it. "Yeah," I say, "I knew that."

I hope someone believes me.

Walter Bartlett speaks with resounding clarity when he says, "This is all absolutely absurd."

"I'll be the final judge of that," Lloyd Holler says before blowing his nose into a handful of Kleenex.

"I've had enough of this idiocy," Walter says. "I want to go home."

"Walter, hang in, would ya?" I say more than ask the man. "It's a party, enjoy yourself."

Mr. Bartlett does his best to suppress his irritation by folding his arms across his chest and grinding his teeth.

I reach into a bowl, grab a handful of party treats and offer them to Mr. Bartlett, "Here, have a chocolate bullet."

I take a minute or two to get my act back together. I take a breath, move back into the center of the room and continue, "Somehow, either Bruno or Guido find out about Oscar's plan, and come up with their own plan to nip this thing in the bud."

"This is worse than a dime store novel, Sherlock," Guido tells me and the assembled.

It is really too bad there are no dime stores any longer, the closest thing we now have are 99 cent stores.

I take a beat before I continue. "So, all is coming into play, all at the same time. A showdown is inevitable. And it all happens the night Tiffany and Alix sit on opposite barstools at the Zanadu Club." I take another beat to heighten the excited party atmosphere. "Bruno and his new employee are going to prove a point to Monroe and Oscar. Bruno spikes a martini with a ton of steroids. A couple of swallows of the PED concoction and Monroe will be knocked for a loop, which should be enough to convince him to mind his own drug business. That was the plan. The problem is the cocktail never reaches Monroe. Tiffany picks it up by mistake, takes one sip, and almost goes into anaphylactic shock when the chemicals hit her system. She drops off the barstool like a boulder in an avalanche."

"See," Tiffany says to Alix, "I told you."

Alix shoots Tiffany an *I don't give a damn* look with her cold, piercing eyes.

I step between Guido and Tiffany. "Am I close here, Guido?"

"You're whacked, asshole. This is all a bunch of bullshit."

"So, you weren't dealing steroids while on the job as a doorman?"

"No."

"And you didn't bash in Bruno's skull with a fireplace poker?"

"No."

"How about you, Oscar?"

"How about me what?

"Did you kill Bruno?"

"No."

"Monroe?"

"Don't be ridiculous."

"You, Mr. DeWitt?"

"Shut up."

I look at the Behemoth. "How about you?"

"Dun't know."

Well, even with his answer, I can safely take the Behemoth out of the mix.

"Somebody in this room killed him. And if you want to make this easier and just own up to it, I'd really appreciate it."

No one speaks up. It was worth a try.

I turn to the barback, still seated in the corner in the back of the room. "You saw Bruno spike the drink, didn't you?"

"*No hablo Inglés.*"

239

"He told you, 'you'll be back in Juarez if you say anything,' didn't he?"

Anybody who listens as intensely as this kid does knows how to speak English.

"*No hablo Inglés.*"

"Then Bruno punches you in the face to make his point clear."

The kid rubs his still swollen eye.

"This is stupid, ridiculous, dumb bullshit," Monroe says.

I move to the back of the room. "Mr. DeWitt," I address my ex-employer, "was the money-man at the Zanadu. He got his drug-dealing buddies to help put up the original dough, he figured out how to launder megabucks through the place, and how to invest it into hedge fund securities. Right, Mr. DeWitt?"

"You're smokin' something, Sherlock," is his comeback.

"But you got greedy, didn't you?"

"Dis is bullshit." Mr. DeWitt's comebacks are going downhill rapidly.

"So, Mr. DeWitt sets off a piss-poor explosive in his own office."

"And why would I do something as stupid as that?" he asks me.

"Because your fellow Zanadu partners suspect you are taking more than your share of the illegal profits and you wanted to throw suspicion off of yourself."

"No way."

"You rig up a lousy explosive device, set it up in your office on an off-night for the club, get under your desk, and detonate it via your cell phone."

"Totally ridiculous," Mr. DeWitt exclaims.

"Then why didn't you get showered with glass? Why didn't you get drilled to the wall when the bomb went off? Why didn't you ask 'How much smoke does one of these things give off?' to the guy who sold you the stuff?"

"I didn't do any of that. And if I did, why would I?" DeWitt questions me.

"I already told you. You knew your buddies were starting to smell a much wealthier rat than themselves."

"No way."

"One of them went so far as to hire a detective, in case you didn't know."

"Who?"

"Me," I say distinctly.

Mr. DeWitt doesn't choose to comment on my revelation. I can't blame him.

"You don't have any proof of any of this," Guido says. "If you did, you would've already made an arrest."

"Correct," I say. "That's why I'm once again going to ask for a confession." I wait. "Which one of you killed Bruno?"

Nobody speaks up.

"Anybody?"

Dead silence.

Darn.

I pace over to where Oscar sits, give him a quick head nod, as if to say *You?*

"I was in no way involved in any drug deals or killing anybody," Oscar says.

"Didn't you get busted for dealing PED's the other day?"

"False accusation," Oscar says. "My lawyer's got me as good as out on that charge."

"And you can thank Monroe for that," I tell him, bringing him down one notch.

"This party's over," Mr. DeWitt says. "Get out of my office."

"Wait," I sound like Jack Wayt. "I've got an idea. Let's play a game within this game."

"We're all tired of playing your games," Monroe says.

I position myself beneath the board game poster. "It'll be like the board game *Clue*. We can go around the room and all come up with who, what, where and how."

"Yeah," Tiffany says. "Colonel Mustard, in the drawing room, with the candlestick."

I can hear Jack's audible sigh from over by the door. Hopefully, this is from too many bacon wrapped avocados.

"I'll start." I pause, walk all the way around the room, and end up right behind Oscar. At this point I don't know who did it. Being wrong with Walter Bartlett has thrown me off my game. I picture *The Original Carlo* in my head, replace the old Bartlett card with a new one, get even more confused, and decide to throw caution to the wind. I blurt out: "It was Guido, in Bruno's apartment, with a fireplace poker."

Guido sits up straight. "You're full of shit, Sherlock."

I'm not sure if it was the way he said it or if something clicked when he stood up to scream at me, but all I can see is Guido in his stained uniform coat with dark, rusty, red dots and blotches going up the sleeve. I got nothing to lose, so I walk towards him "Maybe you were angry, maybe you two had a fight, maybe you wanted to be the boss, who knows? But, the deadbolt on the door was locked, and you were the one with access to the key."

I'm now only a few feet away from Guido, staring right into his eyes. "You killed him. And all I have to do is have the stains on your doorman's coat analyzed and see if they match the bloodstains on the walls."

Guido bolts upright, and throws a fist into my gut. Ouch. I feel it all the way to my sore back. Guido goes left as I go down. I look up to see him snatch the Waterford water pitcher off the coffee table with his right hand, grab Tiffany with his left, wrapping her up in a tight choke hold. He's backing up as Jack and "No-No" come at him. I can hear as well as feel the beginning chaos in the room.

Tiffany screams, "Ahh, I can't breathe … I can't breathe." She kicks and twists her body, trying to get free. "And I hate pain."

I stagger, get to my feet, and straighten up as best as I can. "Let her go, Guido."

I see him go crazy-eyed. He's sweating and shaking. Ears turning red. His muscles tighten and his veins bulge. If I were to Google *Roid Rage* right now, I'd see a similar picture, but I don't know how to Google on my new phone.

Tiffany continues screaming. "Help me, Mr. Sherlock … I'm too … beautiful … to die."

"I'll bash her face in if you don't let me go," Guido says between froths from his mouth.

"Not … my face," Tiffany screams. "Anyplace … but … my … face."

"Shut up, bitch!" Guido swings the Waterford upward; it's now poised to strike Tiffany right in the kisser.

Tiffany's eyes go wide as Frisbees. "Ahhhh." And she faints dead away.

If you have ever had to pick someone up who is fast asleep or maybe even dead, you know it's a very difficult thing to do; hence the term: *dead weight*. Lifting a body with no muscle tone whatsoever is like trying to handle a large, weirdly shaped, unwieldy bag of sand. It's next to impossible. Yet another reason why murderers roll bodies up in carpets before they carry them away.

Tiffany is no exception. She slumps in Guido's arms like a worn-out Gumby doll—a very well-coiffed, well-manicured, well-dressed Gumby doll. The instant Guido tries to secure his grip on her I make my move and throw my entire body on the arm that holds the Waterford. I twist the pitcher out of his hand and it falls on the carpet, thankfully unbroken. Waterford is really expensive.

Now we're a human Hoagie sandwich with me and Guido two halves of the roll and Tiffany as a very limp piece of luncheon meat. Guido pulls one way, I push the other. Neither of us can shake the other off. Others are trying to grab us, but Guido throws his body to the left. I go with him and we crash into the sheet of plywood like a bowling ball scoring a strike. We go down hard and flop around on the floor, half-way in and half-way out of the room, dangling above the packed dance floor below us while some rapper wails out "Slap that Bitch" over and over again on the sound system.

Guido's squirming, I'm holding on, and Tiffany does nothing. We're a very mismatched three-some, heading for a very hard landing. I look down. My entire upper torso hangs out of the room. But so do my companions'. Did I mention that I hate heights? I hold onto Tiffany, whose lithe, slender body is like jelly in my hands.

Guido's got a hold of her too, but his arms are slipping as he screams, "Get away or I'll take her down with me."

I won't let go of Tiffany. Guido is starting to fall. Tiffany and I are going along with him. I'm holding on to a piece of wood frame for dear life. The three of us inch closer and closer to an inevitable quick trip down to the floor below. The dancers below are oblivious to our plight. I wonder if they can break our fall.

And a shot rings out.

This changes everything. Alix screams. Bodies dive for cover. Furniture is going every-which-way. I'm holding onto Tiffany, while my back is going into torturous agony beyond my wildest estimations and capabilities for dealing with pain.

I feel two strong hands latch on to the back of my jacket. They jerk me upward. I clutch Tiffany, struggling to pull her with me. Guido also hangs on tight ... and I see a fist smash into Guido's privates like a sledgehammer. Guido's grip is broken. Tiffany comes with me. Now, with nothing to have and to hold, Guido goes past the plywood, past the floor's edge, and into downward flight to the dance floor below.

Splat.

There are a few screams from the patrons below, but mostly what is heard is the revelry of kids heralding a new exciting dance move.

I'm on the floor, away from the open window, next to the comatose Tiffany. There's noise and commotion all around, but all I can feel is the pain in my back. I twist to my left, "Tiffany, Tiffany, are you okay?" I hold her in my arms and cradle her head. "Get me some water," I yell at the top of my lungs.

The chaos continues. Alix's screaming is joined by Monroe's, who's not too happy to be there himself. Walter Bartlett lies on the floor with his head in his arms. Some of the partiers are scurrying out. "No-No" is rubbing her now-sore hand after throwing the final punch in Guido's life.

"Freeze!" Jack Wayt lets loose at the top of his lungs.

All activity in the room stops, except for Gibby Fearn coming to my side with water. "Hold her head up."

"That you, who fired?" I hear Jack ask "No-No."

"No, no," she answers. "I thought it was you."

"You?" Jack asks a body close to him.

"Dun't know," the Behemoth answers.

A minute or two elapses. We all need a break.

Gibby tries to pour water past Tiffany's lips, but that doesn't work. He takes a little and splashes it on her face."

I hear Alix say, "She's going to be pissed if you ruin her make-up."

Tiffany starts to stir.

"Oh ... Mr. Sherlock," she says softly.

"Relax, Tiffany. Don't talk."

"It happened again."

Nobody listens to me.

I can't, but everyone else in the room rises to their feet. This is due to Detective Neula "No-No" Noonan removing her gun from her purse and pointing it at the assembled. "No, no," she says, "nobody move."

Everyone's hands rise to her direction except D'Wayne DeWitt. He remains quietly seated in his desk chair. His head tilted back, resting on the cushion, a blank expression on his face. There is a small quarter-inch hole in the middle of his forehead. Not much blood leaks out of this wound, but a steady stream is pouring out the back of his head, in the spot the police refer to as the *exit wound*. Due to the amount pooling on the seat, I'm afraid the resale value of this fancy, ergonomic, desk chair is going to be nil.

"Everybody keep their hands up, until I say so," "No-No" orders the partygoers.

As Jack pats each down searching for a firearm, Tiffany flops around in a half-in, half-out, physical and mental state—a different half-in, half-out state than she's usually in. We stay on the floor together for I'm not sure how long until a bunch of Chicago cops run into the room and handcuff everybody except Lloyd Holler.

"If you don't want to be audited for the rest of your life, you get those shackles away from me," he threatens.

"Don't you know who I am?" Alix tells the cop who cuffs her. "Just wait 'til my daddy hears how you manhandled me. He'll have your badge, your ugly uniform, and your flat feet in the cafeteria line serving up mac and cheese."

"Yeah, yeah. We hear that everyday, lady," the cop says.

Two paramedics slap an oxygen mask on Tiffany, and go to work reviving her. Two more run right past me to Mr. DeWitt. What am I chopped liver?

Jack helps separate the good eggs from the bad, lining up two different sets of partiers.

The paramedics continue to work on Tiffany. I insist she be taken into the ER for observation. "She's got great insurance." I assure them.

After Tiffany is on the gurney, one EMT questions me on what I want. I contemplate asking for a ride to the Barnes & Noble to finish the *Oh, My Aching Back* book.

With Tiffany in an ambulance, one group escorted to a waiting paddy wagon, and Gibby, Alix, and the barback released, Jack and "No-No" come over and sit with me.

"Guido dead?" I ask.

"No-No" says, "Let's just say his music's stopped."

"Sorry about your coat," Jack tells me.

"What's the matter with my coat?" I ask.

"No-No" helps me get it off and I can see the entire back panel is ripped beyond repair.

"It gave way when I grabbed you," Jack says.

"Damn. I really liked this jacket," I tell them.

"Why?" "No-No" asks.

"It was the only club that let me be a member," I confess.

We take a few minutes and just sit.

"You have it all figured out before you got here tonight?" Jack asks.

"Every last word of it."

"You're lying."

"Yeah, I am," I admit. "You think I would let Tiffany sit next to a murderer? Her father would have me killed if I did that."

"Tell Tiffany," "No-No" says. "I got a picture of Alix in handcuffs. She can post on the Internet if Alix tries anything funny."

"I'm sure she'll appreciate that." I pause. "You get all the right people in the right paddy wagons?" I ask.

"Yeah," Jack says. "But most of them will be lawyered up and back out on the street before this place closes tonight."

"What about Mr. DeWitt?"

"Whoever shot him was a great shot," Jack says.

"The good news is we got plenty to keep Lloyd Holler busy until he retires," "No-No" says.

"I'll bet he's happier than the Village People during a sold out reunion concert."

Jack gives me a gentle pat on the shoulder. "Thanks, Sherlock. You did a good job."

"I had a good teacher."

Jack and "No-No" help me to my feet and I start to walk, although not very well. "You two back to being an item?" I have to ask.

"I'm going to quit eating," "No-No" says. "And Jack's going to learn how to commit."

I bet that's going to work out real well, I think, but don't say.

"I'll have a squad car take you home," Jack says. "Are you going to be okay?"

"I have to be. We have our last basketball game tomorrow."

"And you're playing?" "No-No" asks the crumbled me.

"No, I'm the coach."

CHAPTER 22

I had a horrible night's sleep; not only was my back killing me, but my head joined in on the fun. My brain is being flogged worse than a galley slave who refuses to row, row, row the boat.

I get myself out of bed, grip my head between my hands, and stumble into my front room. *The Original Carlo* stares down at me like God stared down at Adam finishing his apple.

Something is wrong. It doesn't fit. I missed something. But what?

I retrace every card, every line, every suspect, every scenario, and the only result is that my headache aches even worse. Walter Bartlett selling his house three months before my visit is the monkey wrench thrown into the teeth of my perfectly oiled machine. I'm sure he's the one who finagled the Zanadu money into CEI, but if he wasn't the buddy of Mr. Rogers, who was? Or did Mr. Rogers even have a buddy? And who is Mr. Rogers? I realize now, I never really bothered to find out, amazing how money can cloud your thinking.

I take a shower. I load up with ibuprofen and try to do some *Oh, My Aching Back* exercises, but can't perform a single one. I'm not in as much back pain as I was last night, but I'm still hunched over like an AARP member, ambling along without his walker.

I leave my apartment, giving myself an extra half-hour to pick up my girls and get to the game. I'm glad I did, because it takes me almost ten minutes to navigate the three flights of stairs from my door to the street. When I finally get to my Toyota, which is parked a block away; I'm met with a very big surprise—the Thug. He leans against his limo sporting a brand-new grey fedora with a red feather on the left side of the headband.

"No. You can't kidnap me today. I'm the basketball coach and the game starts in an hour."

The Thug adjusts the gun behind his back. It looks like I'm going for another ride.

The driver's door opens and guess who gets out—the Behemoth.

"What's he doing here?" I ask the Thug.

"Twin brudda."

"You two are twins?"

"I'm older," the Thug says proudly.

"Fraternal twins?" I ask.

"We din't go to college," the Thug replies.

The Behemoth faces me. I ask him, "How'd you get out of jail so quickly?"

"Dun't know."

These two must have had hundreds of fascinating conversations from the womb all the way to today.

"Forget it, guys. I'm not going anywhere with you." I move towards my car, but the bruddas block me like an offensive NFL offensive line. "I'm not kidding. I have to be at this game. It's our last game of the year. I can't miss it. If I'm not there Mrs. Whiner will coach and she could leave permanent psychological scars on the players."

"Dis way," the Thug says pushing me back towards their limo.

"No, I can't."

He opens the back door, as if he's going to unceremoniously shove me in the back seat, but instead he reaches inside and pulls out a white envelope. "Dis is fer you," he says handing it to me.

My name is on the front. The envelope is sealed. "What's this?"

"Dun't know," the Behemoth says.

I tear it open and peek inside. It's all green. I thumb through the contents. All the denominations have three numbers.

"Yer services is no longer needed," the Thug tells me as he walks to the front of the car.

"Wait." My headache vanishes. The rainclouds part, the sun shines, music plays, and all is right with the day.

"What fer?"

"I'm having an epiphany," I tell him.

"What's dat?" the Thug asks.

"Dun't know," his brother answers.

"You killed him."

"What?"

"You killed him," I repeat.

"Who?"

"Mr. DeWitt."

"Da dead guy at da Zanadu?"

"How do you know I'm talking about a guy at the Zanadu?" I ask the Thug.

"I din't."

It all makes sense. A day short and a few dollars long, but it all makes sense.

I think out loud, more for my sake than the sake of the brother combo before me. "This wasn't about the Zanadu, or laundering money, or hiding cash from the IRS. It was hard core business. One drug kingpin moves in on the territory of another and the other guy doesn't like it. A war starts. The street soldiers go at it, but this is a game neither can win. So, the big boys get involved." I take a second, and then say, "I'm not even sure your boss Mr. Rogers even has anything to do with the Zanadu."

A slight smile breaks out on the Thug's face.

"Rogers' problem is he's not sure exactly what is going down, all he knows is a competitor is moving in on his action. He suspects it's DeWitt, who maybe even once worked for him. Rogers needs information, and knowing I'm already close, he contacts me. Our first meeting is interrupted by some dumb street shooter, probably sent by DeWitt, who's not smart enough to consider you in a Kevlar vest. You catch up to him, shoot him, and the kid ends up dying in the ER later that night."

"Naaa," the Thug says very unconvincingly.

"The stakes rise. Kids are still killing each other hourly, and something has to be done before the National Guard starts patrolling the streets in armored Humvees, ruining business for everyone."

I realize that I got used and used big time. Isn't the first time and it won't be the last. I'm a parent don't forget.

I continue, "I don't know what I said, or what information I relayed to your boss, but last night, it was time to kill the competition. And I'll bet you pulled the trigger."

The Thug smiles at me, signals his Behemoth brother to get back in the car and opens the passenger side door. "Nice ta see ya," he says before the limo drives off.

I'm still standing, as best as I can stand. I'm not sure what to do or what to think. In some ways I feel incredibly stupid. It was all there on *The Original Carlo*. I just couldn't put it together. What I don't feel is remorse. I open the envelope and count the money. Twenty-five hundred bucks. I know it is evil lucre and consider giving it back, but that would be dumb. Money is money. And I need money. In my head I add this to the cash in the recipe box. I've got myself a grand total of $5,500.

Cha-ching. Cha-ching. Cha-ching.

On the way over to get the girls, I can't help but come up with a couple hundred ways I can spend my newly acquired fortune. The last time I had this much cash in my hot little hands I was putting down a down payment on the house where I am soon to arrive and which I no longer own. I know it is trite to worship the almighty dollar and that money will never buy me happiness, but it sure feels good knowing I won't be bouncing any more checks, receiving any pink notices in the mail, or having to search the couch cushions for butter and egg money.

Kelly and Care run out the front door as soon as I pull into the driveway. I give them both a kiss as they climb into the car.

"Where's the boat?"

"Mom said, 'that ship has sailed,'" Kelly says in a near perfect imitation of her mother.

"I'm not real sure what that means," Care adds.

"It means that the Commodore decided to fish in new waters," I explain.

I pull out of the driveway and head north.

"I bet it was Mom who dumped him," Kelly says.

"Guys with boats that big, seldom get washed ashore," I tell her.

Another life lesson, she doesn't hear.

As we proceed, I ask, "Notice anything different?"

"No."

"The car's not making noises anymore."

"Oh, yeah," Care says.

"That's what I was going to say, Dad," Kelly says, "but you didn't give me a chance."

"Yeah, right."

"Hey, Dad, did you crack the case?" Care asks.

"Yep. All done."

"Are you going to tell Care how I was the one who did something that helped you figure it all out?" Kelly asks.

"Why don't you tell your sister, Kelly?"

"No, Dad, she wants to hear it from you."

"I'll tell you what happened, but you can't tell your mother."

"Okay, deal."

The rest of the way to the school gym, I go through the entire sordid tale. I leave out many of the gruesome details and the part about the Posedown in Pittsburgh because that would be more difficult to explain than the murders. They, of course, are more interested in what happened with Tiffany and if they will be able to see any of the pictures of the party on the Internet. They don't ask about my well-being. What else is new?

There's quite a turnout for the last game of the season. The stands must have at least ten or twenty parents and fans in attendance. The game before ours is coming to an end, with Delmonico's Pizza the winner over Glenview Car Wash by six points. As these two teams go through the ceremonial high-five handshakes and I wait to take the bench, a tap comes on my shoulder.

"It's your last chance, Sherlock."

"Mrs. Whiner, I'm so surprised to see you here. Is Mr. Whiner here too?"

"There is no Mr. Whiner," she says.

"You're kidding?" What a surprise.

"Just because this team is undefeated, doesn't mean they can't be beaten." She pulls out a stack of papers, hands them to me, and gets down to business. "Listen, Sherlock, there's no reason the girls can't pull this one out today if they stay focused, don't make any unforced errors, keep their heads in the game, and execute, execute, execute."

I'm a non-violent person, but the thought of executing Mrs. Whiner immediately comes to mind.

"I want you to go over these plays with the girls. Tell them to play tight, fight for every rebound, take the open shot, and execute, execute, execute."

"Mrs. Whiner," I say to the woman as kindly as possible, "it's our last game of the season. All I want to do is make it memorable for the kids, teach them what the game is really all about, leave them with smiles on their faces, and maybe even something to put on their Facebook page."

"A victory," she says, "that's what they need. A real, solid victory. That'll show these other teams what they're really made of."

"Mrs. Whiner, I got something even better."

251

"What could be better than winning?"

I refrain from what I really want to say and remember to be polite. "Enjoy the game, Mrs. Whiner." I return her diagrams, turn my twisted body away from her, and head for my team.

Our competition, the Spurs from Harry's Horse Tack and Supply, takes the opposite bench. Their faux leather uniforms boast a patch design with dazzling silver spurs that would be the envy of both Gene Autry and Roy Rogers. I can see in their faces that they are all business. Their two coaches line up the girls at the free-throw line and put them through a series of lay-up, rebound, and passing drills. All are performed flawlessly, but without one smile, snicker, or laugh from one of the players. These kids are just one step removed from being genuine, certified Stepford basketball automatons.

Our team warms up by shooting baskets—or at least trying to shoot baskets.

The ref blows his whistle to announce the tip-off.

I bring the team together and speak from the heart. "Listen girls, there's no doubt in anyone's mind that this team is going to kick our butts. So, here's our game plan."

The girls are surprised at my candor to say the least, but I know that they know I'm right.

"I want you to accomplish one thing today. I want you to have some fun."

"How are we going to have fun, Mr. Sherlock," Allison asks, "if we're going to get our butts kicked?"

"I want you to have a good time while you're playing. Don't get down, get up. Tell jokes. Tickle them instead of fouling them. Sing *Old McDonald* if you want. Dance one of those wacky hip-hop dances. Most important of all, I want you to laugh. Forget about who wins or who loses. Be yourselves, have a good time, have some yucks. Girls, if what you do in your life isn't fun, then find something else that is fun and do that. That's what life is all about," I pause to let it sink in. "What do you say, team?"

Morrie's Bail Bonds Bailouts take the floor and I take the bench. Kelly sits next to me. "What did you tell them, Dad?" she asks, after hearing the loudest cheer the team has ever wailed.

"I told them if you can't have fun with what you're doing, it's not worth doing."

"Oh, Dad, do you ever stop with the life lessons?"

"You know, Kelly, one of these days someone is going to listen to me and the world will become a better place."

"I doubt if that'll be anytime soon."

The whistle blows. The game begins—and chaos ensues.

Shemika cuts some wild hip-hop moves that would put the Zanadu dancers to shame. Annie and Kaylyn sing their hearts out. Care tickles their best player to the point where the kid can't stop laughing. Kelly supplies the music. Even Wilma Whiner gets into the act, laughing for the first time this season—or maybe the first time in her life.

I don't yell one instruction from the bench. I merely sit back as best as I am able and enjoy the spectacle. The opposition coaches go bananas, constantly complaining to the refs that we're making a mockery of the game. Who cares?

The Bailouts actually play pretty well. I'm not sure if it's because we played better, or because the Spurs get totally discombobulated by our style and don't know what to do. Of course, we still lose by the slaughter rule and the game is over at half-time, but my girls are jumping around laughing, giggling, and high-fiving, while the winners look like they're filing out of church after a funeral.

I turn behind me to see Mrs. Whiner, pale as a ghost, leaning back against the bleacher seat, passed out like a drunk at the Zanadu, the stack of basketball diagrams resting on her lap. Her season is over.

Kelly's having such a good time, she puts down her cell phone, and she joins the festivities on the court. The only thing that gets her attention away from the frivolity is a visitor who arrives—late as usual. "Hey, it's Tiffany."

"Oh, Mr. Sherlock," Tiffany cries out as she mars the court with her hard high heels.

"Tiffany," I call out. "You're supposed to be home resting."

"I'll sleep when I'm ninety," she tells me as she greets the team and Kelly. "How'd you guys do in the game?" she asks.

"We got our butts kicked," Allison answers, "but we had a good time."

"Good for you."

Tiffany takes me by the arm. "Mr. Sherlock, I have to talk to you."

"What about?"

"Me," she says. "What else do I ever talk about?"

"Good point."

I wait until the commotion dies down, bring the team together on the court for the last time, and announce, "Pizza party, my treat, for you and your parents, at Delmonico's, right now."

Another rousing cheer from my team. What better way to start spending my windfall than on the worst basketball team ever?

As we exit the court for the next two teams, Tiffany comes to my side. "I really need to talk to you, Mr. Sherlock. It happened again."

"What happened, Tiffany?" I ask as we leave courtside.

"I had another vision."

"Oh, no. Were you in red again?"

"No, blue," she says. "A dainty little print dress with a couple of gold bracelets and a gold pendant around my neck. My hair had this faint little curl in it that really brought out my highlights and framed my perfect cheekbones."

"Well, that's a good sign."

"The vision told me something, Mr. Sherlock."

I can't wait to hear what. And it doesn't take long for her to tell me.

"The vision was like telling me I have to go back to being the old me. So, no more Ms. 'Nice Guy' Tiffany. I'm done with that."

"Really?"

"Mr. Sherlock, I may be rich, self-centered, and a little bit selfish, but that's who I am. I gotta be me."

"You hear that in a song?" I ask.

"I don't think so."

"This is quite a revelation, Tiffany."

"It's amazing what can happen in your brain after your drink gets spiked or some badass dude tries to choke the life out of you," she says.

We're outside, heading for my car. "Did you inform your life coach of this sudden revelation?" I ask.

"I fired her," she says. "I thought that would be an excellent start in getting back to being the real me."

There's a silver lining to every cloud; although it's more of a gold lining in Tiffany's case.

"See, the vision told me that being the same old selfish, self-centered me was actually a positive because when those not-so-fortunate, *More Misérables* types see me parading in all my glory, they'll have something to strive for."

"And how was this revealed in your vision?" I have to ask. But if I didn't, she'd tell me anyway.

"There I was, in my blue-print mini, looking absolutely radiant, walking down Michigan Avenue on a bright, sunshiny day, with hundreds of fashion-challenged girls wishin' and hopin' to be just like me. Their tongues were wagging, and their hearts were pounding, and they all followed me right into Saks where they all picked out the right clothes, and left looking the spitting image of me."

I seem to remember Tiffany already having this vision in the past, but I don't mention it. It's as if she forgot the original episode as she was watching the re-run.

"Well, all I can say is more power to you." I try to sum it all up. "Tiffany, you've had quite an epiphany."

"What's an epiphany?" she asks. "Is that some new kind of software app for my iPhone?"

"I wouldn't know. I'm techie challenged."

"That's right, I forgot."

Kelly and Care meet us in the parking area. "Tiffany, are you coming to the pizza place with us?" Care asks.

"Sure, but I'm not eating any of the crust."

When we reach my Toyota, Tiffany asks Care, "Want to ride with me instead of in that awful car of your father's?"

"Yeah!" Care says.

"Dad," Kelly says after her sister walks off with Tiffany, "I almost forgot."

"What?"

My daughter pulls an envelope out of her back pocket and hands it to me. It has *Richard Sherlock* written on the front.

Before opening it, I react by saying, "I can't take you this weekend. My back is killing me. I can hardly stand up."

Kelly gives me that cute crooked little smile of hers.

I open the envelope, take out the sheet, and read:

Mr. Richard Sherlock:

The orthodontist informs me that Kelly can't wait any longer to get her braces. They will cost $5,500 and must be paid for in advance. His address is on the bottom where you can send the check—ASAP.

The note is signed: *Your Children's Mother*.

I peer down at my oldest and all I can think is: *I'll miss that crooked little smile*.

The End.

Note from the Author

Thank you for reading The Case of Tiffany's Epiphany. I certainly hoped you enjoyed my novel, and if you did, please let others know of your good reading fortune. The easiest way being through cyberspace, via social media networks, such as Amazon, Facebook, Linkedin, Goodreads, and Twitter. Please put out a good review to the above, and to your friends, contacts, and fellow readers. It will be greatly appreciated

About Jim Stevens

Jim was born in the East, grew up in the West, schooled in the Northwest, and spent twenty-three winters in the Midwest. He has been an advertising copywriter, playwright, filmmaker, stand-up comedian, and television producer.

Contact him at: **JimStevensWriter@gmail.com**.
Jim loves to hear from his readers, especially the ones who like his books.

<u>The Richard Sherlock Whodunit Series</u>

The Case of the Not-So-Fair Trader (Book 1)

The Case of Moomah's Moolah (Book 2)

The Case of Tiffany's Epiphany (Book 3)

The Case of Mr. Wonderful (Book 4)

The Case of the Woebegone Widow (Book 5)

The Case of the Missing Milk Money (Book 6)

The Case of the Dearly Departed (Book 7)

The Case of the Comatose CEO (Book 8)

<u>Also by Jim Stevens:</u>

WHUPPED

WHUPPED TOO

Hell No, We Won't Go,
A Novel of Peace, Love, War, and Football

www.ingramcontent.com/pod-product-compliance
Lightning Source LLC
Chambersburg PA
CBHW050024180626
46810CB00002B/562

* 9 7 8 0 9 8 4 9 2 4 7 7 6 *